Advance Praise for *Almost Like Being in Love*

"I love Vogt's layered and masterful romances. *Almost Like Being in Love* was one of those stories you don't want to end, and I lingered over every page enjoying the intriguing characters. Highly recommended!"

—Colleen Coble, author of *Mermaid Moon* and the Rock Harbor series

"*Almost Like Being in Love* is the perfect beach read. Beth K. Vogt delivers a charming romance with a sigh-worthy happily-ever-after ending."

—Rachel Hauck, *New York Times* bestselling author of *The Wedding Chapel*

"In *Almost Like Being in Love*, Beth Vogt once again introduces us to relatable, heart-tugging characters. Caron and Kade are struggling with broken dreams, with both their careers and their love lives in upheaval. I loved the thread of hope laced through this story and the reminder that sometimes the best things in life are waiting for us behind the most unexpected doors. Another keeper for your bookshelf!"

—Melissa Tagg, author of *Like Never Before* and *One Enchanted Christmas*

"Beth Vogt is an author I look to for not only a delightful story, but one that moves me and stays in my heart. *Almost Like Being in Love* is no exception. Moving, romantic, fun—a great way to spend the weekend!"

—Susan May Warren, RITA Award–winning author of the Christiansen Family series

"It's always a pleasure to read a Beth K. Vogt book. Authentic characters with realistic struggles we can all identify with bring her well-written words to life in this touching story about finding love where you least expect it and finding the courage to follow your heart. *Almost Like Being in Love* is another winner that fans and new readers alike will thoroughly enjoy."

—Catherine West, award-winning author of *The Things We Knew*

"Love is complicated. Family relationships are complicated. In *Almost Like Being in Love*, Beth K. Vogt explores the collision of the two with a soft touch and deft hand. Her novel sings with grace and the journey to learn who we are and how to stand on our own. And how to do that while risking all to discover who we are and a love that will sustain us. A beautiful novel that I inhaled."

—Cara Putman, award-winning author of *Shadowed by Grace* and *Where Treetops Glisten*

"Author Beth Vogt has done it again—a story you can curl up with and crawl into. Her characters are so real, I wish we could hang out. She has a permanent place on my favorite's shelf."

—Edie Melson, director of Blue Ridge Mountains Christian Writers Conference

Praise for *Crazy Little Thing Called Love,* Book 1 of the Destination Wedding Series

"Second chances at love, storm-chasing danger, and a destination wedding? I'm in! Beth K. Vogt's newest book, *Crazy Little Thing Called Love*, hits all the right notes, touching on more serious subject matter without losing any of Beth's signature charm. This is sure to be a favorite addition to any fan's Christian romance library."

—Carla Laureano, RITA Award–winning author of *Five Days in Skye* and *London Tides*

"In *Crazy Little Thing Called Love*, Beth Vogt shows us that indeed love is crazy, in the best possible way! This story had everything I've come to expect from a Beth Vogt novel: high-quality writing, a deep spiritual journey, and a poignant love story. Throw in the fun of a destination wedding and you have yourself a story that is sure to touch hearts and entertain readers. I can't wait for the next installment!"

—Katie Ganshert, award-winning author of *The Art of Losing Yourself*

"Curl your toes into the sand and relish the delicious warmth of Destin, Florida, in Vogt's *Crazy Little Thing Called Love*. A must-read with engaging characters, rich scenery, and the high tension of a hurricane that carries us into love, forgiveness, and the joy of discovering treasures once lost."

—Katherine Reay, author of *Lizzy & Jane*

"Logan Hollister is a storm chaser by profession, but he's never been able to tame the storms in his personal life. *Crazy Little Thing Called Love* is an exciting, romantic adventure as Logan and his ex-wife, Vanessa, are forced to confront both a hurricane and the emotional storm that rages between them. Beth Vogt takes readers on a heart-pounding journey through both the present and the past even as her characters try to sort out their future. Second chances are a rare gift, and Beth unwraps this one perfectly."

—Melanie Dobson, award-winning author of
Shadows of Ladenbrooke Manor and *Chateau of Secrets*

"Beth Vogt has done it again! Her heart-tugging characters and writing make you feel like you're right there on a sunny—and sometimes stormy!—Florida coast. I especially loved the underlying themes of mistakes and regrets turned to joy and new hope. Another winner!"

—Melissa Tagg, author of *From the Start* and *Three Little Words*

"Second-chance love at its crazy best! Beth Vogt is a master at wringing tears from the eyes and sleep from the soul in a tender love story that both heals and haunts."

—Julie Lessman, award-winning author of the Daughters of Boston,
Winds of Change, and Heart of San Francisco series

"Beth K. Vogt's amazing ability to create complex, true-to-life characters with realistic flaws and emotions keeps me hungering for her novels before they're even available for sale. The depth of her stories pulls me in, leaving me to ponder the spiritual truth she has woven into the plot long after I've finished the book. Beth's novels are automatic buys for my keeper shelf."

—Lisa Jordan, award-winning author of *Lakeside Redemption*

"Beth Vogt is a master at capturing the sometimes stormy emotions of the human heart. In *Crazy Little Thing Called Love*, Vogt takes the reader on Vanessa and Logan's road back to each other—a journey that is both deeply felt and realistic. She makes us believe in the power of second chances, all the while reminding us that it's never too late to have faith in our first love."

—Kristy Cambron, author of *The Butterfly and the Violin* and
A Sparrow in Terezin

ALSO BY BETH K. VOGT

ALMOST
LIKE *BEING*
L in *OVE*

• ♥ • a destination wedding novel • ♥ •

BETH K. VOGT

HOWARD BOOKS
An Imprint of Simon & Schuster, Inc.

NEW YORK   NASHVILLE   LONDON   TORONTO   SYDNEY   NEW DELHI

Howard Books
An Imprint of Simon & Schuster, Inc.
1230 Avenue of the Americas
New York, NY 10020

First Howard Books trade paperback edition June 2016

HOWARD and colophon are trademarks of Simon & Schuster, Inc.

For information about special discounts for bulk purchases, please contact Simon & Schuster Special Sales at 1-866-506-1949 or business@simonandschuster.com.

The Simon & Schuster Speakers Bureau can bring authors to your live event. For more information or to book an event, contact the Simon & Schuster Speakers Bureau at 1-866-248-3049 or visit our website at www.simonspeakers.com.

Interior design by Jaime Putorti

Manufactured in the United States of America

10 9 8 7 6 5 4 3 2 1

Library of Congress Cataloging-in-Publication Data

Names: Vogt, Beth K., author.
Title: Almost like being in love : a destination wedding novel / Beth K. Vogt.
Description: First Howard Books trade paperback edition. | Nashville : Howard Books, 2016. | Series: A Destination wedding novel
Identifiers: LCCN 2015044092| ISBN 9781476789804 (paperback) | ISBN 9781476789811 (ebook)
Subjects: | BISAC: FICTION / Christian / Romance. | FICTION / Romance / Contemporary. | FICTION / Contemporary Women. | GSAFD: Love stories. | Christian fiction.
Classification: LCC PS3622.O362 A79 2016 | DDC 813/.6—dc23 LC record available at http://lccn.loc.gov/2015044092

ISBN 978-1-4767-8980-4
ISBN 978-1-4767-8981-1 (ebook)

To Rachelle Gardner, whom I am thankful to call
both my literary agent and my friend:
Your influence runs deep in my life and I am a
better person for knowing you. Here's to pursuing
dreams together for many years to come—yours
and mine both.

ONE

• ◆ • ◆ ♥ • ◆ • ◆ •

A new day—another opportunity to prove herself to her boss. Of course, Caron had complicated the whole "prove herself" challenge by working for her father.

She leaned back in the driver's seat of her car, inhaling the faint citrus scent of Armor All lingering in her SUV. From the hubcaps to the dials of the CD player, the car gleamed. Dash and door handles wiped down with cleaner. Windows streak-free. Floors vacuumed so that not a candy wrapper or Hot Tamale lurked beneath her car seats. At this moment, she sat in the perfect car for a Realtor to transport clients to see properties.

Not that her father conducted weekly inspections of his employees' cars. But he could inspect hers, if he wanted to.

Caron unbuckled her seat belt with a sharp metallic click. Time to get to work. It was almost six o'clock in the morning. Showing up before sunrise might earn a brief nod of acknowledgment from her father, but only if he'd been there to see her early entrance into the empty building.

She paused in the reception area long enough to place a fresh arrangement of bright purple irises and vivid blue cornflowers in the vase on the glass-topped coffee table, then switched the outdated copies of *Real Simple* and *HGTV* magazines with more current ones. She returned to her SUV to grab the bags of pillows she'd purchased over the weekend. Removing the teal and muted silver ones set along the back of the sofa, she added the circular pops of yellow, white, and royal blue. The final touch—a single spray of cornflowers added to the tall glass bottle on the receptionist's desk.

Her father might not ever acknowledge her attention to detail, but their—*his*—clients appreciated the welcoming touches. And the coming summer season was the perfect time to update the look in the reception area.

Once she was in her office, the minutes disappeared into the silence, her thermos of cold sweet tea ignored on the corner of her desk as she studied the new homes on the MLS list. She e-mailed a prospective buyer, a military spouse flying in midweek to house-hunt, attaching photos of a few of the houses she had in mind for the family of five. Later today, she'd go visit some of the homes she'd marked down and begin mapping out the showings.

"You heading into the morning staff meeting?" Jackie appeared in the open doorway to Caron's office, holding a mug of coffee emblazoned with the company logo.

Caron rested her chin on her hand, resisting the urge to rub her eyes and smudge her mascara. "Is it almost nine o'clock already?"

"Yep." Jackie nodded toward the conference room, causing her sleek black ponytail to sway. "I think your dad—I mean the boss—brought in some sort of motivational speaker this morning. I only got a quick look, but there's something familiar about her."

"What? My father didn't mention anything during Sunday's barbecue."

Of course, he didn't have to tell Caron everything—or any-thing—just because they worked together. But there were the very rare times they talked business, sitting in his office at the back of the house until her mom came looking for them and demanded that they stop.

"Well, we won't know what's going on until the meeting starts." Jackie took a step back. "And we both know the boss likes his employees to be punctual."

Caron slipped on her floral heels, organizing the top of her desk before joining Jackie and making their way to the confer-ence room. "Did you have a good Memorial Day weekend?"

"Spent it out on the bayou, water-skiing. What about you?"

"The traditional barbecue with my family and Alex's family." Caron lowered her voice as they entered the conference room, nodding to her father. "Alex didn't get called away once on an emergency."

"All the air conditioners on the Panhandle managed to stay functioning for a day, huh?"

Caron muffled her laugh with her hand, turning it into a cough as her father took his place at the head of the long table. It was their Monday-morning staff meeting—only on Tuesday morning, thanks to the holiday weekend. Time to focus, to be professional.

Caron used the logo-branded pen to surround the list of top-ics on the paper in front of her with various-sized arrows as her father worked his way through the list.

- Scheduling for Continuing Education Courses
- Agents' New Listings
- Open House Weekly Caravan
- Office Total Production for Month/Quarter/Year
- Agents' Production for Month/Quarter/Year

"I wanted to single out one agent in particular this morning—Caron Hollister."

At the mention of her name, Caron dropped her pen so that it rolled across the table with a clatter of plastic against glass, her attention pulled away from her doodling.

"Congratulations on surpassing the proposed quota in sales not only for the month, but for the quarter." A brief smile creased her father's face. "If you keep this up, you're likely to be in the top ten percent of sales in the country by the end of the year."

A flush heated her neck, rising to her face—the round of applause from her colleagues mere background noise to her father's public praise. Yes, the sales meant she'd satisfied her clients, but she'd also made her father proud, which made all the early mornings and late nights worth it.

"And now that we've discussed the usual business agenda—" Her father smoothed his royal-blue tie against his starched white dress shirt. "—I have an important announcement that affects the future of this company."

As he spoke, a petite woman, who appeared no more than ten years older than Caron, entered the room and came to stand beside him. She was all polish and poise. Immaculate deep red dress that almost shouted designer-made. Mile-high heels. Airbrushed makeup. Blond hair cut into a classic bob. Bleached-white smile.

Wait . . . who was she? Caron scrolled through her brain, trying to put a name to the vaguely familiar too-perfect face.

Nothing.

A hush settled over the room as if everyone took a collective breath and held it. No exhale.

Wait for it . . . wait for it . . .

"I'd like to introduce Nancy Miller. I'm sure you're all familiar with her reputation along the Emerald Coast as a well-respected Realtor. After some lengthy negotiations, I'm very pleased to inform you that Nancy is joining Hollister Realty . . . as my partner."

The room remained quiet, as if people weren't sure if a round of applause was in order. Caron gripped the fabric edge of her chair to keep from bolting to her feet. *His partner?* Her father didn't share his business with anyone. Caron stared down through the clear glass table. Maybe if she let go of the edge of the chair, she'd fall through the glass like some modern-day Alice. Fall, fall, fall into some other world where things made sense.

Her father's voice chained her to the how-can-this-be-true reality.

"As I'm sure you're all aware, Nancy has a thriving real estate firm in Navarre. I've watched her for years and I respect her business prowess and all she's accomplished in the past decade. We both realized that together we'd be a realty force to be reckoned with."

Her father was standing there . . . praising Nancy Miller . . . announcing she would be his new partner . . . only minutes after he'd finally acknowledged Caron was successful—on her way to possibly earning national acclaim.

"This is going to mean great things for our companies. A name change, for one. We'll become Hollister Realty Group. We're already working on our ad campaign to announce our merger and our new name." Her father beamed like a man announcing the birth of his firstborn. "At this time, no one needs to worry about any adjustments to our staffs."

Around the room, the employees relaxed in their chairs, a collective exhale whispering through the air.

"As a matter of fact, we may need to hire additional employees. But that's all to be determined. This morning, I just wanted to share that today's a new beginning for our company."

Applause splattered around the room.

"To celebrate, I requested champagne and cake. I'm not sure what the delay is." Her father motioned Nancy forward. "I also wanted Nancy to say a few words and to give her the chance to tell you her vision for our future. While she does that, I'll slip out and see what's the holdup on the bubbly."

As a wave of laughter flowed among the employees, Nancy worked the room like a pro, starting off with a joke about her early years as a Realtor. Caron slipped from her chair and caught up with her father in the hallway.

"What was that?" Her words were a timid verbal tap on his shoulder.

Her father didn't slow his stride. "What was what?"

"That." Caron motioned back toward the conference room. "That announcement."

"Just like I said—it's the future of this company."

"I was at the house two days ago for lunch and you never said a word."

"That was a family gathering. You found out today, with the rest of the employees, Caron."

"But I'm your daughter."

"Exactly. At home, you're my daughter. Here, you're my employee like everyone else." He stopped outside the kitchen, where two of the receptionists arranged clear plastic champagne glasses and plastic plates with slices of cake on two rolling carts. "And I decided it was best you found out today."

"How long have you been planning this?"

"Six months, maybe a little longer than that."

Six months? For a moment, the scene in front of her blurred—the receptionists pouring streams of champagne into tiny cups seemed to fade in and out. "You didn't think I would want to know? Didn't realize how this would affect me?"

"My decision affects you the same way it affects any other Realtor who works for me. It's a wise move for the business."

Caron's fingers worried the collar of her linen dress. "Dad, you made Nancy Miller your *partner*. You've always said that this company was yours—a family-owned business—"

"And it still is. I've retained majority ownership in the business."

"But Nancy Miller isn't family—"

"No, she's not. She's my partner. And I chose to expand my business by making the best decision for this company."

Nancy Miller. Her father's partner.

And where did that leave her?

Caron swallowed past the sharp ache slicing the back of her throat. This was not the time to give in to emotion. Her father had taught her the importance of remaining calm when negotiating. "But . . . you knew my dream was to . . . to one day . . ."

Her father stepped away from the other women, blocking them as he turned to face her. Lowered his voice, his gray eyes glacial. "Dreams don't get handed to you. Having the Hollister name doesn't guarantee you anything. I make *business* decisions based on what's best now as well as in the future. Granted, you've surprised me by settling in here and proving to be a good Realtor. But Nancy Miller has years of experience that you don't have. She's rocketed past anyone's expectations for her success. A good employee doesn't question her boss's decisions—in public or private. Given time, you'll realize this was a wise decision."

With that, her father addressed the receptionists, his voice smooth. Caron braced a hand against the wall. With her father's unexpected decision to form a partnership, she'd lost her way. His "surprise" at her success erased any indication she'd made real progress. It was as if he'd removed all the signs, all the mile markers, from the road map of her life.

Her father took a few steps past her, back toward the conference room. Stopped. "Are you coming?"

Was she coming . . . where? Back to the conference room to watch everyone fawn over the woman who'd stolen her dream?

No, that wasn't true. Nancy Miller hadn't stolen her dream. Her father had handed Caron's dream to her, with no thought of how it would destroy his daughter's professional goals.

By aligning himself with Nancy Miller, her father had betrayed her. Was she going to betray herself?

Caron forced herself to stand straight, fisting her hands at her sides. How . . . why had her father done this to her? She'd poured hours into being the best Realtor she could, all the while hoping that one day she'd be her dad's partner. How was she supposed to work under Nancy Miller?

"Dad, you've worked hard for what you've accomplished. Made the decisions you thought best." Her body flushed hot, then cold. "It's . . . only right I do the same."

A nod of agreement. "Now you're talking."

"I don't understand your latest decision . . . how I fit in . . ." Caron searched for the next words. The necessary words. The words that would stamp FINAL on today. "—so . . . so I think it's best that I'm not a part of Hollister Realty Group."

"Excuse me?"

She hesitated for only a moment, waiting until she could say what needed to be said without her voice quavering. "I quit. I'll draw up the standard two weeks' resignation today—"

"Don't be rash, Caron. You're not in high school anymore."

High school.

With those two words, her father reduced her to a seventeen-year-old with streaks of vivid pink in her hair.

"I'm not being rash." Caron maintained eye contact. "I'm making a wise business decision. For me."

Now was the time for her father to tell her that she was too valuable an employee to lose. Maybe even put his arm around her shoulder in an all-too-rare display of affection. Insist they both calm down and talk this out, Hollister to Hollister.

But instead, her father nodded again, his face devoid of any emotion. "You do recall you signed a contract stating that when you leave here, any and all deals in process revert back. That your commission drops down to fifty-fifty, even if you are making a larger commission at the time. I will not make an exception for you, daughter or not."

Of course he wouldn't.

"Understood."

"Fine. You've got until the end of the month under my name. Your MLS access shuts off in two weeks." Her father's words were automatic, as if he was checking off a list. "I'll waive the two-week resignation period. And Caron, don't be foolish enough to think there'll be a job waiting for you here when you realize your mistake."

"I won't."

"You can clean out your desk immediately."

And that meant she'd skip the champagne and cake, too.

.   .   .

What had she done?

Caron sat at her desk, the stillness seeming to crawl up her skin. Everyone else was in the main conference room. Celebrating. Toasting her father's brilliant business venture.

And she . . . she had just thrown away the only job she'd ever wanted. And her father hadn't stopped her. Hadn't done one thing to keep her as an employee, despite praising her less than an hour ago.

Why?

Caron closed her eyes, covering her face with her hands, fighting the increasing desire to burst into tears.

Not here. Not now.

Why didn't her father insist she stay? Was she nothing more than a quarterly statistic that benefited his company? Why didn't he at least try to discuss things with her? Why didn't he . . . understand?

With hands that shook, she moved one of the empty computer-paper boxes from the floor to the top of her desk. Slid open the middle file drawer, the scrape of metal against metal severing the suffocating silence. Within minutes, she'd transferred her transactions in process and future-leads files to the box. Farther in the back she found the folder of thank-you notes from clients, depositing those into the box, too. Sliding the drawer closed, she opened the bottom drawer, where she kept her stationery, a backup makeup kit, a small hairbrush, and a bottle of her favorite hair spray, along with a bag of cashews and another of golden raisins.

Next—the top desk drawer.

Paper clips. Neon Post-it notes. Pens with the company logo, which her father would be changing. A pack of breath mints.

She slammed the drawer shut. She didn't want, didn't need, any of it.

The pen engraved with her name that her parents had given her when she'd passed her real estate license exam lay on top of the desk. Caron balanced it in the palm of her hand, tempted to leave it among the other pens in her desk drawer.

No. She was still a Realtor, albeit an unemployed one. And she didn't have the energy to be petty. Her father likely wouldn't even notice she'd left the pen behind.

Her desk lamp. The chargers for her iPod and iPhone and the speakers she'd brought in so she could listen to music while working. The photo calendar on the wall Vanessa had made her for Christmas, filling it with family photos and pictures from Logan and Vanessa's wedding and photos of Caron and Alex. Of course she'd take that, and the framed photo of Alex and her, taken on her last birthday.

The two watercolors of Destin—one of pale-green-and-gold sea oats, one of a purple-and-orange-tinged sunset—wouldn't fit in the boxes. She'd just carry them out to her car, then come back for the boxes.

On her return, she dumped her business cards in the box, so that they tumbled, helter-skelter, like oversize confetti. Tossed in her datebook. The small glass jar of bright red Hot Tamales she kept on the edge of her desk. Only a few pieces of candy remained inside. She'd meant to bring in a bag to refill it this week.

And that was that.

All that was left of her time here.

She'd have to call her clients, let them know she was no longer working for Hollister Realty. *Correction.* No longer working for Hollister Realty Group. She would try to find out who would be handling their closings. But she'd make those calls from home.

Caron stood in her office doorway. Did she want to wait, take the time to explain to Jackie? To say goodbye to everyone? Make the rounds of the other offices? Hug the receptionists?

No.

She needed to leave with her dignity intact. No wobbling chin, no blinking back tears.

She could always send e-mails or make phone calls later. Maybe bake brownies and drop them by in a few weeks—or better yet, have something delivered.

As she entered the building after depositing one box in her car, people had begun to return to their offices as the celebration broke up. She needed to be done. Gone, before anyone tried to engage her in conversation. She wasn't a coward, but one confrontation was enough for this Tuesday.

.   .   .

She was no better than a thirteen-year-old, running home to her mother, expecting her to dispense just the right amount of love, listening, and momma-wisdom to make everything better.

She'd left her father's office with no real idea of where she was going. She'd driven over the Mid-Bay Bridge, ending up at the Donut Hole, in a booth with a glass of sweet iced tea that the waitress kept refilled and a salad that ended up in a to-go box. And despite several hours at the restaurant, going over listings, trying to create a semblance of order to her life—the life she'd wrecked of her own free will—she was still lost. Now she was driving back across the bridge to her parents' house, just wanting to be with her mom.

Not that Caron expected her mother to fix anything. She couldn't. And most of all, she didn't want her mother caught between her father's red-letter day and her unemployment announcement.

But Caron still wanted to tell her mother herself what had happened—what she'd done—before her father did. She needed to be an adult. First she'd tell her mother. Then she'd tell Alex that his girlfriend was now unemployed. And then, after conquering those two hurdles, she'd start sifting through the shambles of her life tomorrow.

Caron swallowed back the sour taste that filled her mouth, pressing the palm of her hand against her stomach. Right behind the looming question "What had she done?" lurked the question "What was she going to do?" Work for another realty company? Go independent? Or maybe she'd surprise everyone and do something else. Go sell Hawaiian shaved ices in one of those little trucks along the beach in Destin.

Caron shut the front door of her parents' house, kicking off her high heels and heading for the kitchen, the plush carpeting soft on the soles of her feet. "Mom? It's me."

Where would she find her mother? Caron never stopped to consider what her mom did during the day. The house was always immaculate and her mother refused to let her father get a maid service. She nurtured the mini-jungle of plants growing in the sunroom, belonged to a book club, attended a women's prayer group. She planned dinners for her husband's business colleagues—the consummate hostess, Dad always said.

The kitchen smelled of chocolate and vanilla and peanut butter, and a quick glance at the red KitchenAid mixer on the counter—with remnants of cookie dough in the silver bowl and a black wire rack with cookies cooling alongside it—proved that her mother had decided to bake. She couldn't be that far away.

Sure enough, Caron found her mother sitting on the family room couch, her laptop balanced on her knees, a pair of bright fuchsia readers, embellished with gold filigree, perched on her nose.

"Hi, Mom." Caron offered her a small wave from where she stood in the archway separating the two rooms.

"Caron!" Her mother started and then smiled. "I didn't hear you come in, honey."

"Sorry. I didn't mean to surprise you. What are you doing?"

"Nothing important." Her mother moved the laptop aside, shoving her readers on top of her head. "I'm surprised to see you in the middle of the day right after a holiday weekend. The office is usually so busy—"

"I know. Usually."

"Do you have time for some lunch?" Her mother transitioned into the kitchen, offering Caron a quick hug that was like a soft kiss on her bruised emotions. "I have leftovers from Sunday, or I can whip up some tuna salad. It won't take long."

"I'm not that hungry, but some iced tea would be nice."

"Coming right up. I've got it sweetened, just the way you like it."

Unexpected tears stung Caron's eyes, but she blinked them away. That was her mother—always taking care of her and everyone else, too.

"Listen, Mom, something happened at work today and I wanted to tell you myself . . ." Her voice wobbled like a kid's bike with only one training wheel.

"Oh?"

Caron scooped the side of the mixing bowl with the plastic spatula, savoring the leftover cookie dough. "Did you know Dad was going to partner with Nancy Miller?"

Her mother stilled for just a moment, then resumed removing two tall glasses from a cabinet. "Yes. He's talked about it for months."

"Mom . . . you know he's always said Hollister Realty is a family-owned business. His company. Why would he suddenly partner with Nancy Miller?"

"Caron, I don't tell your father how to run his business. Yes, he discusses things with me, but in the end, he makes the decisions." Her mother stopped talking for a moment as she filled the glasses with ice. "I do wish he'd told you before today, but he prefers to keep family and business separate as much as possible. And I respect that."

"Well, there won't be any problem with that now."

Her mother carried a plastic pitcher of tea to the kitchen counter. "What do you mean?"

"I quit."

The pitcher hit the counter with a dull thud. "Caron! Why would you do that?"

"How can you even ask that question, Mom?" Caron abandoned the mixing bowl and held the glasses steady as her mom filled them with tea. "You know my dream has always been to be more than another one of Dad's employees. I wanted to inherit the business one day. By partnering with that woman, he's made it very clear I don't fit in his plans."

"I know that's been your dream. And I know your father's decision is a shock." Her mother paused, seeming to debate her words. "But Caron, have you ever asked yourself if being with Hollister Realty is the right dream for you?"

"Ever since I was a little girl, I've loved going with Dad when he viewed houses, prepped them for showings. I worked in his office during the summer. All I've ever wanted was to be a Realtor—"

"I know that—"

"I kept waiting for him to see that even though Logan didn't want to follow in his footsteps, I did. *I could.*" Caron closed her eyes, resisting the urge to stomp her foot on the tile floor. "And what good did it do me? He joins forces with Nancy Miller. And now I don't have a job."

"Caron, if you really want to be a Realtor, I'm sure your father will understand you were upset. Go back and talk with him—"

"Haven't you been watching me for the last four years, Mom? Or listening to anything I said? I *am* a Realtor." Now Caron did stomp her foot. "And I'm not asking for my job back. Dad may think Hollister Realty Group is the future of the company, but I don't want to be a part of it. I was working for my future—what I hoped would be my future. I made the wrong assumption. I'll figure out something else."

"Well then, I won't try to talk you out of your decision." Her mother slid her readers off her head, setting them on the counter. "You're an intelligent woman, Caron. Your decision to quit may have been sudden, but that doesn't mean God isn't in it. I once heard someone say an unexpected bend in the road can lead right to God's next blessing for us."

God. Right. He was probably standing back and watching her tear her life apart, wondering why she hadn't asked for his help, his direction, when she was upset. Caron sipped her tea, but the sweetness didn't alter her attitude in any tangible way. She didn't have the right to throw a temper tantrum and blame anything on God. Her earthly father had hurt her, not her heavenly one. But right now her emotions were as shattered as if she'd dropped her glass of iced tea on the kitchen floor.

She wanted to blame somebody for the mess her life was. Her father for not making the decisions she wanted. Nancy Miller for being an interloper.

"So, what can I make you for lunch?"

"Mom, I didn't come here for you to fix everything. Or to fix me lunch. I just wanted you to hear about my decision from me, not from Dad."

"Making you something to eat doesn't mean I'm fixing anything—"

"I know. I'm sorry. I'm just not very good company right now."

"Tell you what." Her mother wrapped her in a loose hug and the faint scent of vanilla. "How about you go swim a few laps? That used to work when you were in high school and you were stressed out about exams or a basketball tournament."

"Leave my troubles in the deep end of the pool, right?"

"Something like that. I'll make lunch while I finish up these cookies. No more talking. As a matter of fact—" She consulted her slender gold watch. "—I have somewhere to be in an hour. Lunch and fresh-baked cookies will be waiting for you after your swim. So what's it going to be?"

"I learned a long time ago to never argue with the wisdom of my mom." Caron returned her mother's embrace. "A few laps sound perfect. Who knows? Maybe I'll have an appetite when I'm done."

"Swim as long as you want. I'll have a sandwich waiting for you in the fridge and cookies in the usual container."

Her mother was right. She'd drag her heated emotions through the pool, eventually tempering them in the repetitive motions of kicking and arm strokes, of breathe and hold, breathe and hold. Most days after high school basketball practice she'd come home and cool down with a swim. And when the team lost? She'd endure her father's replay of the game—what she'd done right and everything she'd done wrong—and then muffle the sound of his criticism by swimming lap after lap in the pool. Caron only stopped when her mother stood at the edge, towel in hand, and demanded she get out, dry off, shower, and come get something to eat.

Some teenage habits were worth reviving.

TWO

• • • ♥ • • •

*H*ollisters don't quit.

Her father's voice had chased Caron from her parents' house, following her all the way home. He'd drilled those three words into her from an early age until they seemed an inseparable part of her DNA.

And yet, if she wiped away the steam clouding her bathroom mirror, she'd be staring at the reflection of an unemployed woman.

A quitter.

She scrubbed away at the mirror with her towel, staring into her eyes.

"You made a decision, Caron Hollister. You live with your decision."

And now she was quoting her father to herself? Out loud?

She needed to call Alex and tell him about her ill-fated day. He would provide some much-needed consolation.

Caron towel-dried her hair, any hint of chlorine washed away, thanks to her favorite shampoo. The scent of coconut and shea butter always reminded her of lazy summer afternoons lying out on the white sands of the Destin beach when she was a teenager.

The coolness of the bathroom tile floor changed to the softness of bedroom carpeting. Her rescued-from-a-flea-market wrought-iron bed dominated the area, the off-white comforter shot through with multicolored threads of muted reds, blues, oranges, greens, and yellows—all echoed in the myriad pillows piled at the top of the bed.

She settled herself in the center of the mattress, legs crisscrossed beneath her short cotton robe. Just as she reached for her phone, it came to life with the upbeat tones of "Count on Me" by Bruno Mars.

Okay, then. She was talking to her best friend before she talked to her boyfriend.

Caron flopped back among the accent pillows. "Hey."

Margo ignored her greeting, her voice shrill. "You quit your job?"

Caron jerked her phone away from her ear. "Stop shrieking at me."

Margo inhaled a gulp of air. "You quit your job?"

"We've texted about this all day. Five I-quit-my-job texts from me to your five WHAT? reply texts." Caron tossed the damp towel onto the floor beside her bed. "Yes. I quit my job."

"Why?"

"It was time."

"It was time?" A piercing note tinged Margo's voice yet again. "Come on, Caron, this is me. Your high school best friend. Your college roommate. I know all your secrets. So unless you want me to start posting them on Facebook in the next thirty seconds, start talking."

"Coercion? And you call yourself my best friend?"

"Whatever it takes. Stop stalling."

"I can't work for my father anymore. Not after what he did."

"And what exactly did he do?"

"He brought Nancy Miller on as a partner." Caron sat up, shoving her wet hair out of her face.

"He did not!" There was a pause on the other end of the phone. "Wait! Who is Nancy Miller?"

A half-formed laugh died in Caron's throat. Even after moving cross-country for a job, Margo was such a faithful friend— outraged for her even when she didn't know why.

"Nancy Miller is a top Realtor in town. She may be five years older than me—she's probably no more than ten. She's this prepackaged thirty-or-forty-something professional on the rise." Caron pressed her lips closed to stop the words spewing from her mouth. "To be honest, I respect the woman. She's worked hard to get where she is. Won a ton of awards. Today he announced they merged companies to form Hollister Realty Group."

"Why would he do that?"

Nancy Miller has years of experience that you don't have . . . she's rocketed past anyone's expectations for her success.

The echo of her father's words interrupted her conversation with Margo. The woman was her father's dream employee. She, on the other hand, had merely surprised him by "settling in" as a Realtor. Where did she fit in her father's grand plan for the future?

She didn't.

"Hey, did I lose you?"

"Sorry. I asked my father the same question. According to him, this partnership is the future of Hollister Realty." Caron clutched a round, tasseled pillow to her chest. "But it's not my future."

"What are you going to do now?"

"I have no idea. I just . . . quit."

"This is bad, Caron. Bad."

"I know that. I'm sitting here trying to imagine not going into work tomorrow—"

"You need a break." Margo rushed past her. "Before you make any more life-altering decisions, why don't you come out here for a week or two?"

"What?"

"Come to Colorado. Catch your breath, get your bearings again." Margo's words piled on top of one another as she warmed up to her idea. "And you can help plan my wedding up close, instead of always being long-distance. It's been a challenge, planning everything solo, since Ronny's job transfer isn't happening until right before the wedding. There's a big bridal fair soon. I'm hoping to find some beautiful bridesmaid dresses for you all at these supposedly amazing prices—"

"I can't—"

"Why not? What are you going to do? Stay in Niceville and avoid your dad?"

Margo's question was like running into a towering defender on the basketball court. Blocked. But did it make any sense to quit her job and then run away to Colorado and play bridesmaid instead of figuring out her future?

Her phone beeped, indicating another call.

Alex.

"Margo, I've gotta go. Alex is calling."

"Fine. But think about what I said, okay?"

"Sure. Fine. Love you."

"Wait." Margo's voice stopped her from hanging up. "I need to mention one thing, though—"

"We'll talk tomorrow. And I promise I'll think about coming to visit."

· · ·

Three rings. No answer. Looked like he wasn't going to catch Caron in between his two emergency work calls.

Alex exhaled, scrubbing his palm across his face, the stubble on his chin a reminder he was running well past five o'clock. He'd wait for the phone to roll over to voice mail, leave a message, and then head to the next client's home—

"Hello?"

Caron's voice, when he was expecting to be greeted by her voice mail message, stalled his reply for a moment.

"Alex?"

"Yeah, I'm here. I was expecting to have to leave a message. Thought you must be busy with clients."

"No . . . no, I'm home."

"Nice." Alex started the van, cranking up the air-conditioning to combat the eighty-three-degree heat and one hundred percent humidity lurking outside. "Busy day?"

Caron's voice dropped low. "I would say . . . it's been more of an interesting day."

"Interesting in what way?" Alex pulled a plastic sandwich bag half full of beef jerky from a crumpled brown paper bag on the passenger seat. "Did you find the perfect house for that one family—?"

"I quit my job."

The salty chunk of meat seemed to lodge in Alex's throat, causing him to cough and struggle to speak. "What . . . did you say?"

Caron raised her voice as if Alex were hard of hearing. "I quit my job."

A quick gulp of lukewarm grape Gatorade helped him swallow the beef jerky. "Why would you do that?"

"My father made some changes at work that I didn't agree with, so I quit."

"Your father is your boss, Caron. He can do whatever he wants."

"Nancy Miller isn't that much older than me, but she's earned my father's respect so much that the same morning he compliments me in the staff meeting, in the next breath he announces that she's his new partner."

"Who's Nancy Miller?"

"A hotshot Realtor in town who had her own company."

"Well, I'm sure your father knows what he's doing."

"Would you stop defending my dad and listen to me?" Caron's voice sharpened. "I'm your girlfriend. You're supposed to take my side."

Alex tossed the plastic bag back onto the passenger seat. It was past eight o'clock in the evening and he had one more emergency call waiting for him, thanks to another malfunctioning air conditioner. If he was lucky—and if he didn't get caught up in an unexpected argument with Caron—he'd be home before eleven.

"I know how hard you worked for this job. I hate for you to throw it away without really thinking your actions through. I'm sure if you went and talked things over with your father—"

"There is nothing to talk over with my father. My decision was abrupt, yes, but that doesn't mean I made the wrong decision. My father waived the customary two weeks' notice—"

"Waived the two weeks' notice? Caron, what did you do to upset him so badly?"

"I quit because I couldn't stay and see my father give Nancy Miller everything I've always dreamed of." A soft sniff hinted that Caron might be crying. "I may admire the woman professionally, but that doesn't mean I'd enjoy watching her live my dream. And why are you so worried about my father? Why aren't you defending me?"

"I'm concerned about both of you." He searched for the right thing to say. "I apologize. I'll try to be more understanding."

"Thanks for that."

Too little comfort, too late.

Alex opted to just keep asking questions. "What are you going to do now?"

"I think . . . I think I'm going to take Margo up on her offer."

How did Caron's best friend end up in the conversation?

"And what offer was that?"

"I talked to her right before you called. She invited me to come out to Colorado for a short visit. Catch my breath and get my bearings again."

"Do you think that's the best choice right now?" As soon as he asked the question, Alex knew he'd lost more ground with Caron.

"I realize you don't understand my decisions today, but yes . . . yes, I do. I'll only be gone a week, ten days at the most. I'll get away. Get some perspective. And then come back here and start job-hunting."

"You're upset—understandably so." Best to retreat to the understanding boyfriend stance. "Why don't you sleep on it, and then make a final decision tomorrow morning? If you still want to visit Colorado, let me know. I'll get you to the airport and be waiting when you get back to Florida."

Their goodbyes were brief. An abbreviated exchange of "I love you" and a promise to talk in the morning.

Alex put the work van in gear, focusing on the task ahead of him. He had a customer and a nonworking air conditioner waiting for him. They were his main concern now. He'd talk with Caron again tomorrow morning, when the emotion of the day had worn off and she was calmer. More reasonable.

THREE

• ♥ • •

*I*f he was going to achieve his dreams—at least the professional ones—he needed to continue thinking like an up-and-coming Realtor, but act more like an Army Ranger. When Kade was in the military, he'd demanded more of himself. More physically. More mentally. Why should it be any different when it came to selling houses? Success wasn't going to track him down. And he wasn't waiting around for someone to show up and hand any career victories to him, either.

Kade paced his small office, outfitted with the essentials. A basic oak desk. A high-backed leather chair. Several coordinating dark brown cloth chairs for clients. Oak bookshelves. The requisite art pieces he'd selected because he liked the mountains and the autumn colors reflected in the lake and the perspective of the aspens zooming up against the clear blue of the Colorado sky. Mitch, who knew the quirks of his personality, allowed the quiet to stretch out between them.

"So I've been thinking—"

"Uh-oh." Mitch positioned his wheelchair to face Kade.

"Hear me out." Kade settled into the chair behind his desk, swiveling forward. "This is a good plan. One almost guaranteed to bring in more business, if the other guy goes for it."

"The other guy? You looking to bring in another Realtor?"

"No. Webster Select Realty is doing well for now with just you and me. If this project succeeds, then we'll probably need to talk about bringing on another Realtor."

With two quick motions of his muscular arms, Mitch maneuvered his wheelchair closer to the desk. "Appreciate being included in the process, boss. Now tell me your plan."

"How many times do I have to tell you to stop calling me boss? You invested in this company, too."

"Employee. Boss." Mitch pointed to himself, then to Kade, his grin meant to yank Kade's chain. "Enough of this lighthearted banter. Back to telling me about your *good plan*."

"Right. I have a friend in the homebuilders' association. He told me about this new builder who's entering this year's Peak Tour of Homes. Already entered." Kade leaned forward, resting his elbows on his desk, steepling his fingertips. "He's started a small subdivision. He's got half a dozen new homes in the plans. I'm going to approach him. Offer to pay his entry fee and provide signage—something better than that little sign on a stick you get. Then I offer to be onsite when the people start visiting the homes—"

"Ah. Put the Kade Webster charisma to work."

Kade waved away Mitch's statement. His plan was much more than some personal "razzle-dazzle."

"We can both take turns greeting the visitors. See if they're just looking at all the new homes or if they're actually in the market to buy one."

"I like the way you think, Kade. This is why you moved on from Hollister Realty."

"Mitch, that's the past. I'm focused on the future of Webster Select. Besides, your suggestion to try my luck in Colorado if I was going out on my own was a smart one." He motioned around the room. "It's gone well. But I'm not the only one who's going to see this opportunity and want to take advantage of it."

"So when are you talking to this guy?"

"His name's Eddie Kingston and I'm talking to him tomorrow. Had to get through the holiday weekend. We're meeting for breakfast."

"Turn on the Webster charm—the one that sells houses and attracts the ladies—" Mitch's smile widened with every word he spoke.

"Hey, I sell houses because I've worked hard and learned the business. We both do. And I'm not interested in attracting anyone right now. That's the last thing on my mind."

"The Hollisters really did a number on you, didn't they?" Mitch rubbed his fingers through his dark blond hair, still cut in a military style.

"I'm focused on the future now—the future of Webster Select." Kade shifted his position, reaching for the ballpoint pen labeled with his business information and tapping it on the desk. "So, you still feeling good about the Mudder?"

"Very smooth, changing the subject." Mitch gave him a quick thumbs-up. "And yes, I'm looking forward to the chance to splash some muddy water in your face."

"We'll see who's muddier by the end of the course." Kade knew his grin matched his friend's. "Lacey coming to watch?"

"Yes, and she's declared herself the team photographer, too. She's studying the online map and trying to figure out where she can take pictures along the way. She also said to invite you over for dinner tonight."

"I'm in. It's always good to see Lacey and remind you two—"

"That you introduced us to each other. Yeah, yeah." Mitch rolled his wheelchair a few feet backward. "You'll be best man at our wedding."

"You plan on proposing anytime soon?"

"Did I say anything about proposing?" Mitch broke eye contact.

"Just asking. You don't want somebody to move in on Lacey while you're biding your time—"

"Thanks for the vote of confidence, man." Mitch didn't laugh at the joke. "I'd like to, but . . ."

"But what? Are you worried about Lacey not understanding what life will be like—"

"Married to a double amputee?" Mitch's voice deepened.

"I was gonna say married to someone as ugly-stubborn as you. But okay, we'll go with that. Surely you two have talked about the challenges."

"Sure, we've tried to talk through the challenges. All the what-ifs. Lacey says the unexpected is covered in the 'for better, for worse' clause in the wedding vows." Mitch fisted his hands in his lap. "I'm a little more practical. We can't live in her apartment. *I* can't live in her apartment. What am I supposed to do, ask Lacey to come live with me and my brother, Tony, after we're married? You and the other guys were great, putting the ramp out in front of my brother's house. And retrofitting the shower for me. Even if I opted to buy the house from him, day-to-day living there is . . . well, it's cramped and challenging. We'd have to do a bunch of construction on the house to really make it work for us long-term."

"So you take out a loan. Do what you need to do. Lots of married couples do that."

"Yeah, well, there's no use pretending Lacey and I'll be a normal married couple." Mitch's gaze didn't waver. "But I'm still committed to living as normal a life as possible, Kade. And I want to be able to provide a decent house for me and my wife."

"I understand."

"I keep hoping I can find a bigger house to buy. Something that will work now and in the future . . . if . . . when we have children."

"Have you talked to Lacey about it?"

"No. I want to do this myself. I've had to get used to adapting or asking for help for a lot of things. Buying a house—that I want to do on my own."

"Come on, Mitch. Did you forget I'm a Realtor, too?" Kade waved his hands up and down in front of himself. "Hello? Finding people the right house is what I do for a living."

"If I can't find anything, what makes you think you can?"

"Thanks for that, buddy."

"Besides, I want to keep this quiet. I don't want to get Lacey's hopes up."

"I can be discreet. Tell me your price range, some specifics, what location you'd like to settle in, and I'll see what I can find. Between the two of us, we'll find the perfect house. Something that won't require too many changes."

"We keep this between you and me, right?"

"Absolutely. Part Realtor, part secret keeper. And I like surprises as much as the next guy. When we find the house, we'll put a big red bow on the front door with a tag that says 'For Lacey. Love, Mitch.'"

His comment earned a laugh from Mitch. "I'm going to hold you to that."

"We'll make it happen." Kade pressed his hand against his chest, right where his heart was. "We've had each other's backs for a long time, Mitch. That doesn't stop just because we got out of the military. We'll find your house. I promise. And praying about it—that's going to help, too."

"I needed that reminder."

"How about we pray about finding the right house now. And then we'll plan on praying together at the start of each work day, so long as we're both in the office."

"Sounds good."

The prayer was direct. Brief. But it—and the agreement to work together—reminded Kade that he wasn't the only one with goals.

"Now, what time's dinner?"

Mitch checked his watch. "Not for another hour. Why?"

Kade powered up his computer. "Get over here. Let's browse houses a bit before we head over."

. . .

There were other Realtors vying for Eddie Kingston's favor, but Kade expected to be the one who won.

A four-year stint as an Army Ranger had taught him many things about survival. One of them was: *Know your chances for success. No matter what they are—succeed at any cost.*

He'd heard through the grapevine that breakfast was Kingston's favorite meal of the day, so he'd scratched the idea for a lunch meeting. He'd arrived early at Over Easy, setting his sights on one of the few booths in the restaurant. Before Eddie arrived, he'd tipped the waitress, who'd introduced herself as Felicia, to ensure good service and no need to rush. But all of that was merely the backdrop for today's meeting. Now he had to convince the other man to do business with him—and no one else.

Kade had prepared almost two hours of conversation. Well-thought-out, guided questions aimed to put Kingston at ease. What Mitch called charisma required planning and forethought. Kade was disciplined—had the ability to do the needed work, no matter what it took. His years as a Realtor had honed his natural ability to read people. And despite how things had ended with Russell Hollister, Kade was thankful the man had taught him the importance of taking the time to know his clients. Anticipating their needs.

Once Eddie arrived at nine, it was all about being relaxed. Focusing on the man across the table and keeping the agenda hidden. Like most people, Eddie enjoyed talking about himself. He liked to think Kade was interested in him as a person, not just as a project. Eddie loved his wife and two preteen girls, and owned an extensive collection of Marvel comics. Over breakfast, they talked football, found out they'd both served in the military—Eddie in the air force—and they both liked water-skiing.

They ate huevos rancheros, sharing sides of buttermilk biscuits and sage gravy, and bacon. Kade moved the conversation from personal to professional, first asking about Eddie's work history and his business philosophy—both of which he already knew, thanks to his research—and then finally outlining how he wanted to partner with him.

"Eddie, I realize you're talking with other Realtors. I'll admit I'm not the biggest company in town. But *no one* will work harder for you during the Tour of Homes than I will." Flashing a smile and taking the time to thank Felicia, Kade motioned for her to refill their coffee cups. "I'm prepared to cover the entire amount of your entry fee and purchase better signage outside your home on the tour. And if you want, I'm connected with a great home stager. We can work with you to decorate the house."

Eddie sipped his coffee from the red pottery mug, his scarred

knuckles testimony to years of working in construction. Between the two of them, they'd finished off an entire pot of the
strong liquid fuel. Once this deal was completed, Kade was
going to flush out his system with lots of water and a run along
the Santa Fe Trail.

"I like the way you handle yourself, Webster. No denying
that. The question is, can we work together? We've been talking the Tour of Homes, but let's be honest with one another.
Behind all that, there's the possibility of a long-term business
relationship. Are you the right Realtor to represent Kingston
Homes—not just now, but possibly for years to come? I've got
big plans. I can't afford to make mistakes that are going to cost
me—and I don't just mean financially." Eddie placed his napkin
on the table beside his plate. "I'm going to have to think on
this—"

Kingston was going to walk. And if he walked, Kade knew
he'd end up with a polite "no thanks" at the end of the day. He
knew the importance of closing a deal.

"You're right." Kade leaned forward, holding up his hand
to prevent Eddie from leaving. "Of course this is about more
than the Tour of Homes. Who thinks about just one home?
You've got plans for six homes in just that development. We're
businessmen. We think about the future. It's the way we build
our success. The truth is, we could benefit each other—create a
bigger vision for both of us. I've seen the plans for that house,
Eddie. It's a beautiful home. Spectacular, really. But why not
make it more?"

Kade knew he had the other man's attention when Kingston
settled back into his chair. "What do you mean?"

"We're located in Colorado Springs. Surrounded by the U.S.
Air Force Academy. Schriever and Peterson Air Force Bases.
Fort Carson Army Base. Both retirees and Wounded Warriors

are part of the population." Kade paused for the briefest of moments. "Why not adapt that custom home of yours so that it's handicap accessible for our wounded veterans?"

"Is this some kind of joke, Webster? The Tour of Homes opens the Monday after the Fourth of July."

"I know you're not afraid of a little hard work, Eddie. You wouldn't have started your own custom-home business if you were." Kade forced himself to appear relaxed. This was the moment when he either won or lost Eddie's confidence. "I'm suggesting retrofitting the master bathroom. Reworking some of the kitchen counter space. The sink. Widening the doorways. Replacing some of the carpeting."

"Ramps out front and back." Eddie mirrored Kade's posture. "I know what it would take. Manpower around the clock. My costs could skyrocket."

"But think of the impact of this house. Include these changes, and you would be making a statement to every single person who walks through about how our wounded vets, our retirees, should live in a home that is both functional and attractive. That these men and women deserve it." Kade took a deep breath. "That someone like Mitch Herringshaw deserves it."

"Who's Mitch Herringshaw?"

"He's a Realtor who works with me. We were Army Rangers together. Mitch is a double amputee." A flash of memory— Mitch lying in a hospital bed as Kade waited for him to wake up. How he'd thought *sleep, sleep* with every breath, because then he wouldn't have to tell his friend . . . With a shake of his head, Kade dispelled the memory. "If you want your name associated with that kind of project, then I'm your man."

Kade sat back. He'd played his hand. Not that any of this was a game. He meant every word he'd said. Soldiers like Mitch shouldn't have to settle for barely adequate homes. Now all he could do was wait and see if Eddie was all in. Or if he'd gambled and lost.

"Less than six weeks to do everything you're talking about."

"You know it can get done. And you know no one else is doing it."

After a moment, Eddie rose to his feet, stepping out from the booth and holding out his hand. Kade stood, gripping the other man's hand in his.

"You're crazy, Kade—and I must be, too." The other man shook his head, a grin deepening the lines in his tanned face. "I've got some phone calls to make to see about adapting the house. My subcontractors are going to have a few things to say about this, and then they'll start drawing up their orders. And you, Webster—you need to write me a couple of checks. And contact that home stager of yours. I want to hear some ideas. Soon."

"Yessir." Kade's heart pounded in his chest, thundering in his ears so loudly it drowned out the noise of the restaurant. "Thanks for the opportunity, Eddie."

"This opportunity is filled with all sorts of risks."

"The more risks, the more potential payoffs."

FOUR

• ♥ • •

*M*aybe she didn't have what it took to get married. She'd been in almost-engaged limbo for too long. Or maybe a woman shouldn't go to a bridal fair straight from the airport after an impromptu trip, too much stress, and too little sleep.

Of course, the fact that one of the last things Alex had said to her before she went through airport security was "I still don't understand why you're going to Colorado" pulled her between two places. Alex had kissed her. Told her to have a safe trip. But all the while he'd looked as if he wanted to insist she somehow retrieve her luggage from the airline and come back home with him.

And now here she was in the middle of Denver. Not a drop of humidity in the fast-paced city's air. Mountains that lurked just beyond all the buildings that had been framed by the small plane window during their approach to Denver International Airport.

The bridal frenzy surged around them the minute Margo led her maid of honor and trio of bridesmaids into the convention center. Caron halted just inside the doorway, trying to get her bearings.

Couldn't she go sit in the car with her luggage? Check to see if she had any text messages from Alex? Take a nap?

Margo spun around and faced her. "Come on, we've got to get shopping! I paid extra for the early-entrance tickets."

"If getting all the way down the aisle to 'I do' requires this kind of attack-and-leave-no-survivors approach to shopping, then I'll just date Alex forever."

"Oh, come on." Margo grabbed her wrist, pulling Caron alongside her. "You're braver than this."

"If I'm so brave, then what am I doing playing runaway after I quit my job?" Caron whispered the question to herself.

"What did you say?"

"Lead on. I'm right behind you."

Within forty-five minutes, Margo had each of her bridesmaids loaded down with a selection of dresses in various shades of purple.

"There's an empty dressing room!" Margo marshaled them forward, using her minisuitcase of a purse to clear a path through the crush of women. "Those three girls just walked out!"

Caron averted her eyes from some of the bridal expo attendees who, in their search for the ultimate bargain, had abandoned all hope of securing the privacy of a dressing room. Instead, they chose to try on garments in between the racks of sample dresses. Or while friends formed a human barrier around them. Or wherever they found some open space in the convention center.

"Grab that room before someone else does." Caron tightened her arms around the shifting load of bridesmaid dresses. "I am not changing clothes in public—not even for you, Margo. There was a TV news team interviewing people in here earlier."

Leslie and Brooke, who carried their own loads of purple-hued bridesmaid dresses, nodded in agreement and murmured an endless litany of "excuse me, excuse me" as they tried to keep up with Margo. Emma, in true I've-got-this-under-control maid-of-honor fashion, succeeded first, and positioned herself in front of the prized location of the dressing room with her sister.

"Okay, get in there and start trying dresses on." Margo pulled back the white curtain.

Caron blew a wisp of hair out of her eyes, but didn't budge. "All of four us? At the same time?"

Margo waved the curtain like a flag flapping in a strong coastal breeze. "The sooner you try these dresses on, the sooner we find out if anything works, and if we need to go looking again—"

"Be reasonable. Four women and who knows how many dresses in that makeshift space would be a disaster waiting to happen." Caron shifted the armful of dresses again as the one on top started to slip. "Why not let Emma and Brooke go first? Then Leslie and I'll go."

Emma, who balanced her stack of dresses like a professional juggler, nodded. "Caron has a point. No sense in having your bridal party suffocate under a mountain of purple dresses."

"Fine. But I want to see everything you try on. Everything."

"Yes, ma'am. You're the bride-to-be." Emma motioned Brooke into the room as Margo held the curtain open. "You're in charge today."

"Three months to plan a wedding. Three months." Margo settled onto the expo's concrete floor, which, for today's festivities, was covered in a bold blue carpet. "I must be crazy. Tell me all this will be worth it so Ronny and I can have the wedding we want."

"It will be worth it." Caron joined Leslie and Margo on the floor, setting her selection of dresses to the side, creating a semi-circle in front of the dressing room.

"What about you?" Margo ran her fingers through her short-cropped brown hair and then leaned back on her hands, her gaze focused on Caron.

Caron pointed to herself. "What about me *what*?"

"What about you and Alex? You've been dating for almost two years now. You go to the beach. Have dinner every weekend with your parents. When are you going to make life easy on yourselves and get married?"

The clamor of women's voices seemed to intensify as if someone had found a universal volume control and twisted it all the way up. The air was thick with an overwhelming blend of competing perfumes.

Make life easy. Get married. When were she and Alex going to get married? Good question. One both sets of parents asked with increasing frequency.

"Oh, I don't know. We're both so busy with work—"

"Now you sound like some sort of jet-setting celebrity couple who won't ever set a wedding date. *We're both so busy.*" Margo stopped when the dressing room curtain swished open and Emma stepped into view.

"What do you think?" Emma stood with one hand on her hip, the other holding up the too-long skirt of her plum-colored halter dress.

"I like yours better than this froufrou thing." Brooke hung back in the doorway, plucking at the feathered neckline of her short cocktail dress.

"No to the feathers." Margo waved Brooke back into the dressing room. "Yours, Emma, is a definite possibility. Next."

Without missing a verbal beat, Margo refocused on Caron.

"So do you want a summer wedding? That would mean waiting another year. Fall? That would be a challenge to pull off. Maybe a Christmas wedding?"

"I haven't really given it much thought." Caron played with the zipper of one of the dresses. Up. Down. Up. Down. Up.

"Oh, come on. Every woman imagines her dream wedding. Surely you and Alex have talked about it—"

"A little."

Or not.

"Margo mentioned your brother, Logan, had a destination wedding, right?" Leslie leaned around Margo to join the conversation, her layered black hair falling over her gray eyes.

"Yes—in Destin, at the Henderson Beach Inn. Logan was living in Oklahoma and Vanessa lived in Colorado."

"So what about that?" Margo played with the strand of turquoise beads around her neck. "Or you could do something out of the country. Italy. Or the Bahamas."

"A destination wedding? I don't know."

How long did it take for Emma and Brooke to change dresses? And why couldn't they talk about Margo's August wedding instead of Caron's yet-to-be-scheduled one? She and Alex were in a relationship holding pattern: girlfriend and boyfriend. Marriage would happen . . . sometime.

"I read about a couple who dated for twelve years before they got married. Can you imagine? Twelve years." Leslie shook her head, grabbing her sunglasses just before they toppled off her head. "No, thank you. I would have broken up with the guy long before that."

"Maybe she did." Margo stretched her long legs out in front of her, her white capris showing off her tan. "Maybe they were that perpetual on-again-off-again couple, but somehow she always knew he was the one."

"Or he knew she was the one." Caron averted her eyes as a woman right behind Margo peeled off her sundress to try on a long, electric-orange gown. "Why do we always assume it's the girl hanging around, waiting for the guy to make up his mind and propose?"

"Good point." Margo ducked as a woman walked by, an assortment of dresses slung over her shoulder. "Although, really, you'd think you'd know what you wanted in a relationship after twelve years, right?"

They were surrounded by nonstop noise and motion as Caron searched for some way to change the topic. "Didn't you mention you and Ronny were buying a house?"

Leslie stared straight ahead, eyes locked on the dressing room curtains, while Margo looked everywhere but at Caron. Something between a laugh and a groan wheezed out of her friend's mouth. "Funny you should mention that . . ."

"I'm not following. Are you buying a house?"

"We're still looking." Margo's next words rushed over her. "And Kade Webster is our Realtor."

Kade Webster? *Her* Kade Webster? Well, not that he was "her" Kade Webster anymore. They'd broken up two years ago—or rather, she'd broken up with him.

"Margo, why didn't you say something?"

Emma and Brooke stepped into view again, interrupting Margo's explanation. This time Emma wore a short lavender dress with an Empire waist and a flowing, layered skirt. Leslie wore a long plum sheath.

Margo turned her attention to the other women, tilting her head and tapping her forefinger against her chin. "Yours is fun, Emma. What do you think?"

"This style feels a little young for me. It's more like a junior bridesmaid dress or something I might have worn to homecoming. I like the one Brooke has on."

"I like this one, too." Brooke turned a slow three-sixty, standing on her tiptoes in her navy-blue flip-flops.

"Did all of you find that style in your size?"

Caron couldn't seem to push past the reality that Kade Webster was in Colorado, too. Of course she'd known that. Still remembered the night her father mentioned the news that Kade had left Florida to strike out on his own in Colorado, starting a realty company with a friend. How had she forgotten he was *right here*—and why hadn't Margo told her that she and Ronny were using Kade as a Realtor? Her world suddenly felt small. Too small.

Enough. Today was about Margo's wedding. This trip had nothing to do with her ex-boyfriend. And Margo didn't have plans to go house-hunting while Caron was in town. Did she?

"Caron?" Margo's voice pushed through the haze of questions whirring in her brain.

"I'm sorry. What?"

"Do you have the same style of dress as Brooke is wearing?"

"I lost track. Maybe." Caron riffled through the pile of dresses, the material soft against her fingers. So many purple hues. Maybe if she tried to name them all it'd help fend off any memories of Kade. Dating him was nothing but a momentary stop on her romantic journey to happily-ever-after with Alex.

"Well, keep that style in mind. If we decide we want it, we can look again." Margo rose to her feet and took a closer look at the dress Brooke wore. "I think it will look good on all of you."

The moment Brooke and Emma disappeared into the dressing room again, Caron turned to Margo. "Explain yourself."

"What?"

"You know what. Explain this failure to mention Kade Webster is your Realtor."

Her friend cleared her throat, tugging at her top. "It's the craziest coincidence—"

"Right."

"No, really. One of my coworkers used Kade when she bought a house, and so when I mentioned Ronny and I wanted to buy a house, she recommended him." Margo's words tumbled out faster and faster. "She gave me his phone number, and I called him. We were talking before I realized—"

Caron held up her hand, eyes closed. "Fine."

"Fine? That's all you have to say?"

"What else am I supposed to say? It's done. I'm just too tired for surprises today."

Almost three hours later, they'd conquered the madness on the dress sales floor. Four gowns labeled amethyst, boysenberry, antique fuchsia, and lavender were stowed in the trunk of Leslie's car, and the escape to outside the convention center was a welcome relief—even if it was located in the middle of Denver.

The bride-to-be declared it was time to visit vendors and consider reception decor, wedding cakes, and announcements.

"That was worth it." Brooke linked her arm through Caron's.

"We found bridesmaid dresses for under a hundred dollars apiece. I should say so."

And the topic of Kade Webster had been dropped. Fine. He was Margo's Realtor. Caron was only here for a week. She could evade memories of the man for seven days.

Caron bumped into Leslie, who had come to a halt just inside the event center doors. "What is going on?"

"Prizes." Leslie waved a ballpoint pen and a square entry form. "We're entering for Margo. Saves us time."

"You should enter, too." Brooke gathered several squares of paper, digging through her purse for a pen.

Caron tried to move around her friends. "Me? No. Margo's the bride-to-be."

Margo blocked her path, handing her several entry forms and a pen. "That's a brilliant idea. Go ahead and enter. You could win a wedding dress, jewelry, a photography package—the grand prize is some sort of destination wedding in Telluride. Wouldn't it be fun if we both won something?"

Caron resisted the offer of the pen and paper. "But I'm not even engaged—"

"It's only a matter of time. You and Alex have been together forever." A chorus of agreements followed Margo's statement. "Fill out one or two, just for fun. Put an imaginary date on the form. Besides, what are the odds? There are hundreds of other people here."

"Fine. But just one."

She'd humor Margo. One of the reasons she'd come to Colorado was to join in on the prewedding fun, right? It was all about making the bride-to-be happy today. Caron scribbled her name on the form. She picked a date sometime next fall for the line labeled *Wedding Date*, filling out her phone number, e-mail, and future husband's name.

Caron stuffed the slip of paper into a large box wrapped in white paper covered with silver filigree hearts and topped with an enormous silver bow. She trailed behind the other women into the side of the convention center filled with all things nuptial. Vendors displaying wedding invitations. Tables decorated for wedding receptions in coordinating table linens. DJs playing competing playlists—each advertising the perfect songs to get guests on the dance floor. Floral bouquets and displays. Romantic getaways for honeymoons. Caterers with food displays. All overlaid by a frantic buzz of nonstop conversation punctuated by laughter.

"Where do we start?" Caron had to raise her voice to be heard.

"Let's just go counterclockwise around the room." Emma took charge. "Margo, you let us know when you want to stop at a particular booth, okay? If we get separated, we'll meet back by the display with the huge black-and-white geometric wedding cake in an hour. Sound good?"

"It's a plan." Caron stepped aside as another group of women flowed into the room. One girl with long blond hair wore a white sash emblazoned with the words BRIDE-TO-BE. Did she think this was some sort of bachelorette party? "Let's get moving."

. . .

When, oh when, could they head south to Margo's apartment in Colorado Springs? Caron didn't want to fight crowds of brides and their bridesmaid wannabes. She didn't want to listen to wedding music. Didn't want to ooh and aah over reception favors. Didn't want another stranger to ask her, "So when are you getting married?"

All she wanted was something to eat and then crawl into bed and go to sleep. She'd start having fun again tomorrow.

"Can we leave now?" Caron tapped Margo's shoulder, certain she sounded like a whiny child on an endless road trip asking her mom, *"Are we there yet?"*

"We can't leave before they finish. They're getting ready to announce the winner of the grand prize." Margo bounced on her tiptoes, trying to peer over the shoulders of the rows of women in front of her. "Who knows? Maybe I'll win."

"Or maybe Caron will." Brooke laughed at her suggestion.

"I don't think so." Caron backed away from her friends. "I'm going to wait outside. I need some fresh air."

Well, as fresh air as she could get standing on a street in downtown Denver. Of course, she could be a total tourist and take a photo of the huge sculpture of a blue bear peering into the Denver Convention Center and then post it to her Instagram account.

She made her way through the crowd gathered near the stage that, only an hour earlier, had been the site of a fashion show of wedding gowns. The emcee had described each one in glowing terms. *Perfect. One-of-a-kind. Elegant. Showstopping.* Was that the goal of a wedding—to stop the show?

Now the exuberant emcee in a black tux rattled off the names of the various winners, causing the attendees to erupt in shouts of "Me!" and "I won!" as women rushed the stage to claim their prizes.

She was almost to the door, her gaze focused on the lighted green exit sign, when the crowd erupted again, celebrating the final winner of the day. *Hooray.* She imagined some lucky girl was now vaulting onto the stage to hug Tuxedo Guy while friends and complete strangers jumped up and down and applauded.

Just as she stepped outside, the first hint of Colorado air a welcome relief after hours of stale air filled with marital merriment, someone grabbed both her arms, pulling her to a stop.

Caron whirled around and came face-to-face with Brooke and Leslie, who seemed determined to drag her back inside and toward the stage.

"What are you doing?" Caron dug her heels into the thin layer of carpeting. "I told you, I'm going to wait outside."

"You won, Caron. You won!" Leslie took her other hand and joined Brooke in towing her back to the stage.

"I won—"

"Didn't you hear your name announced? You won the Colorado destination wedding!"

"You have a lousy sense of humor." Caron scanned the stage, spotting Margo and Emma standing beside the emcee bathed in the white spotlight, motioning her forward. They weren't kidding. "I don't want it. Tell them to give the prize to Margo."

"Margo already told them that we were going to get you. Go claim your wedding. Won't your boyfriend be surprised when you tell him?"

FIVE

• • • ♥ • • •

Work—the great distractor.

Except there wasn't much to fix here.

Alex rubbed his forearm across his forehead, rocking back on his heels as he contemplated the air-conditioning unit in front of him. The SOLD sign still planted in the front yard meant a home inspector okayed the thing—and after cycling the unit through, it was running just fine. Despite the mechanical puzzle sitting right in front of him, his mind wandered back to earlier this morning.

Caron had quit her job. And despite his protests, she'd accepted Margo's invitation, disappearing into the slow-moving line of passengers making their way through security at Denver International Airport. His day had started hours before he ever saw his first client.

"Excuse me."

At the sound of a woman's voice behind him, Alex twisted around, maintaining his balance by putting his hand on the patchy grass that covered the backyard.

"Oh, I'm so sorry." The homeowner who'd answered the door when he arrived backed away, sloshing water out of the blue plastic cup onto the ground. "I thought you might be thirsty."

"Thanks. I am at that." He rose to his feet, towering over her like a modern-day giant.

"So how's it look?" She walked around the air conditioner as if she could figure out what was wrong. "Can you fix it so it doesn't keep tripping the breaker?"

"I cycled it through and it seems fine now, ma'am." The ice water eased his dry throat, even as the midday sun caused a slow trickle of sweat between his shoulder blades.

"Oh, call me Jessica, please." Her smile seemed genuine. Friendly, not flirtatious. "I just don't know why it keeps tripping the breaker and then it won't restart. You're the second repairman to come out and check it."

"Compressor could be going bad. That's your worst-case scenario. If this continues to happen, you might need to replace it."

The woman smoothed the hem of her plain yellow T-shirt, shading her eyes. "How much would that cost?"

"For this size house? You're looking at a three-ton unit. So, about twenty-five hundred dollars."

Her face blanched, her eyes widening behind her silver wire-rimmed glasses. "I'd like to avoid that expense if I could." When she twisted her fingers together, he noted she didn't wear a wedding ring. Probably single. A first-time homeowner. Sunk all her savings on the down payment.

"It's only a diagnostic charge today." He'd charge her the standard rate minus 10 percent. Good thing this hadn't happened during the holiday weekend when he'd have to charge extra for an emergency call, as well as overtime. "You can call again if there's a problem."

"I hope not. It's barely the beginning of June and the temps and humidity are crazy high. I need my air-conditioning. Scotty can't sleep without it."

Ah. No husband—but a boyfriend who couldn't sleep without the air-conditioning on. "I hear that a lot."

"I imagine you keep pretty busy."

"Got that right." He drained the cup of water, handing it back to her. "Thanks. I'll write up your bill and be on my way."

"Saving the day at someone else's house?"

He chuckled. Right. He was a real superhero. "Just repairing air conditioners."

His work boots tapped a soft staccato on the sidewalk leading from the front door to his work van, the words EMERALD COAST AIR-CONDITIONING AND HEATING printed across the side in blue block letters. When his phone buzzed on his hip, a quick glance showed that it was his father.

"What's up, Dad?" Alex slipped into the van, turning it on and starting up the A/C, welcoming the blast of cool air.

"Mrs. Carlson called, wondering where you are."

"Just finished the job before her. Can you call her back and let her know I'm on my way?"

"Sure."

There was silence on the other end of the phone. Why wasn't his father hanging up, letting him get back to work?

"You need something else?"

"Have you talked to you mother today?"

"No, I didn't see her before I left the house, but I left early. Had to take Caron to the airport." Alex tossed his cap onto the dash. "Mom seemed fine yesterday—and she did go to the Memorial Day barbecue with the Hollisters."

"Being with the Hollisters helps. But she's been having a tough time. You know."

"She usually does this time of year."

"This year seems worse, for some reason. There's nothing really to say or do—just wait for it to pass. But could you check on her—maybe before the workday's over?"

"Sure." Resting his arm on the steering wheel, he mentally scrolled through his appointments. "I'll run by home sometime today."

"Thanks."

As his father hung up, Alex wrestled with the urge to call him back. To continue the conversation. To say things he'd wanted to say for years, unspoken words that caused him to clench his jaw, his fingers tightening around his cell phone.

No. I'm not checking on Mom.

I don't want to do this anymore.

But so many years of being the good son—the only son—who accepted responsibility without complaint had taught him well. There was no sense in putting up a fight. Against who? His parents? A ghost?

He'd do what needed to be done. Keep the peace, such as it was.

.   .   .

The house was quiet, the curtains drawn so that no hint of sunlight filtered through. Alex shut the front door and unlaced his worn work boots, leaving them in the entryway. He tucked his cap in his back pocket.

"Mom? It's Alex."

No reply.

He balanced the white Styrofoam container in one hand, turning on the foyer light. It was that odd in-between time— too late for lunch, too early for dinner, but he'd stopped and picked up a chef's salad for his mother. Just in case she hadn't eaten breakfast. Or lunch.

The living room was empty. Everything in its place. Neat and dusted, thanks to the maid service his father had decided it was worth paying to come in and clean once a week. Vacuum. Clean the bathrooms. Change the sheets. Make sure the dirty dishes were loaded into the dishwasher and unloaded once they were cleaned.

The kitchen bore evidence that his mother had been up. A couple of wine bottles sat on the kitchen counter—one empty, one half full. A few glasses cluttered the sink, all with a small layer of liquid in the bottom. His father had probably gathered them up from their bedroom. No need to sniff them and find out what his mother had been drinking. It didn't matter anymore what she drank. White wine today. Red wine tomorrow.

Some days he could almost convince himself it didn't matter that she drank at all.

His mother had left her black cotton robe draped on the back of one of the chairs in the breakfast nook. He could only hope she'd decided to get dressed this morning. Or had slept in a nightgown.

Alex picked up the empty bottle. Zinfandel. Threw it in the trash. He drained the other bottle in the sink—also zinfandel—the liquid disappearing down the drain with barely a sound. Then he tossed the bottle into the trash with the first, glass colliding with glass with a sharp clink. Alex piled the glasses in the dishwasher. One less thing to deal with later tonight.

He didn't even bother checking the sunroom. His mother lived like one of those vampires in a gothic novel, preferring darkness to sunlight. In the past, when she used to somehow juggle her drinking and friendships and the occasional business dinner, she'd managed to maneuver between the foyer, kitchen, and the dining room, never coming near a window.

Friends. Who was he kidding? The Hollisters were their most loyal friends, the only ones who knew the Madisons' well-guarded secret. They knew who his mother was. What his mother was. And they accepted that most days she was a functioning alcoholic. And they loved her and Alex and his dad even on the days when his mother struggled and failed.

The hallway leading to his parents' master bedroom used to be lined with framed family photos. Of him, the firstborn son. And then Shawn, the baby. Christmas photos. Easter photos. Birthday photos. The beginning-of-school-year photos, Shawn trailing Alex. And then . . . there had been only photos of Alex. He'd bought each of the inexpensive frames for his school photos. Hammered the nails into the wall, making sure the photographs were lined up, level with one another.

Look, Mom, I'm still here . . .

But now the walls were bare. He'd arrived home from his first year of high school one day to find every single photo gone. No explanation—just empty space.

"Where are all the family pictures, Dad?"

His father tore the plastic wrap off a frozen dinner, placing it on the rotating glass plate in the microwave and punching in the required time. "I don't know. I just got home."

Alex tossed his canvas book bag onto the kitchen table. "Mom had to have taken them down. She was the only one home today. She knows where they are."

"Probably."

Alex continued to talk to his father's back as he pulled a carton of milk from the fridge. "Aren't you going to ask her? Put them back up?"

"No."

No? That was it? Just no?

"Why not?"

"Obviously seeing the photos upset your mother. Putting them back up will upset her again. Let it be, Alex."

And that was the end of that. *Let it be.* No confrontation. Just manage. Maintain.

It was as if he fought an invisible force as he made his way to his parents' bedroom. The carpeting might as well have been thick, clinging mud or quicksand, the way his steps slowed. For all the times he'd gone in search of his mother and never found her . . . hurt . . . there was always the very real possibility that this time . . . this time he'd open the door and find the sum of all his nightmares waiting for him.

Alex knocked on the half-open bedroom door. Waited. No sound. No slurred "Who is it?" The prayer he'd prayed since childhood skittered through his brain:

God, if you're there—and I know you are—please, let her just be asleep . . .

When he opened the door, holding his breath, his mother lay on her bed, her too-thin body tangled up in the comforter and sheets. A pillow was cradled in her arms like a child, her face pressed against it, eyes closed, her brown hair threaded through with gray and pulled into a messy ponytail. A glass sat on the bedside table, and beside it stood a bottle. Cheap and ready comfort. And his mother considered the relief worth the price.

She'd never know the true cost of her drinking. Never be able to reckon it.

Quick, silent strides brought him to her bedside. His hand on her shoulder only reinforced how little she weighed—her form skeletal beneath his touch.

"Mom? It's Alex."

With a mumble, she buried her face in the pillow.

He crouched beside her, raising his voice in an attempt to break through her drugged sleep. "Are you hungry? I brought you some lunch."

Her lids flickered . . . open . . . shut . . . open . . . revealing bloodshot eyes that held no glint of recognition. "Wha—?"

"Are you hungry?"

She closed her eyes, lifting her hand in a feeble attempt to push him away. "No . . . go away . . ."

Alex rose to his feet. Covered his mother with the top sheet. Best to let her sleep it off. She wouldn't remember he was there. And if she did wake up, she'd only get herself all worked up again, talking to him—and then drink more once he left. He knew the routine well. All too well.

Once in the kitchen again, he drained the third bottle into the sink and then threw it in the trash, the rattle of glass too loud in the silence that lurked in the house. Grabbing a piece of paper, he scrawled a note and left it on the counter, letting his mother know he'd left the salad in the fridge.

Crisis averted. Again. He'd report back to his father. He could call Caron and ask her for prayer. But he wouldn't. Not when she was already so stressed. This kind of day with his mother was nothing new. They'd talk later tonight and she'd know just what to say. At times like this he realized how much he loved her. Needed her. This was one of the reasons they were so right for each other. She knew his secrets. Kept his secrets. Loved him in spite of his secrets.

SIX

• ♥ • •

*K*ade could either ignore the growling of his stomach until he got home and scavenged through the few leftovers in his fridge, make himself a protein shake, or stop and grab something to go and reheat it.

A guy had to eat.

He merged into the left-turn lane leading into University Village, mentally scrolling through restaurant options. *Tokyo Joe's. Which Wich. Chipotle. Panera. Noodles & Company.* Or he could just drive through Starbucks . . . but his body demanded something more than sugar and caffeine topped off with cream.

Chipotle. He'd grab a burrito and an iced tea, and get back on the road in less than ten minutes.

After circling the crowded parking lot twice before finding a parking space, he resigned himself to the reality that his wait at Chipotle might be longer than he'd prefer. He moved between cars, his thoughts scrolling ahead to the work waiting for him at home. He needed to check in with Mitch. Touch base with Eddie Kingston . . .

He stopped midstride as the driver's-side door of a white sedan swung open and a woman with short brown hair and sparkly earrings that almost reached her shoulders stepped out.

"Oh! I'm sorry! I didn't see you there—" The woman apologized with a light laugh that ceased altogether when she saw his face. "Kade!"

"Hey, Margo, what are you doing here?"

"Um . . . I'm going to dinner with—" She removed her tortoiseshell sunglasses, her gaze tracking left as someone else stepped out of the passenger side of the car.

Caron Hollister.

The woman gripping the roof of the car was Caron Hollister. Light brown hair that hung past her shoulders. She must have abandoned the blonds-have-more-fun motto. Hidden behind a pair of pink retro sunglasses as they were, Kade couldn't see her brown eyes, the same color as a smoky topaz gemstone. She offered him the smile of a professional Realtor. Businesslike, but with just a hint of practiced charm.

"Kade."

"Caron's visiting me this week." Margo rushed into the looming silence. "Taking a few days off after—"

"Just taking some time off." Caron shut the car door with enough force to rock the car. "We're having dinner at Hacienda."

"Nice choice. I like their fajitas." Kade could maintain a casual tone, too, as if running into Caron Hollister, who should be two thousand miles away from here—and who was two years in his past—was a normal part of his day.

"We'll keep that in mind." Margo took a few steps back.

"Did you see the e-mail I sent you?"

At Kade's question, Margo stopped, sparing a quick glance at Caron, who waited by the front of the car. "No. We've been out and about all day. Garden of the Gods. Glen Eyrie. That sort of thing. I haven't checked my e-mail that much."

"I found a few new listings I thought you and Ronny might want to look out. Let me know what you think."

"Absolutely."

"We can take a look at them later this week if you want to—"

"I'll have to check with Ronny. And Caron is here until Sunday night."

"Don't worry about me, Margo." Caron raised her voice to be heard over the sound of a passing Harley. "I can entertain myself if you want to go look at some houses."

"Just text me. Whatever works." Kade nodded at Margo, then Caron. "Ladies. I'm off to get dinner. Enjoy yourselves."

. . .

He'd tossed the white Chipotle bag into the passenger seat of his SUV, secured the cup of iced tea in the holder, and cranked up the radio, the lyrics to "What We Ain't Got" filling the car—until he twisted the knob and silenced the song. Dinner would be cold by the time he got home, but so be it. Any food he dropped or dribbled, he only had to clean up later.

Not worth it.

His phone rang and he connected to the in-car Bluetooth before it had a chance to ring a second time.

"Kade Webster, Webster Select Realty."

"Hey, boss."

"How goes it, Mitch?"

"It's been a productive day. Although it is good to get my legs off and get back in the wheelchair—"

"Really, man? When are you going to stop saying stuff like that?"

"Hey, the things make me more mobile, but after a while they get old." Mitch laughed. "Gotta have a sense of humor, right? Anyway, I got a good offer on the property out in Falcon."

"Excellent."

"Lacey told me to call you, see if you wanted to come over for dinner."

"Your girlfriend is determined to feed me. Thanks for the invitation." Kade maneuvered the car onto I-25 heading north, allowing other cars to go ahead of him on the on-ramp. He wasn't in a rush. "But I picked up a carnitas burrito from Chipotle. I'm good."

"You sure? A burrito will keep. Have it for breakfast tomorrow."

"I appreciate the offer, but tell Lacey I'll take a rain check this time."

"Everything okay?"

"Sure." He debated saying anything more and then continued. "I ran into Caron Hollister earlier."

"Caron . . . Hollister? *The* Caron Hollister?"

"One and the same."

"She lives in Florida—"

"She's visiting Margo Owens, who happens to be one of my clients. I saw them in the University Village parking lot. They're going to dinner at Hacienda."

"And?"

"And nothing. I saw her." Kade tapped his thumbs against the steering wheel, stuck behind a slow-moving U-Haul van hauling a Jeep. "I'm not even certain we managed a formal hello and goodbye."

"If Lacey were in on this conversation, she'd ask how you were feeling."

"But she's not. And I'm fine. A bit surprised to see Caron on my turf . . . but fine. According to Margo, she'll be gone in a few days."

"Then let's get back to talking business, shall we?"

"It beats talking about old girlfriends. Let's leave that to the country songs." Kade signaled, moving to the left lane to pass the U-Haul. "I know how to sell houses. Caron Hollister? Obviously I didn't know her as well as I thought I did."

SEVEN

• ♥ • ♥ • ♥ •

Quitting her job had its perks.

Caron slipped into a jewel-tone swing tank that comple-
mented her khaki capris. A few days of sleeping in, several
shopping days with Margo that might require her borrowing
a second suitcase to get everything back home, hiking through
Ute Park—she was beginning to remember how to relax.

"You dressed?" Margo rapped on the door to her small guest
bedroom and then walked in.

"Hey! How about giving me a chance to say yes or no?"

"But you're dressed."

"But I might not have been—oh, never mind. Honestly,
you've reverted back to acting like we're living in a dorm
again." Their laughter blended together as she selected a pair of
gold hoop earrings from her zippered jewelry case and Margo
stretched out on her bed. "So, what's on the schedule today?"

"I thought we'd keep it low-key, since we're heading to Telluride tomorrow."

"You know we don't have to do that."

"Oh, yes we do. You're going back to Florida to tell Alex you won a destination wedding in Telluride, right? You need to see the area so you can tell him how beautiful it is."

"I certainly haven't figured out how to tell him over the phone that I won a wedding." Caron slipped on the first earring. "I'm not sure what he's going to say when I come home and tell him that I brought him a destination wedding back from my impromptu vacation. I think he'll be expecting something more along the lines of a Colorado T-shirt or a key chain."

"Like you've never done something surprising, Caron? Remember, Alex knew you back in high school when you went through your various fashion stages, including a toned-down Goth girl, skater chick, and finally settled on the award-winning athlete." Margo gave her a quick once-over. "I bet you go to bed at a decent hour every night now, don't you?"

"Trying to fit in at Hollister Realty." She finished with the second earring and did a quick bend-over-and-back-up to flip out her hair. "Be more of what my dad expects from one of his employees."

"Well, even with the conservative hairstyle and clipping your nails short, that doesn't mean you've clipped your wings, does it?" Margo rolled over on her back and sat up. "You're still allowed to be yourself, aren't you?"

"Of course. Off hours."

"Huh. If I know you, those are few and far between—for the same reason. You're trying to keep your dad happy."

Keeping her father happy. It's what she did best—or rather, what she'd tried to do for so many years, it came easily to her. And yet here she was, unemployed. She wasn't as good at pleasing her father as she thought.

"Can we get this conversation back on track? What are we doing—"

At the sound of her cell phone in the other room, Margo bolted off the bed. "Hold that thought. I'll be right back."

She returned ten minutes later, phone in hand, her red-tinted lips twisted and her well-thinned eyebrows furrowed.

"Everything okay?"

"Yeah." She slumped onto the edge of the bed. "That was Kade. He called to tell me that we could go see one of the houses he found a few days ago. He has an appointment set up today. At noon. But I told him I couldn't go."

"Why not?"

"Because you're here, obviously. We have plans."

"Today's our low-key day. I can hang out here while you're gone. Go ahead and see if it's something you and Ronny would like."

"I don't want to leave you alone here."

"Fine. I'll come with you."

Now why did she say that? Seeing Kade for even those brief, barely-say-hello moments in the parking lot had unsettled her. The man's black hair, his broad shoulders, his brown eyes that she'd recalled even though they'd been hidden behind his dark sunglasses—how easily she remembered the man's attractiveness. Why was she offering to be in the same room—the same house—with him?

Because she could tell her friend was torn—wanting to go check out the house but not wanting to abandon her.

"You will?" Margo had every right to sound surprised. "You'd have to see Kade Webster again."

Caron scrambled for an answer. "I won't have to see him that much. I'll look at the bedrooms while you and Kade tour the living room and kitchen. Then we switch. It'll be fine. Then you and I can go have lunch or something. Go ahead and call Kade back and get the address. Tell him we'll meet him there."

"Are you sure? I mean, I'd like to go see the house—"

"It's not a problem."

"All right." Margo started pressing numbers on her keypad. "I'm calling Kade now. If you're going to change your mind—"

"Not changing my mind. Make the call. I'll start the coffee. And I hope there's time to grab a quick breakfast."

"Hello, Kade, this is Margo." Her friend turned so that Caron was staring at her back. "Have you canceled that appointment yet? You haven't? Good. I want to keep it."

All he needed to do was walk Margo through the house—and ignore Caron Hollister.

Kade would concentrate on his client, highlight the assets of the three-bedroom, one-and-a-half-bath house in Rockrimmon, and be ready to answer Margo's questions. Caron wasn't his concern. She hadn't been for two years.

Both women waited behind him as he removed the key from the metal lockbox around the doorknob and gained entry to the house. Caron allowed Margo to precede her into the house, disappearing down the hallway to the bedrooms as Kade began listing the advantages of the open-concept living room/dining room area.

An eighteen-hundred-square-foot house should be big enough for both Caron and him to survive in for the next half hour.

"It's an older house, but they've remodeled the kitchen." Kade deposited his business card on the kitchen counter. "And put in new wood floors. Both bathrooms are updated, too. And, thanks to the last hailstorm, there's a new roof."

"I like the stone fireplace in the living room area." Margo did a slow turn. "Are those countertops Corian?"

"No, high-quality Formica. They've improved the product quite a bit."

"I wouldn't have guessed Formica."

"There's a decent backyard, too. It's xeriscaped so it doesn't require too much upkeep or watering."

"That's good. Ronny and I both like yard work, but we don't want a yard that costs a lot to keep up."

The house showed well. No lingering scents of cigarette smoke or pets, which were both immediate reasons to say no for a lot of his clients. No odd paint colors that he had to help potential buyers overlook, reminding them how inexpensive it was to paint.

They met up with Caron as she exited the bathroom off the master bedroom.

"I wouldn't label this an en suite, but it's still a good size. It's large enough that you could replace the single sink with dual raised glass bowls. Maybe paint the bathroom a classic gray. New light fixtures will make a difference, too." Caron pressed her lips together, raising her hand. "Sorry. Kade's the Realtor here, not me."

"But I want to know what you think." Margo's gaze switched back and forth between Kade and her friend. "You're Ronny's stand-in."

"We can always talk afterward. I'll let Kade do his job."

"I'm interested in your opinion, too." The comment escaped before he realized what he was going to say. Caron always had a way of casting a design vision for a house. "Realtor to Realtor."

Caron's eyes widened at his statement. "It seems to meet Margo and Ronny's requirements. The layout is nice. And the owners have done some good upgrades. Refinished wood floors will work well with the two Turkish rugs your parents said they're going to give you. The other bedrooms are decent sizes and you could have fun with colors. I could show you how to do some geometric patterns to create an accent wall in one of the bedrooms if you want. It's not that hard. The measurements for the half bath are small, so depending on what's already there, you might want to put in a pedestal sink. I did see that the hot water heater and furnace are older . . . sorry, I scrolled through the listing you e-mailed Margo."

"Understandable. If Margo and Ronny decide to put an offer on the house, we'd wait to see what the inspector said—"

"And possibly request the sellers purchase an extended home warranty?"

"That's always an option."

"Is the price negotiable?"

"It just came on the market a couple of days ago, so I'm not sure how much the sellers are willing to budge."

"The carpeting is in good shape. Not brand-new, but clean." Caron paced the perimeter of the bedroom, stopping by the door where Kade and Margo waited. "Rooms are good sizes. One could work as an office. You could replace the solid wood doors with glass-paned ones to let in more light."

"The third bedroom—the smaller of the two?" Kade tilted his head left, in the direction of the other room.

"Well, if Margo and Ronny want a guest bedroom, it makes sense to use the larger of the extra bedrooms for that, don't you think?"

"Good point."

Caron offered him a smile that might as well have been a sucker-punch to his solar plexus. This was the Caron Hollister he remembered—well, one facet of her, anyway. Talking houses. Suggesting improvements. Self-assured. And an alluring smile that slammed him up against the wall. A dash of Caron's casual beauty mixed with her warmth.

He faced Margo. His client. "So, Margo, you ready to look at the other rooms?"

"Sure."

Caron's voice slipped past any defense he tried to erect. "I'll just get out of your way and check out the rest of the house."

"Hey, you're keeping your skills up." Margo wrapped an arm around Caron's shoulders in a side hug. "Don't want to get rusty before you find another job."

"Margo!" With a quick shake of her head, Caron shrugged out of the other woman's embrace. "We're here to talk about whether this house works for you and Ronny—not about me."

"Right. Sorry."

"It's all good. Go on and finish the tour with Kade." With a soft "excuse me," Caron eased past them, escaping down the hallway and back toward the front of the house.

Kade stilled. What did that exchange mean? Caron was looking for a job? That made no sense at all. Back when they dated, she was focused on achieving success at her father's real estate office.

He released a breath. Inhaled, catching just a remnant of her still-familiar coconut-scented shampoo lingering in the air.

Back to work, Webster. You haven't been able to figure Caron Hollister out for a long time. And if you want to indulge in the scent of coconut, go buy yourself a piña colada cheesecake.

"You ready to see the other two bedrooms?" He ushered Margo forward with a sweep of his arm.

EIGHT

• • • ♥ • • •

Caron slid out of the front seat of Margo's car, Emma mirroring her movements from the passenger door behind her. An eager valet, dressed in a white shirt, black bow tie, and black pants, greeted them as he hauled their luggage out of the trunk.

It was almost one o'clock on Friday afternoon, and all Caron wanted was the key to their hotel room and the chance to relax. To take a nap. Anything but sit in Margo's car, scenery streaming by—no matter how captivating the mountains and glimpses of rocky streams were.

And to think they'd be duplicating this long drive on Sunday, only in reverse, all the way back to Colorado Springs and straight on to Denver, to guarantee she made her late-evening flight to Florida.

"Find me a decent cup of coffee and I may think the drive down here was worth it." Caron stretched her arms over her head. "Is there any time for me to schedule a massage at the hotel's spa?"

"Not this trip." Margo fought to remove her car key from her overloaded key ring so the valet could park her Subaru. "But feel free to schedule massages for us when we all come back here for your wedding."

"*If* I come back here."

"Of course you're coming back. We got up at six and drove for almost seven hours so we could discover all the reasons to convince Alex that he wants a destination wedding here."

"Driving through small mountain towns like Florissant and Lake George aren't going to convince him, that's for sure. Now, if he was a hunter or liked to fish, he might love Gunnison." Caron rolled her shoulders backward, then forward. "Although you managed the whole 'The speed limit's sixty-five, oh, surprise! Now it's forty-five' experience like a pro."

"It only takes getting caught in a speed trap once." Margo tossed the words over her shoulder, navigating her way to the front desk. "And you have to admit some of the scenery was remarkable."

"Yes, it was."

"You certainly said 'Stop the car, I need to get a picture of this' enough times." Margo waved Caron and her sister to move past her. "I'll check us in. Go ahead and look around. Take Emma with you and find coffee."

"You don't have tell me more than once." Emma tucked her arm through Caron's and tugged her forward. "Don't forget to ask if the events coordinator is around. We want to let them know their prizewinner is in the building."

Less than ten minutes later, Margo found them standing on a stone balcony overlooking a valley. "What, no coffee?"

"No, but we discovered this view." Emma motioned with one hand. "If Alex saw this, he'd say yes to a destination wedding, right, Caron?"

Mountains ringed the resort, covered with lush green trees—aspens and pines—with elaborate houses partially hidden within the forest. A grand golf course stretched out before them, golf carts rolling across the well-groomed grass. A patio dotted with tables covered with rust-colored umbrellas was off to the left, surrounded by a four-foot glass wall. To their right, floor-to-ceiling windows allowed visitors to the dining room to enjoy the view, too.

"Nice, isn't it, if you like rustic decor."

Caron rested her hands on the balcony. "I'm a Florida girl, but I like all the leather and stone, and the oil paintings of horses are stunning."

After a few moments, Margo led them back into the hotel lobby, her sandaled feet slapping against the flagstone floor. "Do you think Alex will like it?"

Caron did a slow turnaround. "It's different, but isn't a honeymoon the perfect time for something different?"

Emma rubbed her arms. "I didn't realize it would be so cool up here."

"One of my coworkers warned me that Telluride's weather is capricious. That's why I made sure we brought jackets, even if it is June." Margo waved the plastic keycards for their room. "How about we go unpack, then find the coffee shop and go walk around Mountain Village?"

Caron motioned to the small coffee cart situated in one corner of the lobby. "Change that to get coffee first and then go unpack and that sounds like a good plan."

．　．　．　．

"So do you think you're going to be able to convince Alex to have your wedding here?"

Caron would have laughed at the timing of Margo's question, but she was too busy gritting her teeth and gripping the passenger-door handle as her friend maneuvered her car up the winding, narrow dirt road leading to Bridal Veil Falls.

"I don't know that now is the best time to ask her that." Emma leaned forward from the backseat.

"What's wrong?" Margo pulled over to the right side of the road, close to the sloping edge, so a Jeep coming down from the waterfall could pass them. "This is the best part of the trip, next to the gondola ride in and out of Telluride. I think when we come back for the wedding, we should take a morning and hike up here."

"That might be fun." Caron forced herself to release her hold on the handle. Sit back. Unclench her jaw. "I think I might like this road better if I was walking it."

"This is nothing. You should drive up to Pikes Peak."

"Sorry I'll miss that this visit."

"Liar." Margo tossed her a grin. "Just look out the window and see how many different colors of columbines you can see along the side of the road. Tell me when you want to stop to take a photo."

"Just keep driving—" Caron gasped as the car turned a corner. "Stop! Stop!"

She was out of the car before Margo had parked, careful not to slip on the slick muddy ground. The nondescript rocky road had turned into a forest vale, the waterfall plummeting down the sheer face of the rock in front of them and becoming a cascading mountain stream. Towering mountain pines surrounded the makeshift parking lot, and other sightseers wandered about, necks craning, their faces upturned as they gazed at Bridal Veil Falls.

Alex had to see this.

She took photo after photo, first with her cell phone, then with her regular camera, which she had slung around her neck. Emma and Margo joined her, but she barely noticed them as she tried to frame the best photograph.

"We need a photo of the three of us." Margo tugged her toward the falls. "Get over here!"

The roar of the falls submerged the sound of their laughter, the spray dampening their hair.

"I've never seen anything like this." Caron turned to face the waterfall again. "Can you imagine wedding photos up here?"

"The events planner said you could have your ceremony up at the top of the falls, right?"

"Yes." Caron couldn't stop her shoulders from slumping as she covered her camera with the lens cap. "Let's keep driving. I want to get to the top and see what it's like."

Crouching down, Emma took one last photo of Bridal Veil Falls. "Envisioning a wedding?"

"Sort of."

"What's wrong?" Margo faced her, head tilted to the side, nose scrunched.

"What do you mean, 'What's wrong'?" Caron stood her ground, slippery as it was, but not quite making eye contact.

"You were all excited and then *poof!* It's like someone stuck a pin in you and all the enthusiasm disappeared. You're not nervous about telling Alex about winning the wedding, are you?"

"No . . . yes." Caron tucked her phone back in her jacket pocket. "Alex is wonderful. But what guy wants to hear his girlfriend say, 'Guess what, darling, I won a wedding! Ready to get married now?'"

"I'm sure you'll figure out a way to say it better than that. And besides, according to the rules, you have a year to redeem the prize."

"A year. It sounds like a long time, but when it comes to planning a wedding, it's not."

"So you go home tonight. You tell Alex in the next couple of days—whenever the time is right—and then you start planning.

I'm pulling off a wedding in three months. You can do this, Caron."

"And you'll help me, right? I mean, you'll help me plan the wedding—not to tell Alex."

"Of course. But first, let's finish the drive to the top of the falls and then get you back to Denver so you don't miss your flight."

"Sounds like a plan." Caron took one last photo of the waterfall. "This may be the only time I'm thankful I took a later flight."

NINE

• ♥ • ♥ • ♥ •

Maybe she should have listened to Margo and stayed in Colorado for two weeks. Of course, it was far too late to be rethinking that decision, considering her boarding pass for her flight from Denver to Fort Walton Beach was stuck between the pages of the novel she'd finished on the flight home. She'd returned late last night and spent today unpacking, doing laundry, and sorting through the stack of mail Alex had left on her dining room table.

Alex.

Caron fashioned her hair into a messy bun, clipping it in place. She'd also spent the day waiting for Alex to call—and half hoping he wouldn't.

She practiced her announcement out loud for the hundredth time. "Hi, Alex. Colorado was wonderful. And guess what? I won a destination wedding."

Still didn't work.

Maybe by the time she finished her as-regular-as-they-could-schedule-it Skype session with Logan, she'd know how to tell

Alex about her matrimonial surprise. But for now, she'd do one last check to ensure she had everything she needed for tonight's conversation, and then sign on.

Comfy pair of old sweatpants cut into shorts. T-shirt. Bare feet. *Check. Check. Check.*

Glass of sweet tea. *Check.*

Bowl of pretzel sticks. *Check.*

Smaller bowl of whipped cream cheese to dip her pretzels in. *Check.*

Caron moved the glass of tea closer to the edge of the coffee table before settling into the corner of the couch. Nine o'clock Monday night Niceville time—Logan should be on Skype. Time for her to get online, too. She'd taken her laundry from her washing machine to her dryer, and moved another load from her dryer to a laundry basket so she could fold clothes while they chatted. Home from Colorado for all of one day and her life was almost back in order.

Of course, not having to go in to work provided her plenty of extra time to do what she needed to do—including avoid her boyfriend.

And no matter what else happened in life, some things never changed, including Skyping with her brother. Even though Logan was married and continued to chase tornadoes with his team, the Stormeisters, Logan somehow found time to catch up with her online. The Internet was in a good mood tonight and they connected on their first attempt.

"How's life on the Gulf Coast, Caro?" As the Skype connection activated, Logan's body blocked the computer screen. He adjusted the desk lamp so she could see his face better, instead of staring at a dim blur, and then sat down.

"To be honest, it's been interesting."

"Do tell."

"Where to start?" She sipped her tea, acknowledging to herself that she was stalling. "Well, I went to Colorado last week to visit Margo. While I was there I won a destination wedding—"

"Seriously? Destination weddings are becoming a family tradition. I didn't even know Alex had proposed."

"He hasn't."

Logan almost choked on his gulp of Coke. Even though she couldn't see into his tumbler, Caron knew it was flavored with lemon slices, a long-standing quirk of her brother's. "Now I'm confused. You won a wedding, but you're not engaged yet?"

"I admit things are a little out of order. But Alex and I have talked about getting married. Occasionally. And my winning the wedding was purely accidental—"

"How do you accidentally win a destination wedding?" He held up his hand, blocking the screen. "Don't tell me, I don't want to know. You can explain all that to Vanessa, who wants to talk to you when we're done. Where is this destination wedding going to be?"

Caron adjusted the tasseled pillow behind her back, balancing her laptop on her knees. "Colorado . . . Telluride, to be exact."

"That's in the San Juan Mountains, isn't it?"

"Yes. And they're stunning. It's a National Historic Landmark District, if you can believe that."

"Impressive."

"Anyway, Margo and I drove down there this past weekend before I flew home. Check out my Instagram account if you want to see some of my photos."

"That'll be fun. So, Alex hasn't proposed. You've won a destination wedding. Only you, little sister. Only you." Logan ran his fingers through his dark blond hair. "This is one of the craziest conversations we've ever had."

"You keep hassling me, big brother, and I won't tell you the other reason I wanted to talk to you tonight."

"Hey, I'm hassling you because I *am* your big brother. It's my duty." Logan offered her a smile that charmed her even through the computer screen. "You know I love you."

"Yeah, yeah."

"And besides, after all this, I don't know if I want you to tell me anything else."

"Believe me, you're not going to want to miss this news flash." Caron nibbled on a pretzel dipped in cream cheese. "I'm being serious now, Logan."

"You weren't before?" Logan held up his hands in mock surrender. "I'm sorry. What's up, Caron?"

"I quit working for Dad."

"About time. How's Mom?"

"Wait a minute." Caron dropped her pretzel back into the bowl of cream cheese. "I tell you I quit working for Dad and all you have to say is 'About time' and 'How's Mom'?"

"Caro, you've needed to quit working for Dad for months. Years, even. I'm not sure you should have ever worked for him. Now you can figure out what you really want to be when you grow up."

"I know what I want to be when I grow up." Caron sat up, planting her feet on the floor. "I *am* a grown-up. I want to be a Realtor. I am a Realtor."

"Can we be honest here? You're a Realtor because Dad's a Realtor, just like you played basketball in high school because Dad likes basketball."

"I was good at basketball."

"I didn't say you weren't. But would you have played basketball if Dad hadn't been crazy about basketball? All those times you and he sat around drawing up brackets during March

Madness? I never understood the attraction. But I get it that if you played basketball, Dad could come to your games."

"Well, of course I wanted Dad to come to my games. And Mom and you—"

"But you didn't ask Mom and me how you did. You sat there while Dad dissected every play, and if he said something as simple as 'nice job,' well, you would have thought you'd scored all the points that night."

Caron chose to ignore her brother's assessment of her relationship with her father. "I played basketball because I wanted to play basketball. Nobody made me go out for the team, Logan."

"But why did you want to play basketball?" Logan's tone was almost detached. "And if you love the game so much, how come you haven't touched a ball in years?"

"I . . . I'm busy. I have a job. Well, I had a job." Caron resisted throwing one of the decorative sofa pillows at the computer screen. Barely. "Look, Logan, I wanted to tell you that I quit working for Dad. I didn't ask you to psychoanalyze me."

"Fine. You want to tell me why you quit?"

"Only if you'll listen."

Logan settled back in his chair, hands folded across his chest, obscuring the Stormeisters' logo on his T-shirt. "I'm listening."

"Dad formed a partnership with Nancy Miller."

"Yeah, he told me about that. She's another big-deal Realtor in town, right?"

"He told you?" Caron barely stopped herself from spewing her sweet tea onto her computer.

"What's the matter?"

"When did he tell you?"

"I don't know. I think he mentioned it a month ago, maybe two. The last time we talked. It's not a big deal."

"It is a big deal. I find out with the rest of the employees—but you . . . and Mom . . . probably even Vanessa . . . knew before I did."

"But that's different."

"How? How is that different?"

"I don't work for Dad. Neither does Vanessa or Mom." Logan leaned forward, his face looming closer. "You chose to be his employee, Caron. Why don't you see that things have to be handled differently between you and Dad? You can't expect special treatment because you're his daughter."

"I'm not asking for special treatment—"

"Yes, you are. And when you calm down, you'll realize it. That's called nepotism. Is that how you want to get ahead? Because Dad made things easy for you? Because you had an 'in' with the boss?"

This conversation was spiraling out of control. What had happened to Logan, her big brother who was always there for her?

"Is that what you really think, Logan?"

"Now that you're not working for Dad, I think you have a perfect opportunity to really think about what you want out of life . . ."

"You and Mom . . ."

"What?"

"Nothing." Caron pressed her fingertips against the bridge of her nose. "I've got to go . . ."

"Caro, stop. Don't be like this—"

She tried to muster a smile. To end the conversation on some kind of pleasant note. "Like you said, I need time to think. We'll talk later."

"Vanessa's right here. Can't you at least talk to her?"

"No . . . I'm sorry. Not tonight. I'm tired after a late flight last night and . . ." Somehow this phone conversation had backed her into a virtual corner. "Give her my love."

"Will do. I love you—"

"Love you, too."

Logan's face disappeared as she clicked on the red circle with the white phone emblem on the computer screen. Then she shoved her computer off her lap onto the coffee table and slammed the lid closed. Usually a Skype session with Logan resulted in a huge grin.

But tonight, Logan had poked and prodded her with his words.

Would you have played basketball if Dad hadn't been crazy about basketball?

Is that how you want to get ahead—because Dad made things easy for you?

You can't expect special treatment because you're his daughter.

Is that what she'd done? Expected special treatment because she was the boss's daughter? Somehow her relationship with her father and her role as his employee got all tangled up. And both left her wondering, "What more do I have to do?"

And which came first—daughter or employee?

That ought to be an easy question to answer. She was a daughter first and an employee second.

But if she was honest with herself, she couldn't remember the last time she'd felt as if her father saw her as special—for any reason at all.

TEN

. . . ♥ . .

When he lived on his own, Alex wouldn't put a single drape, curtain, or valence on his windows. Nothing. The sun would pour into every single room all day long. And at night, he'd enjoy the stars, the phases of the moon . . . even the pale white glow of the streetlights. The stream of passing cars' headlights.

Let there be light . . . any and all light.

He shut his bedroom door, moving down the hallway without glancing back at his parents' bedroom. The closed door. He couldn't hear a sound, but he knew what was happening. His father placating his mother, trying to persuade her to get up and get dressed for dinner at the Hollisters'.

Not going to happen.

She'd been missing in action Monday and Tuesday; the only evidence that she even lived in the house was the empty glasses and bottles that littered the kitchen counters and the coffee table in the Florida room, where the TV was left on for hours at a time.

A plate of cold scrambled eggs and two strips of bacon sat on the kitchen counter, right next to yet another empty wine bottle. Alex had stopped counting the bottles years ago, tired of the ever-increasing sum that was a virtual warning flag. His father's attempts to get his mother to eat breakfast before he'd left for work earlier that day had failed, but it looked as if he'd managed to remove one bottle from their bedroom.

Alex scraped the food into the trash can, the sound of metal against the ceramic surface of the plate setting his teeth on edge. A squirt of liquid dish soap scented the air with lemon. With a blast of hot water from the faucet, he scrubbed the plate clean. The already loaded dishwasher worked away on the few glasses, plates, and utensils that he'd gathered up the night before. He and his dad usually ate on the run, dashing out the door to work to meet client after client. The freezer was stocked with frozen meals, not that his mother cared what they ate.

Was it time for him to move out? Finally find an apartment—get a little space from all of . . . this? How many almost-thirty-year-old men still lived with their parents, anyway? Would moving out change anything besides his location? Or would things collapse worse?

"Hey, son."

Alex continued washing the already clean plate, the hot water turning his skin red as it rinsed away any remnants of wasted food.

"Your mother's not up to coming tonight. Says her head hurts."

"Okay."

"You ready to go? The Hollisters will be expecting us."

And it's not like they could call and say, *We're not coming. Mom's had too much to drink.* Besides, the Hollisters knew what the word *headache* meant. No further explanation needed.

He took another swipe at the plate. "Let me just finish up here."

"You want to drive over?" His father paced the kitchen.

"It's only a couple of blocks. A walk sounds good."

"Sure."

The humidity rose up from the asphalt, not quite reaching the chill settling around Alex's mood. The two of them kept to the side of the road, shoulder to shoulder. He got his six-foot-five height from his father's side of the family.

"So, what's going on with you and Caron?" His father's question cut through Alex's silence.

"What do you mean, 'What's going on?'" Alex kicked a rock so that it skittered farther down the road.

"When are you going to propose to that girl?"

"What kind of question is that, Dad?"

"A good question. I'm asking what's going on. You and Caron have talked about getting married, haven't you?"

"Yes." Not that he ever thought he had to report back to his father.

"I thought so. Then why haven't you proposed?"

Alex shrugged. "I don't have a ring—"

"What's the matter? Do you need money?"

"No, I don't need money."

"I can loan you money, if that's a problem—"

"There's no problem, Dad."

"Well, there's got to be a problem if you haven't proposed yet. You two are perfect for each other. You're smart enough to know that."

"I'm saving up to buy a ring, okay?" Alex moved two steps to the left, farther into the road. "You're the one who always preached about not using a credit card."

"Well, you've got a point there." His father scratched at the tuft of gray chest hair poking out just above the collar of his polo shirt. "How much are you planning on spending on this ring, anyway? You don't have to pay a ridiculous amount of money, you know."

"I'll decide how much I spend on Caron's engagement ring."

His father stopped walking. "You know, there's always your mother's ring."

"What?"

"Your mother's ring—the first one I gave her. I replaced it on our tenth anniversary with something better. The first one's got a small diamond. I think it's a third of a carat. But it's a good-quality diamond." His father's bass voice rose as he warmed up to the idea. "It's in a safety deposit box down at the bank. We can go look at it later this week if you'd like."

"I'm sure Caron would like to choose her own ring—"

"Well, how do you know? Have you asked her?"

"We haven't even gone looking at rings yet—"

"Alex, your mother would love it if you gave Caron her engagement ring."

His father's words dropped like an invisible noose around Alex's neck. His mother would love it. Alex twisted his head from side to side, sucking in a deep gulp of the moist night air.

"Let me think about it, okay, Dad?"

"I just want to see you happy, son. Caron's a wonderful girl. You two will have a great life together. Don't blow this by wasting your time."

"I'm not wasting my time. I just want things to be right."

He was entitled to that, wasn't he? To choose when and how he proposed to Caron? To choose what was right for him . . . for them.

.   .   .

Midweek dinner at her parents'. With Alex and his parents. While it wasn't their normal Sunday schedule, it should still be a nice, relaxed evening.

Except she'd quit working for her father two weeks ago.

And she had to tell Alex about what she won in Colorado.

Caron locked her car doors with a quick click of the automatic key. Whose Audi SUV was parked in her parents' driveway? Had Alex's dad splurged on a new car? Not likely. Mr. Madison was content to drive one of the work vans around town, maintaining the illusion that he was on the clock twenty-four hours a day. And Alex had driven the same car for the last seven years, so it was unlikely he would top her destination wedding surprise with an I-bought-a-new-car announcement.

No one greeted her as she entered the front door. If she had to guess, her mother was probably busy with last-minute dinner preparations while Mr. Madison and her father sat out by the pool, talking business, and Alex indulged in whatever appetizer her mother had prepared. An unfamiliar blend of voices, capped off with her father's deep laugh, broke the stillness inside the house.

After slipping off her red ballet flats in the foyer, Caron beelined for the kitchen. Had her mother broken tradition and invited someone else to join them for dinner?

A crisp white tablecloth covered the dining room table, which was set with her mother's Villeroy & Boch Mariefleur china, each plate decorated with watercolor floral sprays. A quick count proved Caron's suspicions correct—two extra places were set. Alex had already texted her to say his mother was staying home. Who else was joining them for dinner tonight?

Just inside the archway from the dining room to the kitchen, she stopped. *Nancy Miller.* Why was she here?

The woman wore a black, white, and red color-block dress paired with white platform wedge sandals. Her makeup was perfect, multiple layers of mascara thickening her lashes. Nancy Miller looked ready to face a bank of television cameras.

"I hope everyone likes cheese-stuffed mushrooms." Nancy picked up a glass tray from the kitchen counter. "This is one of my favorite recipes."

"They smell delicious." Her mother noticed Caron standing off to the side, offering her a welcome hug. "Caron. When did you get here?"

"Just now." Caron returned her mother's embrace, nodding to Nancy over her mother's shoulder. "Nice to see you."

And if she'd been younger, her mother would have washed her mouth out with soap for telling a lie.

"Good to see you, too." The other woman's response sounded genuine.

"Now that everyone is here—"

"The Madisons are here?"

"Yes. Alex and his father walked over." Caron's mother motioned toward the family room. "Alex's mom is under the weather. She's got a bad headache."

Ah. So Mrs. Madison was still struggling with the anniversary of Shawn's death.

The open window between the kitchen and family room framed a quartet of men seated on the leather sectional in the Hollister family room. Had Nancy Miller's husband come, too?

"Why don't I take the appetizer in to the others?"

"That would be great, Nancy. You can tell them that dinner should be ready in about fifteen minutes." Her mother pulled a large ceramic bowl full of tossed green salad from the fridge. "Caron, don't you want to go say hello to Alex?"

"Sure." She'd do that. Once she got used to the reality that Nancy Miller was here. "Do you need any help?"

"Everything's under control." From the vivid colors of the fresh green salad her mother topped with a fine layer of shredded Parmesan cheese, Caron couldn't argue with her mother's assessment. "All I need to do is remind your father to check on the pork loin on the grill and get the side dishes on the table."

"Why are Nancy Miller and her husband here?"

"Your father came home and told me that he'd invited Nancy Miller and her boyfriend to dinner tonight." Her mother set several different bottles of salad dressing on the kitchen counter.

"I thought this was going to be a family dinner. After what happened two weeks ago, don't you think it's going to be uncomfortable enough without her being here?"

"I'm sure since we're all adults, we can manage to have a pleasant evening. It's dinner, not a business meeting." Her mother motioned to the bottles. "Will you put the salad and the dressings on the table for me?"

"Sure."

"Thank you." Her mother handed Caron the salad bowl, the pottery cool to her touch. "I'll remind your father to check on the meat. There's the salad, and the rolls are over there in the basket, and I have a pasta salad still in the fridge."

"Sounds like another one of your great meals, Mom."

Not that she'd taste any of it with Nancy Miller sitting at the table.

And she had approximately ten minutes to grow up.

Alex found her as she set the side dishes out on the dining room table, coming up behind her and wrapping his arms around her waist to pull her close.

"Welcome home—again." His voice was low in her ear, sending a quick shiver of warmth across her neck.

"Thank you." She settled the bowl of pasta salad on the white tablecloth. "Don't distract me. I don't want to spill anything."

She turned in his arms and accepted his kiss, even as she noticed the shadows under his eyes. "You okay?"

Alex leaned past her, lifting one of the water glasses and drinking half the contents. "Busy week. Lots of emergencies. Same old, same old."

Caron rested her hand on his arm. "I'm sorry your mom isn't feeling well."

"This time of year . . . it's always tough."

"I know. But I'm still sorry."

"So, we didn't talk too much when I picked you up last night. Colorado?" He covered her hand with his, the touch of his skin warming her. "It was good?"

"Yes, very relaxing, but I wasn't expecting to come back and have dinner with the woman who stole my dream job—"

"We'll get through tonight just fine. I'll be right beside you."

"Thanks for that."

Compliments about the food were exhausted within the first five minutes of the meal. Caron sat between Alex and his dad, while Nancy Miller sat across the table from her. The two Madison men seemed to treat Caron as a human wall, separating them from one another. They spoke to her, to the other people at the table—but not to one another.

What was going on?

"So, Caron, your father tells me that you worked for him for several years." Nancy scooped salad from the pottery salad bowl and piled it onto her salad plate.

And now she had to engage with the last person she wanted to talk to. Caron could almost hear her mother saying, "Mind your manners," like she had when Caron was a child.

"Yes. I did."

"I'm sorry you're not a part of Hollister Realty Group. I saw your sales figures. You'd be an asset to our team."

Caron sipped her water, swallowing back the bitter taste of defeat. And yet there was nothing peremptory in the other woman's tone. Could she take Nancy Miller at face value and just accept the compliment for what it was?

"I enjoyed my time at Hollister Realty—" That was the truth. "It was a good starting point for my career. But I'm ready for something new."

"And what is that?" Nancy passed the salad bowl to her boyfriend as she lobbed the loaded question to Caron.

"Well . . . I just came back from Colorado. My friend is getting married, and we were doing some wedding planning. Now that I'm back home I'll be concentrating on my job leads."

Not that she had any. But no one needed to know that.

"I think we can all understand the need to move on, to try something new. I certainly didn't stay at the first company I worked with as a Realtor. Did you, Russell?"

"No." Her father sliced into his pork, the knife scraping against his plate.

"Of course not. And while it's wonderful that your daughter wants to follow in your footsteps professionally, she certainly doesn't want to get lost in your shadow." Nancy accepted the basket of rolls from Caron's mother. "I'm sure that's why Kade Webster is no longer your golden boy, Russell."

The conversation came to a sudden standstill, as if Nancy Miller had steered them all into an unexpected traffic jam.

"What are you talking about?" Her father's gruff voice cracked the silence icing the room.

"With you as his mentor, Kade Webster was almost an overnight Realtor success in the Panhandle. Someone that good is going to want to strike out on his own."

Caron struggled to find a way to turn the conversation back to her—anything but talking about Kade. "I don't think—"

"Your situation isn't anything like Kade's, of course." Nancy glanced back and forth between Caron and her father. "I mean, there were rumors of a less than amicable parting between Kade and your father, but I prefer to ignore rumors. I shouldn't have mentioned it at all. I apologize. We probably shouldn't talk business all night."

"Thank you, Nancy." Caron's mother turned toward the other woman's boyfriend. "Now, what did you say you did again, Gunther?"

As Caron's mother steered the conversation to a neutral topic, Caron settled back into her chair. How was she supposed to stay angry with a woman who unknowingly took what Caron had always wanted—and then treated her as a professional peer?

.   .   .

Tonight, the safest place in her parents' house was the kitchen.

Her mother and father sat in the family room, enjoying coffee and fresh strawberry pie with Nancy and Gunther, who managed to hold his own in the conversation, despite being the owner of a charter fishing boat and not a Realtor.

Alex's father had disappeared early, two slices of pie tucked away in a Tupperware container, one piece for him, one for Alex's mom. Both pieces would be eaten by Mr. Madison. Alex's mom ate one meal a day, if that.

And now here she was, playing a sulky Cinderella, hiding in the kitchen as she loaded the dishwasher and scrubbed the pots clean, avoiding interaction with Nancy Miller. And her father.

She was being childish. And stubborn. But there was no changing her attitude this late in the evening.

"Can I help with anything?" Alex scooped the last bite of whipped cream and strawberries off his plate.

"I'm about done here." She sat the last pot in the dish drainer.

"So are you going to stop hiding and join the rest of us?"

"I'm not hiding—"

Alex stopped her protest with a subtle shift of his shoulders.

"Fine. I'm hiding. But I'm also tired. And I really can't play nice anymore."

"But Nancy Miller has been nothing but pleasant—"

"I know that, okay?" Caron gripped the edge of the sink, suds dripping off her fingers. "I didn't think she'd be here tonight. I don't want to like her, but she's making that impossible. I'm confused . . . and just tired."

"Too tired to go swim in your parents' pool for a little bit?" Alex placed his plate and fork in the sink. "They're starting to discuss mortgages and interest rates in there. I'm sure we won't be missed."

"Sounds perfect."

And now she had no excuse not to tell Alex about how she'd won a destination wedding. She could only hope and pray he'd be excited about the idea—and not feel as if she'd backed him into the corner about proposing.

"See you in the deep end."

Caron dried her hands on a dish towel. After a good meal, Alex was usually relaxed. Of course, Alex was always laid-back.

Less than twenty minutes later, she'd slipped into a faded black-and-white tankini she kept in the closet in her parents' guest room and sat on the edge of the pool, the water slick against her legs, the air thick with the humidity and the faint scent of chlorine. Alex swam toward her from the far end, his long, muscled arms slicing through the water, his legs kicking slow and easy. When he reached the wall, he flipped over, disappearing beneath the water away from her again, droplets of water splattering her arms and torso.

So long as he kept swimming, she didn't have to talk.

Caron gripped the cement curves of the pool wall. This was absurd. She and Alex were in a long-term relationship. They'd talked about getting married more than once. For all intents and purposes, they were engaged . . . almost. They just hadn't done anything specific. Yet. She'd tell Alex what had happened in Colorado. They'd share a laugh. And then they'd figure out when they wanted to use the unexpected gift of a destination wedding.

Happily ever after for them. And their parents.

"You're very dressed up tonight." Her father appeared in the hallway as Caron checked the items in her beaded gold clutch.

"Well, it's a special night."

"Really?"

"Alex and I are celebrating our one-year anniversary."

"One year." Her father clapped his hands. "I guess this is a case of fathers and mothers know best, eh?"

Caron paused by the front door. "What's that supposed to mean?"

"All those times you fussed when we teased about betrothing you to Alex—"

"Dad, please. You and the Madisons embarrassed us talking like that. We were in high school. We could make up our own minds about who we wanted to date. Or not date."

"Well, you and Alex ended up together after all. I won't say I told you so—"

And he didn't. But Caron knew what her father was thinking.

"Going to join me?" Finished with his first set of laps, Alex pushed his thick brown hair back off his forehead and rested his crossed arms over the edge of the pool, his hazel eyes tinged a faint red from the chlorinated water.

"I'm good here for now." She spun tiny whirlpools with her feet. Time was up. "So while I was in Colorado, I went to a bridal expo with Margo and the girls . . . and the most unexpected thing happened."

"Really?"

"The vendors gave out all sorts of prizes. Photography packages. Wedding cakes. Music for your wedding reception. All the wedding fun."

"Nice."

"The grand prize was a destination wedding in Colorado. Telluride, to be exact. It's this amazing place, where you have to ride a gondola over the mountains into the town."

"Sounds different." Alex did steady kicks with his legs, seeming ready to turn and launch off the side of the pool again and head for the other end.

"I won it."

Alex blinked. Once. Twice. "You won . . . what?"

Caron plunged her feet into the water, splashing water up onto her thighs. "I won the destination wedding and the honeymoon. In Telluride."

"But we're not getting married." Even as Alex held on to the side of the pool, he straightened his arms, pushing away from her. "I mean, I haven't proposed—"

"I know you haven't proposed, Alex. A woman doesn't overlook something like that. But we've talked about getting married."

"Yes, we've talked about it. But usually there's a proposal before the wedding and honeymoon is planned. The whole 'Will you marry me?' tradition." Alex's brow furrowed. "And usually the future husband has a say in the plans."

"Alex, I filled out one entry form. *One.* Winning was some sort of crazy fluke."

"What if I don't want to have a *fluke* wedding?"

"Excuse me?"

"When I propose, I want to get married here. In Florida. In our home church, with our family and our friends."

"But we haven't even discussed this. And if you look at the

photographs I took, you'll see how spectacular Telluride is. Bridal Veil Falls—"

"You're right. We've never even discussed something like this." Alex released his hold on the wall. "A destination wedding isn't our style. Running off someplace with a small group of people and getting married? Excluding most of our friends and family? Why would we do that?"

"You're dismissing this without even thinking about it!" Caron's raised voice seemed to slice through the air. "We've been given a wedding and honeymoon. It's all paid for. What am I supposed to do with the grand prize?"

"Give it back." Alex spoke as if he'd settled the matter. "Do you think my mother is going to get on a plane and travel all the way to Colorado?"

"Do you think your mother is going to handle some huge wedding here better than a smaller destination wedding?"

Spoken and yet-to-be-spoken words quivered in the air between them.

"This is not just about my mother, Caron." Alex kept himself afloat by kicking his legs. "I don't want a destination wedding."

"And what if I do?" The rough edge of the wall scraped against the back of her legs and the palms of her hands.

The two of them were locked in some sort of verbal tug-of-war about a wedding she had won. By chance. That she hadn't even been certain she wanted. And now she gripped the prize with both hands, almost daring Alex to take it away from her.

"It seems we have a problem." Alex stared at her, his body swaying back and forth in the water with the rhythm of his kicks.

"Yes, we do." Caron could play the stare-down game just as well as he could. "A Colorado destination wedding sounds fantastic."

Alex's jaw tightened, his eyes narrowing. "I don't agree."

"I can see that. And I guess you have our wedding all planned out?"

"Well, I always thought I'd have some say in it, rather than being told where it was so I could just show up."

Yanking her legs from the pool so that water splashed into Alex's face, Caron scrambled to her feet.

"Where are you going?" Alex swam toward the side.

"Home." She wrapped a flowered beach towel around her shoulders. "You know what? Nancy Miller was nicer to me tonight than you're being right now."

"Caron—"

"Good night, Alex."

ELEVEN

• ♥ • ♥ • ♥ •

Caron shoved the teal and purple pillows on her gray couch to one end, stretching out as she held her phone up at the proper angle so she could see the image of her sister-in-law's face.

"Can you still hear me, Vanessa?"

"Yes. I can still see you, too." Her sister-in-law's smile came through even miniaturized by FaceTime.

"I'm sorry I didn't talk with you last Monday when Logan and I Skyped."

"After he told me what you all talked about and what he said to you, I'm not surprised you didn't feel up to more conversation."

"Yeah. He was taking his big brother role pretty seriously." Caron snagged a handful of Hot Tamales from the bowl resting on the coffee table beside the couch. She popped two in her mouth, savoring the sweet and spicy tang of her favorite candy.

"Your big brother's back on the road with the team. I promise to just listen. That's what sisters are for."

"I don't know. Every night when I go to bed, I think about the day I quit working for my dad. Did I do the right thing? Should I have stayed? Could I have swallowed my . . . not my pride, exactly, but my *hopes*, and stayed around and watched Nancy Miller get everything I wanted?"

"And?"

"How do you stay when someone comes in and steals your place? Not that I have her experience. I don't. But she's where I wanted to be—well, eventually." Caron blinked back the hot sting of tears. Useless. "You want to know the funny thing?"

"What?"

"My father invited Nancy and her boyfriend to dinner last night and . . ."

"And?"

"She was nice."

"And that's funny because . . . ?"

"Because I didn't want to like her. It would be easier to not like her if she was pretentious or . . . or—"

"Not nice?"

"Yeah." Caron gathered a few more candies into the palm of her hand.

"Okay. So Nancy Miller is nicer than you thought. And she took your place—what you hoped to be your future. So that door is closed?"

"If by 'that door,' you mean working for my father—yes, it's closed. I slammed it shut. I can't imagine going back there for any reason. And then after what Logan said—"

"He was out of line, Caron."

"No, he wasn't. Not really. I didn't like what he said to me, but I can't stop thinking about it. Questioning why I played basketball in high school. Was it just because my dad liked basketball? Was it a way to get his attention? And then Logan suggesting that I wanted my dad to make it easy on me at work . . . Is there any truth to what he said?"

"Is there?"

"I don't know." Caron chewed on a few Hot Tamales, the flavor burning her tongue. "Or is it that I don't want to know?"

Vanessa stared at her from the small space of her cell phone.

"Nothing to say?"

"I'm trying to hold up my end up of the bargain—the one where I said I'd listen."

"You've been a great listener." Caron sat up, rubbing at the crick in her neck. "I haven't even talked about the other issue."

"What issue?"

"Didn't Logan tell you that I won a destination wedding?"

"Yes, but why is that a problem? It sounds wonderful! I love Colorado. After all, I lived there."

"Well, Alex doesn't think it sounds wonderful."

"What? Maybe he was just surprised—"

"Oh, he was surprised. But he was also angry." Caron adjusted her position on the couch, echoes of last night's scene with Alex filling her mind. "And I . . . I got angry, too."

"And then what?"

"And then I left. Alex and I never argue."

"Never?"

"It's just not what we do. Alex is so easygoing. That's one of the things I've always appreciated about him. But right now I like the idea of a wedding in Colorado more than I like my boyfriend."

Vanessa's laughter pulled a giggle from Caron. "You did not just say that."

"Yes, I did. I know we're supposed to be this ideal couple, but between his response to my quitting work and his reaction to my winning the wedding . . . I feel like I don't know Alex as well as I thought I did."

"Are you having second thoughts about marrying him?"

"How can I have second thoughts when he hasn't even asked me yet? A fact he pointed out, I might add." Caron got up and wandered into the kitchen, setting the dish of candy on her counter. "I am having *thoughts*, though."

"What does that mean?"

"I lost my perfect job. My perfect boyfriend isn't so perfect. There. I said it out loud. I keep asking God what's next—and oddly enough, I'm almost ready for something less than perfect."

"That's a different perspective on things. I'll start praying for some imperfection in your life, how about that?"

"Thanks." Caron released a sigh, her shoulders collapsing. "Hey, next time you talk to my brother, tell him I love him, will you?"

"Why don't you call him or send him a text? He'd probably like to hear from you."

"You're right. I'll do that once we get off the phone."

"Well, I have a date with an exercise video, so go ahead and text your brother."

"Yes, ma'am. Love you, Vanessa."

"Love you back."

Caron leaned into the counter, resting her forehead on her outstretched arms. The kitchen was her favorite room in her house. She'd worked step by careful step to transform it into what she wanted. The glass-fronted cabinets were the perfect display for her Fiestaware dishes, stacked in vivid colors of peacock blue, poppy red, sunflower yellow, and deep plum. And when she turned on the varied lighting choices she'd included—both under-the-counter accent lights as well as vintage glass pendants—her pure white Corian counters almost glistened. Unable to decide between wood or tile floors, she'd opted for tile that looked like wood, smiling at the humor and beauty of it every time she entered the room.

This room was everything she'd ever dreamed of for a perfect-for-her kitchen. Worth the wait. She'd put up with all the in-between stages because she was the only one who didn't see the unfinished steps as "less than." Nobody told her to what to do. Or to hurry up and fix this or that. It would be everything she wanted—one day.

And now she was letting Vanessa pray for imperfection in her life? Should she call her back and ask her to pray for what she wanted? But what was that? She'd already lost her dreams . . . and there'd been no time to replace them with new ones.

Imperfection would have to be enough right now.

TWELVE

• ▾ • ♥ • ▾ •

The walls of the locker room muffled the sounds of the weight room. The clank of weighted plates. The dull thud of barbells hitting the floor. The air was laden with leftover humidity from the showers and the competing scents of sweat and soap.

Kade straddled the bench in front of his locker, using a white hand towel to absorb some of the lines of perspiration trickling down the sides of his face. "Ready for the Mudder at the end of the month?"

Mitch drained the last of the water from his Contigo water bottle, his neon-green T-shirt clinging to his chest. "You keep asking me that. Have I said anything about backing out?"

"Nope. Just checking. I talked with Brady and Zach and they're still a go. What about your brother?"

"He's in, and he invited his CrossFit instructor, a guy named Don. An ex-air-force guy. Seems pretty straight up."

"Sounds good. You want to invite anyone else to join the fun?"

"If Pete was stateside, I'd definitely give him a call. But I think we've got a good-sized team."

"Works for me."

"I'm gonna head home and shower there." As Mitch rolled past, the two men exchanged quick fist bumps. "See you tomorrow at work?"

"Yeah. Don't be late. I want to catch you up on the Tour of Homes project—" Kade paused as his phone buzzed. "Let me grab this. I'll catch you in the morning."

A quick glance at his phone indicated Sheila Mills was calling.

"Sheila, how are you? Ready to give me some of your ideas for staging Eddie Kingston's house for the Tour of Homes?"

"Oh, Kade, I'm so glad you picked up." Sheila's words ran together like an out-of-control train. "Something awful has happened . . . I don't know what to do. I mean, I know what to do, but everything's a mess and I hate to call and tell you—"

"Sheila, take a deep breath and calm down." Kade swung his leg over the bench so he could stand up and pace the floor. "Let's try this again. Are you okay?"

"I'm fine. But my sister, Cecilia, well, she fell down the basement stairs in her house because she tripped on her son's shoes and she broke her ankle and her wrist. Can you believe that? I mean, it would be bad enough if she broke just her ankle or her wrist . . . but breaking both of them? And the doctor said she might need surgery on her ankle . . ." Sheila ignored his advice to take a deep breath and calm down. "And she has four kids. The oldest is eight. And her husband is deployed. You understand, don't you?"

In her frantic state, Sheila hadn't even told him the worst part of the situation—at least what was the worst part for him. But he did understand.

"You have to go help your sister. That's what family is for."

Not that he'd experienced anything like that in his life, not after his parents' divorce. He scrabbled to get his thoughts together, ignoring the flash of memory of spending time with the

Neilson family when he was in high school. That was so long ago it no longer counted.

"She lives in Virginia. The kids and I are leaving as soon as I get off the phone with you. Kade, I'm so sorry."

"I understand."

"I'll text you some other options for people who can help stage the Kingston home."

"Thanks. I'd appreciate that."

"I haven't had a chance to call any of them to see if they're available—"

"Just do what you need to do and get on the road." Kade sat back down on the bench. "Don't worry about me. Mitch and I will figure this out."

His bravado faded as soon as he ended his conversation with Sheila.

What was he going to do? The Peak Tour of Homes opened the first Monday after the July Fourth weekend. He trusted Sheila and her team to stage a house well. They'd worked together on a dozen or more homes. They understood each other. She knew the importance of the tour, and they'd already discussed options for the various rooms.

He'd put his reputation, as well as his hopes for his professional future, on the line when he'd pitched his plan to Eddie Kingston. He had to overcome this setback.

.　　.　　.

"I appreciate you letting me interrupt your dinner for this impromptu business meeting, Lacey." Kade shoved his spaghetti coated with a marina sauce, fragrant with oregano and basil, around on his plate with a piece of French bread, but not even the scent of butter and garlic lifted his spirits. "I just need some help figuring this out."

Lacey filled their glasses with sangria, and then served both men additional pasta without asking if they were ready for more. "Didn't you say Sheila sent you the names of other stagers?"

"Yes." Kade tried to wash away the dryness that kept building in the back of his throat with a quick sip of wine. "But I haven't worked with any of them."

"But if Sheila recommended them—"

"I'm not sure how well I can trust her at this moment. She was pretty frazzled. When I called the first number on the list she gave me, I got someone at a pizza parlor asking if they could take my order. The other two were actual home-staging businesses, but all I could do was leave my name and phone number, asking them to call me back as soon as possible—and hope I didn't sound desperate."

"Why don't you call Sheila again?" Mitch wiped the corners of his mouth with his napkin as he finished off a bite of meatball. "Recheck the numbers?"

"She was getting on the road right after we talked. I have to accept Sheila's out of the loop now."

"Is there anyone you can think of that you know could pull this off on such short notice?"

"Yes, but only one person."

"Then why don't you call her? Or him? Whoever it is."

"Because it's Caron Hollister."

"Oh." Lacey sat down at the table and rested her chin in her upturned palms, her black hair with teal tips falling about her shoulders. "Nothing like calling an ex-girlfriend for help."

"Not to mention the fact she lives in Florida." Mitch shook his head.

"I wouldn't even think of calling her for all those reasons— except for the fact I'm desperate and because of something her friend said when we were looking at a house together."

"And what was that?"

"Something about Caron needing to find another job."

Mitch paused with a forkful of pasta suspended over his plate. "You're not thinking of hiring Caron Hollister long-term as a Realtor, are you?"

"No. I've worked with her once in that capacity and it was a disaster because it became personal. I'm thinking immediate need only. Asking her to help me stage Eddie Kingston's house for the tour."

"And then she goes back to Florida."

"Exactly."

"Do you think there's any chance Caron will say yes?" Lacey sipped her sangria. "I mean, given your history together?"

"It's a crazy gamble. But if anyone can pull off staging a home on short notice, Caron can. I've seen her decorate homes for her dad. She even helped stage a Parade of Homes house for him once. She has a natural flair. Her own house is this eclectic, fun reflection of her personality. Only Caron Hollister would paint her front door purple—"

"Purple?" Lacey's laughter morphed into a snort.

"Yes, and it's a fun glimpse of what's waiting for you inside the house."

Lacey clapped her hands. "Kade, you have to call her."

"What do you think, Mitch?"

"I think it's ridiculous to even be talking about this. But I also know you." His friend crossed his arms over his chest, a smile twisting his lips. "You think asking Caron Hollister is the right thing to do. You're going to do it. Make the call."

"I will. But can we pray first? Because this is one of those times when doing the right thing scares me."

THIRTEEN

• ♥ • •

$\mathcal{T}$he name and address of the work order on the metal clip-board had looked familiar. As soon as he turned down the tree-lined street in the older part of town, Alex gave a low exhale. Jessica Thompson was the new homeowner with the boyfriend who couldn't sleep without the air-conditioning on.

So much for his superhero status—his "It's working now" assessment had been pronounced not quite two weeks ago. Ac-cording to the notes on the paper, she'd called back in with the same complaint: the circuit breaker flipped. She turned it back over. No air-conditioning. Again.

While he hated that Jessica's A/C wasn't working, it was another opportunity to stay busy. Air conditioners he could fix. And the broken-beyond-repair ones, he could replace. But when it came to figuring out how to fix his mother's broken heart . . . convincing her that drowning her sorrows . . . her life . . . in a nonstop stream of alcohol wasn't helping . . . well, that he couldn't do.

Caron had smoothed over their argument from the other night with a brief voice message this morning. An

I-love-you-we'll-talk-and-it-will-be-okay run-on sentence that, once again, covered any tension between them and ended their brief standoff.

Things were back to normal. Pleasant and peaceful.

This appointment wouldn't take too long. He'd check the unit again, but he already knew he'd have to deliver bad news and recommend Jessica buy a new one.

She answered the door, a smile lighting her pale blue eyes behind her glasses. "Hi. I didn't know if you'd be the one to come back today."

"Afternoon." He tipped his hat. "The company tries to send the same repairman out to a job when we can."

"It's nice to see you, but please take this the right way: I was hoping I wouldn't see you again."

"Most people feel that way about repairmen. Part superhero, part bearer of bad news."

"Think you can maintain your superhero status today?"

"I'll do my best—"

Small footsteps sounded behind her as a young boy with the same strawberry-blond hair as Jessica's ran up, wrapping his arms around her leg. "Who's this, Mommy?"

"This is . . ." Jessica stopped to read the name patch on his shirt. "Mr. Alex. He's going to fix our air-conditioning."

"Yay!" The little boy hopped from one foot to the other, still clinging to her leg. "It's hot in here."

"Yes, it is."

Alex squatted down so he was eye level with the boy. Well, almost eye level. "You know my name. What's yours?"

"Scotty."

"Nice to meet you, Scotty." So Scotty was her son, not a boyfriend. Alex eased to his feet. "Named after his dad?"

Jessica wrinkled her nose at him. "No. He's named after Mr.

Scott in *Star Trek*. I'm a huge fan. I can show you my action figure collection if you need proof."

"No need." Alex held his hands up in mock surrender. "But I'm a die-hard fan of the original series."

"Of course." She stepped back, holding Scotty's hand. "Why don't you come through the house to the backyard?"

Alex stayed where he was. "I don't want to tromp dirt through your house."

"Are you kidding me? I'm the mom of a five-year-old. I spend hours sweeping up dirt. Scrubbing it off of him, too."

Alex allowed Jessica to lead the way through her house, Scotty in between them. The rooms were furnished with the bare essentials, most of which looked worn. But everything was clean. Neat. And soft music came from an iPod dock set on a bookshelf in the living room.

"So, the same thing happened?"

"Yep."

"I'll take another look and let you know what I find."

A few minutes later, Jessica and Scotty reappeared in the backyard as she brought Alex a cup of water in the same plastic blue cup as before.

"I thought I wouldn't wait until the end of your visit today." She motioned Scotty away. "Don't bother Mr. Alex while he's working. Go play with your trucks while I start the burgers."

Alex's stomach rumbled at the word *burger*. His dinner would have to wait, and it wouldn't be fresh-off-the-grill anything. As he worked, the aroma of grilling meat wafted through the air, causing Alex's mouth to water. Jessica hummed a familiar popular tune as she entered the house again, admonishing Scotty to behave until she got back.

"Whatcha doing?"

Alex couldn't hold back a grin. He knew the little boy would make his way over here, but he needed him to stay back.

"Trying to figure out why this big old thing isn't working."

"Can I help?"

"Sorry, I can't let you do that. You have to go to school to learn how to do this."

"Really? Did you go to school?"

"Yep."

"I'm going to kindergarten soon."

"Well, that's a start, but you have to go to a few more years of school than that to repair air conditioners."

"I bet you're smart—"

"Scotty!" Jessica slid back the screen door and crossed the backyard. "I told you not to bother Mr. Alex."

"I just wanted to help him, Mommy."

"And I explained to Scotty that he needed to go to school a while longer before he could be my helper."

"I'm sorry. I really thought he'd obey for longer than three minutes—"

"Are you married, Mr. Alex?" Scotty squinted up at him. "My mommy's not married—"

"Scotty! That's not something you need to ask Mr. Alex." Jessica's fair skin flamed red as her hands pressed to the sides of her face. "I am so sorry. He just says whatever he's thinking—"

"It's okay. And I have a girlfriend, Scotty." His phone buzzed on his hip, indicating a text. "Let me take this and then I'll tackle your A/C."

His father—adding yet another appointment to his day.

As Jessica flipped the burgers, she glanced over at him. "Everything okay?"

"Just another emergency call added to the list."

"So I'm not your last job?"

"You were, but things changed."

"Don't you get a dinner hour? Aren't there union rules or something?"

"We do what we have to do to keep our customers happy."

She motioned to the air conditioner. "Well, I'll stop interrupting you so you can finish up here and get going."

Less than a half hour later, Alex knew he wasn't going to maintain any sort of superhero status today. No matter what he did, even pulling out every trick in the book, the unit refused to start.

Tipping back the brim of his cap, he shook his head. He'd like to find that home inspector and give him a piece of his mind. He—or she—hadn't done Jessica any favors letting this unit pass inspection. She could either buy a new unit or sweat out the upcoming Florida summer.

She scooped half a dozen burgers off the grill onto a chipped white plate as he approached. A bag of buns, sliced tomatoes and onions, and lettuce were arranged on another plate, next to plastic bottles of ketchup and mustard. Scotty straddled the bench, munching on potato chips.

"It's not good news, is it?" Jessica poured her son a cup of lemonade.

"How can you tell?"

"It didn't start back up. I feel like Captain Kirk when McCoy says, 'He's dead, Jim. He's dead.'" Her smile wavered. "And my A/C is one of the red-shirt guys who doesn't survive the expedition."

Her attempt at bravado was endearing. "I hate to have to put on my bearer-of-bad-news alter ego, but you need a new unit."

Her voice barely registered a whisper. "I was afraid of that."

"I can see about finding a sale unit, cutting back on labor costs."

"Are you okay, Mommy?"

Jessica put a bright smile on her face as she turned toward her son. "Of course, sweetie. Mr. Alex and I are talking about that silly old air conditioner. It's being cranky and doesn't want to work."

"But Mr. Alex said he went to school, so he knows how to fix it."

"Well, yes, but sometimes things can't be fixed."

"Like the washing machine—"

Jessica refused to look at Alex. "Yes, like the washing machine. But don't worry about that."

"Maybe Mr. Alex knows how to fix washing machines, too. You could ask him—"

"Mr. Alex fixes air conditioners, not washing machines. And he has another job to go to." She refocused on Alex. "Don't mind him."

"Your washing machine is broken, too?"

"It's an older model that came with the house. Obviously it and the air conditioner are in cahoots." She shrugged. "Isn't that the way it always goes? They say trouble comes in threes, but I'm hoping to dodge the third problem somehow. Maybe get off for good behavior."

"Here's hoping." Pulling a blue bandanna out of his back pocket, Alex wiped his hands. "Listen, would you mind if I washed up in your bathroom?"

"No, of course not. It's down the hall, first door on the right."

When he came back outside, Jessica greeted him with a paper plate loaded with two hamburgers on buns, along with a couple of packets of ketchup, all covered with plastic wrap. A plastic sandwich bag filled with tomato, onion, and lettuce slices was set on top. Scotty bounced up and down beside her, holding a bottle of water and a bunch of napkins.

Alex faced off between mother and son. "What's this?"

"Dinner."

"What?" Alex held up his hands, even as the sight of the impromptu dinner-to-go caused his mouth to water again. "No—"

"It's all packed and ready for you." Jessica held the food out to him. "I hate to think of you missing dinner. Besides, I always make extra food, just in case a friend or even a stranger drops by. It's something I learned from my mother. She was always taking meals to neighbors and people in the church when I was growing up."

"So what does this make me?"

"Well, you're not a stranger—"

"You're Mr. Alex." Scotty bumped against his leg, offering the bottle of water.

"Exactly. You're Mr. Alex." Jessica moved the plate closer so that he could smell the aroma of the burgers fresh off the grill. "And now, Mr. Alex, your girlfriend doesn't have to worry about you not eating a decent meal."

FOURTEEN

• • • ♥ • • •

*T*he key to the conversation was to be impersonal, professional—and to not sound desperate.

Kade tossed his cell phone on his desk, shoved his chair back, and stared at a framed photo of Pikes Peak at sunset on the opposite wall. The competing demands of "Have to" and "How?" clawed their way across his nerves, forcing him to make a choice he'd never imagined.

Would he do everything possible to showcase Eddie Kingston's house for the Tour of Homes?

Yes.

Then he needed to replace Sheila with the absolute best home stager he could find. His repeated attempts to contact the three stagers she'd recommended had been a waste of time. The last thing he wanted to do was start searching Google for random recommendations.

Which left him with this farfetched option.

Might as well make the call, hear the no, and move on—to what, he had no idea.

Funny how even after two years, he still remembered Caron's cell phone number.

"Hello, this is Caron Hollister."

Her greeting, after just one ring, caught him off guard. All he had to do was stay focused. Ask the question. Get it over with. It wasn't as if Caron Hollister hadn't rejected him before—only this time she'd actually do the rejection straight up.

"Hello?"

"Caron. This is Kade. Kade Webster."

A moment's silence and then: "Kade. I wasn't expecting to hear from you."

If that wasn't the understatement of the year.

"Understandable." He sat up straight, anchored his feet to the ground. "How are you?"

"I'm . . . good. You?"

"Enjoying Colorado, even if it is a landlocked state. A friend keeps telling me to buy one of those artificial sound machines since I miss the sound of ocean waves so much."

"There's a thought."

A brief response, without a hint of humor. He needed to ask the question and be done.

"I'm sure you're wondering why I called—"

"Yes."

Kade tugged at his tie, loosening it. "I want to offer you a job."

"Excuse me?"

"Look, I heard what Margo said when I was showing her the house—about you needing to find another job. I assume that means you aren't working for your father anymore." His statement was met with silence. "Am I correct?"

"Yes, you're correct. I'm no longer working at Hollister Realty."

She wasn't sharing details. Fine. He didn't need to know if she was fired or if she quit.

"I'm not calling to pry into your personal life—" Might as well settle that from the start. "But if you haven't found a job yet, I'd like to offer you a temporary position with Webster Select Realty."

"You want me to come work for you—temporarily—as a Realtor? Kade, you know that's not possible—"

"No. I need a home stager for a major project. That's the job I'm offering you."

"I'm not a professional home stager, Kade."

"I know you're not a professional, but you're a natural. You're even better than some of the home stagers I've worked with in the past. I've seen some of the houses you've decorated for your father, remember? I've also seen your home. That's all the résumé I need."

"What kind of project are we talking about?"

Was she actually considering his request?

"I'm helping a custom homebuilder who's participating in the Peak Tour of Homes. Paying his fees, buying him better signage, that kind of thing. I also said I'd stage the home for him. But the stager I usually work with just left town to help take care of her sister, who fell and broke her wrist and ankle."

"Not good."

"I know, and I should be feeling bad for that woman, but I'm panicking here. Sheila—the home stager—gave me some other people to contact, but they're all dead ends."

"So you're panicked and I'm your last resort."

Kade pressed his fingertips into his temple. What did she expect him to say? "Caron, you know as well as I do that I'm calling you under less than perfect circumstances, and not just because I'm up against a deadline. But I have no doubt you can come through on this. I've asked the question. Now I need to know if you're interested. I'll fly you out here, put you up in a hotel, pay you per diem, cover your meals, car, whatever—"

"I can't give you an answer right now, Kade—"

"That is an answer, Caron. It's a no."

· · ·

This was not the time to be having this conversation with Kade Webster.

She shouldn't be talking to the man at all, but especially not now when she was already facing one major decision.

Caron held up her hand in the universal "just one minute" sign, offering the receptionist at the hair salon a smile that begged for understanding.

She'd had to force herself to walk through the door, reminding herself this wasn't the first time she'd done something different to her hair. That she could trust Paula, her stylist. But it was as if the shadow of her father lurked in the back of her mind, causing her to question what hairstyle to choose.

Surely she was capable of getting her hair done without worrying about what her father would say. He wasn't her boss anymore. She could do whatever she wanted, including dye her hair blue or even shave half her head.

Not that she was considering anything that drastic.

And then Kade had to call, the sound of his voice throwing her into some two-steps-into-the-past, one-determined-step-back-to-the-present dance. Reminding her of the times when she'd anticipated hearing his voice.

And then the verbal dance lumbered to a stop when he offered her a job.

"Are you still there?"

She faced away from the receptionist, marching back outside the salon into the smoldering afternoon humidity, shutting the door on the hum of conversations interwoven with the whir of blow dryers, the air laden with the scent of shampoos and styling chemicals.

"Yes. I'm at . . . an appointment."

"I apologize. I didn't mean to interrupt."

"It's not like you know my schedule—" Caron caught fractured glimpses of herself in the glass storefronts. "Can you give me until tomorrow morning to think about this?"

"I suppose that's fair. But you need to know that, if you accept the job, I would need you here as soon as possible."

"I will consider it—" Time for a quick about-face back toward the salon. "And I will call you back by nine o'clock in the morning, your time."

"You can call me earlier. I'll be up."

"I'll talk to you tomorrow, then."

"Perfect."

Kade's conversation replayed in her head moments later as Paula motioned her back into her private room in the salon.

Less than perfect circumstances.

There was nothing perfect about the possibility of working for Kade Webster. Even considering it made no sense at all. When Vanessa promised to pray for some imperfection in her life, Caron never imagined a job offer from Kade, temporary or otherwise, as God's answer to Vanessa's "Caron's life needs to be less than perfect" prayer.

"So, the usual shampoo, cut, and blow-dry?" Paula ran a wide-tooth comb through Caron's wet hair.

Caron clasped her hands beneath the long plastic cover draped over her shoulders. "No. I think it's time for a change."

Why not be deliberate about her life changing? Have a say in the matter? Of course, she'd been the one to quit working for her father, but only after he'd sprung Nancy Miller on her.

"Okay. What are we doing?"

"I'm thinking—" Caron threaded her fingers through her shoulder-length brown hair. There was nothing wrong with her natural color, except she'd gone back to it only to please her dad. "—blond."

"Blond." Paula's smile widened into an oh-yeah agreement. "How blond are you thinking?"

"I know the long process for getting to platinum. We've done that before. Let's just start with a fun, shimmery blond for now and go from there."

"Are you thinking like Reese Witherspoon in *Legally Blonde*?"

"Maybe more like January Jones in *Mad Men*."

"Sounds great. I always liked you as a blond."

"I did, too. And who knows what the future holds, right?"

Maybe when Paula was done working her magic on her hair, Caron would recognize the woman in the mirror again. Reclaim a little bit of control in her life by having a say in her hair color. Someone else might laugh at her feeble follicle attempt at retaining power, but they hadn't been living her life for the past few years.

· · ·

The deed was done.

The proof was there whenever Caron fingered the long layers Paula had added to her hair, or whenever she'd stopped at a red light and snagged another glimpse of the blond hair framing her face in the rearview mirror.

Was her decision an I'm-my-own-person action or a stubborn I-can-do-what-I-want stomping of her foot?

Whichever it was, she'd paid for it, adding a hefty tip.

While Paula had mixed the hair color, applied it to her hair, set the timer, and then taken a quick call from her daughter, Caron prayed. A silent, stuttering, start-and-stop kind of prayer with a lot of "Should I?" and "How would this work?" and "Am I crazy to even consider this?" kinds of questions thrown at God.

Her emotions mirrored the first time she tried to read a real estate contract. Confusing. Impossible to sort out. She wanted to forget Kade had even called her.

But she couldn't. She'd promised him an answer by tomorrow morning.

Once home, Caron went straight to her kitchen pantry and retrieved the tall glass apothecary jar from the top shelf. Half full of bright red Hot Tamales, it was just what she needed—her favorite candy, the perfect accompaniment to a phone conversation with Margo.

The minute Margo said hello, Caron started talking, digging a handful of Hot Tamales out of the jar and spilling them onto her kitchen counter.

"I need you to tell me what to do. Because I can't believe I'm even considering this. It's . . . it's impossible." Caron lined the red candies up, side by side. "But then a part of me thinks, Why not? Why not get away from here for a little while? Get some space from my father? I mean it's only for, what, a month maybe?"

"I'd be happy to tell you what to do—if you want to give me a hint about what exactly you're considering. Are you thinking of doing the Pamplona Bull Run in Spain? Count me out. Are you considering going skydiving? I might join you. Want to run away to Tahiti? I'm all in. We could have some kind of besties getaway before I get married."

Caron's laughter dissolved into a half sob. "Oh, Margo . . .

remember back in college at Alabama when we had all those adventures?"

"Roll Tide! We had a few, including that semester abroad in Paris. That was fun, right?"

"Yeah."

"And then I came back and Ronny had missed me so much he didn't want to be 'just friends' anymore—"

"Focus, Margo. This is not the time to remember your romance with Ronny."

"Sorry. Tell me what's going on. Why are you laughing and crying?"

"My life's a mess. I thought I had it all figured out. Who I was. Where I was going. Even who I was getting married to. And now . . ." The threat of more tears caused Caron to stop talking.

"And now you don't know anymore?"

"No. I don't. I quit my job. And I told Alex about the destination wedding . . . and he hates the idea just as much as I love it."

"But he didn't say an absolute no, did he?"

"We stopped talking about it, just like we always do when we teeter on the edge of a full-blown argument. It's ridiculous to want to argue with my boyfriend."

"But don't your parents say Alex is the perfect—"

"Don't say it, Margo. Okay? Just listen for now."

"Sorry. That was a bad joke. Listening."

Caron abandoned the line of candies, opting to pour herself a glass of sweet tea and escape to her bedroom. "When I told Alex about what happened at work, he spent more time supporting my dad than listening to me."

"I'm sorry. So what did you do?"

Caron sniffed and giggled. "I dyed my hair blond."

"O-kay."

"I know dyeing my hair red might have been more daring, but the point is, my hair looks like I want it to look—not how my dad expects me to wear it." Caron set her glass on her bedside table and then climbed into her bed. "I like my hair blond."

"I do, too. You make a great blond."

"Thanks. I have the support of you and my hairstylist." A sip of tea rinsed away some of the tightness in her throat. "And right before that, I got a job offer."

"A job offer? Really?"

"It's a temporary one. And I just might do it. I think I might want to get away from here for a little bit before I do any serious job-hunting."

"It's not in Florida, then?"

"No. It's in Colorado."

"*What?*"

If Margo shrieked at the mention of the location, what would she do when Caron told her who her boss would be?

"Kade Webster called and asked me to come out and stage a home for him. It's a Tour of Homes project."

"You did not just say that Kade Webster offered you a job."

"Yes, I did. What do you think?"

"You . . . and Kade. Together again . . ."

"Not together again. *Working* together again. There's a big difference."

"When are you coming out?"

"*If* I come out, Kade sounded like he needed me there yesterday. I told him I would call him tomorrow and tell him my decision. He said he'd pay per diem, pay for a car, put me up in a hotel—"

"Absolutely not! You're staying with me!"

Caron sat up, careful not to spill any liquid on herself or her bed. "Margo, you're talking like I've made the decision to do this."

"You have. You asked me to tell you what to do. Tell Kade yes."

"Why?"

"For all the reasons you said. Get away from the stress of your dad. Take a break before you jump into a new job. I know how hard you've been working the past few years. Do this short-term project for Kade."

"But we dated—"

"That was two years ago. You both have moved on. He knows you're with Alex, right?"

"I don't know. I mean, he probably knows I'm dating some-one."

"Mention it and your relationship is an instant do-not-cross-this-line barrier. And you and I get some time together. It's perfect."

"No, it's not perfect. But it seems like God is answering a prayer."

"Pardon?"

"Nothing. It's a joke between me and Vanessa." Caron tapped her fingers against the side of her glass. Margo made it all sound so simple. "Okay. I'll do it. Now all I have to do is tell Alex. And my parents."

"But first tell Kade, because then no one can talk you out of it."

"Right. I'll tell Kade first."

"Call him tonight."

"I'll call him tomorrow."

"I can call him for you—"

Her friend's insistence pulled a laugh from her. "No, I will accept my own job offer. Thank you very much."

Caron contemplated her half-empty glass of tea like a woman attempting to divine the future by reading tea leaves. But she had no ability to foretell her future. Once she called Kade, she set events in motion . . . but she had no control over them. She'd have to trust that if God was saying *yes* to Vanessa's prayer for less perfection in Caron's life, then he'd make it all turn out for the best. For her good. And for Kade's, too.

. . .

He'd offered Caron the job.

Now all he could do was wait for her to call him back tomorrow morning with her answer. Her *no*. Kade dropped onto his couch, grabbing the remote control and turning on the TV, surfing the channels. Cooking shows. Movies. Reality TV. Sports.

Nothing worth watching.

His cell phone buzzed where it lay on the couch beside him. A Florida area code . . . could it be—?

"Kade Webster here."

"Kade. This is Caron." Her tone was direct, businesslike.

"Morning came fast."

Lame joke.

"I thought about your offer . . . made my decision . . . and decided there was no reason to wait until tomorrow to call you."

"Fine." He could manage direct and businesslike, too.

And if Caron was going to turn him down, he appreciated that she told him now. He could start scrolling through the Internet tonight, rather than waiting until tomorrow morning.

"I'm in."

"You're . . . in?"

"Yes. It sounds fun."

"You'll stage the home?"

"Yes, I'll stage the home." A hint of laughter tinged her words.

"That's great!" Kade stood, running his hand through his hair. "How soon can you get out here?"

"Well, you said this is urgent, so how about if I fly out to Colorado on Sunday and come to work on Monday?"

"That would be fantastic." Kade sat back down. "Do you want me to make your flight reservations for you?"

"Why don't I do that and you can reimburse me? And I'm staying with Margo—so no hotel costs. But per diem and a car—"

"Of course. Just pick up a car at the airport. I'll draw up a contract tonight and e-mail it to you. While I'm at it, I'll include the floor plan of the house so you can start thinking about what kind of furniture you want."

"Sounds good, but I can't guarantee how much I'll get done. I have some things to do here before I leave."

"Understood."

"I would like to know what kind of budget we're working with and if you have any furniture in storage we can use."

"I'll include that information, too." No need to tell Caron that she was starting from ground zero on this project. He wanted her yes to stay a yes.

"All right, then. I need to get online and make a plane and car reservation."

"And I need to start compiling some information." Kade stood again, the up-down-up movements mirroring his emotions. "Thank you."

"Glad to help."

"I'll see you in a few days."

"Yes. See you in a few days."

Kade turned his cell phone over and over in his hands. Caron Hollister would be here Monday morning. She was now the home stager for Eddie Kingston's home.

There was no going back now. He'd made the call, and against all the odds, Caron had said yes. He was two years older, two years wiser, when it came to Caron Hollister. He knew she could stage the home. But he also knew he'd already given her the opportunity to break his heart. He wouldn't let that happen again.

FIFTEEN

• • • ♥ • • •

$\mathcal{A}$lex hunched over the bathroom sink, holding himself steady with one hand as he made short work of brushing his teeth.

Brush. Rinse. Spit.

Time to shave.

Friday. Another too-full day of work, thanks to a rival company poaching their new tech. The business had enjoyed a couple of weeks of breathing room, and now they were back to being understaffed, scrambling to keep up with customer calls.

Once he was dressed, Alex cleared his stuff off the top of his dresser—wallet into his back pocket, watch strapped onto his left wrist, a few pens slipped into his shirt pocket, cell phone—

Wait. He'd missed a text from Caron?

Good morning! Are you awake?

Alex tucked his work cap in his back pocket, texting a reply on his way to the kitchen.

Getting ready for work.

Caron replied as if she'd been doing nothing else but waiting for him to answer.

Got time to talk? Need to tell you something.

Huh. Maybe she'd found a job, or maybe she'd managed to smooth things over with her father and gotten her old job back.

Sure. Want me to call you?

No. Just come to your front door.

Come to his front door?

Sure enough, Caron stood on the porch in the early-morning sunlight, the air already drenched with humidity, dressed as if her next stop was the gym, her hair pulled into a messy bun.

"Good morning." She offered a small wave before stepping into his embrace. Her head barely reached the middle of his chest, but she fit just right in his arms. Familiar. Comfortable.

"Good morning. This is a pleasant surprise."

She brushed a quick kiss across his lips. "I know you don't have time to chitchat, but this can't wait. And I know once your day gets started, you never know when it will end."

"True." He rested his arm around her waist, moving her toward the kitchen. "Can you tell me what's up while I get coffee?"

"Sure." She lowered her voice. "Is your dad here?"

"He already left. And Mom is . . . sleeping." Alex inhaled the strong aroma of coffee as he filled his thermos. He held up the glass carafe. "Want some?"

"No." Caron paced a small circle around the kitchen, stopping to grip the back of one of the wooden chairs. "So, Alex . . . I got a job."

"You're kidding me." He settled the coffeepot back on the burner.

"I most definitely am not kidding about this. It's unexpected—"

"I didn't even know you'd started looking."

"I hadn't. Someone called and offered me a job. It's only temporary."

"A temporary job? Okay. That's good to have while you look for something permanent."

Caron held up her hand. "Let me just tell you about it, okay?"

Alex rubbed the back of his neck, the memory of their too-recent argument seeming to skulk into the kitchen. He would do better this time, even if doing so made him late for work. He pulled out a chair, the scrape of the feet against the worn linoleum like a whispered complaint. He took Caron's hand and tugged her down into the chair next to him. "Okay. I'm listening."

"I was asked to stage a home. It's not buying or selling homes, but since it's out of state, I can't work as a Realtor anyway."

"Wait. This job isn't here in Florida?"

"It's in Colorado." Caron laced their fingers together and offered him a smile—the one that he'd noticed back when he was fifteen and realized Caron Hollister was more than just his parents' friends' daughter. "It's only for a month. And I think it'll be good to get away. Not from you, of course. But things are so tense with my dad right now. Four weeks away will allow everything to blow over. Let me get used to the idea of his partnership with Nancy Miller. And then I'll be back and start looking for a permanent job."

"Who knows? Maybe you'll come back and you and your dad will talk and he'll offer you your old job back."

Caron shook off his hand, standing. "Alex, stop. I know you like my dad. And I know that you've listened to me talk about working for him ever since we started dating. But I'm done. Okay?"

He needed to keep the peace and still hope and pray things could change. "Okay. My bad. So, tell me more about this job in Colorado."

· · · ·

And now came the most difficult part of the conversation. No matter how many times she'd practiced saying "I'll be working for Kade Webster," there was no way to be nonchalant about accepting a job with her ex-boyfriend—especially since she hadn't mentioned seeing him while she was visiting Margo.

"Kade Webster called yesterday and offered me the job and I accepted. I fly out to the Springs on Sunday morning." The words rushed out, one after the other, the resulting silence making it seem as if she'd shouted at Alex.

"Kade Webster?"

"Yes."

"Why would Kade Webster offer you a job?"

"I saw him when I was visiting Margo. I mean, the only reason I saw him is because he's Margo's Realtor." Caron sat back down, her knees almost touching Alex's. "And she slipped up and mentioned that I was job-hunting."

"And why didn't you tell me that you saw your ex-boyfriend?"

"I didn't mention it for that exact reason, Alex. He's my ex. I dated him for a few months. I've been dating you for two years." Caron reached for his hand again. "And I saw him for an hour because Margo wanted me to go see a house with her. To be Ronny's stand-in. I saw Kade for less than an hour and I spent most of my time avoiding him. End of story."

"Except now you're going to work with him for a month."

"Exactly. I'm going to work for him. *For a month.* I'll get out of town. Stage a home. Talk wedding stuff with Margo. Come home and job-hunt. Simple as that."

Alex's phone rang, stalling his reply. He stood as he answered. "Yes, Dad, I'm going to work. I won't be stopping by the shop before I go to my first appointment. I'll talk to you later."

Caron stood, too, waiting to resume their conversation until he was done speaking with his father. "Are we going to finish talking about this?"

"I, uh, I've got to get to work." Alex grabbed his thermos and keys from the kitchen counter.

She stopped him with a light touch of her hand on his arm. "I wasn't hiding anything from you, Alex, because there was nothing to hide. It just wasn't important that I ran into Kade. I mean, I won the destination wedding and was already trying to figure out how to tell you about that—"

"Yeah." Alex's huff of laughter held no humor.

"I guess we can talk about that when I get back, too."

"Sure."

She slipped her hand into his on the way to the work van parked in front of the house, allowing the sound of buzzing insects and frogs to fill the silence between them.

Alex opened the van door, standing with it between them. "Do you need a ride to the airport?"

"I've got an early flight—"

"I'm always there for you, you know that."

"I know. And there's no one else I'd like to take me to the airport—and pick me up when I get back."

"Think we can squeeze in a quick date before you leave?"

"Absolutely. It's going to have to last for a month." She savored Alex's kiss. "Pray for me, okay? I still have to tell my parents."

.   .   .

Either she got out of her car and marched into her father's office and told him her plans, or she'd have to admit she was a coward.

That thought alone forced Caron from her car.

Yes, she was trembling in her high heels, but Caron refused to just tell her mother she'd taken a job in Colorado with Kade Webster, and then make her mom break the news to her father.

The same bright white, blue, and yellow pillows adorned the couch in the waiting area, but the fresh flowers had been replaced by a formal array of white calla lilies. Something Nancy Miller had suggested, perhaps?

Shelby was on the phone as Caron entered, her eyebrows skyrocketing as Caron waited in front of the receptionist's desk.

"Caron!" Shelby leaned over the phone console and hugged her as soon as she hung up the phone. "It's so good to see you."

"You, too. How are you?"

"Insanely busy. This whole merger thing . . . everything is in an uproar—"

"I can imagine."

"Are you coming back to work?"

"No. No." Shelby's question sent an unwanted jolt of electricity through her already-on-edge nervous system. "Just need to talk with my father, if he's available."

"He was in a meeting with Miss Miller, but I just saw her go out." Shelby picked up the phone. "Do you want me to check?"

"No. I still know the way to his office. This won't take long."

The building pulsed with activity—ringing phones, the interwoven threads of multiple conversations, people moving in and out of offices. An occasional "Caron! Hey, Caron!" broke through her concentration, and she acknowledged the greetings without stopping. A smile. A nod. But always moving forward to her father's office. The smaller of the three conference rooms in the middle of the building was a shambles—empty of the long table and chairs, carpeting pulled up.

What was going on?

The answer to her unspoken question was no longer any of her business.

Her father hung up the phone as she stood in his open doorway, rising to meet her. Had Shelby notified him of her arrival? Fine. It's not as if she was going for the element of surprise. That would happen soon enough.

"Good afternoon, Caron. I'm assuming this is a social call."

She could read between the lines. Her father's "Don't come back looking for a job" edict still held.

"Of course." Caron stood behind one of the chairs situated in front of his desk, so similar to his office at home. Her father was a creature of habit. "And I realize I'm interrupting you at work. I would have waited to talk to you this Sunday at lunch, but, well, I won't be there."

"You won't? Have you and Alex made other plans?"

She started to grip the edge of the back of the chair, and forced herself to release her hold. Exhale. Relax her stance. Her father knew how to read people. "Alex and his parents may very well still join you and Mom on Sunday. I, however, will be on my way to Colorado."

"Didn't you just get back from a trip?"

"That's correct." Caron clasped her hands in front of her. "I'm going back for a job."

"A job? You're not licensed as a Realtor in Colorado."

"No, sir, I'm not. I'm going to be staging a home . . . for Kade Webster."

She had to give her father credit. He was not one to give away his emotions or his thoughts. His movements were deliberate as he removed his glasses. Pulled a clean, starched handkerchief from his pocket. Cleaned one lens, then the other. Replaced his glasses on his nose. Began to fold his handkerchief.

"Do you think that's wise, Caron?"

Caron thought she'd prepared herself for this confrontation. She'd prayed. Reminded herself that she was an adult. That she could make her own decisions. That she didn't need her father's approval. But somehow she'd forgotten his ability to use one well-aimed sentence to reduce her to a mere teen, trying to defend herself to her all-wise, all-knowing father who did not approve of her actions.

Her bottom lip trembled, but she refused to catch it between her teeth. Or to acknowledge that her face flushed. But she couldn't hide how her breathing ratcheted up, so that her shoulders jerked beneath the soft material of her short-sleeved blouse.

"I do." Her words were breathy. "I—I know I can stage this home for Kade. I'm excited about the opportunity."

"I thought you'd learned your lesson about not mixing business and personal relationships."

"This is purely business between Kade and me. His regular home stager had an emergency and he needs to stage a home on short notice. He offered me the job, and I accepted."

"I see."

A whiff of floral perfume scented the air, followed by the sound of Nancy Miller's voice. "I apologize, Russell. I didn't realize you were talking with someone."

"Come in, Nancy." Her father came around his desk, leaning on the corner. "My daughter came to tell me that she's taking a temporary job in Colorado."

"Oh, hello, Caron. I didn't realize that was you." Nancy remained standing in the doorway. "I don't want to interrupt."

"You're not interrupting—and this is quite an interesting story. She's working for my former protégé. Kade Webster, as you know, learned everything he could from me about the realty business, thanked me by dating my daughter behind my back, and then walked away to start his own company."

"I wasn't aware of all those details."

Caron waited. Now was Nancy Miller's chance to align herself with Caron's father. Confirm in a few short sentences that Caron had made the wrong choice by dating Kade Webster, and that she was making the wrong choice now.

"And we both can probably think of relationships in our pasts we should have avoided, too. Right, Russell?" Nancy's laugh sounded forced.

Her father's jaw tightened.

"I just think we have to let our children find their own way. Make mistakes all their own. We certainly did."

Nancy Miller was defending her?

With the other woman's words, Caron could leave with some semblance of dignity intact. There was nothing more to be said.

"I have to pack and catch a plane." Caron backed up into the doorjamb, the impact jarring her spine. She sidestepped around Nancy and found the space to make her exit. "And I'm sure you two have business to discuss."

"Have a good trip, Caron." Nancy Miller touched her arm. "Good luck in Colorado."

Nancy Miller said something, eliciting a response from her father—what it was, Caron couldn't decipher as she moved farther and farther down the hallway. She'd come to tell her father about her decision, and she had accomplished that.

She hadn't expected her father to congratulate her and wish her well. That would have been expecting the impossible.

SIXTEEN

• • ♥ • •

*A*s long as Alex remembered Caron's time in Colorado was short term, he was fine. And as long as he ignored the fact she was working for Kade Webster.

In the end, she'd come back home to Florida. To him.

The drive to the airport was quick, the road empty of traffic, the occasional streetlights providing the only break in the predawn darkness.

"You checked to make sure your flight wasn't delayed?"

"Yes. It's still leaving at seven. I'll be there in plenty of time." Caron rummaged in her carry-on bag, securing her phone charger in an interior pocket. "Thanks again for taking me to the airport."

"I don't mind. I'll park and help you carry your suitcases inside when we get there."

"You don't need to, Alex—"

"I want to."

"I just hope what I packed in two suitcases will be enough for the next month . . . well, two suitcases and my tote." Caron tucked a lock of her hair behind her ear. "Of course, Margo and I can always go shopping, right?"

"I guess." Alex drained the last of the coffee in the insulated travel cup. "She's picking you up at the airport?"

"No. Kade is paying for a rental car while I'm there. I told you that, didn't I?"

"I don't think so. I guess that makes sense."

Caron set her bag beside her feet, turning to face him. "I'll be busy working and I don't want to have to ask anyone else for a ride. He was going to put me up in a hotel, too, but Margo insisted I stay with her. I admit that I like this option much better."

Another mile marker slipped past. They would be at the airport in ten minutes at this rate.

"Caron, I wanted to talk to you about something before you left."

The early-morning darkness shadowed her face. "Okay. What's on your mind?"

"We've been dating for two years now. And we love each other. We've talked about getting married—" Alex tilted the travel mug to his lips again. Nothing. "I've been thinking about that . . . and you know, why don't we?"

Caron remained still. Silent.

"Did you hear what I said?" He reached for her hand, but she didn't respond to his gesture.

"I did. I'm trying to figure out . . . if you just proposed to me or not."

"Well, it's not a formal proposal, obviously. I mean, I don't have a ring—"

"Oh. So is this considered a *casual proposal*? Tossing a why-don't-we question at me while we're driving to the airport before dawn when I'm leaving for a month?"

"Like I said, I've been thinking about it—"

"Alex, the last time we talked about getting married you were telling me how much you disliked the idea of a destination wedding in Colorado." Caron's words ricocheted through the car. "Am I supposed to believe that our . . . our argument caused you to think about proposing to me now?"

"No."

"Then what did?" Before he could reply, she rushed ahead. "Because if your 'not formal' proposal was prompted by my leaving town to work for Kade Webster, it feels more like you're marking your territory."

"Caron, I realize this is less than ideal—"

"Less than ideal? You weren't even looking at me when you sort of asked me to marry you!" Caron's shoulders were rigid, her words rupturing his hopes. "You know I'm not a morning person . . . and I don't even have any makeup on and you didn't even notice that my hair is blond!"

"Your hair is blond?" Alex allowed himself a quick glance. "What does that have to do with me proposing to you?"

"Nothing. And everything." She sniffled. "And I am not crying. I'm mad."

Right. The sounds she was making were angry sniffles.

"Can we forget what I said?"

"Yes. Please."

The lights of the airport loomed ahead. Maybe while they waited in the terminal for Caron's flight he could figure out a way to fix the mess he'd made.

"I think . . . it would be better if you drop me off at the curb."

"Caron, don't be like this."

"I'm not *being* like anything." A sigh filled the car. "I'm tired. The last few days have been stressful. I want to get through security and go sit at my gate, okay?"

"I'm sorry."

"I know."

A few moments later, Alex lugged her suitcases over to the curb, his car idling in the no-parking zone. Caron stepped into his embrace.

He pressed a kiss on the top of her head. "I love you."

She tilted her face, offering him a glimpse of the barest hint of a smile. "I know you do. I love you, too."

"Forgive me?"

"Of course." She stepped back. "Now get moving before that security guard comes over here and tells you to."

"Right."

"I'll call when I get to Colorado."

Maybe by then he'd have figured out a way to undo his informal proposal and make things right between them again.

.   .   .

We've talked about getting married . . . I've been thinking about that . . . and you know, why don't we?

Alex's words weighed on her like invisible—and unwanted—carry-on baggage.

Caron slumped into a seat at her gate, setting her leather bag at her feet. She pressed her fingers to her temples, willing away the pressure building there.

What was Alex thinking, tossing a last-minute proposal at her? Was he that insecure about Kade Webster—and that sure of her, thinking she'd be happy with nothing more than a "Why don't we?" for a marriage proposal? Yes, they'd been dating for two years, but she still wanted romance. Still wanted him to put some effort into their relationship.

She understood his long work hours. Sympathized with his family situation. And forgave him when he didn't notice things like a new hairstyle . . . or realize that she needed more than an offhanded "Will you marry me?"

She'd miss him, but she knew this trip was exactly what she needed.

For the next few weeks, she'd be on her own, experiencing unexpected newfound independence. Untangling herself from the grip of her father's assumptions.

By nightfall, she'd be at Margo's apartment. Again. Unpacked. Ready to face tomorrow.

Maybe not ready.

But she'd give Kade her absolute best effort when it came to staging the house. Work. Go back to Margo's. Work. Go back to Margo's. Toss in some wedding fun with her best friend if time allowed.

All Kade wanted from her was a well-staged home. She could do that, so long as she wasn't lured into the past by the "might-have-beens" that lingered around Kade Webster.

Maybe, just maybe, there'd be time for her to find clarity. Figure her life out.

Maybe in Colorado she'd find the space to hear God better, to discover the answers she needed to move forward with her life.

Who am I, God?

I mean, truly . . . who am I? Not who do I have to be to keep my dad happy . . . Just . . . who am I? I know I should know this by now . . . but I don't. I let someone else fill in the answers for me.

Caron closed her eyes, blocking out the sight of the terminal beginning to fill up with passengers rushing to their gates. Maybe she needed to be more eloquent. More specific. But this early in the morning, with too little sleep and too much travel ahead of her, that's all she could come up with.

She could only hope it was enough.

SEVENTEEN

• • • ♥ • • •

Irst day. New job. Clarification—new interim job. Three and a half weeks. Twenty-one days to do what she needed to do to prove herself again. To Kade Webster, the man approaching her with a long-legged stride. Familiar—and yet this was totally unfamiliar territory.

Kade was her boss. She was his employee. So long as she kept that fact straight while she was here, everything would be fine.

"Are you ready to get started?"

"Absolutely." Caron gripped the handles of her mulberry leather tote. Dug the three-inch heels of her matching shoes into the plush cream carpeting in the waiting area. Pasted on a smile she hoped looked natural—and not overly caffeinated, which she was, thanks to a night spent tossing and turning in Margo's spare bedroom. Last night was a blur of too little sleep mixed with frantic prayer. Kade turned toward the young woman behind the front desk, who rose to meet Caron. "This is Miriam. She's worked with me since day one. She's reliable, catches on quickly, and keeps everything organized. I never miss a message, thanks to her."

"Hello, Miriam. I'm Caron." She peeled her fingers away from the handle of her tote and shook hands with the young woman, who couldn't be a day over twenty-one, if that. She wore a trendy multicolored wrap around her shoulder-length dreadlocks and a breezy white top over wide-leg pants.

"Good morning. It's nice to meet you. After Mr. Webster shows you around, I'll check in and see if there's anything you need." As the phone rang, she whispered "excuse me" and returned to work.

"I have one other Realtor working for me. I hope we can catch him before he heads out this morning. I know he had some early showings." He rapped on the open doorway of the first office. "Mitch? Good, you're still here. I wanted to introduce you to Caron Hollister."

A muscular, broad-shouldered man with dark blond hair moved his wheelchair around from behind his desk. "Ah, the infamous Caron Hollister."

"Infamous?" Caron shook her head, even as her skin flushed. "I hardly think so."

"Just a joke. Although I will say Kade almost cartwheeled into the office today knowing you were coming to stage the Tour of Homes house. He's talked you up quite a bit."

Caron scrambled to remember what Kade had told her about Mitch. They'd met during army boot camp, and their bond was forged a couple of years later when they reconnected during Ranger training. "He did, did he?"

"Don't be modest, Caron." Kade leaned back against the doorjamb, the epitome of relaxed confidence in his navy-blue blazer and tan slacks over a white dress shirt. "Hollister Realty—Hollister Realty Group now, right?—is one of the top companies on the Gulf Coast. And you were one of their top Realtors last year."

"Just hard work paying off, that's all."

"She's modest. You didn't mention that." Mitch's smile held a hint of bad-boyishness. "Good to have you with us. Kade's a good boss. He believes in that one-for-all-and-all-for-one stuff."

Caron shook his hand. "Thanks, Mitch. I'm excited about being here."

And now she sounded like some mechanical doll. Just pull the string and she'd say the appropriate phrase. Her frayed nerves and lack of sleep were getting the better of her.

Kade led her down a hallway decorated with photographs of aspens, mountain streams, and autumn foliage.

"Very Coloradoan."

"Of course. Setting the appropriate tone." Kade pointed to an office on the left, stepping back to let her enter. "This is your office. Do whatever you want to make it your own."

A basic dark brown desk. A high-back fabric chair. Small window. That was a plus. A computer.

She stepped inside, pivoting to face Kade. "I don't need all this, not when I'm here for less than a month."

"You still need someplace to work. It's a spare office, Caron. Go ahead and put a plant in here." As he continued down the hallway, she dropped her tote off and resumed the tour. "My office is to the right. Conference room is in the middle area. Break room to the left. Bathrooms are straight back. As you can see, we're not that large—yet."

"It's a good size."

"A good size to begin. I didn't want to waste a lot of money on overhead at first. I'm already looking around for what's next. I want to rent something larger. Maybe buy a building. Who knows what will happen after the Tour of Homes."

"You have a lot riding on that, don't you?"

"Yes and no. I believe in the adage 'Don't put all your eggs in one basket.'"

"So not all your business hopes are pinned on the tour?"

"Of course not." He stuck his hands in his pant pockets. "We've worked together before, Caron. You know me better than that."

She didn't have to worry about being uncomfortable working for Kade Webster. The man had met her at the office, introduced her to the receptionist and Mitch, gave her the grand tour, and then told her to have a great day and disappeared out the front door.

Which suited her just fine.

She needed to get settled. To focus on the Tour of Homes project. The easiest way to do that was to do what she had to without worrying about where Kade was.

"Do you need anything, Caron?" Miriam appeared in the doorway of her office.

"I don't think so, but thank you. I'm just trying to get set up here." Caron returned the girl's friendly smile as she plugged in her iPad.

"Mr. Webster said not to order you any business cards, correct?"

"No. I'll be gone after the Tour of Homes."

"If you don't mind me saying so, I think you'll love working here. Mr. Webster is a great boss."

Was that the slight echo of an office crush in Miriam's voice?

"He has high standards, but he pays well and he's very fair." Miriam stepped into the office. "I need to get you a desk lamp in here. I'll talk to Mr. Webster about that. Anyway, he's a straight-up kind of guy."

"A straight-up kind of guy?"

"Yes, I might as well tell you this is my first real job. My mother warned me not to get any ideas about my boss, but I mean, have you seen Mr. Webster?" Miriam giggled. "Of course you have. He could be on TV, don'tcha think? What girl wouldn't get a crush on him?"

Bingo.

Caron found Miriam's naïve honesty endearing and couldn't help responding. Oh, to be that young again. "You had a crush on Mr. Webster?"

"I hate to admit it, but I did." Miriam twisted a dreadlock. "It was pretty obvious. I tripped all over myself and kept forgetting to do things the way he asked. Kept messing up the phone calls. He should have fired me."

"What did he do?" There was no way Caron would ever confess to Miriam that she once had similar feelings for Kade. Even though she was older and wiser, Caron couldn't help smiling at the girl's romantic travails in the midst of a stressful situation.

"He called me into his office and told me it was time for my first month's review. He thanked me for being punctual and always being pleasant with the clients and for keeping such an orderly desk."

"And?"

"And then he said if I didn't stop acting like a schoolgirl, he'd have to fire me and find someone else to do my job."

"He did not." Despite her protest, Caron wasn't too surprised Kade had been so blunt with the girl.

"He did. I about died from embarrassment. But honestly, he was as nice as he could be about it. He asked if I could please make it easy on him so he wouldn't have to hire anyone else because overall I was doing well. And then he said he was a committed bachelor or something like that—"

"A confirmed bachelor?"

"Yeah. And that he was too busy starting up his business to get involved with anyone. And besides, good bosses do not date their employees."

"Good point."

"Mr. Webster said it's company policy, although there's nothing in the employee handbook. I looked. Not that I was going to argue with him or anything, I love this job. I'm saving up so that I can go to college eventually. And I don't think I'm going to find a better boss than Mr. Webster."

"I would have to agree. Some bosses might actually take advantage of your, um, schoolgirl crush."

"That's what my best friend said," Miriam said, and backed toward the door. "Anyway, I really do think you're going to like working here."

"I'm excited about staging the house." Caron smiled at the young girl. Unwritten rule or not, the no-dating-employees rule was best. Miriam didn't need to know Caron herself had learned that truth the hard way.

EIGHTEEN

• • • ♥ • • •

*T*ime to be the boss.

Kade had kept busy with his clients, giving Caron two hours to set up her office. He'd treat her like any other new employee and give her space. Let Miriam answer any basic questions. But he couldn't do evasive maneuvers all day, every day while Caron was here. They had to work together at some point. Go over their employment agreement. And get started on Kingston's house.

Kade pushed away from his desk. He'd been staring at his computer screen for the last five minutes. Neither of them had time to waste, and it was up to him to get things started. All he had to do was find his new employee and invite her to go see the Peak Tour of Homes house. Not that he was offering a real say-yes-or-no invitation. They needed to start planning how Caron was going to stage the house.

Finding her office empty, Kade checked with Miriam.

"Have you seen Miss Hollister? Did she head out to buy something?"

"Did you check the break room? She came by a bit ago and asked if we had any pitchers."

"Pitchers? Okay, thanks."

Caron was faced away from him as he entered the break room. A pile of torn foil tea-bag wrappers littered the counter.

Kade tucked his hands in his pockets. "You planning on drinking a lot of hot tea?"

Caron whirled around, creating enough of a draft that the pile of wrappers fluttered to the floor. "What? Oh, Kade, it's you. No . . . no, I'm making a pitcher of sweet tea."

"Ah." Caron's drink of choice. "How did I forget your addiction to that stuff?"

"It's not an addiction—" Caron waved him away and knelt to gather the debris on the floor, her once-again blond hair spilling across her shoulders. "It's a preference. And while I'm here, there will be a pitcher of the best sweet tea you've ever tasted in that fridge over there."

"No complaints here. Will it have a 'For Caron Hollister Only' sign on it?"

"Hardly. I don't mind sharing."

"Just mark it 'Sweet Tea' in nice bold letters. Can't have Mitch and Miriam victims of an unexpected sugar high."

"Got it." Caron added one more tea bag to the pitcher. "Did you need to talk with me?"

"I was wondering if you're ready to go see Kingston's house?"

"Absolutely. I've got some preliminary ideas, of course, but I'm eager to do a walk-through and get a feel for the house."

"Perfect. Meet me in the parking lot in five?"

"Sure."

Thanks to an unexpected phone call, Caron waited for him beside his car, dark purple leather tote in one hand, two bottles of water balanced in the other.

"Miriam sent these." Caron nodded toward the plastic bottles. "She said to remind you that she deserves a raise."

"Yeah, she tells me that about once a week. It's an ongoing joke." Kade hit the keyless entry to unlock the car. "Be careful when you sit down, okay? I left something in the passenger seat."

"What? Kade Webster, Realtor, keeping a less-than-spotless car?"

"Hardly. For your information, I just had it detailed. I got you something."

Caron deposited the bottles of water in the cup holder, slid her bag in front of the passenger seat, and found his offering. Slipping into her seat, she shook the red box of Hot Tamales so the candy rattled around. "What's this?"

"I believe you used to refer to that as 'brain food.' I need you at your creative best."

"Thanks." Before he even pulled out of the parking lot, she'd opened the box and indulged in a couple of pieces. "So tell me more about the Tour of Homes house."

"Well, it's located out in the northern part of town in a new subdivision." Kade maneuvered the car onto Powers Boulevard heading north. "I convinced Eddie Kingston to make some last-minute changes—"

"You convinced the builder to make some changes? I would have liked to listen in on that conversation."

"Yes, well, he was surprised at first, but I'd done my research well enough to know he was an innovator—"

"Smart, Kade, very smart."

"Thank you, but this conversation will go a lot easier if you stop interrupting me." Kade raked his fingers through his hair. "Some things never change."

"Did you just say 'Some things never change'? What does that mean?"

"It means you still have your tendency to interrupt when I'm talking, Miss Hollister."

"I do not interrupt conversations. I participate in them."

"Well, participate in this one a little less so I can explain what's going on before we get to our destination."

"Whatever you say, boss."

"Boss." Kade nodded, unable to hold back the smile curving his lips. "I like the sound of that. Feel free to use that term whenever you wish."

When Caron popped another Hot Tamale into her mouth as a response, Kade twisted to look at her.

"What's the matter? You can't say 'boss' more than once a day?"

"I'm not hijacking the conversation."

At her reply, Kade chuckled. "All right. Since I have your undivided—and uninterrupted—attention, I'll continue. Eddie is redoing the house so it works for a handicapped person—a Wounded Warrior or maybe an elderly person who has to use a wheelchair or a walker."

"You mean someone like Mitch." Caron covered her mouth with her hand, muttering a muffled "sorry."

"Yes, someone like Mitch. He was my inspiration." He held out his hand. "You owe me one Hot Tamale, please."

"Are you making up rules as we go along?" Caron doled out the required single Hot Tamale. "And I thought this box of candy was a gift, not some sort of penalty box."

He popped the candy into his mouth. "We're running up against an almost impossible schedule, what with widening doorways, pulling up carpeting, retrofitting the master bathroom, lowering some of the kitchen cabinets and counters, and the sink, too. Ramps for the front and back doors."

Kade stopped talking and silence filled the car.

"So what do you think?"

Caron formed a *T* with her hand and the box of candy. "I just called a time-out. So, when I speak, I do not forfeit a Hot Tamale."

"Fair enough."

"I think this is a brilliant idea. I can't wait to walk through the house and see how much has been done."

"Eddie promised to meet us there today so he can give us a tour of the home himself. He huffed and puffed at first about making the changes—"

"I can imagine—"

Kade held out his hand for another piece of candy, his eyes still on the road.

"What? Oh, fine." Caron dropped another candy into his palm.

"As I was saying, he blustered a bit at first about the added work, but things are moving fast now. I'm eager to see what he's done."

Out of the corner of his eye, Kade caught Caron's silent nod. It was surprising how a box of candy had helped them relax with one another.

But was that what he wanted? To relax? Get comfortable with Caron Hollister again? Was he maintaining proper business demeanor?

He shifted in his seat, as if putting a few more inches between him and the woman beside him would reestablish the needed boundary. He'd asked her to come to Colorado to help him, not to get involved with her again. And he wasn't about to open himself up to getting hurt by her again.

"Is there anything else you want to tell me, or do you want to hear some of my ideas?"

Caron's voice pulled Kade from his musings.

"We'll be there in about fifteen minutes. Why don't we talk more once you've seen the house? Discuss it as we go room to room?"

"Good idea."

Kade switched on the radio, filling the car with a current country hit. He'd avoid conversation, filling the silence with someone else's thoughts set to music. By the time they arrived at the house, he'd be back in the proper mind-set.

Two professionals working together. Nothing more.

*   *   *

Caron left Eddie and Kade inside the house, her iPad on the kitchen counter, easing open the sliding glass door that led to the backyard.

She'd accompanied the two men through all the rooms, dodging workers laying cream-colored Berber carpet and painting walls a muted eggshell as she typed notes in her iPad and took photos of each room. Possible ideas for colors, furniture, and accent pieces competed inside her head—ones she'd thought of back in Florida and new ideas now that she'd seen the house. All she had to do was sort everything out, room by room, into a plan that would best showcase the house.

The Front Range, capped by Pikes Peak, stretched out against a cloudless Colorado-blue sky. Now, how would that color be described if it were paint? She squinted, trying to remember some of the names she'd come across in store displays. *Parade Blue. Baby Blue Eyes. Atlas Blue.* Nope. Nothing but *Colorado Blue* worked. And even with the bright June sunshine, Caron savored the lack of humidity that would have caused her blouse to cling to her skin by now. Rolls of sod were positioned around the yard, as well several flats of bright red, purple, and white petunias.

"Can I help you with anything?"

The man's deep bass voice caused Caron to turn. He was tan, a faded brimmer hat shading his face and a wide grin reaching all the way to his eyes.

"No, I'm fine. Just stepped outside to think."

"Can't say I blame you. It's noisy in there." The man extended a hand, then pulled it back to dust off the dirt caking his skin onto his jeans. "Sorry about that. I'm Austin Barret, the landscaper."

"I'm Caron Hollister. I'll be staging the house."

"Great. We'll be seeing each other again."

"Possibly." Caron couldn't help but like the man and his natural friendliness. "Although I'll be inside and you'll be outside."

"Well, a guy's got to get a drink of water now and then. And I might need advice on where to place a petunia or two."

"I'm sure you will."

"I'll wager you're not from Colorado."

"What gave me away?"

"That little Southern drawl of yours is charming."

Caron had to laugh at the man's blatant flirting. "I bet you use that line on all the ladies, Austin."

"Only the Southern ones." Austin tossed her a wink.

"Everything okay out here?" Kade's voice sounded across the yard.

Caron's laughter stilled as Austin's eyes narrowed. "That your boyfriend?"

"No. That's my boss."

"I see."

"He's probably ready to discuss this project. We're on a tight schedule."

Austin tipped the brim of his hat, flashing another of his teasing grins. "Been a pleasure to meet you, Caron. I hope to see you again. Soon."

"See you around, Austin."

Kade stood, hands on hips, at the top of the wooden ramp that had been constructed on one side of the small patio. Caron chose to use the stairs on the other side.

"Everything okay?" A slight breeze lifted her hair off her neck, and she relished the coolness.

"You tell me."

What did Kade mean by that?

"You and Eddie were discussing retrofitting the second shower or not. I stepped outside to gather my thoughts—"

"Looked like you were flirting with the gardener."

"If by 'flirting' you mean that he came over and said hello and that I said hello back, then yes, I flirted with the gardener." Caron huffed out a breath. "And I don't see why that's any of your business."

"It's my business because I'm paying your salary for the next few weeks, which means I am paying you to work for me—not to fool around."

"Fool around . . ." Caron kept her voice low, stomping her foot so that a sharp pain zinged up her calf. "I was talking to the man for less than five minutes."

"I had to come looking for you. Eddie wants to know if you have any preliminary ideas to share with him."

"Yes, I do. I just need to get my iPad." Caron straightened her shoulders and stood as tall as she could, marching past Kade, but pausing long enough for one last verbal volley. "And if you plan on keeping track of me, I'll just tell you now you'll have to pay me extra to wear a bell."

NINETEEN

· · · ♥ · · ·

*A*lex grabbed the washing-machine belt from the passenger seat of the van, knocking the crumpled fast-food bag to the floor, where it lay next to an empty Big Gulp cup and a Baby Ruth wrapper. He needed to clean the van in his spare time. But how often did he have any of that? Days like today were rare. The previous two appointments had been easy fixes and he'd finished up early, providing him with an extra hour to stop by Jessica's and tell her about his idea for her air-conditioner replacement. Yes, he'd be eating on the run again, but if everything went well with this impromptu repair, he'd still be on schedule.

Everything seemed quiet as he stood on the small front porch decorated with a white plastic planter filled with red geraniums. He knocked on the door. Waited. Knocked again. Waited. He tried ringing the doorbell, which gave an odd one-note jangle. How many things in this house were broken?

After a few moments of waiting, Alex had to admit Jessica wasn't home. Why did he assume she didn't work during the day? She'd obviously taken off when he came to repair her A/C the first time, and the second time it was after five o'clock.

Just as he got back to the van, Jessica turned the corner at the end of the street and came toward him.

"Alex?" She quickened her pace.

"Hi." He tapped the rubber belt against his leg.

"What are you doing here?" She stood on the sidewalk, a narrow strip of dry grass separating them.

"I came by to check on your washing machine."

"My . . . washing machine? But you repair air conditioners."

"Turns out I also know a little bit about other appliances. And I snuck a look at your machine the other day when I washed my hands because I needed to know the brand. Based on what you described, I think it's just a matter of replacing the belt."

"Alex, you didn't—"

"I'm here. I have the belt. Is it okay if I take a look?"

She shrugged, a smile curving her lips, her strawberry-blond hair held back from her face by a plain white headband. "Of course it's okay. I don't mean to sound ungrateful. I just don't want to take advantage of you."

He followed her lead to the front door. "Where's Scotty?"

"I walked him over to a friend's house for a playdate." She ushered him inside with a flourish. "You obviously know the way."

"Guilty as charged. Are you off work today, too?"

"Off work?"

"I assumed you were off work the first time I came to repair your A/C—"

"I work from home. I'm a medical transcriptionist."

"Really? I don't think I've ever met one of those."

"I listen to different doctors' dictations of their reports and medical notes and I type them up and then send them back for their review. It's nice because I'm home, and I can be here for Scotty. I might look for something else once he's in school full-time, but for now, it's a great job for a single mom, if you don't mind all the medical jargon."

"Scotty's a great kid."

"He is that. But today he was getting a little tired of hanging around the house while I tried to catch up on my work. Hence, the playdate." A soft laugh wrapped around her words. "Some days it's all I can do to keep up with his never-ending appetite, his creative imagination, and his curiosity that leads to a million questions."

"I bet he's got a lot of those."

"Everything from why puppies can't talk to him, to why can't he eat all the ice cream he wants, to why doesn't his daddy live with us." Jessica had switched from sunglasses to her regular glasses. "I have to admit, that last one is the toughest."

Her last comment was said with raw honesty. "Does Scotty see his dad often?"

"No. I have sole custody of him. Our divorce was rough. I guess Wayne expected me to tolerate his not-so-secret girlfriends forever. I didn't wise up soon enough not to marry the guy, but I didn't stay stupid forever."

Her admission surprised him. A brief explanation that didn't ask for pity.

"Anyway, you didn't come here to find out about me. I'll get out of your way and go wrangle with some long, complicated medical words."

Alex disconnected the water and electricity before moving the washing machine away from the wall. Once he removed the back panel, he pulled out the broken belt—just as he suspected.

But his victory was a short-lived one. Yes, Jessica's washing machine needed a new belt, but he'd brought the wrong size. So much for his good deed for the day.

Jessica sat at a small wooden dining room table, laptop open, headphones in place, eyes intent, fingers flying over the keyboard. Alex positioned himself at the other end of the table, standing silent, waiting until she finished typing. She paused the dictation machine next to the computer, removing the headphones and rearranging the headband that held her hair in place.

"So?"

"Well, I'm right . . . and I'm wrong."

"Okay."

"Meaning, it *is* your washing-machine belt, but I bought the wrong size." He scratched the side of his jaw. "So, give me another chance to get the right one and I'll fix it for you."

"Alex, really, I didn't expect you to do this—"

"You can't expect me to be this close and quit now."

"I'm going to lose this argument, aren't I?" At his nod, she smiled. "So, do you win all the arguments with your girlfriend?"

"Caron? We don't argue." Except about her winning the destination wedding in Colorado. And about her quitting her job. And about her working for Kade Webster. He wouldn't call his near-miss of a proposal a true argument.

Why were there so many missteps between them lately?

"Oh, one of those we-never-argue kind of couples."

"We've known each other for years. It's . . . easy."

"Easy would be nice. Are you two serious?"

"We've been together two years—so yes. We're talking about getting married." That was one way to put the disastrous conversation in the car.

Jessica leaned back in her chair, sliding her glasses back up on her nose. "Congratulations. But oh, boy, when it comes time to propose . . . well, you've got your work cut out for you."

Proposing. Between his dad and now Jessica, it seemed there was no avoiding the topic. "What do you mean?"

"Where have you been? You can't just hand a girl a ring and say 'Will you marry me?' anymore." Jessica shook her head. "It starts in high school nowadays. Guys are supposed to come up with these elaborate ways to ask a girl to homecoming or prom. Flowers. Banners. Gigantic stuffed animals. By the time a girl expects a wedding proposal, a guy has to have some sort of grand, romantic gesture she'll tell all her friends and family about and remember for the rest of her life."

No wonder Caron had shut him down. There was no way he was telling Jessica Thompson how badly he bungled things the other day. No flowers. No ring. And no eye contact. "I'm not much of a grand-romantic-plan kind of guy. Caron knows that."

"All the more reason to surprise her."

"Maybe." Alex tapped the palm of his hand with the useless belt. "Oh, man, I can't believe I forgot to tell you something."

"More bad news?"

"No. I figured out a way to save you some money on a replacement air conditioner."

"Really?"

"We had to pull a unit at a customer's home because they're remodeling and they wanted a larger unit. The unit they had works fine and they had a planned service agreement, so it's well maintained. It should last awhile without problems."

"It sounds wonderful. But how much am I looking at spending?"

"Only twelve hundred dollars. We can arrange a payment plan. Think about it." He pulled a business card out of his shirt pocket and handed it to her. "Call me and let me know and we'll set up an installation time."

"I'll need to check my finances."

"I understand. I'll let you get back to work." Halfway to the door, he stopped. "You still good with me fixing your washing machine?"

"Am I still good? What kind of silly question is that? Believe me, going to the Laundromat is not high on my list of favorite things to do. And Scotty doesn't like it any more than I do."

"I can imagine." Alex tugged on his cap. "I might not be back until the weekend, or whenever you decide about the air conditioner."

"I'll give you a call. And I really do appreciate you thinking of me—I mean, for the used air conditioner. And don't worry about my washing machine, Alex."

"One good deed deserves another."

"Oh, that reminds me! Wait there." She disappeared into the small kitchen, reappearing with a small brown lunch sack.

"What's this?"

"Not much, really. Just a snack. An apple and an orange and some homemade cookies. Now get going."

He raised the sack and saluted her. "Thanks."

By the time he'd turned off her street, Alex had already finished off two of the oatmeal raisin cookies. He was going to have a hard time keeping up with Jessica in the good-deed department. It was second nature to her. Seemed like she was determined to carry on her mother's tradition of feeding both friends and strangers.

Too bad Scotty hadn't been there today. He'd missed the little boy's nonstop chatter and questions. Not that he had the time to get attached to him. Or Scotty's mother. He could help out someone in need, too. And then focus on work, and getting things back to normal with Caron as best he could while she was several thousand miles away.

TWENTY

· ♥ · ♥ · ♥ ·

The noise reverberating through the gym minutes earlier faded as the basketball players exited, the wheels of their chairs squeaking against the polished wood floor. A few of the men called back and forth to one another, their T-shirts and hair damp with sweat, laughter punctuating their words.

With a wave, Mitch separated himself from his teammates and made his way to where Kade leaned back against the lowest set of bleachers.

"You should have joined us." Mitch wiped his arm across his forehead.

"Didn't have the appropriate mode of transportation. Besides, I couldn't keep up with you on the basketball court before, and I still can't."

"Got that right. Ready for a swim?"

"Yeah."

Mitch stayed in place. "You going to tell me what's going on?"

Kade slumped forward over his knees. "It's that obvious?"

"An artic breeze blew through the office late yesterday afternoon, man. And Miriam warned me that Caron came in to work today muttering something about checking the office manual about wearing a bell." Mitch's laugh rang through the empty gym. "Caron Hollister works for you less than a day and you two already had a fight?"

"It's my fault. I got out of line."

"And what does that mean?"

"I got jealous, okay? Stupid, I know. She was talking to the landscaper out at Kingston's house yesterday and it . . . it bothered me."

"What did you do?"

"I accused her of flirting and . . . fooling around . . ."

"With the landscape guy? What did you do, find them in a passionate embrace behind the begonias?"

"Very funny. And you don't have to say anything. Caron already did." Kade gripped his knees, pushing himself back up. "I was out of line, I know it. I haven't been around the woman for two years and I overreact because she's talking to another guy? What's my problem?"

"You tell me. Isn't she practically engaged to her boyfriend?"

"Probably. I haven't kept tabs on Caron Hollister."

"Lacey would be asking if you're still in love with her—"

"Well, it's a good thing you're not Lacey, isn't it? I hired Caron Hollister to do a job for me. She'll be gone right after the tour. Back to Florida and her boyfriend."

"So what are you going to do?"

"I owe her an apology. And then I need to push reset on this whole work relationship."

"I'm sorry this is tougher than you expected." Mitch's tone sobered. "I'm praying for you."

"Thanks." Kade scrubbed the palm of his hand across his

face. "You know, I hated losing Russell Hollister's mentorship when I decided to go out on my own and start my own company. I learned a lot from the man. How to read clients. To separate what people in search of a home wanted from what they needed. How to close a deal. How to settle disputes. My decision to go out on my own strained—no, it killed our relationship because Russell Hollister felt betrayed. He couldn't see that I only wanted the same thing he'd wanted as a young man—the chance to be my own boss."

"I've seen that happen more than once when someone breaks away from a mentor or a coach."

"Yeah. Caron and I had been dating about six months . . . and I never thought she'd choose her dad over me."

"Is that what happened?"

"I think so. I don't know. She never told me."

"She never told you?"

"Nope. It was just . . . over." Kade rose to his feet. "What's the use of talking about it? Let's hit the pool. Cool down. Clear our heads."

"Sounds like a plan."

"And tomorrow it's back to work and doing what we do best. Selling houses. We need to spend some time looking for something for you and Lacey."

"It's not a priority."

"Yes, it is. I haven't forgotten. The home tour is demanding a lot of time, yes, but we'll do it."

"Maybe we should wait until after the tour. Are we crazy to still try and do the Mudder in two weeks?"

"We are not backing out of the Mudder. It'll take up a Saturday. One day, that's all."

"Okay, fine. But I've waited this long to find a house for Lacey and me. I can wait a little longer."

"It doesn't take that long to scan the new listings." Kade rested his hand on his friend's shoulder. "I'll go in a little earlier tomorrow and let you know if I find anything."

. . .

Kade swiveled his chair around so he faced away from the door leading out of his office. Now he could enjoy the view from the rain-dampened window—a sky filled with clouds that had rolled in over the mountains throughout the afternoon, dumping intermittent showers accompanied with rumbles of thunder.

Facing one way, needing to go in the exact opposite direction.

He knew what he should do, but the "how" eluded him.

Closing on several home sales—the discussion, signing of papers, the smiles and congratulations—had kept him out of the office and derailed his thoughts for the better part of the day. He'd even driven by Kingston's house again as a distraction. He'd sat outside as the workers scurried back and forth, completing their frenzied tasks on the house.

And now here he was, the woman who had rejected him without an explanation, without a goodbye, just down the hallway. Why had he let pursuing his dreams get him tangled up with Caron Hollister again?

Avoidance was not the Ranger way. He needed to go forward, accomplish the task, and put it behind him. He could call Caron into his office and keep things on a more formal boss–employee status.

But the memory of the few times he'd been summoned to Russell Hollister's office kept him from buzzing Miriam. A brief nod from the older man, indicating that Kade was to sit in one of the chairs in front of the older man's desk. Conversation kept to a minimum, mostly one-sided.

Despite his admiration for Hollister's business savvy, he'd never liked some of the man's high-handed ways. And yet he sounded as arrogant as Caron's father when he talked to her on Monday. His attitude had shadowed him like an unpleasant odor lingering in a seller's home. He was the boss and he wanted to develop a certain type of relationship with his employees—even if Caron was only temporary. And what happened between him and Caron after he saw her talking with the gardener did not reflect his employer–employee mind-set. He'd handled Miriam's silly crush better than he'd dealt with Caron. And if he was honest with himself, he'd overreacted.

They were both here now. Mitch had left earlier with a get-it-done nod in the direction of Caron's office. Kade might as well choke down his slice of humble pie and be done with it.

.   .   .

How had she so easily . . . so blindly . . . run from one set of expectations she couldn't live up to only to collide right into another wall of expectations she had to scale?

Caron dumped what was left in the box of Hot Tamales into a plain white bowl on her desk, the red oval candies clattering against the ceramic dish. She'd go shopping for something nicer to store the candy in if she was staying. But a twenty-one-day job warranted nothing more than a cereal dish found in the break room cabinets.

She ought to toss the candies in the trash, but she needed the zing of her favorite snack. Let Kade Webster joke all he wanted to—chewing a few Hot Tamales did get her creative juices going. It was part of her regular workday routine. And despite Kade's moronic behavior on Monday, she had a job to do. She'd work here as late as she could, and leave when Kade left, since he hadn't given her a key to the building.

She hit speed dial on her cell phone, waiting for Margo to answer. "Hey, I wanted to update you on my plans for tonight."

"Going out with your handsome boss?"

"Just . . . stop." Caron fisted a handful of Hot Tamales. "I'm going to work here as late as I can—"

"But Emma and the other bridesmaids are coming over to start making their jewelry. We need you here."

"Oh, I'm sorry. I forgot." Not lying to her friend because she had truly forgotten the craft night planned for this evening. "I'm so swamped—"

"Well, I'll start your necklace, but you should come anyways! It'll be fun."

"Um, yeah." For someone who wasn't craft-challenged.

At that moment, Kade stopped just outside her office. Caron paused, waiting for him to move past. Even at the end of the workday, he still looked good in his charcoal-gray suit jacket and khaki pants.

Caron closed her eyes. Not that she should be noticing how he looked.

When she opened her eyes, the man still stood in her office doorway. He tilted his head, eyebrows raised, asking a silent "Can I talk to you?"

Caron mirrored his head tilt, pointing to herself, responding with a silent "Now?"

With two swift steps, Kade entered her office. That would be a yes.

Margo interrupted the silent standoff. "Are you still there?"

"Yes. But I have to go. I'll see you later tonight."

Kade started talking as she disconnected the call.

"I apologize for interrupting—"

"No problem. It was just Margo." Caron unclenched her hand. Ugh. Sweaty Hot Tamales. She needed soap and water. "I wanted her to know I'd be working late tonight . . . well, as late as I can."

"How late were you planning on being here?"

"I'll stay until you leave. I don't have a key."

"I apologize again. I didn't even think about getting a key made for you. I'll have Miriam do that tomorrow."

"It's not a big deal, but it would make it easier. I like to come in earlier, stay later—and my hours may be erratic, trying to get the job done as soon as possible."

"Understood." Kade cleared his throat, tugging at his blue paisley tie as if it choked him. "I've managed two apologies already in this conversation. I can certainly manage a third."

Oh.

"I was out of line the other day. I could give you all sorts of excuses, but none of them matter. Somehow I let my past feelings for you get mixed up with the reality of today." Kade had maintained eye contact with her the entire time—and oh, how she recalled getting lost in Kade Webster's gaze. Losing track of time . . . of what she'd been doing . . .

"Caron?"

Her attention jerked back to the present. "What?"

"Did you hear what I said?"

She hadn't. Not a single word. "I-I'm sorry . . . You lost me there for a moment."

Kade cleared his throat. "I admitted I overstepped our professional relationship saying what I did. I apologize."

"Thank you. I accept your apology." How formal she sounded. "I guess this means I can stop looking for an assortment of bells to go with my different work outfits."

"I deserved that." Kade's smile gave way to a snort of laughter. "Look, let's just both acknowledge the elephant in the room—that we dated once, a long time ago—and then show the elephant the exit door. Deal?"

"Deal."

"I appreciate your help and I am well aware your boyfriend is counting the days until you get back home."

"Right." There was no need to mention Alex's messy attempt to propose to her before she left. But she could still maintain distance from the man she once loved by positioning her boyfriend between them.

"You're all good with your rental car?"

"Yes, thank you. I kept it small, since it's just for driving around town."

"And Miriam gave you the spreadsheet detailing our agreement, as well as the contract?"

"Yes. I signed and returned it."

"Then we're all good here." Kade stepped back. "Let me know when you're ready to discuss ideas for the tour house."

"End of the week good?"

"Perfect. I'll be a while longer if you're still working—"

"Thanks. I'm trying to move from brainstorming to specifics."

"I'll leave you to it, then."

Once Kade disappeared, Caron unclenched her hands that were hidden behind her desk. Apology given and accepted. Invisible boundary line drawn, thanks to Alex.

Time to get back to work.

TWENTY-ONE

• ♥ • ♥ • ♥ •

Caron rested her elbows on Margo's wooden dining room table that was covered with magazines and the various pages she'd torn out for inspiration. They were scattered about like oversized bits of autumn foliage, adorned with glossy photographs and captions. The only hint of the jewelry-making party she'd missed were several stray pearls and the photo of her partially assembled necklace Margo had texted her.

Caron leaned forward so her hair fell around her face, pressing her fingertips to her eyes, which were dry and gritty from lack of sleep. What time was it, anyway? The tiny clock at the top of her laptop screen declared it was four o'clock. In the morning.

Kade Webster hadn't asked her to work all hours of the day and night, but agreeing to stage Eddie Kingston's home was a lot like facing the obstacles in the Emerald Coast MudRun—without the mud.

And she'd run that course with a group of other Realtors from her dad's office to raise money for charity. She'd had teammates who helped each other conquer the obstacles that demanded balance, upper-body strength, and the ability to slog through mud that sucked the shoes right off your feet.

Her scrawled list of things to do was her virtual obstacle course that she faced all by herself. Kade might supply the finances to help her, but being her boss wasn't the same as being her teammate.

Or being her boyfriend.

Kade had risked a lot calling and asking for her help after she'd walked away from him. She'd hurt him two years ago. While staging the house wasn't an act of penance or payback, she wasn't going to disappoint him again.

Caron scanned her list again, rubbing her eyes when the words blurred.

Decide how to decorate each room.

Find the right furniture and accessories for each room.

Transport furniture/accessories to Kingston home.

Stage each room.

Take it all down after the tour.

That about covered it. Now all she had to do was make it come together. Do her job. Her absolute best. Make Kade happy. Make Eddie Kingston happy.

Her brain buzzed like a light bulb that was about to short out. She needed to step away from all of these ideas for the living room, the bedrooms, the family room. Her mind swirled with furniture and fabrics, all hazy with fatigue and an overload of caffeine, carbs, and sugar.

Caron dumped her watered-down glass of sweet tea into the kitchen sink and tossed the empty bag of white cheddar popcorn and its companion empty box of Hot Tamales into the trash. She couldn't eat another piece of candy. Her tongue and teeth were coated with sugar and spice—and it was anything but nice.

Her comfortable, still-made bed in Margo's small guest bedroom tempted her, inviting her to snuggle between the blankets and pull a pillow over her head. Close her eyes for a few moments. But that would be a mistake, leading her to sleep through an alarm, ending up late for work.

That would impress her boss.

Kade.

The memory of his apologies trailed behind her as she made her way to the bathroom to shower, the heat of the water washing away the tiredness weighing down her limbs. Why hadn't he taken the easy way out and just let things blow over? Acted like nothing had happened at the tour house? But then, Kade had always been about working on their relationship when they were dating.

Caron hurried across the parking lot. She'd kept Kade waiting. She was late for their dinner date because her father needed to talk with her. She should have told her father she had to go because she was dating someone. That she was dating Kade Webster.

"I'm sorry." Caron met Kade as he moved around to the passenger side of his car. "I didn't realize I'd be this long."

"Something important?" Kade remained standing beside her, taking her hand in his.

"I, um, had a meeting with my father."

"I know. I got your text." He intertwined their fingers, his thumb stroking the soft skin on the inside of her wrist. "And you can't tell your dad you had a date, can you?"

"You know I can't. He's not just my father, he's my boss. If he calls a meeting—"

"That's not what I mean, and you know it. I was talking about us." He motioned back and forth between them. "Are we going to skulk around like this forever, Caron? I feel like I'm some sort of teenage derelict, instead of a grown man in a relationship with a woman he happens to—"

"I just don't know what he'll say——" Caron rushed past Kade's words. As much as she wanted to hear them, she wasn't ready. It would change everything. Demand things of her and force her to make tough choices. *"——how he'll react."*

"Is there an office regulation that says we can't date each other?"

"No."

"Then what's the problem? I've worked here for three years. Your father's mentored me and helped me learn the ropes. I'm respected in this town because I'm associated with this company." Kade pulled her closer, resting his forehead against hers. *"And yet you won't tell him that we've been dating for four months. Why?"*

"What if he thinks you're dating me because I'm the boss's daughter?"

Kade's eyes darkened. *"Is that what you think?"*

"No, of course not. I'm trying to keep my father happy . . . trying to keep you happy . . ."

Kade pulled her into his arms, up against his chest, locking her there. *"Look at me."*

His dark eyes glittered in the glow of the streetlight, the planes of his face a contrast of light and shadow.

"This is our relationship. You. Me. I am sick and tired of feeling like your father is some invisible third person tagging along." His words were low and intense. *"I'm in love with you, Caron Hollister. And I don't care what your father—or anyone else—thinks about it."*

She expected his kiss to be as forceful as his words, but the touch of his lips was a gentle wooing. He sought and found a response she didn't even know was hidden inside of her. His kisses left her breathless, and then his lips found the soft skin of her neck, just below her ear. Her breath caught, warmth flooding her body. As she struggled in his arms, he loosened his hold, allowing her to wrap her arms around his neck and pull him even closer.

But as he started to kiss her again, she pressed her fingers against his lips. "I'm sorry."

"If that was your apology——" Kade's breath was warm against her skin. "——I may still be a little upset. Tell me again."

Caron risked kissing him—savoring the enticement of his kisses for a few seconds before pulling away. There was no reason to be afraid of this man. Of the future. "I do love you, Kade. I know we need to tell my father. My entire family. Just let me figure out the right time."

"Knowing you love me, I can wait."

And then Kade had decided to start his own real estate business, announcing his decision a mere two months later. And that was the end of their relationship. Her father's accusations that Kade was untrustworthy, scheming, and manipulative had backed her into a corner. Who did she know better? Her father? Or Kade? Her dreams had been entangled with her father's for so many years . . . how was she supposed to choose Kade over her family? She'd made the only choice she could.

And that was all for the best.

"Did you sleep at all?"

Margo's question followed a quick rap on the bathroom door, which she eased halfway open.

Caron pulled her robe closed, tying the belt. "Come on, Margo! Do you ever knock and wait for someone to say 'come in'? What if I was still in the shower?"

"I knew you weren't. I heard the water go off. You've been up all night, haven't you?"

"Yes. I've been thinking." Caron towel-dried her hair.

"About?"

"Staging the house, of course."

"And?"

"And what?"

"How does it feel to be working for Kade?"

"It's . . . fine."

Margo yawned, running her fingers through her short hair so that it stood up in little spikes. "*Fine.* O-kay."

The traitorous memory lingered in the back of her mind, not that she'd share it with Margo.

"What do you want me to say, Margo? I don't even recognize my life anymore. My father partners with Nancy Miller. My professional life looks like a house that's been gutted for renovation. My boyfriend tosses an offhand proposal at me on the way to the airport—" At the sound of Margo's gasp, Caron paused. "I must have forgotten to mention his romantic so-do-you-want-to-get-married proposal."

"What did you say?"

"Nothing. I didn't have time to say anything because we were almost to the airport. We're okay. As soon as we figure out my destination wedding misstep and his blunder of a proposal, we'll get married. Happily ever after. Simple, right?"

"Caron, I've always been your honest friend—sometimes too honest. There is nothing simple about your life right now."

"On that we can agree."

"So back to my original question—it doesn't feel odd, working for Kade?"

"Kade is happy pursuing his career. I'm here temporarily. We both know that. And we both acknowledged, like two mature adults, that we dated once and that our brief relationship is all in the past."

"If you say so."

"That is hardly a rousing vote of confidence." Caron hung the damp towel on the rod.

"Sorry. It's not even five o'clock. If you want more enthusiasm, you'll have to ask me later today."

"Says the woman who did get to sleep through the night."

"How about if I go put some coffee on while you get dressed?"

"That would be wonderful." Caron waved her toward the kitchen. "Right now I don't have time to discuss my messed-up past and the unclear future. I need to get ready for work. Concentrate on this project. And somehow figure out how to be productive after pulling an all-nighter."

"I'll make the coffee extra strong."

"And I'll have to apply an extra layer of makeup to try and hide the bags under my eyes."

"You primp. I'll prep the coffee."

TWENTY-TWO

• ♥ • • ♥ • •

*I*t was going to be a good day.

If he had a Superman T-shirt, Alex would wear it to work today. Under his uniform shirt, of course, keeping his identity hidden just like any other superhero.

He was being ridiculous, but the knowledge that he would fix Jessica's air-conditioning today had him fighting back a huge grin the entire time he showered, shaved, and brushed his teeth.

He'd made sure she was his first appointment, marking off the entire first half of the day to install the unit. If he had time left over, he'd fix her washing machine, too. If not, he'd let Jessica know he had the right belt now, and ask when he could come back to install it. She had to be tired of hauling both her dirty laundry and her rambunctious son to the Laundromat by now.

A quick stop in the kitchen to heat up a breakfast burrito in the microwave and then he'd get on the road.

The sight of his mother slouched at the breakfast table stopped him short. She wore her black robe over her thin frame, her hair loose and uncombed.

"Morning, Mom. Dad still here?"

"Haven't seen him."

When had his mother's voice gotten so faint, so rough—her words like verbal sandpaper worn thin?

"He must have left for work already." Which was where he needed to be going. Soon. "Do you want anything to eat?"

"Not very hungry."

She never was. He shouldn't have bothered to ask.

"I could make you some toast—" He stood with the fridge door ajar. "Maybe some hot tea?"

"I'll get myself something to drink in a little bit."

Alex shut the fridge door, his fingers tightening around the handle. Breakfast or try to reason with his mother? Eat . . . or waste his time fighting a never-ending battle he couldn't win?

When he sat across from her, she refused to look at him, eyes downcast.

"Mom." He rested his hand on top of hers, willing himself to curve his fingers around her hand. Her skin was dry, her hand skeletal. "I know you're having a tough time right now—"

"You don't understand." Her words rasped out. "I'm his mother."

"But I am . . . was Shawn's brother."

"It's not the same." Her eyes were bloodshot. Unfocused. "And his birthday . . . it's always the worst."

They hadn't celebrated a birthday in the house in years. Maybe his brother's birthday was the worst, but any family birthday was a day of mourning.

"But drinking like this . . . it doesn't solve anything."

"It helps me forget."

"You don't really want to forget him, Mom." Alex's words felt like so many pieces of loose gravel tossed against a closed window. "Maybe I could take you to the cemetery, to visit his grave again—"

"No!" His mother jerked her hand away. "I want to forget him. I want to forget everything."

She stumbled to her feet, the chair behind her teetering back and forth.

"Mom, let me help you—"

"There's nothing you can do." She pushed her hair from her face. "I'm tired. Need to go back to bed."

Alex stood in the center of the kitchen, the sound of his mother's footsteps fading down the hallway. The bedroom door opened, closed with a click. He wasn't foolish enough to think his mother would go to sleep. No, she'd wait until she heard his car pulling away from the house and then make her way back to the kitchen to get a bottle and glass.

Why hide the bottles from her anymore? He and his dad limited the amount of wine in the house instead. Hiding the alcohol only made things worse—sending his mother out to shop for her relief. Preventing her from driving anywhere controlled things somewhat. His father had abandoned the battlefield years ago. An all-out surrender.

Alex had done what he could here. He'd tried—and failed—again.

Just outside the house, Alex stopped, staring at his cell phone. What time was it in Colorado? Would Caron be up yet? He'd call her, say good morning, relax into the familiar sound of her voice, allowing her to calm his frayed emotions.

"I love you."

"I know you do. I love you, too."

"Forgive me?"

"Of course."

The snippet of their conversation outside the airport terminal offered him some comfort. And she'd called him to let him know she'd arrived safely in Colorado Springs, as she'd promised.

He pocketed his phone. He was running late, and Caron probably wasn't even up yet. He'd text her a quick "I love you" midmorning, promising to call her later.

They were fine. They understood each other. Loving Caron was easy—their relationship was the one reliable, good thing in his life.

.   .   .

Pulling up in front of Jessica's twenty-five minutes later restored his mood. Some. He'd learned a long time ago to leave personal stuff behind the closed doors of his home. He couldn't fix his mother. But he was at work now and he could install air-conditioning for one deserving single mother and her very active son, who would sleep better tonight.

The scent of cinnamon filled the air when Jessica opened the front door.

"It smells like a bakery in there." Alex tucked his hat in his back pocket, smoothing his hair back from his face.

"Good morning." The sound of feet pounding on the wooden floors caused Jessica to brace herself as Scotty ran up behind her and wrapped his arms around her leg. "I made cinnamon rolls this morning. Can I interest you in one?"

His "No, thanks" was interrupted by a loud stomach rumble.

"You sure about that?" Jessica's grin indicated she'd heard his stomach's complaint.

"I confess, I skipped breakfast this morning."

"Do all repairmen have as bad eating habits as you do?"

"I haven't participated in that poll, ma'am."

"Hi, Mr. Alex." Scotty stepped forward. "Are you going to fix our air conditioner?"

"I'm going to do even better than that."

"Really?"

"Yep. I'm going to give you a different air conditioner. I've got it in my truck." He winked at Jessica. "If it's okay with your mommy, you can unlatch the gate and wait until I bring it around to the backyard. Deal?"

"Deal." Scotty tilted his head up. "Can I help Mr. Alex?"

Jessica waited for Alex's nod. "Sure. And while you do that, I'll get Mr. Alex some breakfast."

"I appreciate it. I've always been partial to cinnamon rolls."

"Then this is your lucky day. My mother's recipe is the best ever. I'll bring breakfast out when it's ready."

"Are we gettin' started soon with the new air conditioner?" Scotty hopped from right foot to left and back again.

Alex ruffled the little boy's hair. "Yes, we are. You've been very patient. Meet me by the gate, okay?"

"Yessir!"

Jessica's laughter followed him out to the truck. Just a few minutes talking with her and Scotty had improved his attitude. Of course, the promise of homemade cinnamon rolls would help anyone have a better day.

Scotty stood waiting for him by the gate like a pint-sized sentinel, waving him through, his eyes serious. He hopped and skipped his way beside Alex to the old unit.

"Mom says not to ask if I can help anymore." His voice bobbled with his bouncing body. "But can I watch?"

"You can stay and watch—" Alex pointed to the picnic bench. "—so how about if we carry that over here and you sit on that while I work? Sound good?"

"Yep!"

As they carried the bench over, Scotty's end considerably lower than Alex's, Jessica exited the house with a paper plate and a tall blue tumbler.

"What did I tell you about not bothering Mr. Alex?"

"He said I could watch, Mom."

"It's true, I did." Alex accepted the plate of not one but two cinnamon rolls and a glass of cold milk. "Thanks."

The first taste was a blissful bite of still-warm cinnamon-flavored roll, topped with drizzles of sugary icing and nuts.

"My compliments. This is the best cinnamon roll I've ever tasted."

"Thank you." Jessica bobbed a small curtsy, holding out the corners of her white denim shorts. "So, have you figured out how you're going to propose to your girlfriend yet?"

Alex choked on his gulp of milk. "Pardon me?"

"Proposing. You know, have you thought about how you're going to do it?" She straddled the bench.

"I don't know." He thought for a minute. "How would you want to be proposed to? I'm open to suggestions."

"I'd be fine with my guy showing up at my door with a pizza for our regular Friday movie night. And then proposing when the closing credits are rolling—but definitely not during the movie."

"Really?" Alex chased the question with a gulp of cold milk. "Nothing fancy, then?"

"Nope. I got fooled by fancy talk and an elaborate proposal the first time. Fell for it all. Next time—if there is a next time—I want a simple, straightforward 'I love you. Will you marry me?' "

"Why can't I just do something like that for Caron?"

"Because this is her first—and hopefully her only—proposal. You're a good guy, Alex. I can tell. So do it right. Do a little research on diamonds—or emeralds or rubies or sapphires—whatever it is that she likes. Then find out what type of ring she prefers before you go planning the proposal."

Too bad he hadn't heard Jessica's advice before he'd bungled the proposal with Caron on the way to the airport. But he'd get it right the next time. Might as well take advantage of Jessica's willingness to offer suggestions.

"I still don't know how to actually ask her. Got any ideas on how I should pop the question?"

"Does she like horses? I had a friend whose boyfriend took her horseback riding and then proposed to her at the end of the trail ride."

"No, she's not into horses, but she did play basketball in high school." Alex finished off one roll and started on another.

"Oh, you could take her to a basketball game and do the whole Jumbotron-proposal experience in front of thousands of people. But that's been done to death, don't you think?"

"Yeah, plus I don't want to drive all the way down to an Orlando Magic game just to propose."

"Is she adventurous? Instead of a hot-air balloon ride, you could go parasailing in Destin and propose then."

"And drop the ring in the Gulf? No, thanks."

"I thought Mr. Alex was here to fix our air conditioner, Mommy, not talk to you."

With a laugh, Jessica stood and stepped away. "You're right, Scotty, that's exactly why he's here."

Alex chased his last bite of pastry with a gulp of cold milk. "I just had to finish these yummy cinnamon rolls your mom gave me. I didn't have breakfast this morning."

"You mean your mom didn't make you breakfast this morning? You're lucky. Mommy always makes me eat breakfast."

"Don't be silly, Scotty. Mr. Alex is an adult. He makes his own breakfast."

"That's right." And Jessica didn't need to know he still lived at home. "And you've got a very nice mommy. I bet she makes you really good breakfasts."

"Most of the time. I don't like oatmeal."

"I didn't like it when my mom made me oatmeal, either."

Not that he could remember the last time his mother made him breakfast. Or lunch. Or dinner. It was sometime around when he was ten years old—he just couldn't remember it.

. . .

"Everything going okay?" Jessica's voice sounded behind him.

"Yep." Alex focused on the task at hand. So far no problems. "Scotty get to his friend's house okay?"

"Yes, you were very nice to let him watch you work all that time. But I figured it was best to get him out of your hair."

"He's a good kid." He sat back on his heels. "Does he see his dad much?"

Now what prompted him to ask such a personal question, he didn't know. Idle curiosity. Keeping the conversation going, maybe? Or maybe because Jessica had brought up his relationship with Caron earlier? Conversational tit-for-tat.

"No. He lives here—well, in Panama City. If he wants to see Scotty, all he has to do is ask. He just doesn't ask. And I am fine with that. Makes it easier all around."

"The guy doesn't want to see his son?"

"No. Not that I'm surprised. Being a father cramped his style. Scotty and me—that's my normal." Jessica sat on the picnic bench, pulling her legs up and wrapping her arms around her knees. "So, what about you?"

"What about me?"

"What's your normal?"

What was his normal? He had two ways to answer that—the life hidden in the darkness of his parents' house or the life he lived outside. Jessica might as well have showed up at his front door, knocked, and invited herself in.

"Hello? Did I lose you?"

"Oh, sorry." He picked up a voltmeter. "Double-checking something here. I have a small family. Father. Mother. One younger brother, Shawn, who . . . um, who died when I was ten."

"Oh, Alex . . ."

"That was a long time ago. I've learned to live with it."

"What happened? I mean, if you don't mind me asking—"

"Car accident. He was six. He loved riding his bike. After dinner one night, he went back outside and no one noticed. Shawn went through the intersection at the end of our cul-de-sac without stopping—"

"How tragic."

"Yeah." Alex shifted his attention back to the air conditioner. "I need to get this finished if I'm going to get to my next appointment on time."

"Sure. I'm sorry, I shouldn't have—"

"It's okay. Not a problem."

The rest of his work was done in silence. No Scotty asking questions a mile a minute. No Jessica wanting to know what his "normal" was.

He had a split-personality life. Out of control at home. Manageable at work. His relationship with Caron balanced on the tightrope between two lives. She was the one who kept his secrets. The one who offered him an escape from his secrets.

TWENTY-THREE

• ♥ • ♥ • ♥ • ♥ •

$\mathcal{Y}$ou weren't dozing off, were you?"

Caron's head jerked upright, her eyes opening. Her hands rested on her keyboard and several long lines of vowels and consonants—gibberish—strolled across her open Word document. Proof positive that she'd fallen asleep at her desk. No sense in denying the obvious, even if Kade Webster was the one who had caught her asleep at work.

So much for impressing the boss.

"I have no excuse." She shut down the offending document before Kade could see that, too. "I was up so late—"

"Thinking about Kingston's house. I get it. And then I had to cancel our earlier meeting. I apologize." Kade's half smile disarmed her. "Do you have time to talk now?"

"Absolutely." Caron resisted the urge to run her fingers through her hair. Pat the corner of her mouth, checking for drool. "I'm ready when you are. I wasn't doing anything."

Except napping.

"Meet me in the conference room in ten?"

"Sure."

Caron fast-timed it to the break room and filled a tumbler with an abundance of ice and sweet tea, dropping it off in the conference room first. Then she went back to her office and gathered her iPad and her leather folder, stopping to organize her papers into a more orderly pile. A quick brush of her hair, a refresh of her lip color, and she was ready to go.

Wait. She backtracked and grabbed a few Hot Tamales from her candy dish on the corner of her desk. Brain food. Get the creativity flowing again. And just as good as a breath mint.

She still didn't know why Kade hadn't shown up for their meeting this morning. She'd arrived at eight o'clock to find Miriam at her desk, but no Kade in sight. And then Miriam delivered a brief "Kade can't make it and apologizes" message. Not that Kade had to provide her with an explanation. And this reality was a reminder of her employee status.

Kade positioned himself at the head of the table, a bottle of water paired with his own glass of tea.

"I see we think alike. I'd forgotten how good your sweet tea was." He loosened his tie. "I know these things are part of the business, but sometimes I wish I could wear jeans and a T-shirt to work."

"I've always been glad I can skip the tie." She arranged her papers on the table. "You ready?"

"The question is: Are you ready?" His dark eyes glinted with a challenge.

"More than ready."

And just like that, an echo from the past tripped her up. How many times had she and Kade challenged each other by tossing the " 'You ready?' 'The question is: Are you ready?' " taunts back and forth when they both worked for her father? They'd always enjoyed challenging each other to try harder to achieve the monthly business goals.

"Caron?"

Her attention jerked back to the present. "Sorry. I just have to decide where to start. I'm not sure how to set this up so you can see everything—"

He stood, moving his chair around the edge of the table and positioning it next to hers, and then sitting back down. "This should do it." He rested his elbows on the glass tabletop. "Go ahead. I'm all yours."

And that comment was just a turn of phrase. Nothing more. Kade probably wasn't even aware of what he'd said.

Boss. Employee. Boss.

She pulled out her numbered list. "I know that not all home-builders stage every room in their homes for the tour, but we're going to."

"We are?"

"Of course. You want to give Kingston your best, so that's what we're going to do. We're going to decorate every room. A full-court press." She used her purple gel pen to tick down her handwritten list. "The nice thing is, we don't have to worry about decluttering like I have to when I stage a home that goes on the market."

"True."

"Okay. The kitchen is minimal, except for accents. Same with the bathrooms—rolled towels, baskets, candles—a spa feel for them. The focus is on the three bedrooms, the family room, and the dining room. And I'm trying to decide whether I want to make the small den an office or a workout room."

"Okay. You planning on outfitting the laundry room, too?"

"It's not my major concern, even though people are crazy over the laundry room these days. Eddie's built a nice-sized room with good shelving and I'll accent that with baskets."

"What's wrong with sitting in the living room and folding laundry while watching sports?" With nothing but a numbered list to look at, Kade's attention never wavered from Caron. "What about outside?"

"Curb appeal—and we have to think about the access ramps. We have to be extra attentive to make the outside of the house look good while we work around those."

"Agreed."

"I know the house will be sodded by the time the Tour of Homes starts—" Caron stumbled over even the slightest reference to the landscaper. "—but do you know if Eddie is working with Austin beyond that and the flowers I saw the other day?"

"I didn't think to ask."

"Okay." Caron scribbled another note on her list. "I'll check with him . . . with Eddie, I mean."

"What else have you got for me?"

She hesitated over the one question Kade hadn't answered yet—and she hadn't broached. "I haven't asked you what our budget is for this project."

"What our budget is." Kade tapped his fingertips against his lips. "Interesting question. What if I told you that my usual stager gives me a deep discount because her husband and I are friends?"

"So you're saying our budget is small."

"Yes."

"I'd rather you'd told me that we had an unlimited budget. A girl can dream, right? Your stager didn't leave you access to her storage unit, by any chance?"

"She called in crisis mode. It never occurred to me to ask—"

"Okay, then, we'll go with plan B."

"Which is?"

"You telling me how much money you want to put toward staging the home. And then I start contacting furniture stores and asking if they'd like to take part in the upcoming Tour of

Homes for strategic advertising. It's too late to get their names in the tour booklet, but we can print up our own flyers. Miriam can work on that, if you're okay with her helping me. We'll have them available during the tour. And we can see if we can borrow any pieces—"

"Borrow furniture? What are you planning on doing, going door to door?"

"No. But Margo's parents have this beautiful dining room table—"

"And you think they'll loan you something for a week—"

"It doesn't hurt to ask, Kade. Providing someone with, say, four tickets to the tour is a lot less expensive than buying dining room furniture." She held her hand up. "If you plan on staging homes in the future, you might want to consider purchasing some key pieces of your own."

"What else?"

"Depending on the budget, I'd like to go antiquing and visit a flea market or two to see if I can find anything. Maybe purchase a couple of pieces of art for the walls."

"You're going to start filling up that nonexistent storage unit for me, is that it?"

"Yes, I guess I am." Kade couldn't fault her for thinking long-term. "And we need fresh flowers during the week. And—"

"There's more?"

Caron couldn't help laughing. When Kade joined in, the boyish, natural sound was a tempting invitation to go back in time. Kade's laughter had disrupted the seriousness of a Monday-morning staff meeting at Hollister Realty more than once—their glances meeting across the table and him tossing her a quick, conspiratorial wink as her father called the meeting back to order.

Boss. Employee.

"Of course there's more." She shifted in her seat. How had she moved close enough to Kade that their arms brushed up against each other's? And why was she just now noticing the faint eucalyptus scent of his shampoo?

Boss.

"We're going to need to rent a U-Haul to get the furniture over there. And we'll need to have some help loading and unloading the stuff, as well as arranging it."

Kade leaned forward, turning the paper scrawled with her notes so he could scan it. "You've obviously got a plan to accomplish all this."

"I'm making a plan. It's quite the undertaking, but I'm excited to see it all come together."

"If anyone can pull this off, you can do it, hotshot."

Hotshot—the nickname he'd first tossed at her across the conference table in her father's office after she'd closed a difficult deal.

"I won't let you down, Kade."

Her words dimmed the tenuous camaraderie that had built between them. He couldn't say "I know you won't"—because she had once before.

But she'd see this job through. She owed him that.

"Do you want to hear about any of my preliminary decorating ideas? I want things streamlined, with some bold punches of color. I've even put a call in to Eddie and asked for an accent wall in the living room—"

"I think we're good for today." Kade rose to his feet. "As far as the budget goes, I will need some specific numbers from you. I'm not ready to write you a blank check, but I can give you some initial funds."

"No blank check?" Caron remained seated as Kade backed away, her question a feeble attempt to infuse humor back into the situation.

"Sorry, nope." Kade shoved the chair back into place. "I'll see about rounding up some people to help get the stuff loaded and unloaded and put in its proper place in the house. Sound good?"

She put Kade's initials by one item on the list. "Perfect. One less thing on my list. But I will check back with you about what you find out."

"Of course you will." Kade rubbed the palms of his hands together. "So we're good here?"

"Yes."

"Great." He readjusted his tie. "Time to go join the fray again."

"I'm going to sit here and see if I can come up with a preliminary budget. Is that okay? You don't need the room right now, do you?"

"It's all yours." He paused. "You've got my number, right?"

"Yes, from when you called me. Why?"

"I realized we probably need a way to get in touch with each other until we get through the tour. Just text or call me if you have a question, and I'll do the same, okay?"

"Sure, that's fine." Caron fought to keep her voice casual. There was a time when Kade's number was at the top of her favorites list. "You've got my number, too, right?"

"Never forgot it." He flashed her his trademark smile, the one that was all professional Kade Webster—nothing personal—as he strolled out of the conference room.

That had gone well.

So long as she concentrated on things like lamps and chairs and beds for Eddie Kingston's home . . . and insisted that her untrustworthy mind keep the past in the past . . . she'd survive the next few weeks just fine.

●   ●   ●

He needed to find a reason to get angry with Caron Hollister again. To get really angry—and stay that way.

Kade's combat boots pounded the ground, the backpack weighted down with fifty pounds of bricks pressing against his shoulders, as he tried to outrun his thoughts. His desires.

He'd offered the woman a job, knowing he could do it because he'd dealt with his emotions—the tangled mess of hurt, disappointment, longing, anger—years ago when she broke up with him.

"Right, God?" He spat the words out into the dust-laden air. "You and me, we got this? I forgave her. Now I'm helping her. And she's helping me."

Except now . . . now he remembered all the reasons he fell in love with Caron.

Some men liked blonds. Some men preferred brunettes. Or redheads. Some guys could rattle off entire lists of what attracted them to women. And him? He met Caron Hollister and tore up any sort of list because she made him stop looking.

She wasn't perfect—not with her Hot Tamale addiction, and her I've-got-an-idea way of taking over a conversation, and her tendency to overload her schedule. But to him, she was the most captivating woman he'd ever met.

And she still was.

He didn't care if she dyed her hair blond or silver or purple. She was smart, a go-getter, and creative. She responded to his ideas, listened to his plans for the future, encouraged him, and made him feel as if he could accomplish his dreams—and more.

Sweat trickled down his face into his eyes, causing him to blink.

"On your left." Kade upped his pace, moving past two teen girls walking up the Incline. He was near the top of the almost vertical climb over rugged railroad ties. He'd stop, drain his water bottle, enjoy the view of Colorado Springs stretching out below, and then start back down Barr Trail.

Could he un-forgive Caron? Go back to being furious at how she ended their relationship? Just until the tour was over? And then he'd thank her for helping with the tour, and they'd go their separate ways.

He'd been trained as a Ranger to believe that losing was not an option. One minute he'd been in love with Caron Hollister. Imagining the whole marriage-and-family-forever-and-ever-amen future with her. Re-create the kind of family he'd experienced when he'd been friends with Drake Neilson and would hang out at his house all the time. And then Caron had walked away from him. No explanation. Just . . . days and days of silence that left him reeling. Left alone again. But he'd survived that unexpected emotional ambush.

And now he'd invited her back into his life because he needed her help, not because he wanted to get involved with her again. He was the one in control of the situation. He already knew the outcome. He was staying in Colorado. Caron Hollister was going back to Florida. Back to her boyfriend.

So be it.

Tonight's workout would clear his head. Then he'd go home. Shower. Grab something to eat. And get back to work.

TWENTY-FOUR

• ♥ • • •

One thing was for sure. Caron was not a professional home stager. Even so, for all the challenges facing her, there was a part of her that loved imagining just how she was going to decorate each room in Eddie Kingston's house.

The diagram on the conference room whiteboard was rudimentary at best. And the Post-it notes she'd positioned in each room to indicate where pieces of furniture would go were haphazard, some torn in half to designate smaller pieces of furniture—an end table or coffee table. But still, the exercise helped her visualize what she wanted to do in each room.

Placing a rectangular orange Post-it note labeled *couch* in the family room, Caron stepped back, careful not to trip over her red high heels that she'd kicked off more than an hour ago as she worked on the two-dimensional house. Couch—*check*. Chair—*check*. Coffee table—*check*. If only she knew someone with a pool table . . . no, too heavy. Maybe a foosball table? Too casual and also too tempting for the kids who were sure to accompany their parents through the tour. As it was, she planned on asking Eddie for cans of touch-up paint so she and Kade could check the walls each night after people came through the house.

She closed her eyes, pursing her lips, visualizing the room again in her mind. It was large, easily twenty by thirty feet. Maybe another grouping of a love seat and two coordinating chairs with another table? More furniture to be added to the list.

"And just what have you done to my whiteboard?" Kade's voice intruded on her musing.

"Oh!" Caron whirled around, dropping her handful of multicolored Post-its. "I was mulling . . . planning out the rooms."

"Is that what this is?" Kade's voice brimmed with laughter, even as he came forward, kneeling to help pick up the scattered notes.

Caron knelt, too, blocking the sight of her kicked-off shoes—and her bare feet—at least for a few seconds. "Yes. It helps me to see things . . . well, a little better."

"Here you go." Kade held out the Post-its he'd gathered for her.

This close up, she could see how his eyes were different shades of brown—a darker, richer color surrounding the irises, radiating out to a warmer honey brown.

"Thank you. I didn't mean to be so clumsy."

"My fault. I startled you." He offered her his hand. "Let me help you up."

Unlike Alex's, Kade's hands were smooth, his nails clean and cut short. He used to hold her hand all the time when they walked along the beach. During church. Grocery shopping, steering the grocery cart with one hand. When he drove. While they ate out at a restaurant, often choosing to sit beside her on the same side of a booth.

"Thanks." Caron pulled her hand away, tucking it behind her. "So what do you think?"

"Um, why don't you tell me what I'm looking at, and then I'll tell you what I think."

"It's not that bad, is it?" At his silence, she laughed. "Okay, I admit, it's a bit of a hodgepodge."

"Good description."

"This is the basic layout of Eddie's house. Keep in mind, nothing is to scale." At Kade's snort of laughter, she paused. "I will ignore that ungentlemanly comment."

"No comment. No comment."

"That ungentlemanly sound, then."

"Continue, please."

"The Post-its represent furniture, again not to scale." She hurried on before Kade could say anything else—or snort again. "This is a couch—a sectional would be nice, or an extra-long couch. A coffee table. End tables. Lamps."

"The, um, lamps are represented by the little circles drawn on the squares of paper?"

"Of course." Caron refused to look at Kade to gauge his assessment of her drawing skills. "I never said I was a graphic artist, Kade."

"No, no. Quite ingenious. Continue, please."

She worked her way from imaginary room to imaginary room, detailing her ideas, explaining where she hoped to use borrowed furniture and where she hoped to utilize items on loan from a furniture store.

"I have to admit, when I walked in here, I wasn't sure what was going on." Kade straightened a piece of paper that represented the couch in the family room. "But you've put a lot of thought into this."

"It's coming together." Caron motioned to the whiteboard.

"When I look at this, I don't see all the scraps of paper, I see the house becoming a home. I don't know how to describe it. Imagining how to decorate a room—the possibilities of color, of style . . ."

"You get a real kick out of this, don't you?"

"More like a power surge." She wouldn't tell Kade she'd skipped lunch because she'd been so busy consulting her laptop, searching different options for the rooms. "There's a real satisfaction selling a house—helping a family find what they want. Making the sales quota."

"Making your dad proud."

His words stalled her for a moment. "Yes, that, too. He was my boss, after all. But there were days that selling homes became nothing more than endless hours of work. I don't stage that many homes, but when I do, well, it taps into my creative side in a way that being a Realtor doesn't."

"Kind of an adult, professional version of playing house—" Kade's grin pulled a smile from her, too.

"With a whole lot of professional success on the line."

"True."

"So what's your idea for the master bedroom?"

"Still mulling." Caron folded a Post-it note into quarters. "I keep thinking of Mitch . . . what if this were his home? What if he was married and living here? So I don't want anything too feminine."

"I know we're trying to cut costs. What if we used mine?"

"What?"

"What if we use my bedroom furniture?"

"I . . . I don't know . . ."

"I have a fairly new bedroom set. It's a four-poster bed, dark wood. Dresser, side tables—the works. Believe it or not, I bought the set from another Realtor in town who ordered it from Italy, but ended up not liking the dark finish. I can always sleep on my couch during the week of the tour." Kade leaned back against the conference room table. "We can take a look tonight. Or not. Just a suggestion. You may need to go some-where or have plans—"

"No . . . I mean, no, I told Margo that I was working late tonight."

"Well then . . ."

"Fine."

"Do you want to ride over to my house together?"

"No, just give me your address and I'll take the rental car. That way when we're done I can head back to Margo's. No need for you to bring me back here."

"Okay. Perfect."

. . . .

Why had he invited Caron to his house—to look at his bed-room furniture?

They had spent less than an hour talking about the Tour of Homes house—her eyes lighting up, her words tumbling over one another as she described her ideas, her hands moving faster and faster, switching scraps of paper back and forth on the whiteboard as her body moved back and forth in front of him . . .

Kade skidded to a stop beside his car, gravel rocks spurt-ing out around his feet. How could he un-invite Caron—tell her the last thing he wanted was her invading his personal space again? Seeing her at work was one thing—having her in his apartment, looking at his bedroom, even if it was work-related . . . *no*. She'd been pure temptation when they'd dated. He'd had to do a lot of praying to ensure he didn't go past their personal boundaries when they sat on the couch together and watched either one of her favorite rom-coms—*What's Up, Doc?* or *Hitch*—or his preferred choice of reruns of *American Ninja Warrior*. And if he went for long, exhausting runs after their dates . . . well, she didn't need to know that.

He needed reinforcements—and that's what friends were for.

Kade slid behind the steering wheel, starting the car as he waited for his friend to answer his phone. "Mitch?"

"Yeah, man. What's up?"

"I need you and Lacey to come over to my house. Tonight. Now."

"What? It's Friday night, man. We're getting ready to go out—"

Kade put the car in reverse, wheeling out of the parking lot, catching a glimpse of Caron exiting the building in his rearview mirror. "Caron Hollister is coming over to look at my bed—I mean, my bedroom furniture—"

"What?"

"I don't have a huge budget to stage the house, you know that. Caron's plan is to have furniture stores donate pieces or else borrow items from people she knows. So I suggested we use my bedroom set. And now Caron's coming to look at it. I need you and Lacey at my condo when we get there."

"You want me to tell you how brilliant you were before or after Caron comes over?"

"I want you to back me up—preferably without an 'I told you so.'"

"Can't promise you that. You on your way now?"

"Yes."

"Okay. See you in twenty. And you owe me."

"You don't even need to say it." Kade hit the brakes as the light up ahead turned red. "Listen, you'll get there before I do. You've got a key. If the place is a wreck—"

"We'll hide your dirty clothes and dishes."

He caught some green lights, and Kade dashed through his front door twenty minutes later, shucking off his coat and tie. He had a good ten minutes on Caron—more if God answered his prayers and all the traffic lights were red for her.

"Hey, boss." Mitch appeared from the kitchen, holding a bottle of water.

"Hey. Where's Lacey?"

"She's making sure everything is all clear in your bedroom. This apartment doesn't accommodate a wheelchair all that well."

Kade bit back a groan. "Sorry about that—"

"It is what it is. It just meant Lacey had to be sent on a search-and-destroy for your dirty laundry. But the place looks great, if you ask me."

"I forgot I had the cleaning service come in today."

"No dirty clothes—" Lacey's voice floated down the hallway moments before she appeared. "Oh, Kade's here."

"Yeah." Kade pulled open the fridge door. "You want some water?"

"I'm good. Have you figured out how you're going to explain our being here?"

"No."

"Then just keep it simple. We dropped by."

"You . . . dropped by."

"Yeah. Friends do that. Or you could say Mitch wanted to talk about something work-related—"

"Like what?"

"I don't know." Lacey lounged on one end of his sectional sofa. "You're the one who had to invite your ex-girlfriend to look at your bedroom. Mitch and I are here as the chaperones."

"Very funny."

The sharp peal of the doorbell interrupted Kade's conversation with Lacey. "She's here."

"Sounds like it, unless you invited someone else over to look at your bed."

"Hardly." Kade tossed his coat and tie to Lacey, who sat there with a what-am-I-supposed-to-do-with-these look on her face. Mitch moved over to the living room as Kade opened the front door.

"Hey, Caron. I see you found your way here without a problem."

"Google Maps is a wonderful thing. And having the mountains to the west is a great anchor, too." Caron took two steps into the apartment and then stopped at the sight of Lacey and Mitch. "Um . . . hello."

"Caron, you know Mitch from work. This is Lacey, his girlfriend."

"Nice to meet you, Lacey."

"Lacey's a professional photographer—" Kade twisted the cap off the water bottle. "I, uh, called her and asked her to come by because I thought maybe you might want to use some of her photographs in Eddie Kingston's house."

"Really? That's a great idea." Caron set her handbag on the love seat, slipping off her shoes. "I'd love to see some of your photographs. Did you bring any with you?"

Lacey shrugged, offering an apologetic smile. "No. I didn't. Mitch and I were already out when Kade called. Going to dinner."

"Right. Right. But I asked her to stop by anyway, just to meet you." Heat crawled up Kade's neck. He was a lousy liar— and Caron knew it. He should have just admitted to being a coward and that he didn't want to be alone with her again.

"O-kay."

Lacey launched into the awkward silence. "And besides, the guys needed to talk about the Mudder they're running next weekend."

"Right." Mitch chimed in on cue.

Caron's glance swiveled back and forth between Kade and Mitch. "You're running in a Mudder?"

"Yes. The Aspen Mass Mudder." Mitch joined the conversation. "We have a team of six of us."

Lacey pointed to herself. "And I'm the photographer."

"I was part of a team that did an obstacle course run. I'm sure it's not quite as intense as what you're doing, but we had fun—and we raised money for Heart of the Bride, a ministry that cares for orphans in Africa, Haiti, and Ukraine."

"You ought to come along with us." Lacey rushed past Kade's attempt to interrupt. "You'd enjoy seeing the race—it's all over a mountainside. A number of Wounded Warriors participate. It'll be fun."

"Oh, I don't know—"

"You can hang out with me. I'm going to be walking the area, going to different spectator sites and trying to get photos of the guys doing the obstacles. I'd enjoy the company."

"Sounds like fun, but that's right before the Tour of Homes."

"Which means you'll have most of the work done by then, right?"

"That's the plan."

"I'm just thinking out loud here—" Lacey paused for a moment. "—I know you're retrofitting the house, right? Maybe we could use some of the photos in the house . . . I could print up a few—"

"That's a great idea!" Caron's eyes lit up. "Maybe in the office."

"Speaking of the tour, weren't you going to check out some furniture?" Mitch interrupted the two women, who seemed intent on becoming fast friends.

"Right."

"Is it okay if I come along with you?" Lacey paused beside Mitch. "Who knows? I might have a photograph that would coordinate with Kade's furniture—if you decide to use the bedroom set, that is."

Caron nodded. "Great idea."

"We'll be right back, Mitch."

"Don't worry about me." Mitch waved the remote. "Got all I need."

It took less than five minutes for Caron to approve his furniture. The entire process was simple, with Caron conferring with Lacey about possible coordinating artwork.

"Well, that's one more thing off my list." Caron slid her shoes back on. "I'll just head out with Lacey and Mitch."

"And you are coming with me to the Mudder, right?" Lacey stood beside Mitch. "It'll be nice to have another woman along. The four of us can ride up together."

"I don't know—"

"You've got to do something besides work while you're here. It'll be fun, won't it, guys?"

"Yeah. You should come." Mitch echoed Lacey's invitation, seemingly immune to Kade's heated stare.

"There—Mitch agrees—and I'm sure Kade does, too."

"Absolutely. Sure." Kade tried to infuse enthusiasm into his voice.

"All right, then. I'll do it."

"Terrific. We'll coordinate everything when we get together this week."

Kade shut the door, blocking out the sound of their conversation fading down the hallway. He'd averted the come-see-my-bedroom fiasco with Caron only to end up agreeing to spend an entire day with her.

TWENTY-FIVE

• ♥ • ♥ • ♥ •

What was it about Jessica's home that invited Alex in? Situated in an older part of Niceville, it was small, probably not even a thousand square feet. The outside needed a new coat of paint, and the yard needed to be reseeded. But the inside? She'd arranged what furniture she had in a semicircle that invited people to sit and talk—a worn, brown leather couch with a coordinating recliner covered in a floral pattern, and a coffee table that was nicked and scarred but still polished so it gleamed. A light wood rocking chair finished off the room decor. Had Jessica held a much younger Scotty as she sat in the chair, lulling him to sleep?

"I notice something different about this place." Alex stepped over a small pile of green, blue, yellow, and red Legos.

"Really?" Jessica stood with her hands on her hips, glancing around the room. "I can't think of anything. I haven't even bothered to have Scotty pick up his toys yet today."

Alex stepped over another pile of plastic building blocks. "I was talking about the air-conditioning. The room's nice and cool."

"Oh. That." Jessica's smile bore a hint of Scotty's little-boy grin. "Some guy came and fixed it the other day."

"Some guy, huh?"

"Yeah. And Scotty's been asking me when he was coming back—" Footsteps pounded down the hallway. "Brace yourself. I think my son just figured out that you're back."

Sure enough, Scotty ran into the room and barreled right into Alex. But before he could lock his arms around his legs again, Alex hoisted the little boy up into his arms. "Hey, kiddo, didja miss me?"

"Where ya been, Mr. Alex?"

Alex plopped his work cap on Scotty's head so it slipped down over his eyes. "Well, I've been working on other people's air conditioners—"

"Scotty, I told you that we're not Mr. Alex's only customers."

"I know, Mommy." Scotty twisted around in Alex's arms. "But you said he was coming back."

"I said maybe."

Alex released Scotty from his arms, allowing him to jump to the floor. "Why only maybe? I said I was going to fix your washing machine."

"Alex, you do not have to keep being my Good Samaritan. I can get the machine fixed myself."

"Did you?"

"Did I what?"

"Fix the machine?"

"No. I was waiting until my next paycheck—"

"Good. Then let me finish what I started and save you any more trips to the Laundromat." Alex waved the washing-machine belt he held in one hand. "You're not going to argue with me, are you? I've got the right part this time."

"Fine. But can I at least feed you dinner?"

"What is it with you and needing to feed repairmen?"

"What is it with you and fixing things? You fix. I feed. Fair deal if you ask me." Jessica knelt and began dropping Legos into the clear plastic bucket beside the pile. "Unless you're on a tight schedule. Do you have a date tonight with your girlfriend?"

The mention of his girlfriend caught Alex off guard. "Caron?"

"Caron—right." Jessica leaned back, her hands resting on her knees. "You can't work all the time. I thought it might be a date night for you two."

"No . . . no, we're not going out tonight. Caron's working out of town right now." No need to share that he'd rather be here, fixing Jessica's washing machine, than go home and spend a Saturday night alone. And that he felt alone even with his parents in the house. Jessica was just being friendly, not expecting him to be honest about his family situation. "She was asked to help stage a Tour of Homes house in Colorado."

And he wasn't going to mention she was working with an ex-boyfriend.

"I love visiting those kind of events. All the gorgeous houses with the perfect rooms." Jessica stopped Scotty from running past, motioning for him to help pick up the rest of the Legos. "So then you can fix my washing machine and I'll feed you dinner. That is, unless you don't like chicken cacciatore."

"Another one of your mother's recipes?"

"Sorry, not this time. But it's still delicious."

"Well . . . even though it's not your mother's recipe, I guess I'll say yes."

"Very nice, Mr. Alex. Very nice."

Scotty looked back and forth between the two. "Is Mr. Alex staying for dinner, Mommy?"

"Yes, he is."

"Then can I help him fix the washing machine?"

"You may watch him fix the washing machine—after you help me pick up your toys."

"And if it's okay with your mommy, maybe you can hand me a tool if I need it, okay?"

"Okay. That's like helping, right?"

"It sure is."

Jessica followed them down the hallway. "So how long will this take?"

"If all goes well, thirty minutes."

"And if not?"

"It'll be a long evening of me running back and forth to the parts store."

"We'll plan on things going well, then. I'll have dinner waiting."

Even with Scotty's help, Alex managed to replace the belt in under an hour. He insisted they both wash up after, like proper workmen, before joining Jessica in the kitchen. The aroma of chicken and tomato sauce with spices had been wafting down the hallway for the last half hour.

"Smells delicious."

"I hope you like polenta. And spinach. I don't cook the spinach to death, like my grandmother used to." Aiming the remote at the TV, Jessica clicked it off, using the remote like a baton to motion him to sit down. "I add garlic to it, too."

"Garlic makes anything taste better—even spinach."

"Thanks for that rousing vote in favor of spinach."

"Sorry. Didn't like spinach as a kid." He whispered and nodded toward Scotty. "But I'll be a good role model."

"Scotty loves my spinach, don't you?"

The boy sat in a chair beside Alex. "Yep. It's yummy."

Alex held his plate up. "Bring it on."

Jessica loaded his plate down with chicken smothered in

tomato sauce, polenta, and spinach fragrant with garlic. "There you go, sir. Would you hand me Scotty's plate?"

"I want just as much as Mr. Alex."

"I'll start you with just a little less, okay? If you want seconds, that's fine."

As Jessica filled her own plate, she nodded toward the glasses sitting beside their plates. "I hope water is okay. I don't keep soda in the house. It's my one weakness. If I buy it, I'll drink it for breakfast, lunch, and dinner."

"Soda is your one weakness. Got it." He ignored Jessica's smirk. "Water is fine."

"So did you have a good week at work?"

Alex savored his first bite of chicken. "This is delicious."

"Thank you. Try the spinach."

Alex held his fork, loaded with another bite of chicken, suspended over his plate. "Give me a chance to ease into it." He winked at Scotty. "Yes, it's been a good week. Not too many emergencies. No accidents."

"Accidents? Do those happen a lot?"

"Not a lot, but they happen. About eighteen months ago, one of our techs slipped carrying a unit upstairs to an attic. Hurt his back. He was out of commission for a couple of months. Bad for him. And for us."

"I understand why it's bad for him—"

"We're always shorthanded as far as techs go. That means even more hours for me and my dad."

"And Caron's understanding of all this, right?"

"We've known each other for years. My family moved down the street from hers when I was in fifth grade. And then my dad installed some air conditioners for her father. He's a Realtor. So she knows what my job is like."

After a few minutes of silence, Jessica had another question for him. "So, any more ideas about proposing?"

Alex choked on his sip of water. "No . . . no. Haven't had the time. I thought I'd, uh, take her looking at rings like you suggested."

"Like I suggested?"

"You said to make sure I knew what kind of ring she wanted. I figured the best way to do that was to take her ring shopping."

"You've known her for how long?"

"Since I was eleven. Seems like forever. And before you say anything, I mean that in a good way."

"And you've dated . . . ?"

"Two years."

"And you don't know what kind of ring she likes?"

"It's not an everyday topic of conversation."

"What's her favorite color?"

"I don't know . . . blue, maybe."

"Does she wear gold or silver jewelry?"

"Both?"

"When you buy her flowers, does she like tulips or roses?"

"I buy her roses."

"But what does she *like*?"

"Why all the questions?"

"After all this time, I would think you'd know some of these things. And that you'd know your future wife well enough to know what kind of ring she wants. Even if you do take her ring shopping—"

"I just told you that I was going to take her looking at rings—"

Jessica shook her head. "You can still surprise her with the ring you choose for her. That's why you need to plan something fun and creative."

"If you say so."

"What about a treasure hunt?"

"A treasure hunt?"

"You know, plant little notes that she has to find and follow the messages . . . maybe they lead to special places that mean something to both of you . . . and then you meet her at the last place and you propose there. Where do you spend most of your time?"

"At her parents' house. We eat there just about every Sunday."

"Well, that's not very romantic. Don't you have a favorite restaurant or—"

He needed to figure out some way to change the topic. Ask her about her job. Or compliment her on the spinach.

"Mommy, what happened to that car?"

Scotty was swiveled around in his chair, his attention riveted on the silent TV screen. Some sort of breaking news played out across the screen. A car accident.

"Oh, my gosh. I thought I turned that thing off. I must have hit the mute button by mistake." Jessica jumped up to grab the remote. "I don't want him seeing that."

Alex stared at the scene. An older-model four-door black sedan in the middle of a grocery-store parking lot, rammed into a line of parked cars, shoving them all akilter. The camera zoomed in on the woman sitting in the driver's seat, blood streaming down her face into her neck and the collar of her . . . black bathrobe.

"Wait." His voice was too loud. Harsh.

"What?" Jessica stopped, the remote control aimed at the TV.

"I need to see this . . . I . . . I know the woman in that car."

"What?" Jessica stepped in front of the TV. "Scotty, honey, go to your room."

"But, Mommy, I haven't finished eating . . ."

"Go to your room—"

"It's okay, Jessica." Alex shoved his chair back, the wood scraping against the floor. "I need to leave."

"I don't understand. What's going on?"

He lowered his voice so Scotty wouldn't hear him. "The woman in the car . . . she's my mother. I need to leave. Now."

TWENTY-SIX

· ♥ · ♥ · ♥ · ♥ · ♥ ·

How could you let this happen, Alex?" His father's words assaulted him like a verbal slap as the two of them waited in the hushed hospital hallway.

"Me?" Alex jerked to attention. "Why is this my fault?"

"I was out on an emergency call, you knew that." His father's boots thudded as he paced the corridor. Six steps to the left. Turn. Six steps to the right. Turn. "Why weren't you home?"

"I was on a repair call—"

"There was nothing on the books—and don't say there was. I checked."

"I was helping a client . . . who's also a friend . . . with a broken washing machine." Alex shoved his hands into his pockets. "And just because I live at home doesn't mean I have to tell you where I am at all times."

His father motioned to the room where his mother lay, medicated into a fitful sleep. "If you'd been home, this wouldn't have happened."

"You can't expect me to stay home twenty-four hours a day just because something might happen—"

"A broken nose. Fractured wrist. Mild concussion." His father continued on as if Alex hadn't spoken. "Not to mention being ticketed for the accident and a DUI."

"Look, I'm sorry this happened, but Mom is the one who chose to get in the car and go buy more alcohol—"

"Don't you realize how this could affect the business?" His father scrubbed his hand down his face, which was shadowed with a scattering of dark whiskers flecked with gray. "The news channels have already linked your mother to me and the business. What will our customers think?"

"So that's what this is really about, huh? Your reputation? How this affects business?" Alex stepped in front of his father, forcing him to stop pacing. "For once I thought you might actually care about Mom."

"Hey!" Alex's father poked his finger in his chest, pushing Alex back against the wall. "What kind of talk is that? I love your mother."

"Well, you have a funny way of showing it. You're always asking me to check on her. For your information, I am not Mom's babysitter. You're gone so much there were times I wondered if you had a girlfriend—"

His father took a step closer, breathing heavy, hands fisted. At that moment, a nurse exited the room where Alex's mom rested, and stepped in between them. "There is an injured woman in there, in case you've forgotten. I suggest both of you quiet down. And you—" She moved Alex's father toward the door. "—go sit with your wife. Your son can go get some coffee."

Without another word, his father disappeared into the hospital room. Alex shrugged off the nurse's hand. He needed fresh air, not coffee.

As he stepped off the elevator, his cell phone buzzed—a number he didn't recognize. Great. Another customer who couldn't make it through the night without air-conditioning. What did it matter that his mother was in the hospital?

"Emerald Coast Air-Conditioning and Heating, Alex speaking. How can I help you?"

"Alex, it's Jessica." Her words were rushed. "I hope it's okay that I called. Your number was on the business card you gave me."

He was surprised at how hearing her voice seemed to calm some of the pounding in his head.

"Hey, Jessica. Don't tell me, I know. The unit fritzed out, right?"

"No."

"The washing machine?"

"No. And even if they had, I wouldn't call you about that now."

"Then why are you calling?" The hospital doors slid open, allowing Alex to step outside, the humid night air swallowing him in its grasp.

"I'm calling because I'm worried about you—and your mother."

Her words tangled around his heart, making it difficult to breathe. To speak. Jessica was breaching invisible boundaries. Couldn't she read the NO TRESPASSING sign?

"Alex, are you still there?"

"Yes . . . I'm here."

"And where is 'there'? Are you at home or the hospital? I've been watching the news to get updates, so I know they took your mom to the hospital."

"We're still here. My mom has a mild concussion, a broken nose—that's why she had so much blood on her face—and a fractured wrist."

"Oh, how awful. Did they admit her?"

"Yes, just overnight for observation."

"I'm so sorry, Alex. Is there anything I can do?"

Anything she could do? Swear to keep his secret, maybe? If Jessica watched the news, then she now knew his mother had failed a Breathalyzer test and been ticketed for a DUI. No alcohol was found in the car, but only because she had been going to the store to purchase more wine before she crashed.

"No, but thanks for asking." Alex paced the sidewalk. "For calling."

"I'm praying, too. And Scotty prayed for your mom before he fell asleep."

"Scotty?"

"Yes, he kept asking about the lady in the car accident. And when I tucked him in bed tonight, he asked if we could pray for her. Of course I said yes."

Alex stared at the mostly empty parking lot, his grip on the phone tightening. He scraped the back of his fist against his dry lips.

"Alex?"

"Yeah." His answer came out on a rough exhale that burned his throat. "Tell Scotty that I said thank you for praying for my mom."

"I didn't tell him it was your mom."

"It's okay. I trust you with that information. And Scotty, too."

"You sound tired. I guess that's stating the obvious, huh?"

He slumped against the side of his car. "I don't think I thanked you for dinner."

"No need."

"Thank you."

"I have some leftovers put aside for you."

"Your mother raised you right."

"That she did." Jessica's voice softened. "Can you go home and get some sleep now?"

"Yes. My father . . . is staying with my mom tonight." Jessica didn't need to know how unusual that was. "So I'm heading home."

"Drive safely. And sleep well."

"Thanks. You, too."

The memory of his conversation with Jessica replayed in his mind as he drove home. She cared enough to call. Enough to pray.

But Jessica also knew who his mother was . . . what his mother was. And she still prayed for her. It was one thing for an innocent little boy like Scotty to pray for his mom—an unknown woman who'd been in a car accident. He was sure Jessica had whitewashed the details. Leaving out words like *driving under the influence* and *drunk* and *police* when explaining the situation to Scotty.

What did it matter, anyway? It wasn't like he was going to see them again. The air conditioner was fixed. The washing machine, too. And there was no need for him to pick up the leftovers, no matter how good a cook Jessica was.

Her words were laced with concern—not judgment. She'd prayed for him, and encouraged her little boy to pray for him, too. For all the history he had with Caron, he fought against calling Jessica back. Just to hear her voice. To lean into the calm understanding she offered. Maybe she'd pray for him again . . . something he seemed unable to do.

Pulling up outside his parents' house, Alex turned off the engine, palming his keys. And just sat.

The crisis, like so many others, was past. If Caron were in town, he'd call her. Tell her what had happened. She'd understand, having been through countless other crises with him. She knew the routine. Knew his secrets. And it wasn't the first time his mother had gone the drinking-and-driving route. It was just the first time in a long time. Years.

Alex pressed speed dial for Caron's number. Yes, it was late, but he'd woken Caron up before—

"Hello?" Caron's greeting was whispered.

"It's me, Alex. Were you sleeping?"

"No, I'm up. Working."

"I don't think Kade Webster is paying you enough to go without sleep to stage that home—"

"Alex, I'm two hours behind you. It's only eleven o'clock here."

"Are you working this late every night?"

A sigh preceded her answer. "What's wrong, Alex? You didn't call me because you thought I might be working late. Is it your mom?"

Alex tugged at his collar, the cab of the truck too hot. He shoved open the door, but that only allowed the humidity to seep in. "My mother's in the hospital."

"What?" Caron's voice sharpened. "What happened?"

"She wrecked the car driving to the liquor store. She's got a broken nose and wrist and a concussion."

"Oh, how awful."

"That's not the worst of it."

"What do you mean?"

He cleared his throat, forcing the words out. "The accident made the evening news."

"Oh, Alex—"

"You can imagine how thrilled my dad was about that."

"I'm sure he's more worried about your mom—"

"No. No, he was more concerned about ripping me apart. Asking why I didn't stop her from leaving the house."

"Were you there?"

"No, but that doesn't stop my father from blaming me."

"Alex, you know this wasn't your fault."

Did he? When was the last time he didn't feel responsible for his mother?

"The accident wasn't your fault, Alex." Caron's voice broke through his doubts. "I know you're upset, and I'm sorry. I wish I was there."

"I wish you were here, too." Right now he ached to hold Caron. To be held.

"Where are you now?"

"Sitting outside my house in the work truck."

"Enough talking." Caron's voice lowered as if she was reading him a bedtime story. "You need to go inside. Go to bed. You'll feel better after you get some sleep."

"I'd feel better if you were here."

"I'll be home soon. Go on now—get some sleep."

"I love you, Caro."

"I love you, too. Everything's going to be okay, Alex."

Everything's going to be okay. He clung to the assurance of Caron's words as he lay in his darkened bedroom. How many times had she told him that, her words the promise he believed when his mother's *headaches* ruined yet another family meal? And how many ways had he redefined what was *okay* so that life could include his mother's behavior?

TWENTY-SEVEN

• ♥ • ♥ • ♥ •

*I*t was a good thing Kade couldn't dock her pay based on what her office looked like.

Caron shoved her chair away from the desk that was obscured by magazines piled one on top of the other, as well as pages torn from various ones that flowed from the desk onto her office floor. A tumbler half full of sweet tea sat near her computer, where at least a dozen tabs were open—diverse images of lamps, carpets, floral arrangements, and children's bedrooms.

Miriam, Mitch, and Kade had left hours ago, but they weren't staring down a calendar of disappearing days trying to stage Eddie Kingston's house. She'd get back to an organized life—one where she slept—when she got back to Florida. For now, it was back to making decisions. Tomorrow she'd be visiting another furniture store to see if they'd want to donate items for the family room.

"I knew I'd find you here."

At the sound of Kade's voice, Caron bolted to her feet, scattering magazine pages to the floor. "Stop!"

Kade paused in the doorway. "I wouldn't think of stepping one foot into your office. It looks like the periodical section of the library exploded in here."

"Very funny. It's my decision-making process, thank you very much."

"You need a bigger office. Why didn't you go to the conference room?"

"Because my computer is here." Caron rescued papers from the floor, mindful of her bare feet—and her high heels abandoned beneath her desk.

"Have you had dinner?"

"What?"

Raising his arm, Kade shook the brown paper bag in his hand. "Food? Have you eaten?"

"No. I lost track of time."

"That's what I figured. Can't have one of my employees starving to death. So, dinner is served. Get your stuff organized here and meet me in the break room."

Kade disappeared before she could argue with him, leaving her to shut down her computer and stow everything else in her desk drawer. She ran her fingers through her hair, debating whether she should take the time to touch up her makeup. But Kade had already seen her end-of-the-day disheveled. No shoes. He was being nice to her, but that was no reason to primp.

She'd keep it real.

Kade had set two places at the table in the break room, and put a plate with several deli sandwiches in the center, a variety of chip bags beside it.

"I didn't buy drinks because I figured sweet tea would suffice."

"You figured right."

"Go ahead and pick what you'd like." Kade removed the

pitcher of tea from the fridge. "But I did get a ham and Swiss cheese with lettuce and tomato, light on the mayo and mustard, in case you're interested."

Her favorite.

"Thanks." Her tummy rumbled. "I guess I was hungrier than I realized."

"When I called in earlier, Miriam mentioned you'd skipped lunch."

"Part receptionist, part intel asset." Caron accepted the glass of tea with a nod as she settled into a chair across the table from Kade. "I see how it works now."

"Every good receptionist keeps the boss informed about what's going on around the office, you know that."

"True. Sometimes I wondered if my father really needed three receptionists or if he just wanted more access to office intel."

"You have a point. Your father definitely believed the boss needed to have his finger on the pulse of his business." He chuckled. "Pardon the cliché."

"I'll overlook the cliché, but only because you brought me my favorite sandwich."

"Oh, I see—you can be won over with ham and Swiss cheese, is that it?"

"Absolutely."

"I'll keep that in mind." A wink accompanied another chuckle. "Anything else?"

"Chips, of course." Caron selected a bag of salt-and-fresh-ground-pepper potato chips. Had Kade remembered she preferred those, too?

Caron fought to open the chip bag. Kade remembering her favorite sandwich and chips didn't mean anything.

"Need some help?"

"No." The bag refused to open. "Yes."

"Allow me."

When Kade's fingers brushed hers, Caron refused to be tripped up by an electricity-tingled-through-her-hand moment. Talk about a cliché.

Still, she couldn't help but remember the times Kade had held her hand. Twined their fingers together, his skin warm against hers. The evenings he told her to stretch out on his couch at the end of a long day, rest her head in his lap, and then ran his fingers through her hair until she'd fallen asleep. And then he'd woken her up with a trail of light kisses from her temple to the corner of her mouth, whispering, "Dinner's ready."

"Voilà!" Kade rattled the bag. "Your chips."

"Thank you. I always have a problem opening those things and I end up spilling half the chips all over the floor."

"Well, your chips are saved this time." Kade put a roast beef sandwich on his plate. "So, do you want to share any details about the Kingston house with me?"

The house. Safe ground. Much better than remembering Kade's kisses.

"I'm focusing on the children's bedroom tomorrow. And I'm meeting with Lacey at the house in the afternoon so we can talk about possible photographs."

"Sounds great."

"Yes. Thanks for suggesting her." Caron savored a bite of her sandwich, washing it down with a sip of sweet tea. "I'll be meeting with a florist next week to see if they'll donate flowers during tour week. And yes, I'll offer to mention them in our advertisements."

"Speaking of flowers, I suppose I have you to thank for the arrangements that have shown up on Miriam's desk?"

"It's no big deal, Kade."

"I wanted you to know I noticed them and appreciated them, too. Quite honestly, it's not something I'd thought about."

"Well, now you have—and you can have Miriam keep it up after I leave."

"I'll do that. You've reminded me that our clients appreciate little things like flowers in the reception area."

The brief sense of satisfaction at Kade's praise disappeared. He probably didn't even realize what he'd said.

Our clients.

It shouldn't matter that much that Kade noticed something as insignificant as her putting flowers on Miriam's desk. She shouldn't be trying to earn his approval. And any clients were his and his alone.

.   .   .

She either had come up with a brilliant idea or Kade was going to remind her that he was paying her to stage Eddie Kingston's home—and nothing else. Not even floral arrangements.

The only way she'd know was by presenting her proposal to him, and then waiting for his reaction.

"Mr. Webster just pulled up." Miriam leaned into Caron's office, her dreadlocks framing her smile.

"Thanks. His morning's free, right?"

"No appointments on his calendar. I triple-checked."

"Okay. Well then, I'm going to wait in his office for him."

"You want me to hold his calls?"

"Unless it's something urgent, yes. This won't take long." Caron slipped past Miriam. "Wish me luck."

"You asking for a raise?"

"No, nothing like that." The sound of the front door buzzer had Caron scurrying out from behind her desk. "Get back up front."

By the time Kade walked into his office, Caron sat in one of the chairs, a tumbler of sweet tea in hand, another waiting on Kade's desk for him.

"Good morning." Kade paused. "Did we have a meeting scheduled that I forgot about?"

"No, we didn't. But I wanted to discuss something with you."

"About the tour?"

"No . . . and yes."

Kade deposited his faded briefcase beside his desk, sitting on the front edge and lifting up the tumbler. "This for me?"

"Yes. I've noticed you've been partaking in the sweet-tea pitcher in the fridge."

"Guilty. Miriam's a fan, too."

"Not a problem."

"So what's on your mind?"

"Your suggestion for Eddie Kingston to retrofit the house was a gamble and it paid off. The house is beautiful and functional. I know it's already getting some pre-tour buzz."

"Thank you."

"I know Mitch, or someone like him, would love to live there." Caron clasped the plastic cup in her hands. "It's too bad the home is more expensive than Mitch can afford. When Lacey saw it the other day, she loved it."

"I'm not surprised. And I admit I've thought the same thing myself. I've even had a few discussions with Eddie about it."

"Really?" This was even better than she'd hoped. "We both know he's a businessman, Kade. We can't expect him to just give Mitch the house."

"I know the financial realities, Caron. It just seemed like maybe we could work out something. Mitch wants to buy a house. I'm looking for a house for him." He held up his hand. "And that information I just shared with you is confidential. I know Eddie has already built the perfect house for Mitch and Lacey."

"For a hundred thousand more dollars than Mitch could probably afford."

"So did you come in here this morning to talk about why this house is more than ideal for Mitch, but then remind me why he can't have it? I can think of better ways to start the day."

"I wasn't reminding you why it wouldn't work." Caron set her cup on the floor, jumping to her feet. "I mean, on the surface it looks like it won't work, but maybe if we get creative, we can think of a way Mitch can buy this house."

"What? Maybe we should take up a collection?"

"That's exactly what I was thinking."

"A collection . . . to help Mitch buy the house?"

"Why not, Kade?" Caron rested her hand on Kade's forearm. "You already said the subcontractors donated time and supplies to retrofit the house. What if . . . what if Eddie sold the house at cost? And . . . what if we took up a collection for the down payment? Mitch already has some kind of down payment, doesn't he? Or was he going for a VA loan?"

"He has a down payment of ten thousand dollars."

"So, we take his ten thousand . . . and we raise more for a bigger down payment—and lower his monthly payment. We could talk to some of your Ranger buddies . . . relatives . . . I don't know. We'd have to brainstorm. Maybe you could cover closing costs—"

He gave a brief laugh. "Of course I will."

"This is for Mitch—"

"Keep talking, hotshot."

"I'm still brainstorming this." The warmth in Kade's brown eyes urged Caron on. "I wanted to talk with you before I got too far into it. Will you let me draft a letter to send to people about donating money to the down-payment fund?"

"Yes, just let me see it before you send it out. I'll talk to Eddie. He did mention that a few buyers were already interested in this house, so I need to get to him sooner rather than later." Kade covered her hand with his. "What else do you need from me?"

"Any suggestions on who to send the letter to. Family. Friends—both his and Lacey's family and friends. Military buddies. I'll talk to some of the Tour of Homes folks, see if they want to chip in—"

"They've already donated time and materials—"

"I know that, Kade." She took a breath, scrambling to keep her thoughts focused on the original topic. To not be distracted by Kade's nearness. His touch. What was she doing clinging to his arm? How unprofessional. She slipped her hand from beneath his and stepped back. "I . . . I'm just giving them the opportunity. Every dollar helps, right?"

"Can't argue with that."

Taking her seat again provided a few seconds to gather her thoughts, as well as the needed space. "So, is it okay for me to ask Miriam to help? I mean, could she type up the letter once I draft it and get your approval? Mail it from here?"

"I don't see why not. Just remember, Mitch works here, too."

"I think Miriam knows how to keep a secret."

"Right. You say this about the girl who couldn't hide the fact that she was crushing on her boss."

"That's old news, Kade. Miriam does good work."

"I know she does. If there's one thing your father taught me, it's how the people at the front desk make the first impression for your business."

The mention of her father provided an additional barrier between them.

"My father does know business."

"That he does. I've never regretted working for him."

"You . . . haven't?"

"No. Russell Hollister taught me a lot about being a Realtor—things I still use today. The importance of focusing on future success, not past failures."

"A key Hollister principle." Caron stood, picking up her cup, and backed toward the door. "And I need to focus on making phone calls to furniture stores. Maybe doing a little shopping."

"You got my e-mail with the budget, right? Do you have notes on how much you've spent?"

"Yes. Thank you."

"Good. Anything else I can do for you?"

"No, not at the moment."

Caron escaped to her office, closing the door behind her. She buried her face in her hands, willing her heartbeat to slow down.

Why was her heart tripping her up, her emotions tugging her toward Kade? Was it just because her life was so unsettled? Because Alex was so far away?

She was in transition, caught between what she'd planned for the future and all the unclear choices. It was as if she'd been sitting in an old canoe tied to a dock. Everything was safe. Familiar. And then someone had cut the canoe loose from its moorings and sent her floating down the river. But she had no paddles to use to guide her course. No control. Her only hope was to hang on and pray until she was anchored somewhere safe again.

.   .   .

She ought to resign as one of Margo's bridesmaids.

"I'm sorry I missed the last get-together to work on our bridesmaid jewelry." Caron had thought the idea of being around to help with Margo's wedding would be fun, but it was becoming just one more thing to do.

"I understand." Margo's hug was almost an afterthought as she pulled her toward the table covered with wedding invitations and envelopes and a package of stamps. "You can make it up to me by helping address the invitations now. And there's always the trial makeup session."

"The what?"

"A friend of mine is a makeup artist and she's offered to do my makeup on my wedding day. We're going to meet and do a trial run. Come with me?"

"If I can, sure. But life's only going to get busier the closer we get to the Peak Tour of Homes."

"I understand. I know you came out here to work, and I'm just glad you're here. But Kade Webster must be some sort of slave driver. You're living with me, but I barely even see you—"

"It's not Kade, it's me. I've got to make sure I pull off staging this house. I'm either on the phone talking to someone at a furniture store, or I'm driving back and forth to different furniture stores, or I'm looking at websites—" Caron settled into one of the white ladder-back chairs encircling the table.

"Surely you've got it figured out by now. The tour is only a couple of weeks away."

"I think so. I just want to impress Eddie Kingston . . . and Kade. I don't want him to regret asking me to do this."

"You're a natural decorator, Caron. Even back in college, we had the coolest room in the entire dorm."

"Decorating a dorm room or my own house—that's just having fun. Staging Eddie Kingston's house for the tour where judges are flown in from out of state—that's business. I didn't feel this much pressure the few times I helped stage homes for my dad."

"Just pretend this is your own home, Caron. I know you can

do this. Relax. Try to have fun with it. This sounds like a dream project for you."

"This house is a little different, especially since it's being modified for a handicapped person. Maybe a Wounded Warrior." Caron couldn't hold back her smile. "But I have to admit, even though I keep telling myself that I can't let Kade or Eddie Kingston down, I am enjoying myself. I love staging this house. As a matter of fact . . ." Her voice trailed off.

"What? As a matter of fact what?"

"Okay, don't say anything . . . a part of me likes staging a house more than I like being a Realtor. And—"

"And?"

"And . . . I don't know. Sometimes the idea of switching career fields crosses my mind. But I can't even think about that until I finish this job."

"Then don't. For now, relax. And believe me when I tell you that you can do this because you are good at it. That's why Kade called you." Margo set a pile of envelopes in front of her, along with the stamps "So your goal is a beautiful house, right?"

"Yes. But with someone like Mitch in mind, I'm thinking practical but not sterile. Practical with personality."

"If anyone can pull it off, you can, Caron." Even as Margo encouraged her, she opened her laptop and pulled up an Excel spreadsheet of her guest list. "Okay. How about you forget about work for a little while and help me with these invitations?"

"Anyone else joining us tonight?"

"No, it's just you and me. I figure the two of us can handle this. You've got stamps and return-address-label duty." Margo settled into the chair beside Caron. "Tell me what's going on, besides working for Kade. How are you and Alex?"

Alex.

Caron opened the roll of stamps and began affixing them in the upper right-hand corner of each of the envelopes. After adding the return address labels, she stacked the envelopes into piles of ten. Margo worked alongside her.

After a few moments, Margo's voice broke the silence. "So, no comment on Alex?"

"We're fine."

"Well, that's not exactly a rousing endorsement of your relationship."

"Things have been a little off between us the past few weeks."

"Explain what you mean by 'off.'"

"Alex didn't like the idea of the destination wedding in Telluride. At all. And he didn't understand why I quit working for my dad. Honestly, it felt as if he was taking my dad's side instead of supporting me."

"And I can only imagine how he felt about you coming out here to work for Kade Webster."

"That didn't go over well." Caron affixed another address label to an envelope. "And I already told you about how Alex proposed on the way to the airport."

"Yes—where he didn't look at you and he didn't have a ring."

"That was pretty much it." Caron shifted in the chair, unraveling the roll of stamps. "But there's always proposal number two, right?"

"Can I ask you something?"

"Sure."

"Do you really think you're going to marry Alex Madison?"

Caron re-rolled the stamps. "What kind of question is that, Margo?"

"A question I expect you to answer."

"Just because he didn't handle the first proposal all that well—"

"You're being gracious, giving the guy a practice run. But that's not why I asked the question. There are other things . . ." Her friend trailed off. "Never mind."

"Oh, no. You can't say something like that and then say 'never mind.'" Caron waited until Margo looked at her. "What are you thinking?"

"I'm all for the marry-your-best-friend adage. Sometimes. And then sometimes I think you fall in love with someone and you get married and then you become best friends."

"Your point?"

"You and Alex . . . you're just friends. Always have been—and I think you always will be."

"Alex and I haven't always been friends. I couldn't stand him during high school."

"Back then you were still family friends." Margo hooked her arm over the back of the chair. "Your parents were friends. And there was that whole we-betrothed-you-guys-at-birth stuff. What a crazy expectation to have put on you."

"I never bought into that."

"Well, you certainly pushed back against it for a lot of years. But then, I think you caved."

"I . . . caved?" Caron dropped the roll of stamps so that it unwound again.

"You started dating Alex awfully fast after you broke up with Kade—"

"So?"

"Well, he is the parentally approved choice, isn't he?"

"Margo, I am not dating Alex just because my parents like him. We get along—"

"Like friends, Caron."

Caron pushed her hands against the table, causing several stacks of envelopes to topple. "We *are* friends—"

"Let me finish. You act like friends—and nothing more." Margo plunged ahead, overriding Caron's protest, her blue eyes sparking. "Oh sure, you hold hands. You even kiss. Yay! But for the most part, your relationship with Alex is so . . . so casual. And if it's casual now, what's it going to be like five years from now?"

"We're comfortable with one another. Is that so bad?"

"I like my jeans to be comfortable. Or my old, reliable shoes that I run around town in when I'm doing errands all day. But I don't think being in love with someone should be described as 'comfortable.' "

"Well, when you compare my relationship with Alex to a pair of old shoes or worn-out jeans—"

"Answer one question for me, and then I'll drop this whole subject."

Caron straightened a stack of white envelopes. "Ask away."

"When you were dating Kade, would you describe that relationship as comfortable?"

What was Margo doing bringing up Kade?

"Kade is not Alex. You cannot compare the two men."

"Exactly!" Margo leaned forward. "So?"

"So what?"

"Answer the question."

Her relationship with Kade—comfortable? The man intrigued her. At times he infuriated her. He almost dared her to be more than she imagined for herself. And then there were his kisses . . . times when the passion was both enticing and almost frightening. When she was thankful he never asked more of her than she was willing to give because maybe she would have said yes.

"I wish I had a mirror so you could see your face right now." Margo's voice sounded triumphant.

"I don't need to answer the question because it is irrelevant."

Caron looked away. "I am no longer dating Kade Webster. I am not getting engaged to Kade Webster."

"So you're willing to settle for comfortable."

"I am not settling!" Caron stomped her foot, her knee jarring the table and causing several stacks of envelopes to fall over again.

"Then forget I said anything. If Alex is your choice, I'm happy for you."

"Don't say that. You think marrying Alex is the wrong choice."

"I don't know why you broke up with Kade. You refused to talk about it. And yes, I still have my opinion about things, but I won't say anything else. I just don't want you to spend the rest of your life wondering 'what if.' Alex is some safe, approved, passion-free zone. Don't you want more than that for your marriage?" Margo grasped Caron's hand. "When I see you talk about Kade—even now—your entire face lights up with emotion."

"I thought we were addressing invitations, Margo. Not discussing my love life."

"I'm done. But I will say just one more thing—" Margo picked up her pen again. "When you were with Kade . . . when he was around, you shimmered like one of those Fourth of July sparklers. I miss that."

TWENTY-EIGHT

• ♥ • ♥ • ♥

The slightest chill clung to the mountain air, even as the clouds overhead rolled back to reveal a slate-blue sky. Energy pulsed through the area, strongest where the participants for the next heat of the Aspen Mass Mudder assembled in the waiting area. The constant rumble of voices, threaded through with laughter and the blare of music through loudspeakers, was an unrelenting wave of vocal thunder—rising, receding, and rising again.

People wove in and out of the vendors' tents dotting the base of the mountain—sports drinks, energy bars, athletic wear. Men and women who'd already finished the obstacle course—some still covered in mud, some wet from hosing down in the rinse-off area—relaxed in small groups, hugging and high-fiving, recounting their experiences with elaborate hand motions.

"Are you glad you came?"

Lacey's question tugged Caron's attention away from the starting line, where Kade and Mitch, along with the four other members of the team, waited for the start of their race. All six men wore identical orange T-shirts emblazoned with the words MUD DEVILS and a stylized cartoon of a mud tornado on the front. Mitch wore pants with extra padding to protect his stumps from being torn up on the course.

"Are you kidding? This is fantastic!" Caron held up her cell phone. "I'm taking photos, too, but they're going to be pitiful, compared to yours."

Lacey shifted the black bag on her shoulder, her camera slung around her neck. She'd braided her hair and then pulled on a wide purple headband. "Let me know if you want any particular shots. I'll be glad to give you copies."

"Thanks."

"We'll watch the start of the race and then hike up to the next observation point. If we're fast, we'll get there before the guys do."

"Whatever you say. I'm playing follow the leader today."

The group of a couple hundred men and women, some carrying flags, some wearing superhero costumes or camo fatigues and combat boots, quieted as a man shouted final instructions through a megaphone. Kade and Mitch, along with the rest of the team, were front and center in the crowd. As the race organizer reminded the participants that the Mudder was about sportsmanship and camaraderie—and that runners could skip any obstacle they wanted to—Kade positioned himself behind Mitch, gripping the handles of his wheelchair, leaning forward and saying something so that Mitch laughed.

"He probably just told Mitch to hang on." Lacey knelt and braced her camera on a jean-clad knee. "And Mitch warned Kade not to dump him onto the ground."

"They've done this before, right?" Caron crouched beside her, the rough terrain digging into her knees through her jeans, using her cell phone camera to zoom in on the group.

"This is their second Mudder. Last year it rained most of the time."

"You're kidding me."

"It doesn't matter." Lacey talked while she took pictures. "They're all soaked by the third obstacle anyway."

The prolonged screech of the megaphone interrupted their conversation, drawing Caron's attention back to the team as they surged forward, Kade hunched over Mitch's wheelchair to gain traction on the rocky hillside.

"Go, go, go!" Caron jumped up and down, her cheers swallowed up in the roar of the crowd.

"Almost makes you want to be down there, running with them, doesn't it?" Lacey trained her camera on the men advancing up the mountain.

"Me? I don't think so. This is more intense than the race I participated in."

"Come on." Lacey nodded upward once the last of the runners disappeared from sight. "Time to get moving."

As they headed toward the next observation point, Lacey stopped now and then to take photos of the surrounding mountains and of the base area, teeming with spectators' visiting booths.

"So have you and Mitch dated for a long time?"

"We've been friends since high school." Lacey placed the cover on the camera lens. "And then Mitch started dating my best friend. When we graduated, he was headed to boot camp, where he met Kade. Mitch asked everyone to write him. Mostly girls. I promised to write him. It was my good deed, you know? When he and Brianna broke up, I kept it up."

"I see."

"It wasn't like that. We were just friends. And then . . ." Lacey's smile widened. "About a year later, he came home on leave. I'd broken up with a guy that I'd been dating, and he was flying solo, too, so we went out for pizza . . . and he let me cry on his nice, very broad shoulders . . ."

"And you've been together since then?"

"No. After he was injured, Mitch wouldn't answer my calls. I charged a plane ticket and showed up at the hospital—" Lacey's voice broke. "It was awful. I mean, Kade called me and warned me. And I thought I was prepared. But it was still . . . hard to see Mitch like that. I broke down . . . and Mitch yelled at me to leave. Said he didn't want me there."

"Of course it was hard." Caron dug her heels into the dirt and rocks, scrabbling to keep up with Lacey. "Did he expect you not to cry?"

"He didn't want me sticking around because I felt sorry for him. So he told me to get lost. Later, he told me that he broke up with me because he thought it was the right thing to do."

"Well, obviously you got back together."

"It took about six months. And both of us being miserable. And a lot of praying." A smile twisted Lacey's lips. "And Kade."

"Kade?"

"Mitch and I are both stubborn, which can be both a good and a bad thing. We never stopped loving each other. But Mitch was struggling to adjust to life as a double amputee. He wasn't going to ask me to commit to that kind of a future. And to be honest, I wondered if I was ready. I surfed the Internet to understand what Mitch was dealing with. How would we manage a family? And I even dated some other guys. None of them made me forget Mitch."

"So how did you two get back together?"

"That's where Kade comes in."

"Kade played matchmaker?"

"He called me again. He told me that Mitch was struggling. That Mitch needed me, but that he wasn't going to admit it. And Kade reminded me love is about being brave, about making the choice to love someone no matter what. Asked me point-blank if Mitch losing two legs was all it took to change how I felt about him. I was on the next plane to Colorado, praying the whole way."

"And that was it, huh? Happily every after?"

"Hardly." Lacey's laughter seemed to bounce off the mountains. "Mitch yelled at me when I showed up. I won't even tell you what he said to Kade."

"What did you do?"

"I yelled right back at him. And then I cried. And yelled some more. We both cried. That's when Kade left us alone."

"And so?"

"And so?" Lacey shrugged. "Oh, you're asking the when-are-we-getting-married question."

"I guess I am."

"It will happen when it happens. But between you and me, if Mitch doesn't ask soon, I may propose to him."

"You're kidding, right?"

"Nope. Absolutely serious. There comes a time when a girl's gotta do what a girl's gotta do. I love Mitch and I want to be his wife, not just his girlfriend."

Their conversation trailed off and Caron slowed her pace, allowing Lacey to wander ahead, snapping scenery.

Why was she struggling against comparing her relationship with Alex to the kind Lacey and Mitch had? The kind of love that dug in its heels when it faced a battle, instead of turning its back on troubles and pretending they didn't exist.

Was this the reason she was content with her long-standing girlfriend status with Alex? Did she long for something more?

The Mudder took a good six hours, what with the team helping Mitch through obstacles like the ten-foot angled wall named the "Skidmarked" or cheering him on as he conquered the "Pole Dancer," two wobbly, slippery poles, without landing in the muddy water below him.

Between posing while Lacey took their celebratory photos—both before and after rinsing off the mud that soaked their clothes and hair—and finding someplace to eat a post-race meal, they didn't get back to the Springs until almost ten o'clock that night. Caron drove, dropping Lacey and Mitch off at Mitch's house first, where Lacey had parked her car, while Kade dozed in the reclined front passenger seat.

"It was a great day." Caron kept her voice low, trying not to wake Kade.

"It was that." Lacey leaned in to hug her. "We're getting together early next week to select photos for the tour house, right?"

Caron had almost forgotten about the tour while shouting herself hoarse today.

"Yes. I'm down to the wire. And now I'm going to try and get out of here before this guy wakes up."

"He'll sleep well tonight. They all will."

Caron pulled back onto the highway before addressing Kade. "You can stop pretending to be asleep."

"I don't know what you're talking about." Kade shifted in the seat, uttering a soft groan, and spoke without opening his eyes.

"You haven't been asleep. And I know you're hurt."

"I am not hurt—"

"Oh, come on, Kade. I saw you after the Mud Mile. Something changed in your gait . . . your expression—"

"Watching me, were you?"

"Stop it! I was watching the entire team. But I'm concerned about you. I don't know what you did, whether you hurt your back or your leg, but something's wrong."

"Everybody's sore, Caron—"

She barged past his excuses. "And then you let me drive the car home . . . well, that was proof enough. You never hand your car keys over to anyone."

"Fine. I pulled a little muscle in my back." Kade's sigh filled the car, as if he'd held on to it for the entire ride back from Aspen. "Are you happy now?"

"That is probably the stupidest thing I've ever heard you say. Of course I'm not happy you're hurt. I've been worried. I prayed for you while you finished the course."

"Thank you. Now if you'll just drive me home, I'll take a hot shower and get a good night's sleep and be fine in the morning."

Caron drove the rest of the way in silence. Pain made Kade irritable, which was understandable, and there was no need to fuss at him. Not now, anyway.

Lacey had programmed Kade's address into Caron's cell phone, allowing her to get back to Kade's house, where she'd left her car at five o'clock that morning. Kade sat silent, his brow furrowed, arms folded across his chest.

Caron hadn't expected Kade to quit, to walk off the course, just because he'd gotten hurt. She knew him better than that. But the race was over. He could let his guard down. And she wasn't going to abandon him without making sure he was okay for the night.

.   .   .

It had been a good day. A long, hard day. He was already looking forward to running the Mudder next year. But right now all Kade wanted to do was go stand in a hot shower for the rest of the night. But there was no doing that, not when Caron had pulled his car into the garage and shadowed him into the house.

"Okay. I'm home. Are you satisfied?" Kade resisted the urge to slump against the island in the center of his kitchen in an attempt to ease the burning in his lower back.

"I'll be satisfied when you're in bed."

"Oh, really?" Even in the dim light of the kitchen, there was no mistaking the blush creeping across Caron's face.

"Oh, stop it. You're not going to get rid of me by trying to embarrass me." Caron fisted her hands on her hips. "You know what I mean. Now tell me how badly you're hurt."

The sooner he told her, the sooner she'd leave.

"I told you that I pulled a muscle in my lower back—a major one. It's happened before. I'll take a muscle relaxant and grab a hot shower. I'll probably have to sleep on the couch for a couple of nights."

"So, first things first. Go take some medicine and get a shower."

"And you, Miss Hollister, can head home."

"True. I know how to let myself out."

"Then I'll say good night. See you on Monday."

There was no response from Caron. He couldn't blame her for leaving without saying goodbye. She was . . . well, not as tired as he was, but still worn out from the long day. She'd been a great sport today. Had a great time with Lacey. Driven all the way back from Aspen, covering for him by saying she liked long drives through the mountains.

The hot shower lasted less than twenty minutes, but that's what he got for indulging in not one, but two muscle relaxers. He wasn't going to doze off in the shower and wake up tomorrow morning a waterlogged human prune.

Kade managed to pull on a pair of pajama bottoms with minimal groans. He couldn't imagine wrestling on a T-shirt tonight. And if he didn't want to wake up tomorrow with an upset stomach, he needed to eat something before sacking out on the couch. A spoonful of peanut butter. Or a yogurt.

Now, why did his house smell like someone was making a grilled cheese sandwich?

The aroma of toasted bread and melted cheese only got stronger as he shuffled into the kitchen, his hand pressed against his lower back.

Caron Hollister tilted a frying pan, allowing a sandwich oozing with cheese to slide onto a plate waiting on the counter.

"What are you still doing here?" Kade ground the words out through gritted teeth.

"Feel better?"

"I asked you a question."

"It's obvious I'm making you something to eat." Caron waved the plastic spatula over the plate. "Now it's your turn to answer my question. Are you feeling better?"

"I was—until I realized you were still here."

"It's a good thing I remember how cranky you get when you're in pain." Caron moved past him with the sandwich and a glass of milk. "Remember when you had your wisdom teeth pulled out?"

"Don't remind me." He fought against the way the world seemed to be slowing down. "So that sandwich is for me?"

"Yes. Your meds are kicking in, I see. I know we're not talking about why I know this, but I do remember how meds upset your stomach. Come on, the couch is ready for you."

"You made up my couch?"

"That's where you're going to sleep, not just because of your back pain, but also because your bedroom furniture is over at the Kingston house. It was pretty easy to find sheets and a spare blanket and a pillow in your linen closet.

"Caron, go home." Kade collapsed on the couch, causing his back to spasm. Who had signed him up to be an actor in a slow-motion film? All he wanted to do was stretch out on the couch. Or shake Caron very slowly and tell her to stop being so nice. To stop acting like she cared about him.

"Just humor me for a few more minutes, okay? Eat your sandwich. Drink your milk. Hydration, remember? And then I'll turn off the lights and go home."

"Going to tuck me in?"

"If you want me to." Caron sat across from him on the coffee table. "You had a rough day."

"Me? I've got nothing to complain about. Mitch showed us all up today."

"You were all amazing out there—a great team."

"I'll run the Mudder every year Mitch wants to do it."

"It's inspiring—"

"No . . . no, it's humbling." Kade took another bite of the sandwich and set it aside.

"I don't understand."

"It's one thing to run a course when your arms and legs are working. Sure, I hurt my back. That's temporary. But to see Mitch . . . forgetting who he was before the firefight . . . and accepting who he is now . . . facing those obstacles. Refusing to let them stop him. He lives that every day. I couldn't stop him from being hurt . . . but if I can help him live the life he wants now . . . well, I'm all in."

"You're a good friend, Kade."

Kade swallowed against the burn in his throat, his eyes closing. "There was a moment today when I was carrying him on my back . . . and I remembered after the firefight . . . how I wanted to just pick Mitch up and carry him as far and as fast as I could away from danger. But I couldn't. There was blood everywhere . . . and his legs . . . I needed to apply tourniquets. And he was conscious for a moment and I said, 'You're gonna be okay, buddy. You're gonna be okay . . .'"

The warmth of Caron's hand on his, the softness of her skin, saved him from going all the way back into a memory that still woke him some nights. Kade turned his hand palm-up, curving his fingers around her hand.

"He lost both his legs . . . I couldn't prevent that. But I made a promise that I'd help him any way I could."

"Because that's who you are."

"It's the right thing to do. You stand by someone when you love them." Kade gave in to the need to lie down.

Caron adjusted the soft material of the blanket over his shoulders, her fingers brushing his skin. Why was she still here? Why had she come back? He caught her hand in his again.

"Why did you leave without saying anything?"

She stilled. Just like that, with one question, they were facing their past relationship again. "I thought . . . it would be easier."

"Was it? Easy?" He tightened his grasp, determined to have an answer this time.

"No. No, breaking up with you wasn't easy, Kade." With her free hand, she ran her fingers through his hair. "I did love you. It just wasn't going to work . . ."

He closed his eyes, allowing himself to relax as she continued to brush her fingers through his hair. "Are you happy with this other guy?"

A moment's hesitation and then "Yes."

"Well then . . . that's that, I guess. You're happy. He's happy. And I'm . . . well, I'm sleepy." Kade knew his voice was fading.

"And you can go on and leave. It's all right. I should be used to people leaving me by now . . ."

·   ·   ·

Even after Kade had fallen asleep, Caron stayed where she was, his medicated condition allowing her to dare to hold his hand.

His insistence that she leave—that it didn't matter because he was used to being left—kept her at his side, his hand in hers. She'd convinced herself that leaving him with no explanation would be easier. But she knew better.

She knew him.

As Kade tucked her beneath his arm, Caron leaned closer, falling in to step with him. Moonlight shimmered across the Gulf, creating shadows along the sand dunes.

"I like these nighttime walks along the beach."

"Me, too." Kade's voice was low. "No need to wear sunscreen."

"That's not what I meant. I like the quiet. Just you and me and the moonlight."

"My thoughts exactly."

"So I was wondering something."

"And what was that?"

"You know about my family. I mean, you work for my father, after all—"

"True. Although I haven't done the guess-who's-coming-to-dinner routine yet."

"All in good time." She rested her head on his shoulder. "You don't talk much about your family. You do have one, don't you?"

"Everyone has some sort of family."

"Well?"

"I grew up in Maryland. My parents divorced when I was in elementary school. My father remarried and decided family number

two was more important than me. End of that story. My mom lives in Connecticut now, and we keep in touch."

"She never remarried?"

"She has a long-standing boyfriend. It works for them." Kade shifted, pulling her closer to his side. *"The closest thing I had to family were the Neilsons."*

"And they were?"

"Neighbors. A military family that moved next door to my mom and me when I was ten. I became friends with their son, Drake. Man, they let me hang around all the time. Meals. Game nights. Took me to the base pool."

Kade fell silent.

"Do you and Drake keep in touch?"

"I have no idea where he is now."

"What? Why not?"

"When we were fifteen, Drake's dad was diagnosed with cancer. He died six months later. The family moved to be near relatives. End of story."

"Oh, Kade, how awful—"

"It is what it is." Lurking behind the flat statement, Caron knew, were all sorts of stuffed emotions. *"I joined the military right out of high school. Mr. Neilson had always told me that he thought I'd do well in the air force. I'd like to think he'd be proud of me."*

Caron brushed Kade's hair back from his forehead—something she loved doing when they were dating.

She'd obeyed her father's demand and ended the relationship when Kade decided to strike out on his own. But in doing so, she'd hurt Kade even more than she'd allowed herself to realize. She'd proven to him once again that people leave.

But how could she not do as her father expected? Kade knew how much she valued her father's opinion. And he knew how invested she was in her father's company. He knew she'd never imagined working anywhere else. She couldn't stand up to both her father's demands and to Kade's insistence that he loved her—that they defy her father. So she'd simply not shown up for their next date. Never returned a single one of Kade's what's-going-on phone calls. Deleted his texts. Every single one of them.

Yes, it was easier. For her. And as time went on she'd convinced herself that her heart wasn't broken. That what she had with Kade was nothing compared to what she found with Alex.

Then why were there times when she ached for Kade all these months later? Why were memories of their time together closer and closer to the surface of her heart? She couldn't still be in love with Kade. She couldn't be.

And what did a woman do if she realized she'd been wrong to walk away from one man in the hopes of keeping her father happy? That maybe . . . the perfect man for her . . . wasn't the right man for her after all?

TWENTY-NINE

• • • ♥ • • •

aron backed out of the passenger-side door of Kade's car, exhaling as she stood straight. At only nine in the morning, the cement of the driveway was cool beneath her bare feet, the sky overhead still a mix of blue skies and white clouds.

And thanks to a small piece of sleight of hand, she'd retrieved Kade's car keys from the kitchen counter where he'd left them last night. Now the interior of his SUV gleamed. Maybe she didn't own a car with leather interior. Yet. But she knew how to do the basic detail of one. She'd ransacked Kade's garage until she'd found his plastic bucket of car-care supplies. If she was going to clean his car, she was going to do it right.

Of course, she could have just driven through a car wash, but there was no risking the muscle relaxers wearing off and Kade waking up to find his car missing and thinking someone had stolen it while he slept.

Her cell phone buzzed in the pocket of her jeans shorts. A text from Margo.

Where are you?

Instead of texting back, she opted for a phone call.

"You didn't see my note, did you?"

"What note?"

"I left you a note—never mind. I'm going to miss church today."

"Why?"

Caron shut the car door, wiping away the sweat beading along her forehead. "I'm cleaning Kade Webster's car."

"What? He's paying you to stage a home, not clean his car—"

"I'm helping him out, Margo. He hurt his back running the obstacle course yesterday." Switching the phone to speaker and setting it on the front hood of the car, she released her hair from the pigtails she'd adopted for the morning, her hair falling to stick to her damp neck. "His car is filthy after driving to Aspen and back yesterday. He's going to want it clean come tomorrow."

"You Realtors and your insistence that you have spotless cars."

"Just part of the job. I've got the interior done, now all I need to do is wash the outside and I can get out of here before Kade wakes up."

"Doing your good deed in secret, is that it?"

"I guess I am. I want to get this done and be gone before Kade wakes up. It's . . . it's best that way."

"What do you mean by that?"

"Nothing." Margo and she always spoke the truth to one another. Why was she hedging now? "I mean, nothing I can talk about right now, okay?"

"Okay."

"I will talk to you, Margo—"

"I know. Just finish what you're doing and then come on home. I'll be here, ready to listen when you're ready to talk."

She should have gone to church with Margo today. Refreshed herself with the praise and worship music. Found some guidance from the pastor's teaching. But surely God understood that she was helping Kade, stopping him from hurting his back any further.

She'd left the now-empty plastic bucket near the corner of the garage where she'd spied the hose. As she turned away from the car, Caron tripped over her bare feet at the sight of Kade standing in the open garage bay.

"Good morning." His dark hair was tousled, and he wore his long pajama bottoms . . . and a confused smile.

"What are you doing out here?" Caron pushed her sunglasses back up on her nose.

"Shouldn't I be the one asking that question? I mean, my house . . . my driveway . . . my car."

"It's pretty evident what I'm doing. I'm cleaning your car." Caron tried to keep things nonchalant. Go about her planned business of washing Kade's car. Not stare at him in half of his pajamas. Watching Kade take on the Mudder yesterday had reminded her how he benefited from his frequent workouts. Now she had another unobstructed view of his muscular torso.

Focus on something—anything—else. Liquid soap in the bucket. Turn on the outside faucet, and place the bucket beneath the steady stream of water. "I know you need your car cleaned up after the drive through the mountains yesterday."

"I can handle that myself."

"With a strained back? I don't think so." Caron tossed a large blue sponge into the bucket. "Besides, I'm halfway done. I'll finish what I started . . ."

"All right, then. How about I rinse the car off?"

Kade still had to be groggy because he wasn't even arguing with her. With a swift motion, Caron retrieved the hose. "I'll rinse the car off."

"Caron, I'm perfectly capable of—"

"Kade, you're barely awake, and besides, I know how sensitive you are to medication."

"Hey, I'm awake. I'm walking." He offered her a lazy smile that made it seem as if the sun had warmed her body. "Besides, I just invested in a fireman's nozzle for my hose—"

"A fireman's nozzle? Isn't that a little overkill?"

"So I bought into the advertisement." He held out his hand. "I'll rinse the car and you can start soaping it down."

"Bossy today, aren't we?"

"My driveway—my car."

"I know, your house." Caron relinquished the hose. "This is probably safer than letting you wash the car. Just take it easy with that thing, okay?"

"Of course. I've washed a car before, Caron."

Caron jumped back when Kade pointed the nozzle toward her. "Hey!"

"Sorry. I wasn't pulling back on the grip." His gray eyes seemed remarkably clear. "I promise to behave."

For the next few moments, they worked in tandem, Kade moving around the car, aiming a steady stream of water at the exterior and the hubcaps, and Caron following behind him with the bucket and sponge, scrubbing the dirt off.

"I need some more water over here, boss." Caron stepped back, motioning to the bucket with the sponge.

"Sure thing. You want to add more soap? The bottle's right near the rear tire."

"Okay." She squirted more soap into the bottom of the bucket. "There ya go."

Kade aimed the stream of water into the bucket, adjusting the strength, but not before some of it splashed onto Caron's bare legs.

"Hey! What happened to being careful?"

"Oh, please. It's just a little bit of water." Kade moved the hose so that the spray landed full force on her bare feet. "No big deal, see?"

"That's cold water, Kade." She picked up the bucket. "I think it's time I took over rinsing the car."

"You're in charge of the sponge, Miss Hollister." Kade backed up, positioning his hand on the grip that controlled the flow of water. "Don't make me do something you're going to regret."

"You wouldn't. And I seriously doubt that you could, with a sore back."

Kade raised the hose, easing the handle as he pointed the nozzle directly at her heart. "Don't be so hasty to throw down a verbal gauntlet, Miss Hollister."

Oh no he did not! Caron took two quick steps forward and tossed the bucket of water straight at his bare chest—and then dropped the container onto the driveway and ran.

Kade's bellow was followed by an immediate blast of water against her back that sent her running to safety on the other side of the car, her feet slapping on the wet cement.

"You can't outrun me, Caron—"

She tossed the soggy sponge at him. "Drop the hose, buddy!"

"I don't think so." Kade rounded the front of the car, aiming a nonstop stream of cold water at her.

She had no water bucket, no sponge . . . nothing but bravado to try and get out of this one-sided battle. Putting her hands up in front of her face, Caron ran toward Kade, trying to grab the nozzle away from him. But the man only laughed as he pulled her close, wrapping his arm around her waist and anchoring her against him.

"Stop! You're all wet!"

"I'm all wet, am I?" Kade's words were laced with laughter. "And whose fault is that?"

"I'm sorry—"

"Oh, right. You sound sorry." He directed the spray toward her again. "Ready to give up?"

As Caron sputtered and tried to squirm out of his arms, Kade held the hose over her head. He manipulated the grip, allowing it to shower down, dousing her with a cold spray that soaked her hair and T-shirt.

"Kade Webster, you stop right this instant!" She closed her eyes against the downpour and pushed against his shoulders.

A few seconds later, the stream of water stopped. She opened her eyes, and found herself staring into Kade's eyes, tiny droplets of water clinging to his eyelashes. He dropped the hose, not even seeming to notice how it clattered to the driveway. He moved his arm so that it encircled her back, pressing her up against the length of his body. With one hand, he pushed her wet hair back from her face.

"Caron—" Kade's voice pitched low, his fingers tangling in the wet strands of her hair and tugging her toward him with the lightest of pressure.

"What?" The one word was a mere whisper.

"Kiss me—please."

Caron closed her eyes, her kiss an immediate yes to his request. His lips were damp and cold from their recent battle, but within seconds heat flared through her body as his mouth warmed, his kiss slow and insistent.

"Oh, how I've missed you—" Kade's words were whispered against her ear, sending a shiver down her neck.

The embrace . . . the taste of Kade's mouth . . . it was achingly familiar, causing Caron to press herself closer as his arms tightened around her and his mouth found hers again.

Kade's kisses were so much more potent than Alex's kisses.

Alex.

"What am I doing?" Caron pressed her hands against Kade's chest, turning her face away from him.

"I think . . . it's pretty clear what you're doing." Kade pressed his lips to her jaw, trying to find her lips again. "I asked you to kiss me . . . and you did. Amazingly well, I might add."

Even as the huskiness of his voice lured her closer, she forced herself to step away. "I'm sorry."

"You're sorry . . ."

"I can't do this, Kade. I'm with Alex—"

His hands encircled her upper arms, pulling her toward him. "Don't be."

"*Don't be?* That's it? Just end my relationship with Alex like that?"

"There's obviously still something between you and me, Caron—"

"And how would I explain this to Alex? To my father?"

"Fool me once . . ." The light disappeared from Kade's eyes, his hands dropping to his sides. His inhale was sharp as he stepped away from her. "Our relationship never worked because there were always three people involved. You. Me. Your father."

"Kade—" A shiver ran through Caron's body.

"And ultimately, you chose your father. You just never bothered to tell me." He stepped away, increasing the distance between them. "You'll have to excuse me . . . the effects of those two muscle relaxers I took last night are wearing off. I'll finish washing the car later."

As Kade disappeared into the shadows of his garage, Caron wrapped her arms around her waist, water dripping from the hem of her T-shirt onto the ground. There was nothing else to say. No way to apologize for what had just happened . . . or to apologize for what had happened two years ago.

THIRTY

• ♥ • • •

$\mathcal{H}$e didn't know which hurt worse—the heat coursing through his back or the remnants of Caron's kisses that scorched his lips.

The first kiss ignited all his longings for Caron like the initial spark of fire to an abandoned building. He wanted her even more fiercely than he had when they dated two years ago. Like a man who'd been locked in the darkness of solitary confinement and been offered an unexpected pardon, kissing Caron overloaded his senses. Was he shaking because he was wet . . . cold . . . in pain, or because he was resisting the urge to walk back outside and grab her in his arms again and kiss her until the ache lodged in his chest disappeared?

Not going to happen.

He wasn't going back outside—and kissing Caron Hollister again wasn't going to ease all the hurt that had surged past the protective barrier he'd thought would keep his heart protected.

He'd played a dangerous game, hiring her to stage Eddie Kingston's home. But he'd been flat-out stupid to go outside when he saw her in his driveway this morning, washing his car. Why hadn't he taken his meds and gone back to sleep? Let Caron finish her little good deed for the day all by herself?

Kade shrugged into his dry robe, tossing his wet pajama bottoms into his tub. It didn't matter. The damage was done. He'd made a fool of himself over Caron Hollister—again.

He wanted nothing from Caron Hollister except for her to stage Eddie Kingston's house. He couldn't want anything more from her. All he needed to do was reestablish the professional boundaries and get through the next week. Pacing his empty bedroom, which was the room farthest away from the front of his house, Kade voice-dialed Mitch. Waited for him to answer. Groaned when it went to voice mail.

"Hey, it's Kade. Hope you're not too sore after the Mudder. I know it's Sunday. I slept through church. Can't go into the office, but I'm going to look at listings. Give me a call when you get this message, okay? Thanks."

He might as well do some work—or try to before the muscle relaxers kicked in. Put his effort into finding his clients the houses they were looking for since he'd failed—again—at getting what he'd wanted. Who he wanted.

.   .   .   .

"Caron, you know I will walk all the way to Denver and back with you if it takes that long for you to talk to me. That's what girlfriends do." Margo matched Caron's pace. "But I gotta admit I'm trying to figure out why you showed up here soaking wet just as I was getting home from church."

Caron paused on the sidewalk, her arms hanging by her sides, her T-shirt still damp. "He kissed me, Margo."

"What? Kade kissed you?"

"Yes."

"Glory hallelujah, girl!" Margo grabbed Caron's arms and tried to twirl her around, but when Caron stayed rooted in one place, she settled for a modified happy dance. "Why aren't you dancing in the street with me?"

"Because he kissed me. And I kissed him back . . . and it shouldn't have happened. I'm almost engaged to Alex—the perfect guy for me, remember?"

"If you recall, I don't think you should be marrying Mr. Perfect—and it's nothing against Alex. Besides, kissing another guy should have you seriously rethinking whether you really want to say 'I do' with Alex."

"The kiss was an accident."

"On whose part? Yours or Kade's?"

"Both." Caron swallowed back a sob. "I forfeited any chance with Kade two years ago when I broke up with him, Margo. I made my choice—"

"Did you make the choice you really wanted to make?"

"I made the only choice I could."

"Really, Caron?" Margo put a hand on her arm, stopping her from walking away. "You made the only choice you could? I'm going to have to disagree with you. A *choice* implies more than one option. You could have chosen to stay with Kade—"

"Not if I wanted to keep working with my dad."

"Well, not to be obvious, but how did that work out for you?"

"It was going well, until he made Nancy Miller his partner."

"So, you're saying life would be perfect if you could go back to things the way they were before Nancy Miller? You working for your father and dating Alex—being almost engaged."

"Yes."

That was the right answer, wasn't it?

"Then tell me this—"

"Margo, are we really going to do a Q&A out here on the sidewalk?"

"These aren't just random questions, my friend. These are life-changing ones. Why did you kiss Kade Webster? You had a choice there, too. Why didn't you stop it?"

"I did."

"Before or after you got lost in the moment? You don't have to answer that question out loud, but even if you don't, I think we both know the answer—"

"I can't talk about this anymore, Margo. I can't. I'm so confused . . ."

Margo stepped forward, wrapping her arms around Caron, not seeming to mind her damp clothes. "I know. I know. Come on home, get dry, and we can talk about this later—if you want to."

True to her word, Margo gave her space, waiting until Caron sought her out in the kitchen after she'd showered and changed into jeans and a long-sleeve Henley.

"So, any advice for me?"

Margo handed her a glass of iced tea, motioning for her to join her at the small table and picking up the conversation as if it hadn't been interrupted. "Have you ever thought that maybe you've got love all wrapped up with approval? That for you, love is a bunch of if-thens?"

"What does that mean?"

"If you do this or that or something else, then somebody will approve of you. And someone's approval means they love you. And for most of your life, you've wanted your father's approval so much you'd do and be anything he wanted—including walk away from Kade Webster, even though you loved him."

"I understand what you're saying, Margo. And I know you're saying it because you're seeing something I don't . . . that maybe I'm just beginning to see . . . but what do I do now?"

"Just think about what I said. Pray about it. I'll be praying, too. Nothing has to change today."

"But I'm afraid something did . . . and I don't know what to do. I didn't come out here to turn my personal life upside down." Caron shook her head. "And I can't think about Kade. Or me. Or what any of this means. Right now, I have to make sure everything is ready for the Tour of Homes."

"Okay, then you concentrate on the tour. I'll pray about this whole mess and you finish your job."

THIRTY-ONE

· · · ♥ · · ·

*I*n less than twenty-four hours, the first ticket holders for the Peak Tour of Homes would walk through the front doors of Eddie Kingston's house. And she was ready for them.

Almost.

Caron had been orchestrating the actual staging of the house for two days, all the while ignoring Margo's repeated protests that she had to relax. Her invitations to do something fun. Insisting she was content to watch the Fourth of July fireworks on the television while she rearranged furniture and moved accent pieces. And keeping so busy that she fell into bed exhausted every night so she couldn't agonize over the Sunday water battle that ended with Kade's heated kiss.

His bedroom set graced the master bedroom, accented with an untraditional bohemian-style quilt and a riot of pillows—something she knew Lacey's artistic eye would appreciate. Rustic twin platform beds and a matching dresser from Pottery Barn, complete with dinosaur-themed covers and a trio of well-placed stuffed reptiles, transformed one room into a boys' bedroom. The third bedroom was a nursery—all woodland-animal accents in muted oranges, greens, and browns, with a white crib and rocking chair. She'd opted for a traditional office, imagining Mitch working there as she hung some of Lacey's vivid photos of the Mudder on the walls, including the team helping Mitch conquer a high wall.

The living room would greet visitors with an expansive gray sectional sofa, a few throw pillows set along the back—white, muted teal, an abstract outline of a tree. One side table was set with a pewter vase of fresh wildflowers, while the other contained a well-placed set of classic books. Sunlight streamed through the floor-to-ceiling windows, unadorned with any sort of window treatment so that the backyard was showcased.

Caron paced through the kitchen. Clean. The counters gleamed, the breakfast bar lowered to accommodate a wheel-chair and set with yellow crockery plates and mugs. An oval glass bowl filled with oranges and lemons on loan from Margo's mother provided another burst of color.

All she needed was the furniture for the family room. Where was the delivery truck? Kade would be here any minute with Eddie Kingston to inspect everything. She'd remembered Vanessa's prayer for less than perfect in her life and was trying to embrace it—but how was she going to explain a less than tour-ready house to Kade?

After the horrible I'm-sorry-I-kissed-you blunder in his drive-way, she was all the more determined not to fail Kade Webster. She couldn't. The only reason she was here was to stage this house. And once that was done, she was going home to Alex.

There was nothing left to do but make a phone call.

"Hello? This is Caron Hollister. I'm calling about a delivery for a Peak Tour of Homes house. Yes, yes. Two chairs. A sofa and a love seat. Floor lamps."

"Oh, yes . . . Miss Hollister. We were going to call you . . ."

"Is there a problem?"

"Let me get my manager."

The manager? Something was wrong. But what could be wrong? The store manager had been eager to participate in the tour. The brochures were already made . . .

"Miss Hollister, this is Brian Woods."

"Brian. I was calling to check on the furniture you agreed to loan me for the tour this week. Everything was supposed to be delivered by now."

"Well, yes. I meant to call sooner—"

"Is there a problem?"

"Our warehouse flooded."

"Your warehouse . . . flooded?" Caron pivoted to stare out the sliding glass doors, where the summer sunshine lit the blue sky. "But it's not raining."

"There was some sort of electrical short and the emergency sprinklers were activated. We think it might have been a lightning strike. The fire department is here now and . . . well, we're still dealing with the mess. I'm afraid we won't be able to provide the furniture. I'm so sorry."

Caron covered her eyes with her hand, unwilling to face the sight of the empty room—the room that would remain empty. What could she say? "I understand. I'm . . . I'm sorry about what happened."

"Thank you. And I apologize if this creates a problem for you."

"No. No." Venting her panic on someone struggling to deal with problems of his own wouldn't do any good. "Don't worry about me. I'll figure something out."

Just as she ended the call, left alone to face four walls, a ceiling, and a floor, the front door opened.

"Hey, hotshot! You ready to give us the grand tour?" Kade's voice sounded through the house. "Where are you?"

"Here." Caron cleared her throat and forced herself to speak louder. Might as well get through the worst of it now. "I'm in the family room."

"The house looks great. I knew you'd pull it off—" Kade appeared in the archway leading from the kitchen, Eddie right behind him. "What's wrong?"

"There was a lightning strike."

"Where?" Kade and Eddie Kingston resembled a modern-day duo of Keystone Cops as they stumbled to a stop. "Here?"

"No. No, at the warehouse—the one that was donating furniture for this room." Caron motioned around the barren space. "You might notice there's nothing here."

"So what's plan B?"

Kade expected her to have plan B? Of course he did. She had to figure this out—that's why he'd hired her. And she had until the tour started tomorrow morning.

"Don't worry about it." Caron's high heels snapped against the wood floor. She needed to get the two men away from the starkness of the family room. "I'm on it. Let me show you the rest of the house and then I'll get back to handling this situation."

"Do you need any help?"

"Of course not. I've got it all under control." She moved past Kade, refusing to look him in the eye. If she did, he would know she was bluffing. And today was all about maintaining a professional distance.

Of course, at this moment, she had no plan B. Or C. Nothing. But she would handle this. She just didn't know how—yet.

Don't be rash, Caron.

Who invited her father into her head?

She hadn't been rash when she quit her job. Or when she took on this one. She'd had so much fun staging this house she had almost forgotten her life as a Realtor back in Florida. Almost.

She'd finish this job if she had to drive to Denver, buy what she needed at IKEA, and stay up all night assembling furniture.

Kade had waited for her by the kitchen island. "All right, then, it looks like you've got things under control here . . . except for—"

"Not your concern, Kade. I'm on it."

"I'm sure you'll figure it out. Eddie likes everything else you've done. And to be honest, I've got so much else to do, I'd be very little help to you today."

"Like I said, I've got it. Go on. Don't keep Eddie waiting."

. . .

Of course, now it was raining.

Caron parked her rental car behind Margo's building and stepped out into the deluge. Her hair and clothes were soaked within thirty seconds. As she took the wooden stairs leading to Margo's apartment, her feet seemed to land in every single puddle.

She stumbled through the door, kicking off her waterlogged high heels, her hair hanging limp around her face and shoulders.

"Are you going to make it a habit of showing up at my door soaked to the skin?" Margo teased with a warm smile, dropping the bridal magazine she'd been reading onto the floor.

"It's raining." Caron raked her fingers through her hair, shoving it back out of her face. "I need your couch."

"It's raining . . . and you need . . . my couch? Why?"

"And your floor lamp, too. If you had a coffee table, I'd take that. Do you know anyone I can borrow a coffee table from?"

"Caron, what are you talking about? Are you trying to outfit an ark?"

"I'm desperate. One room of furniture didn't show up for the tour—thanks to a lightning strike at the warehouse." Caron buried her face in her hands, muffling the slightly crazed laugh that escaped. "Can you believe it? An act of God is going to ruin my efforts to stage this home for Kade Webster."

Margo gripped her shoulders, forcing Caron to look at her. "Calm down. Deep breaths. What can I do to help?"

Caron could have just collapsed on the floor, but settled for leaning against the wall.

"I can't blow this, Margo. I—I just can't."

"You won't. If you need my couch for the next five days, fine. It's yours. What else? You can have every single piece of furniture in this apartment."

"I need to rent a U-Haul truck. And maybe . . . let me call Lacey and see what she might have. If she doesn't have what I need, then we're going shopping."

"Call Lacey. I'll call the U-Haul place."

"Okay. Let me give you my credit card—" Caron stopped. "Where's my purse? Oh, Peter, Paul, and Mary! I left my purse in the car! I'll be right back."

Margo blocked her exit. "I'll get your purse. Call Lacey. Figure out what she does or doesn't have. Let me know if you need a mirror or something. My coworker has some interesting antiques, and she might let us borrow them."

As Margo barged out into the rain, Caron dialed Lacey, analyzing the couch in an effort to determine how to pull the family room together, starting with a red-fabric sofa.

Hours later, Caron stood in the Kingston house family room, Lacey on one side of her, Margo on the other.

"What time is it?"

"Just after midnight." Margo looped her arm through hers. "Are you satisfied?"

"I'm so bleary-eyed, I'm having trouble seeing the room. How does it look?"

"Spectacular. Doesn't it, Lacey?" Margo slung her other arm over Lacey's shoulder, anchoring the trio together. "Caron, what you had planned couldn't have been better than this."

"I love how just a few fun decorative pillows add a little zing to the couch." Lacey moved back and forth, causing the group to sway.

"Just don't rearrange them again, Lacey. Speaking of the pillows, Caron, can I buy those? I don't want to go back to a plain old couch after seeing this."

"After coming to my rescue, you can have them. Consider them a thank-you gift." Caron ticked items off her fingertips. "Couch, end tables, lamps, your friend's mirror . . . what am I forgetting?"

"Nothing. It's great." Margo grabbed her hand to lead her out of the room. "You just need to do one last walk-through, turn out the lights, and go home and get some rest."

"The room's a little emptier than I'd planned, but it can't be helped."

"It's marvelous. The entire house is. You've showcased what can be done for someone in a wheelchair like Mitch." Lacey sighed. "I confess I've let myself daydream about this house ever since the first time I saw it. Maybe one day Mitch and I'll have something even half as nice. I'll be content with any type of house that convinces Mitch that we can get married."

With everything else going on—the good, the bad, the confusing—Caron hadn't checked back with Miriam on the donation total for Mitch in days. Were they even close? She added another item to her diminishing mental to-do list.

"Okay, one last walk-through. Then we all get some sleep and I'm back here to meet Kade in the morning to make sure he likes what he sees—" She stumbled to a halt. "And then I'll be getting ready to head back to Florida."

"What? No." Lacey sounded as if she wanted to block the front door to keep Caron from leaving.

"Yeah. I mean, I'll stay around to un-stage the house, but that doesn't take long at all. After that, my work here is done. Time to go home."

"But you'll be back for my wedding the first weekend in August." Margo linked her arms through Caron and Lacey's. "That's only a couple of weeks away."

"Right." Caron mustered up a smile. "We can look forward to that."

"Is Alex coming?" Margo's question was spoken into the darkness as Caron turned off the lights.

"That's the plan."

"Plans can change, right?"

Caron shouldered her purse. "There's no reason for plans to change . . ."

"Caron, we've talked about this—"

"And I've told you, I can't think about this right now—"

Lacey stepped between them. "And I have no idea what you two are talking about. But I do know it's late. We're all tired. It's time to head home."

"You're right." Caron whispered a quick *thank you* as they moved toward her car.

"We're not done talking about this." Margo leaned around Lacey.

"Yes, yes we are."

And come tomorrow, she'd be so busy that she wouldn't see Margo until it was time to pack her bags and head back to Florida.

THIRTY-TWO

• • • ♥ • • •

What was he doing, showing up at Jessica's on a Sunday? Alex couldn't hide behind the excuse of a malfunctioning air conditioner or a broken washing machine. Or that he was here to pick up those leftovers she'd mentioned. Too many days had passed for that.

No, he wanted to talk to her—it was that simple and that complicated, all at the same time. There was nothing easy about trying to explain what Jessica had learned about his family on the evening news. His mother, bloodied and battered. And drunk. Her car surrounded by two police cruisers, blue and white lights flashing, after sideswiping several other parked cars in the shopping center, and then crashing into the back end of another.

Jessica's words of comfort had echoed in his mind for days, luring him back to her house. He'd thank her for praying and understanding. Ask how Scotty was.

And then be on his way.

A soft rap on the driver's-side window interrupted his attempt to untangle his thoughts. Jessica stood beside his car, motioning for him to roll down his window.

"Hi." He cut the engine, the car's air-conditioner-cooled air mixing with the sun-warmed air and humidity outside.

She rested her hands against the edge of the half-rolled-down window, bending low to see his face. "You gonna sit here all day? You pulled up a good ten minutes ago."

"Uh, yeah. I mean no. I was . . . thinking."

"You came to sit in front of my house and think?" She scrunched her nose, causing her glasses to tilt. "Okay. I'll leave you to your thinking, then."

"No." As he eased open the car door, Jessica stepped back onto the sidewalk. "I wanted to see you—and Scotty."

"Afraid you're stuck with just me. Scotty was invited to go swimming with a friend." She motioned back toward the house. "I've got a backlog of work to catch up on."

Alex halted at the edge of the walkway leading to Jessica's front door. "I'm sorry. I didn't mean to interrupt."

"You're not interrupting. I needed a break. Join me for some lemonade and tell me how you're doing."

Since your mother's car accident.

Jessica didn't say the words, but they hung in the air between them. And he was here to talk about his mother. Kind of.

"You good with lemonade? It's homemade."

Of course it was. The woman probably made her own bread. He wouldn't be surprised to show up one day and find chickens wandering in the backyard. Her reddish-gold hair was pulled up in a ponytail, but soft tendrils floated free and framed her face, a few pieces laying against the nape of her neck. A red T-shirt dress skimmed her slender frame, and she slipped off casual black flip-flops as she entered the house.

"Sounds perfect."

Files and her dictation equipment covered the dining room table, but other than that, the house was picked up, no sign of a five-year-old. A bouquet of yellow roses sat in a glass vase in the middle of the table.

Who was bringing Jessica flowers?

"Nice roses."

"They were marked down at the grocery store. Scotty insisted on buying them for me. Cute, huh?"

"Yeah. Raising him right and teaching him young to buy a woman flowers." Something akin to relief coursed through him. Not that he had any reason to be bothered that some other guy might be paying attention to Jessica.

"I'll make sure he knows there's more to treating a woman right than bringing her flowers, although it's a start."

She handed him a glass of lemonade and motioned him back to the living room.

"Oh, really? What else are you going to teach him?" He settled on the couch, Jessica taking the corner opposite him.

"I know people say actions speak louder than words, but I consider what a man says is just as important. The whole let-your-yes-be-yes-and-your-no-be-no principle." She stared into the depths of her glass. "I want Scotty to be a man of his word. To say what he means and mean what he says. That kind of guy is hard to come by."

"I take it his father was not that kind of guy?"

"No, he was not, and short of a miracle, he never will be. Not that I don't believe in miracles, but—" Jessica waved her hand, as if dispersing her words into thin air. "Enough about me. How is your mother?"

"She's better. She's going to be in the cast for a while, but her headache is gone and she's off her pain meds."

Jessica paused, tilting her head, hesitating just a moment before she spoke. "And . . . she realizes she made a mistake?"

"What?"

"Your mom realizes drinking and driving was a mistake, right? I mean, you and your dad had that conversation with her?"

He should have expected Jessica to shoot straight. Giving her honest answers after years of dodging and ducking reality? That was the hard part.

"There's . . . no point in having that conversation with her."

A small V formed between Jessica's eyebrows. "Why would you say something like that?"

"Because this isn't the first time my mother has been arrested for a DUI." The admission seemed to increase the pressure building behind his eyes. "It's the first time in a long time . . . but not the first time."

"Are you saying your mother is an alcoholic?"

"Yes." The word came out low—almost a whisper, the one syllable caustic. "She usually doesn't end up in the news. Her doctor's labeled her a 'functioning alcoholic.'"

Jessica shook her head. "What does that mean?"

"Most days she manages. And we manage. Her drinking is controlled. Things seem normal. At least, it's my family's normal. My mother knows her limits. She doesn't drive."

"Okay. Then can you help me understand what happened?"

"The anniversary of my younger brother's death was in mid-May—" Alex swiped his hand across his face. He was mangling this. "I told you about my younger brother, Shawn, right?"

"Yes."

"I can't believe it's been twenty years." Alex shook his head. "My mother always struggles around the time of Shawn's death, but this year it seems harder for her. I don't know why."

Saying it out loud to Jessica—the reality of how long ago Shawn died—ran through Alex like an electric current. One year had bled into the next . . . trying to find a way out of the despair that suffocated his mother. Failing. And then adapting.

"My father and I tried to help her at first. We went to a couple of different counselors early on. My mother hated them. She drank before the sessions. After the sessions. I don't know if she was sober when she went there. I was ten when my brother died. What did I know back then? After a year, my father insisted she go to rehab. She left the program. We hid the alcohol. She found it. My father refused to have any in the house. She would go out and buy it on her own, or hang out at the local bar. I never knew what I was coming home to after school." The words spilled out like sewage from a drainpipe. "Do you know what it's like to get called to the principal's office and have to go home because your mother's sick? Only you know she's not sick? She's drunk?"

"Alex, I'm—"

"And my father . . . after a while, he bailed on the whole situation." Details he'd blocked for years forced their way past the barricades he'd erected. "I'm at the grocery store one day. I'm maybe twelve years old. Trying to buy groceries so I have something for dinner—something for lunch the next day at school. And I don't have enough money. The cashier asks me where my mother is. I can't tell the lady that my mother's passed out at home. So I just ran out of the store. I was able to scrounge enough change to call my dad. And he tells me to just handle it. He's busy at work and he tells me to stop bothering him. Did he think I wanted him to lose the business? Not be able to pay the bills?"

His words seemed to pollute the air with unwanted memories from the past, unlocked from some hidden room in his memory. The broken silence afterward was filled with his harsh panting.

"Oh, Alex." Jessica tugged at his shoulders, pulling him into an embrace. "I'm sorry. I didn't know."

"No one knows. It's the family secret. And I'm responsible for it."

Her touch, gentle and soothing as she rubbed light circles on his back, caused a shudder to run through him. "Maybe you can't help your mother or your father. But you have to help yourself, Alex."

"Help myself? I'm not the one with the drinking problem."

"Have you ever talked to anyone about this?"

"Only Caron. She knows my secret."

"I mean someone who can help you sort through all this. A counselor."

"I don't do counselors."

Jessica sat silent for a few moments, just letting him rest. When she spoke, she continued to hold him, offer him the comfort of her embrace. "What do you do when an air conditioner or heater is broken?"

What kind of question is that?

"I fix them."

"I know you can't fix your mom. And you can't change your dad. But you can take care of yourself. They have Al-Anon meetings for families of alcoholics. Have you ever attended one? Your mother isn't the only one who needs healing—you do, too. Pray about going to a meeting or finding a counselor to talk with about losing your brother and how much it has affected your family."

He shifted away from her. Why couldn't she understand? "I was talking about my mother."

"But this affects you—"

"I'm handling this the best I know how."

"Alex, I'm not trying to argue with you." When she reached out to him, he shifted farther away. "You've been so honest with me tonight, and you didn't have to even talk to me at all. I just think . . . maybe you should consider changing how you've handled this situation because it's hurting you. You've shoved this family secret into a closet, thinking you can ignore it. But it's still there—banging at the door, screaming to get out. Your brother's death . . . your mother's drinking . . . even your father's choices . . . they're still hurting you. Keeping secrets in your family certainly hasn't helped you, your mother, or your father, has it? Maybe it's time to be honest about all that."

"Just because you've fed me a couple of times . . . that doesn't give you any right to butt in on my private life—"

She retreated to the opposite corner of the couch, but not before he glimpsed the tears welling up in her eyes.

"I . . . care about you, Alex. You've been kind to me . . . and to Scotty."

"Look, I'm sorry—"

"Don't apologize." She sucked in a breath. "The truth is, I'm not going to apologize, either—not for anything I said to you. I can't. I believe with all my heart that you need help. You need to recognize how your brother's death is still controlling your family all these years later. Maybe you're right. You can't change your mother or your father—but you can save yourself."

"I don't need saving."

"That's where you're wrong. I can hear in your voice how this is killing you. God doesn't want us to live trapped in desperate situations, without hope."

"God . . . don't talk to me about God. The driver of that car didn't just kill my brother. He destroyed my entire family. And God allowed it." He hurled the words at Jessica and then recoiled as if they had backlashed and hit him. "I—I didn't mean that."

"Yes, you did." Jessica reached for him again, and then pulled her hand back. "God knows our thoughts, Alex. Do you think you've hidden any of that from him all these years?"

"I didn't even know I felt that way—"

"Being honest is where healing begins. God is big enough to handle our honest emotions, no matter what they are."

"I need to go." Alex pushed himself to his feet, his lemonade untouched. "I'm sure you need to get some work done."

"I know. You do, too." She stood in the doorway, forcing the semblance of a smile. "Thank you for coming by."

"Thank you for listening." This all felt so final, but what else could it be? "Tell Scotty that I said hi."

"Of course I will."

"And you know who to call if you have any trouble with your air conditioner—"

"But I won't. You installed a reliable unit."

"Keep up on the annual maintenance."

"I will." She stepped back into the house. "Goodbye, Alex."

He couldn't think of anything else to say. Couldn't think of another reason to continue talking with her. And why should he? She was a customer who had become an acquaintance. Nothing more.

"Take care, Jessica."

"You, too. Thank you for everything. I'll be praying for you."

Her words followed him as he drove away. He needed her prayers. He certainly couldn't pray for himself.

THIRTY-THREE

· · ♥ · ·

*O*ne more day to go.

After tomorrow night, the Peak Tour of Homes would be over. Considering that he'd won two awards from the panel of judges, Eddie already considered the tour a success. And Kade had his own victories, connecting with a number of potential real estate clients as well as looking forward to discussing a future business relationship with Kingston.

Carrying one of the cans of touch-up paint, Caron surveyed the hallway leading to the bedrooms. Last day or not, she still needed to ensure the walls were mar-free. At least she could paint in bare feet.

"Caron?" Kade's voice sounded through the house. "Are you here?"

"Of course I am." She applied paint to a small spot on the wall. If she focused on a chore, she could maintain a professional distance with Kade. "Doing the nightly touch-up work."

"Good. I wanted to talk with you."

"Can we talk while I paint?"

"I don't see why not." He motioned for Caron to hand him the paintbrush. "Let me do that."

Caron couldn't hold back a laugh, half turning away. "You're still in your suit and tie, Kade. There's no way I'm handing over this paintbrush. I'm almost done—"

"What if the boss says hand it over?"

"Oh, please. You're going to pull the boss line on me again? Besides, I just finished the last mark."

"Fine. You win this time." He nodded back toward the main area of the house. "I need to show you something."

Caron exhaled a sigh. They'd managed to regain some sort of normalcy during the tour week, both of them too busy to stay in the past. "What?"

Kade waited while she deposited the can of paint, the paintbrush inside, on the kitchen island, and then pulled an envelope out of the inside of his coat pocket. "This."

Caron rinsed her hands with soap and water, drying them with a length of paper towel. "And what is this?"

"Open it." Kade's infectious grin almost slipped past her defenses. Almost.

"O-kay. You certainly are having fun with all of this."

The envelope wasn't sealed, and she removed a check, her eyes widening at the amount. "Kade! This is a cashier's check for . . . for thirty-five thousand dollars!"

"I know."

"And it's made out to Mitch."

"I know." Kade's smile widened, his eyes glinting.

"Is that all you can say? *I know?*" Caron threw her arms around him, erupting in a high-pitched yell. "Thirty-five thousand dollars! For Mitch."

His arms came up around her, his laughter low and alluring. "Glad you're happy about this, hotshot. Just lower the decibels a bit."

Their laughter blended together for a moment and then faded into the silence of the room. Caron stilled. She was in Kade's arms. Her heart pounded against her ribs, her breath hitching as her fingers almost strayed to the softness of his hair at the nape of his neck. Kade's eyes locked with hers. He waited, his arms locked around her waist.

With a slight pressure against his shoulders, Caron slipped from his embrace. "I . . . apologize. I got a bit excited when I saw the amount of the check."

Kade remained still. And then he blinked, his Adam's apple working in his throat. "Understandable. It's an amazing amount of money. And you know what is even more amazing?"

Caron couldn't suppress the shiver that coursed through her body. "There's more?"

"Yes. Even with several offers on the house—good offers— Eddie agreed to sell it to Mitch at cost."

Caron stepped back, clasping her hands in front of her. She needed to focus on being happy for Mitch and Lacey. Nothing else. "Have you told Mitch yet?"

"No, I want to do it right. There's still a bit of prep that I have to do."

"What kind of prep work?"

"Just a little promise I made to him about when we found the right house—something involving a big red bow."

"Then I need to give the check back to you—" She stopped. Where was the cashier's check? There. On the floor. Probably dropped while they were . . . distracted. "Oh, wow. I'm so sorry."

She scrambled to pick it up before Kade could move, holding it out to him with a flourish. "There. Don't want to delay the surprise any longer than we have to."

"You're part of this, too, you know. The letter you put

together and sent out worked wonders. Donations started pouring into the office. Miriam said she had a challenging time keeping up with all of the letters and checks."

"I only started the process. So many people made it happen."

"Miriam kept the letters people sent. She said she wanted Mitch and Lacey to read them."

"You know you need to give her a raise, right?" Caron began rinsing the paintbrush again—anything to distract her from that too-close moment. "She's been a great help during the tour prep."

"You're right, I do."

"I'm so glad you stopped by to tell me this. What a wonderful end to the week."

He put the crumpled check back into the envelope, sliding it into his pocket. "No worse for a little celebratory wear."

"Good. I still can't believe it." She rinsed and rerinsed the paintbrush. "I'll just finish up here and then head home."

Kade stood next to her. "Caron, I want to—"

"It's been a long week, Kade." Caron stiffened. "Let's just get through the tour, okay? Please."

.   .   .

Kade wrapped the light cotton blanket around his bare shoulders, huddling on the edge of his couch. Despite the dull ache in his lower back, he refused to take a painkiller. Time to tough it out. In a couple of days, he'd be sleeping in his bed again.

His life would be back to normal.

But as he sat in the darkness of his living room, he couldn't escape the reality that he'd bungled those few moments he'd spent with Caron earlier that evening.

Kade had showed up after the end of the tour to tell her about the huge amount of money people had donated for

Mitch and Lacey. Show her the check. Share a few celebratory moments. And leave.

But then she'd jumped into his arms and his traitorous heart was wide open to her again. Defenseless. He wanted to hold her and never let her go. Forget about the guy waiting for her back in Florida. Kiss her until she remembered him and what they'd had.

With a muffled groan, Kade fought against the heated wave of desire that rose inside of him. Caron was leaving him again, but at least this time there was no surprise. She was staying true to her word. She'd done the job he asked of her and now she was going home.

Kade stretched out on the couch, resting his head on his pillow and staring at the ceiling.

He'd survived losing Caron Hollister once before. He'd do it again.

THIRTY-FOUR

• ♥ • ♥ • ♥ •

*T*his was her last day in her office at Webster Select Realty and she'd never bothered to bring in a plant as Kade had suggested.

Caron rested her elbows on the desktop, surveying the bare walls. If things went as well as Kade expected following the success of the tour, he'd be hiring a full-time Realtor who would decorate this office. Hang some pictures on the walls. Stash favorite snacks in the bottom drawer. Have Miriam order business cards.

In just a few short hours, the Peak Tour of Homes would be over. Her job almost done. There'd be a few more phone calls—reminders about picking up loaner furniture and confirming the two U-Hauls she needed on Saturday, as well as connecting with the team of movers to load and unload things, and she'd be almost to the end of her responsibilities. Then she'd check in for her flight back home on Sunday.

Would there be any time for her and Kade to talk? To somehow say goodbye and end this standoff between them?

"Caron?" With a metallic buzz, Miriam's voice came through the intercom on her phone console.

"Yes, Miriam?"

"You've got a call on line one. A Russell Hollister."

Caron's hand froze over the phone panel. Her father? Why was he calling her—and at work?

"Thank you, Miriam."

The small red light beckoned, even as Caron hesitated taking the call. She hadn't seen or talked to her father in weeks. But his easy dismissal of her and his disapproval of her decision to work for Kade even temporarily had shadowed her, adding fuel to her determination to do well.

Why was she avoiding a conversation? What could her father do to her over the phone?

Or rather, what could he do that he hadn't already done?

Flexing her fingers to stop them from shaking, Caron straightened her shoulders. "Hello, this is Caron Hollister."

"Caron. How are you?"

Okay. They'd start with the basics.

"I'm fine. Just wrapped up the tour."

"I trust that went well?"

"Yes. Very well."

"Glad to hear it. Knowing you, I'm not surprised."

Even such an inconsequential compliment stalled Caron's response. "Th-thank you."

"And Alex says you're heading home now."

"Yes. I have a flight back on Sunday."

"Good. That's why I'm calling. I tried reaching you on your cell, but you didn't answer."

Caron hauled her handbag out from beneath her desk, digging through it to find her phone. Sure enough, there was a missed call from her father. She'd been so distracted she hadn't even heard her cell phone ring.

"Caron, are you there?"

"I'm sorry. Yes. I'm here."

Her father's tone transitioned from casual to businesslike. "Good. I was saying that I'd like you to come back and work for me again."

Caron dropped her phone onto the top of her desk. What? She couldn't have heard her father correctly. How many times had she replayed her last day at work with her father? His don't-be-foolish-enough-to-think-there'll-be-a-job-waiting-for-you-here-when-you-realize-your-mistake response to her decision to quit.

"Caron? I assume you haven't found another job yet, have you?"

"No, sir."

"Good. I was discussing plans for Hollister Realty Group with Nancy Miller. She asked me why I let such a valuable employee like you go." Her father cleared his throat. "My explanation of the situation didn't deter her from insisting I call you. We'd like . . . I'd like you to be part of the Hollister team again."

"But you said—"

"It'd be wise if we both forget what we said the day I announced the partnership with Nancy Miller, don't you think? Things can't be unsaid, but we both know there are some decisions that can be undone. Your office is empty. Shall I tell Shelby to expect to see you next week?"

Her father had done the unthinkable. He'd offered her a job with him again. Another chance.

"I—I'd love to come back to work. To be honest, I have some ideas—"

"Of course you do. We can talk about it next week."

"Wonderful."

"Have a good trip."

"Thank you." Caron bit back the words *Tell Mom I said hello.* Best to keep family and business separate. "Goodbye."

She pressed her palms against her face, staring at the phone as if she expected it to ring again. When she picked up the receiver, someone would announce the whole conversation had been a joke. Or an exhaustion-fueled hallucination.

Caron resisted the urge to twirl around in her chair, swallowing back a just-contained jubilant yell. How had this happened? She'd hoped the last few weeks would provide space enough to ease the tension with her father. She'd never imagined that coming to Colorado would be the way God worked reconciliation between them.

.   .   .

At the click of the front door closing, Kade rolled his shoulders and loosened his tie. What a subdued ending to all the planning, all the anticipation, and all the hard work that had gone into the Peak Tour of Homes. Weeks of mental and physical labor were over. No more people streaming through the rooms. No more splitting shifts with Mitch, networking with potential clients while maintaining their regular workloads.

And no need to maintain a controlled distance with Caron. She'd done what he'd asked of her and staged the home with enthusiasm and creativity. It was no one else's fault but his own that he wanted more with her. That he still wanted the future he'd lost two years ago.

With a shake of his head, Kade dispersed the thoughts threatening to pull his emotions under. He may not have reason to celebrate, but Mitch did.

Kade found his friend in the living room, his wheelchair facing the glass doors that led out to the backyard.

"And that's that." Kade clapped Mitch on the back.

"I never realized how much work was involved in a Tour of Homes."

"Nonstop people. Nonstop PR."

"Kingston's house got a lot of good press."

"Eddie told me that one of the local news stations is coming through tomorrow."

"That's great." Mitch shifted his shoulders, positioning his hands on the sides of his wheelchair. "Well, I'm going to head home."

"Mitch. There's just one more thing—"

"Can we table it until tomorrow? Lacey's making her world-famous grilled pizzas to celebrate the end of the tour—"

"World-famous, huh?"

"Yeah. As far as I'm concerned, they should be."

"Can I contribute a little something to the celebration?"

"Okay."

"If you'll just follow me." Kade did an about-face.

"Where are we going?"

Kade waited to say anything until he stood next to the front door. "Right here."

"And we're at the front door because . . . ?"

"Because I need you to see this."

Kade pulled open the door to reveal the huge red bow he'd put in place just moments ago. A white envelope labeled *For Mitch and Lacey* was taped beneath it.

"What is this?" Mitch never took his eyes off the bow and envelope.

"I can understand your confusion. It's not exactly what I promised to do when I found you a house."

Mitch shook his head, a grimace marring his face. "You have never been good at jokes, buddy."

"I would not joke about this." Kade removed the envelope and handed it to his friend.

"What is this?"

"Open it."

Kade bit back a smile as Mitch opened the envelope and slid out the check. Stared at it and then looked at him. "Kade . . . what is going on?"

"You're a homeowner, Mitch. Well, you are if you want this house." The grin he'd been hiding threatened to split his face. "That is your down payment. And Eddie Kingston is dropping the price of the house by a hundred thousand dollars."

"What?" Mitch's hand shook. "How did you do this?"

"I can't take all the credit. Caron started the process. She drafted a fund-raising letter and Miriam sent it out. To family. Classmates. Other Rangers. Donations flooded in. People spread the word. And when I approached Eddie with the idea . . . well, he didn't hesitate. He's former military. There's military all through his family. His niece is hoping to make it into the naval academy."

Mitch dropped the check into his lap, covering his eyes with his hand.

"Hey—" Kade crouched beside the wheelchair, gripping the arm. "What's going on? I thought you'd be happy—"

"How do I . . . accept this?"

"Don't overthink what you've been given. People wanted to do this. Everyone was excited to help you and Lacey." Kade waited until his friend made eye contact with him. "Say thank you. Buy the house. Set a wedding date with Lacey. You've both waited long enough, don't you think?"

"Yeah. Yeah, we have." Mitch replaced the check in the envelope. "Looks like Lacey and I are going to be celebrating a lot more than the end of the tour tonight."

Kade rose to his feet. "Then I won't keep you."

Mitch gripped his hand. "Thank you, Kade. You don't know what this means for me . . . for Lacey . . ."

"You're welcome. Now go on home. Surprise your girlfriend."

"You mean my bride-to-be."

"Oho! Are you proposing tonight, too?"

"Not tonight. But soon." Mitch exited through the door Kade held open. "Soon."

Kade followed Mitch out to his specialized van, waving one final goodbye. Maybe one day he would know how his friend felt. When suddenly what you wanted—*who* you wanted—became a beautiful certainty.

THIRTY-FIVE

* * ♥ * *

Margo stood in the doorway of the guest bedroom, her lips pressed together into a thin line. Caron tried to ignore her friend's silence as she folded another blouse and laid it on top of the clothes already placed in her suitcase on top of the bed covered with clothes waiting to be packed.

As Caron selected another top, Margo shifted her stance, a deep sigh invading the room.

"Oh, for goodness' sakes, Margo. *Say something.*" Caron shook out the blouse with a sharp snap of the silk material. "Your just standing there and sighing is torture!"

"I can't believe you're really doing this."

"Doing what? Packing? It's what people do before they get on an airplane and fly back home."

"Ha ha. You're hysterical. You know what I mean."

"No, I don't know what you mean. I'm packing. I'm going home. It was the plan all along."

"But you love—"

"Alex. I love Alex. And I'm working with my father again."

"And that's the most ridiculous part of all. Why are you going back to work for your father? When you talked about how much you enjoyed staging the house, I thought maybe you were thinking about being a home stager."

"I still am. I'm going to talk to my dad about eventually transitioning out of being a Realtor and becoming the company's home stager." Caron added a dress to the suitcase. "I can work as a Realtor while we build up that part of the business. It won't happen overnight."

"And you'll marry Alex and live happily ever after—"

"Margo, you're marrying the man you want to marry. Why can't I do the same thing?"

"Because you're marrying the wrong guy!"

"Well, you don't get to decide for me, do you?"

"Does Kade know about any of this?"

"It's been the plan all along, so yes, he knows I'm leaving. He doesn't need to know anything else."

Margo shook her head. "Did you say goodbye?"

"Not exactly."

"And what does that mean?"

"He was still at Eddie Kingston's house when I left Friday. And I didn't see him today while we un-staged the home. Eddie came by and thanked me for everything."

"So you're going to do it again?"

"Do what again?"

"Leave Kade without having the decency to say goodbye."

"We are not in a relationship—"

"You worked for the man for almost a month, Caron. You say goodbye."

"Fine. I'll call him—"

"Face-to-face. Finish it right."

"I'm packing."

"You're being a coward."

She whirled around to confront her friend, rather than continue the conversation by talking over her shoulder. "What do you expect me to do? Call him and ask to come over to his condo to say goodbye?"

"No. Just drive over there. Tell him thank you for the job. Say goodbye. It's called closure." Margo was almost pleading with her. "You're going to see him in a few weeks again, you know, when you come out for my wedding. Ronny and I decided to invite him because he's helped us so much with house-hunting. Maybe if you do this the right way now, things will be less messy then."

"I need to pack—"

Margo shouldered her way in front of the suitcase. "I can finish this. But I can't say goodbye to Kade Webster for you."

•   •   •

His life was almost back in order.

Kade shut his bedroom door, where his furniture was in place. He pressed his hand against his lower back, where an unexpected hot twinge had slowed his movements as he'd made up the bed with clean sheets. Sleeping on the couch had ensured the success of the tour, but too many nights he fought faint memories of Caron sitting beside him, her fingertips caressing the side of his face.

Had he dreamed that?

He hadn't dreamed their water battle. Or their kisses. There was no doubting the passion that flared between them. Or how Caron's rejection extinguished it.

And come tomorrow, she'd be back in Florida and he could breathe again, with thousands of miles between him and all the ways she still tempted him.

The sound of his doorbell detoured him from the kitchen to his front door. It was almost nine o'clock. Who would be—

"Hello, Kade." A hesitant smile accompanied Caron's greeting.

Kade gripped the door. "Caron. I wasn't expecting you."

"Yes. Well, I hadn't expected to come over, but—" She tilted her head. "May I come in?"

No.

"Sure."

With a wave of his arm, he ushered her past him. He closed his eyes, forcing himself to ignore how good she looked in a pair of casual black jeans and a scooped-neck top, her blond hair loose around her face.

He sat on the back of his couch while Caron stood in the area between his living room and dining room, twisting the strap of her leather purse.

"I, uh, assume the crew delivered your furniture."

"Yep. Set it up for me, too. I'll be a happy man tonight, sleeping in my own bed."

Caron's soft laugh almost slipped past his defenses. Almost. "I imagine the couch gets old after a few days."

"Well, we all had to do our part to make the Tour of Homes a success." Kade nodded. "And it was that. Thank you."

"You're welcome. I loved being a part of this project, Kade. Thank you for asking me to help."

"I knew you could do it."

"You've always believed in me . . . and that means a lot."

"You're welcome."

Not that believing in her—loving her—was enough . . . because she was here to say goodbye.

The reality caused Kade to stand, as if he could ground himself by placing his two feet on the floor.

"I came to say—"

"Don't." With two quick strides he closed the space between them. "Don't do it."

"Don't say goodbye?"

"Would it make any difference if you knew I still loved you?"

"Kade—"

"Because I do." He grasped her shoulders, pulled her close enough so that he could see how her topaz-brown eyes widened. "I love you, Caron."

Without waiting for her response, without asking for permission, Kade kissed her, allowing his hands to slide down the soft skin of her bare arms, reaching around her to pull her close. For a moment, Caron stiffened, but then her lips softened beneath his as she returned his kiss. As her hands stole up and gripped his shoulders, Kade began to lose himself in their kiss . . . the warmth of Caron's body against his . . .

But then she groaned and pushed against him, stepping away, one hand pressed against the side of her face. "Kade . . . no. We can't do this . . . I'm going back to Florida."

He covered her hand with his own, even as her words chipped away at his courage. "Stay with me, Caron. We're good together. You know we are."

"There's Alex . . ." Her glance wavered. "And my father."

Kade's hand dropped to his side. He'd expected Caron's heart might waver between him and her boyfriend—but the mention of her father hit him like she'd thrown a bucket of cold water in his face. How was he supposed to know he was fighting not one but two opponents? "What does your father have to do with this?"

"My father called and offered me a job again."

"Oh, that's rich." Kade pressed the heel of his hand against his forehead. "A month after you quit working for him—after you declared your independence—and you're ready to go back to work with Daddy."

"Kade, after slamming the door in my face, *my father called and asked me to come back*. You know what my father is like. He never changes his mind about anything."

"You're right. I do know your father, Caron. Well enough to know he never does anything that doesn't benefit him."

Caron's words were a ragged whisper. "Can't you be happy for me? I'm getting my dream."

"You ask too much of a man, Caron. I'll give you this—at least this time you had the decency to tell me why you were leaving. " Kade turned his face away as he moved past her. "I'll save you the need to say goodbye."

·   ·   ·

The gate for her upcoming flight was empty, but the automated sign confirmed she was at the right location, despite the rows and rows of empty seats. Caron separated herself from the ever-moving crowd of people still searching for their gates—hauling carry-on luggage, clutching insulated cups of coffee, some so disheveled they looked as if they'd spent the last week lost in the airport with no hope of rescue. With a sigh that deflated her shoulders, she deposited her tote on a chair facing the expansive windows.

With a muffled roar of its jet engines, a single plane backed away from the row of other airplanes, a lone man wearing an orange safety vest and protective headgear motioning the pilot to continue moving toward the runway. The area outside where her plane would arrive stood empty. What with allowing more than enough time to return the rental car and get through security—and just needing to get out of Colorado—three hours stretched before Caron before her departure for Florida.

Too much time to think.

Not that she hadn't done just that ever since Kade had left her standing in his apartment, disappearing into his bedroom, slamming the door behind him.

"Why didn't you go after him?" Margo followed her outside to *the rental car as Caron stowed her luggage in the trunk.*

"What? Knock on his bedroom door and continue a useless conversation?"

"Yes."

"Why?" Caron faced her friend, arms folded across her chest.

"Caron, come on! You still have feelings for Kade! You know you do."

"I'm not arguing about this anymore, Margo. I came here to stage a home, not get involved with Kade Webster again. My job is done." She pulled the keys out of her purse. "Now tell me goodbye because I'm going home. To Alex."

Margo said nothing as Caron hugged her. "I'll see you for your wedding—and Alex will be with me. And I hope as my friend, you'll support me."

A plane lifted off the runway, seemingly effortless in its defiance of gravity. Within seconds, it was a mere speck on the horizon.

Alex would enjoy Sunday lunch with their families and then be waiting for her at the airport tonight. She'd leave all this . . . confusion behind her in Colorado. Return home to the stability of two years with a man who knew her. Trusted her. Needed her.

THIRTY-SIX

♥ ♥ ● ♥ ● ♥ ♥

*A*lex needed to get up and get dressed. He'd slept through church, but he needed to pull it together and show up for another Sunday afternoon at the Hollisters'. And then he'd pick Caron up from the airport.

Everything would get back to normal.

The alarm clock by his bed—the one he'd used since high school—warned him that it was almost noon. If Caron had been in town—instead of returning from working for Kade Webster—she'd have called him hours ago. Checked on him. Insisted he made it to church.

Once she was back home, she'd make everything okay again.

An image of Jessica's face appeared, and just as quickly dissipated. He wouldn't be receiving any more concerned phone calls from Jessica. They'd both made sure the customer–repairman boundary was well in place when they said goodbye three weeks ago.

And now here he was—wide awake and still in bed. Of course, sleep had evaded him for days as he alternated between going to work, coming home to pace the confines of his bedroom, and crawling back into bed, only to toss and turn, staring at the ceiling. What was he waiting for? Some still-invisible handwriting to appear and reveal the answers he needed? During his brief phone calls with Caron, he'd managed to hide his struggles from her. No need to add any more stress on her, when she'd been wrapping up the Peak Tour of Homes.

Jessica's words had taunted him, lyrics to unwanted background music of his disastrous life story.

"You've shoved this family secret into a closet, thinking you can ignore it. But it's still there—banging at the door, screaming to get out. Your brother's death . . . your mother's drinking . . . even your father's choices are still hurting you. Keeping secrets in your family certainly hasn't helped you, your mother, or your father, has it? Maybe it's time to be honest about all that."

Who did Jessica think she was, telling him things needed to change? That secrets needed to be told? They barely knew each other—and she thought she had the right to tell him what to do to fix everything that was so wrong with his life?

And yet . . . he couldn't escape the harsh ring of truth in her words. How her probing had found the wound he'd ignored for years. He couldn't summon the strength to get up. Get dressed. Go over to the Hollisters' and pretend everything was okay. Not without Caron sitting beside him. Holding his hand.

After the car accident, life returned to the family routine. His mother in a self-medicated haze. His father at work. Always at work. The empty hallway, devoid of any family photos, seemed longer than ever.

He was so tired of doing and saying the right thing.

My mother's an alcoholic.

What if he finally said the truth out loud? What would change?

Nothing.

His mother wouldn't suddenly realize she needed help. She'd never exchange inebriated unreality for sober truth. She'd still choose memories of her dead son over the living and breathing son standing right in front of her. His father wouldn't be there for him after years and years of expecting Alex to handle it. If he wasn't there for Alex when he was a young boy, why would he be there for him when he was an adult?

How did he do life without secrets? If he kept the secret—all of the secrets—no one got hurt.

But where was the truth in that kind of life?

A knock sounded on his door, followed by his father's voice. "You in there?"

"Yes, sir." His voice sounded hoarse. Gravelly.

His door opened halfway, his father standing shadowed by the hallway light. "You sick?"

"No." Alex cleared his throat and forced himself to sit up, the blankets falling around his waist. "Didn't sleep well."

"Caron's mother called and I told her that we'd be over later. Your mother's having a good day, so it'll be the three of us."

"Great."

"You'll make it, right?"

"Of course. And I go get Caron later tonight. She gets back from Colorado."

"I forgot about that." His father was nothing more than a dark figure in his doorway. "Your mother and I already ate breakfast, so there's coffee. Do you want anything?"

"Coffee's good."

Alex welcomed the darkness as his father closed the bedroom door again.

He wanted a lot of things. Years of his life, lost in the twin vortices of his mom's drinking and his dad's absence. He wanted to know what it felt like to wake up and not wonder if his mother was sober or drunk. Not to have to adjust his day around his mother's choices.

He wanted to be able to miss his brother . . . not resent Shawn for dying and twisting their lives into a misshapen family tree bent over into a never-ending posture of mourning.

No healing. No comfort.

His cell phone clattered on his bedside table. Kenny G's "Songbird," the song Caron had programmed in as her ringtone.

Alex leaned back against his pillow as he answered. "Hello?"

"Hi." Caron's voice was a soft whisper. "I just called to say I'm looking forward to seeing you soon."

"Thanks." He swung his feet over the side of the bed, shoving aside the blankets. "Your flight on time?"

"So far. I got to the airport extra early, so I've been watching everyone else's plane take off."

"Feel good to have the job done?"

"Yes. Everyone was happy with how things went." Caron paused, the sound of an overhead announcement playing in the background. "I wanted to share some surprising news with you."

"What's that?"

"I've got a job."

Alex clutched a handful of blanket. He couldn't have heard her right. "A job? In Colorado?"

"No. I mean, yes, I got a job in Florida. My father called and told me that he wanted me to come back and work for him again."

"Caron, that's fantastic!"

"I can hardly believe it myself. Are you going to have lunch with our families today?"

"Of course."

"Well, don't say anything, please. I'm going to try harder to keep business and family separated this time."

"Whatever you say." Caron didn't need to know he'd be lucky to manage any sort of conversation at all.

"I know you're probably getting ready to head over to my parents'."

"In a bit."

After he showered. And shaved. And downed a couple of cups of coffee.

"See you soon. Love you."

"Love you, too." His response to Caron was automatic. He could only hope it was enough to cover up his exhaustion. His lack of any sort of emotion.

.   .   .

Despite a quick shower and two cups of hot coffee, Alex arrived at the Hollisters' home half awake. Even though he'd shaved and caffeinated himself, he still sat at the dining room table with his emotions scraped raw.

How many Sundays had he sat in this house? Eaten lunch. Participated in pleasant small talk. Enjoyed a home-cooked meal. And tried not to count how many drinks his mother indulged in before lunch. Watched as his father accepted another glass of wine for her as Alex resisted the urge to say, "No. She doesn't need another one."

It was a well-practiced dance, this routine between his parents, one where Caron's parents watched without intruding. Where Caron provided a buffer. But not today.

His mother had started the day in a pleasant enough mood, chatting in the kitchen with Caron's mother, sipping a glass of sangria while Mrs. Hollister tossed a green salad and removed a steaming tray of lasagna from the oven.

But now, as they finished lunch, Alex couldn't pull himself away from the mental math. Had his mother had one or two drinks before they came over? She'd become less and less talkative, her focus more inward, the piece of bread and lasagna on her plate untouched. His father and Mr. Hollister talked business, and Mrs. Hollister began to clear the table. As his father started to pour his mother another serving of sangria—her second glass? Third?—Jessica's question echoed in his mind:

And you just accept that things are like this? That things will never change?

"No."

He hadn't realized he'd spoken the word out loud until Mrs. Hollister asked, "*No* what, Alex?"

He blinked, focusing on Mrs. Hollister. Mr. Hollister. His own father, who stared at him, the glass pitcher of sangria suspended above his mother's goblet. "No . . . no, my mother doesn't need anything more to drink."

"Alex, I don't think that's your decision to make." His father tipped the pitcher so the sparkling liquid flowed into his mother's glass.

"And whose decision is it, then? Yours? When was the last time you told Mom no? When was the last time you decided she had enough?"

"This is not the time or place for this conversation—"

"What? You don't think the Hollisters—your oldest, dearest friends—don't realize Mom has had too much to drink? Again?"

"Alex—" Mrs. Hollister set the empty salad bowl down, moving to sit beside his mother.

"What? I know we don't talk about this. We never talk about it. But you and your husband are hoping your daughter will marry me, right? Marry into my family. My secret will become her secret. Let's be honest—it already is your secret. Are you certain you want to pollute your family tree with alcoholism?"

"That's enough—" His father's voice cut across the room.

"Oh, now you want to tell me what to do—after all these years of telling me to handle everything? To take care of Mom? To not bother you at work?" Alex rose to his feet, shoving his chair away from the table. "It's a little late for that, don't you think? I'm tired of handling it. Of taking care of . . . everything. Mom stays in her room and drinks. You go to work—the only place you have any sort of relationship with me. And what do I have?"

A throbbing silence descended on the room. His mother sat, cradled in Mrs. Hollister's embrace, tears streaming down her face. His father stood immobilized, his face flushed red. Mr. Hollister remained seated at the head of the table.

"I know you're upset, Alex." Mrs. Hollister's voice was an echo of Caron's calm, measured tone. "But I think you've said enough."

He clenched and unclenched his fists, his chest rising and falling. What was he thinking, saying all of that? What good had he done?

"I need to go." He shoved past his chair, causing it to fall to the floor. "I know you all think I should apologize. But I can't. I'm sorry for how I said what I did . . . but it doesn't mean I wish I hadn't said it."

THIRTY-SEVEN

· ♥ · ·

*H*er street was shrouded in darkness, the houses seemingly sketched in pen and ink, with an occasional porch light creating a small circle of color. Two boys played basketball in a driveway, illuminated by a light over the garage, their laughter and jests punctuated by the thud of the ball against the backboard, breaking the silence.

After Alex greeted her just past the security area, the ride back from the airport had been an odd mixture of extended silences interrupted by brief bits of conversation. He'd hunched over the steering wheel, making no attempt to hold her hand, his gaze straight ahead. Without a word, he pulled the car alongside the curb in front of her house, turning off the engine, palming the keys.

"Can I come inside so we can talk?"

After barely saying a word to her, now Alex wanted to talk?

"Tonight? Alex, you look exhausted. And I've spent all day traveling—"

"Please."

Seemed like she didn't really have a choice.

Alex carried her luggage into her house, leaving it just inside the door, while Caron kicked off her shoes, tossing her purse on the nearest chair.

"Do you want to sit down?"

"I'm sorry. I know it's late." Alex's shoulders were stooped, his face hidden in the shadows.

"It's not a problem—"

"I just thought, since you're home and I'm here—"

"You obviously need to talk about something."

Alex shoved his hands into his pants pockets. "I don't even know why I'm here."

"You just said—"

"I know what I said. I'm sorry. I've had a rough couple of days."

Caron stopped in the middle of her living room, turning to face Alex, who stepped forward and all but collapsed on her sofa, not even bothering to toss aside the decorative pillows. "What's going on, Alex?"

"I'm trying to finally make sense of my life. Figure out how I got here—and if I want things to stay this way."

Caron eased to the ground beside the couch, struggling to catch up. There'd been no *It's good to see you again* and *I missed you while you were in Colorado* from Alex tonight. "I'm sorry. I don't understand."

"A . . . friend asked me some pointed questions a while ago. About why I let things go on the way they are with my mom. Why I didn't try to get her help. And when I said I couldn't change her, this friend said I should get help for myself."

"What kind of help did this friend recommend?"

"Counseling." Alex stared at the floor. "And I think she may be right."

"She?"

"Jessica is a single mom I met when I was installing a new air-conditioning unit in her house."

"Oh." Since when did Alex have conversations about family problems with customers? Female customers?

"Nothing's going on, Caron—"

"I didn't think there was."

Nothing . . . except this unknown woman having personal conversations with Alex, the man she was supposed to be marrying.

"So do you want to go to counseling?"

"No. No, I don't want to go to counseling." Alex leaned forward, his elbows on his knees, his head resting in his hands. He paused for a few moments before going on. "But I think . . . I need help."

"Help with what?"

"Getting my life unraveled from my mom . . . and my dad. I'm thirty years old and I still live at home with my parents."

"But that's because you want to be there for your mom."

"Exactly." He fell back against the couch, shifting his focus to the ceiling. Looking anywhere but at her. "Dad told me to handle things after Shawn died, and I obeyed him . . . and it's twenty years later and I'm still handling things. Trying to make sure my mother doesn't drink too much. Making her meals, hoping she'll eat something. Doing the laundry and the grocery shopping . . . breathing a little easier on the days when Mom is doing okay . . . and holding my breath on the days when she's not. What kind of life is that?"

Caron reached for Alex's hand. "You've been a good son."

"Have I? Do I even know what a good son is? Does honoring your parents mean you do everything they want you to do? If it does, then when do I get to have a life?"

"Isn't that what our getting married is about—starting your life—our life—together?" Even as she asked the question, Caron wasn't sure she wanted to hear Alex's answer.

"All this . . . these questions . . . they affect you, too. Us. Getting married." His shoulders shuddered with a sigh. His words hollow. "And I thought, if nothing else, I could try being honest with you."

"What do you mean . . . being honest? Haven't we always been honest with each other?"

"Caron, don't you see how you . . . us . . . our relationship is all tangled up in my family's secrets? You know everything about me—the good and the bad—and that makes you both safe . . . and very, very dangerous."

"I don't understand." Caron pulled back, rubbing her hands up and down her crossed arms as his words seemed to chill her.

"As long as I'm involved with you, then my secrets are safe. *I'm* safe. But the minute I even consider trying to have a real relationship with someone else . . . well, that's dangerous because it means they have to know my secrets, too. And if I let you go, you have the power to tell my secrets to someone else."

Why was Alex talking about having a *real relationship* with someone else? Had he found someone else while she was in Colorado? This Jessica, perhaps? And why was there this almost indefinable feeling of . . . of relief to think that Alex might have fallen in love with another woman? She didn't want that to happen—did she?

"Alex, I would never tell someone—"

"I know you wouldn't. All these years we've been friends . . . dated . . . you've kept my secrets. But is a relationship supposed to be based on secrets?"

Secrets. Relationships. Safety. Danger. She'd never heard Alex talk like this before.

"So what are you saying?"

"I'm saying that . . . you're a wonderful friend. My best friend." Alex's eyes were shadowed. "But I'm tired of keeping secrets . . . and of expecting you to keep my secrets, too."

When he reached out to her, she placed her hand in his, allowing him to pull her up to sit beside him on the couch.

"I'm not . . . ready to get married, Caron. Marriage, at the very least, demands honesty. This is the first time I've ever been completely honest with myself. With you." Sweat beaded along his upper lip. "Who knew being so truthful would be this exhausting? And it's painful to say it out loud, but . . . my mother's an alcoholic. My father refuses to deal with her problem. And I . . . I need to figure out how to get a life. My own life."

She waited for Alex's words to hurt . . . to wound her . . . but they didn't. There seemed to be some sort of buffer around her heart that allowed her to listen to Alex . . . to be his friend . . . even as he verbally dismantled their romance. He wasn't rejecting her—not really. He was asking for freedom to figure out who he was as he extricated himself from the emotional web created by his mother's alcoholism. Maybe this unexpected calmness came from recognizing that.

At this moment, Alex needed a friend more than anything else. She could be that for him. She'd always been his friend.

"I understand, Alex." At least, she was trying to understand. She leaned close, resting her head on his shoulder. "And you're right. You need time to sort things out—and the freedom to do it without worrying about me."

"You do know I love you, Caro—" Alex's voice was so low Caron had to strain to hear it. "But I can't ask you to wait while I try to figure my life out. Who knows how long that will take?"

"I know you love me, Alex." Caron could say the words, knowing they were true. "And I love you. You're one of my best friends. And I know the all-wise 'they' say you should marry your best friend . . . but in our case, I think they're wrong."

They sat in silence for a few moments, as if unsure what to say next, or who should say it.

Alex tapped their paired hands against his knee. "So . . . we're not getting married then, right?'"

He sounded so detached. Is that what happened when you realized you were marrying the wrong person? Or you were marrying the right person for all the wrong reasons?

"Correct. We're not getting married." Something pierced her heart as she said the words, but she squeezed his hand, trying to keep any emotion from her words. The last thing he needed right now was for her to cry. "You need to take care of your-self—and not worry about me."

"And we're both okay with this decision?"

"Yes. We made the decision together."

"I suppose we'll need to tell our parents we've ruined their plans—"

His parents. Her parents.

Her father.

"Not right away. Please."

"What?"

"I just got back from Colorado. I'm exhausted. Give me a couple of days to get my bearings again. To get settled back into my job. Can you do that?"

"Sure. I understand." At last Alex shifted on the couch and looked at her. "So, not to ask an awkward question, but what are you going to do with that destination wedding you won?"

The wedding in Telluride. How funny that Alex would re-member that before she did.

"Oh, I don't know." Caron tried to keep her voice light. "There's still time before the expiration date. Maybe I'll donate it—surprise some other couple who is ready to get married. Don't worry about it. You have more important things to think about right now besides a destination wedding you never wanted in the first place."

Alex had the decency to look apologetic—but only a little. "Still friends?"

"Always friends."

"Who knew being an adult was so tough?"

"Who knew?"

"I guess I need to get home." Alex rose to his feet and Caron followed him to the door. "Thank you for listening. For understanding."

"Of course."

Only as Alex hugged her, his embrace so familiar, did something inside of her seem to shift. To crumble. How was she supposed to let him go? His heart beat beneath her ear—steady and strong—an echo of his long-standing presence in her life.

They'd agreed to this . . . this new definition of their relationship. Friends—and only friends. She would not make Alex think she wanted more, not when he was hurting, struggling to find his way. She wouldn't demand something of him that he couldn't give her. And she'd stop pretending she could give him everything he needed from the woman he'd marry.

"Go on, now." She stepped back, face averted, so Alex wouldn't see the tears pooling in her eyes. "It's late."

"Take care."

"You, too."

Only when she was safe in her bed, the covers pulled up over her shoulders, did Caron release a shuddery sigh that became a tear-soaked sob.

She'd done the right thing. It was time for her and Alex to stop using their relationship as a safety zone. Despite her tears, they'd done the right thing.

THIRTY-EIGHT

. ♥ . ♥ . . ♥ .

*O*ne week of work behind her, another week about to start, and Caron had settled back into the routine of working for her father—and Nancy Miller—easier than she expected.

Yes, the sign outside the building now read HOLLISTER REALTY GROUP. And the smaller conference room had been transformed into a private office for Nancy Miller. But the summery pillows Caron had purchased still decorated the couch in the reception area, and she had rescued the vase from the break room, refilled it with vivid pink zinnias, and centered it on the glass table.

Following the Monday-morning staff meeting, Caron waited as the other Realtors left the conference room, some pausing to talk with her father or with Nancy Miller. As the other woman ended her conversation, Caron caught her father's attention.

"Could I talk to you for a moment?"

"Will this take long?" Her father closed his leather folder. "I was about to meet with Nancy."

"No. I wanted to share an idea with you—" She realized Nancy was watching their exchange. "—and Nancy's welcome to listen, since this involves the company. I'd like her opinion, too."

"Well?"

"As you know, I staged a home while I was in Colorado. And you—we—often recommend that our clients use a professional home stager before they put their homes on the market."

Her father remained standing behind the table. "Yes, we do."

"What would you think about developing a home staging branch of Hollister Realty Group?"

"We're a realty company, Caron. We do not stage homes."

"But I can stage homes—"

"You're a Realtor—"

"Yes, I'm a Realtor, but I loved what I did for Kade Webster—" At the mention of Kade's name, her father's posture stiffened. "And I've considered doing it full-time."

"Don't be absurd, Caron. You are not a home decorator."

"But I have the skills. I could show you photographs of the Peak Tour of Homes house—"

"I'm not interested." With a glance at his watch, her father headed for the door. "You've studied real estate. You still have a lot to learn about that. I'm finished with this conversation."

Caron's father didn't even spare her a glance as he left the room.

So much for her brilliant idea.

Nancy Miller lagged behind. "I'm sorry, Caron."

"It's not your fault."

"No, although I do want to say I think your idea has merit." Was the woman merely trying to soften her father's rejection of her idea? "I realize that is not the same as your father being willing to listen."

"No, but I appreciate it."

"Don't let his reaction stop you. Keep gathering information about establishing a home staging division in this company. I've known your father for a long time, and sometimes he forgets that other people have ideas worth considering."

"Yes, well, other people aren't his daughter."

"True. And I hate to say it, Caron, but being his daughter only makes working for him all the harder. Sometimes it's successful, but this is your second attempt to be both his daughter and employee. Do your best, but realize, no matter what you do, you're not ever going to be able to satisfy your father."

• • •

You're not ever going to be able to satisfy your father.

Hours later, Nancy Miller's statement resounded in her mind, as if it was on nonstop playback.

Caron moved her laptop off her lap, scrunching her eyes shut and letting her head fall back against the couch. Her bottle of water had warmed to room temperature, and her container of blueberry Greek yogurt sat beside it, uneaten.

How could the other woman see the truth when Caron couldn't?

She'd failed.

Any indication she'd earned her father's notice as a Realtor? Fleeting, at best.

She'd denied her heart—walked away from Kade—all for her father, who thought Alex was the right man for her.

What would her father say when he knew they'd broken up?

What was she going to do?

The trill of her phone ended her introspection. Okay, easy answer. She'd answer her phone.

"Caron, it's Vanessa. Do you have time to talk?"

"Absolutely. I'm more than happy to talk. I've spent too many hours trying to sort out my life."

"Sounds like there's a story there. Logan's on the road with the team, so I've got lots of time to myself. The last time we talked, you'd quit your job and things were a little strained between you and Alex."

"Yeah, a lot has happened since then." Caron eased off the couch, stretching her back with a soft groan.

"So how's life been treating you since you quit your job?"

Caron tucked the phone between her shoulder and ear as she scooped a handful of Hot Tamales out of the glass jar she'd set out on her kitchen counter earlier in the day. "You want an honest answer?"

"No, I want you to lie to me." Vanessa's words were laced with laughter. "Of course I want an honest answer."

"Let's see . . . weren't you the one who prayed for imperfection for me?"

"I did say something like that the last time we talked. But I've really been praying for clarity and for direction for you."

"God's said yes to the imperfection . . . but not so much to the clarity and direction."

"Why don't you tell me what's going on?"

"The most recent life change is that Alex and I broke up. We both know it's the right thing to do. And we also know our decision isn't going to please our parents at all."

"Oh my gosh, Caron! We have got to talk more often. First you quit your job and now you break up with Alex? You're just making one huge life change after another, aren't you? What happened?"

How did she explain the breakup to Vanessa?

"Well, Alex wasn't very happy when I told him I was going to work for Kade Webster—"

"*What?*"

Vanessa's shriek had Caron holding her phone away from her ear. "I guess I deserved that. So much has happened in the past month—including my working for Kade Webster, although that's not why Alex and I broke up."

When silence was Vanessa's only response, Caron asked, "Aren't you going to say anything?"

"Me? I'm not the one whose life is in upheaval. Keep talking."

"The condensed version is that Kade Webster offered me a temporary job staging a house for him. I accepted, thinking the tension between my dad and me would disappear while I was gone. Alex wasn't crazy about it, but, being Alex, he understood."

"And?"

"Things got . . . a little confusing between Kade and me when I was in Colorado."

"Confusing how?"

"Romantically."

"Caron, we've been talking for, what? Two, maybe three minutes? And I feel like I've been riding a Tilt-A-Whirl."

"You? Hey, I've been living all of this." Caron paced her kitchen, returning to the pile of Hot Tamales. "It's okay, though. I got my head on straight and remembered I was with Alex—"

"But you said you broke up."

"That happened after I came home. Alex admitted he's been dealing with a lot of family stress and that he's not ready to get married. To me or anyone else."

Once again, Vanessa didn't say anything.

"Are you still there?"

"Oh, I'm here all right. But I'm waiting for the next installment in 'Caron Hollister, This Is Your Life.'"

"More like 'This Is Your Life *Unraveling*.'" Caron tossed two Hot Tamales into her mouth. "Alex and I were finally able to admit we are just friends. Nothing more."

"And what do your parents think about all this?"

"We haven't told them yet. Being honest with one another

was hard enough. I needed a little time to gather my strength for the conversation with my parents."

"That's understandable. So, what else?"

"What else—what?"

"Is that all?"

"No, although I wish it was." Caron huffed out a breath. "My father offered me my old job back—"

"What?"

"Believe me, you're no more shocked than I was."

"And?"

"Of course I took the job. What else would I do? But . . ."

"But . . . ?"

"It's not going to work." Speaking the truth out loud seemed to drain the energy from Caron, causing her to slump onto her kitchen floor and lean back against the island.

"Why not?"

"Let's just say Nancy Miller was right."

"Are you going to explain that comment?"

"She said I'm not going to be able to make my father happy." Caron closed her eyes. "Did I ever tell you about what happened in high school?"

"High school?"

"Sophomore year. I participated in a class prank that got labeled as vandalism."

"I imagine that didn't go over too well with your father."

"Just another transgression, along with poor grades and pink hair." Caron sighed. "After that, I decided I was going to stop being the reason my parents dreaded parent–teacher conferences. Put all my time and efforts into my grades and basketball."

"That must have made your father happy."

"Sure. But every basketball victory gave way to the next game and the need to win. To make my father proud, whether he was in the stands or not."

"And then you became a Realtor . . ."

"Yes."

"I would have to agree with Nancy Miller—you are never going to make your father happy."

"I'm just facing that truth for the first time."

"You're not the only person to get tripped up by wanting someone's approval, you know that, right?"

"I know that's true . . . but it doesn't change anything. It doesn't help me figure out how to change."

"Can I share one thing with you?"

"Sure."

"There's a passage in Scripture—John, I think—that talks about the rulers who believed in Jesus. But they didn't confess their belief because they were afraid of the Pharisees and that they might be put out of the synagogue."

"Okay . . ."

"The passage says, *They loved the approval of men rather than the approval of God.*"

Her father's approval. God's approval.

"Those rulers who believed in Jesus? They wanted the approval of the Pharisees more than they wanted everything a relationship with Jesus would give them. Things like freedom. And grace. A new identity." Vanessa paused before continuing. "Can I ask you a couple of questions?"

"Yes."

"What do you want out of life, Caron? And why are you so afraid of losing your father's approval that you aren't truly being you?"

"I . . . can't answer those questions, Vanessa."

"Didn't mean to throw a pop quiz at you—"

"No. No, I'm an adult. I should know the answers. I've never stopped to really think about it before." Caron ran her fingers through her hair. "You've given me even more to think about."

"I'm sorry—"

"Don't apologize. I've got to figure this all out on my own."

"Not on your own. Talk to God. Listen. Wait before you make any more decisions. Maybe if Logan and I'd done that, we wouldn't have made such a mess of our marriage the first time."

Talk to God. Listen. Wait.

Caron lay awake for hours after her phone call with Vanessa, puzzling over the same five words. Maybe talking, listening, and waiting were the right steps to discovering what she wanted out of life.

THIRTY-NINE

. ♥ . ♥ . ♥ . ♥ .

*A*fter hours of nonstop talking and laughter following Margo and Ronny's rehearsal dinner at the restaurant, all was quiet in Margo's apartment.

Emma, Leslie, and Brooke had already said their goodbyes, promising to be back by ten o'clock the following morning to get ready for the wedding. Only Caron remained, gathering up glasses and soda cans and carrying them to the kitchen.

"You, my friend, need to go to bed." Caron tried to shoo Margo out of the kitchen.

"Do brides-to-be really sleep the night before they get married?"

"I wouldn't know, but I highly recommend it."

"I can't believe my wedding day is almost here." Margo moved from the kitchen, but only as far as her couch, decorated with the pillows from the Tour of Homes, collapsing onto it with a sigh. "We've been planning it for months, and now here it is."

Caron moved from the kitchen to sit on the padded arm of the chair across from her friend. "It's going to be a beautiful wedding. The handmade necklace and earrings are perfect with our dresses."

"I'm glad you like them. Maybe that means you'll wear them again."

"I will. But everyone will be looking at you anyway. Tomorrow is all about you and Ronny."

"How are you doing?" Margo sat up, wrapping her arms around her knees.

"Me? I'm fine. A bridesmaid is kind of like background furniture or an accent piece—"

Margo reached for her hand. "I'm serious, Caron. Is tomorrow going to be hard for you after breaking up with Alex and the fact that you'll see Kade again?"

"Breaking up with Alex was the right thing to do."

"And what about Kade?"

Kade.

Her longing for Kade was like the faint sound of wind chimes on a breeze—turning her heart toward something that beckoned her closer, but that she couldn't grasp.

Caron slipped down into the chair. "It's so odd, Margo. I left here knowing there was no chance for Kade and me to ever be together. I thought I would go home and that Alex and I would get married, not end our relationship. I can't deny that I've thought about Kade, even though I've tried not to think of him. But I have to figure out who I am . . . what God expects of me. That's new for me . . . to ask God what he wants from me."

"And does he ever mention Kade?"

Caron couldn't help but laugh. "You are so persistent."

"Well?"

"I miss him. I regret the choice I made two years ago, trying to make my father happy. I was so wrong."

"Then do something about it."

"I have been doing something about it. I've been praying. Asking God what I should do."

"I'm telling you what you need to do." Margo leaned forward. "You have to make the first move."

"Margo—"

"You still love him, right?"

"I . . . might . . . Margo, don't rush me."

"Then prove it. Go after him. Put it all on the line for love."

"Now you sound like some sort of country song—"

"You know what I'm saying. You're the woman with the destination wedding. If you want a chance with Kade Webster again, risk it all."

"What? I'm supposed to ask the man to dance tomorrow and then propose?"

"That's one idea—"

"Oh, right. And what if I risk it all and he doesn't want me?"

"Then you're right back here, trying to figure out what to do with your life. But at least you made your own choice. You went after what you wanted. You didn't worry about your father's approval—or anyone else's."

Is that what God wanted of her? Not to worry about her father's approval—or anyone else's? To love Kade enough to admit to him that she still loved him . . . wanted a future with him . . . even if all she ended up with was a rejection?

What would she do tomorrow when she saw Kade again? Would he ignore her? Would she find a way to talk with him, to let him know how much she'd missed him? Ask him if there was any chance he still loved her?

Given the chance—and the slightest hint that he'd missed her—she wouldn't hesitate to ask him to dance with her. But anything else? Maybe . . . if she caught the bouquet.

"I thought I'd find you here."

Mitch's voice pierced the stillness of the office building, his form backlit by the hall light.

"Hey." Kade kept one hand on the computer keyboard, offering his friend a wave with the other.

"You didn't go to the wedding, did you?" Mitch advanced into the office, his gait so normal most people wouldn't have suspected he wore prostheses.

"Yeah. I got tied up with some things here. Lost track of time."

"Lacey said not to believe you if you said you lost track of time and missed the wedding. She said if you were here that you were avoiding Caron Hollister."

"Really?" Kade swiveled his chair to face forward. "Well, you can tell your fiancée that she was wrong. Besides, I'm Margo and Ronny's Realtor—an acquaintance, really."

"Oh, I think my fiancée is one hundred percent right. But a guy covers for his best friend." Mitch set a plate covered with plastic wrap on the desk. "And he brings him something to eat, too. Lacey made chicken salad."

"Thanks."

"To be honest, that was Lacey's idea, too."

"Then you can tell her I said thank you."

"So you're just going to let Caron go back to Florida?"

Kade knew Mitch wouldn't just drop off the chicken salad and then leave him be. They'd always spoken their minds with one another. "Yep. Didja bring me a fork, too?"

"It's in there." Mitch settled into a chair, linking his hands in front of himself. "I expected better of you, Kade."

Kade unwrapped the paper plate, tossing the plastic wrap into the trash can beneath his desk. "Expected better of me?

Look, the woman chose her father over me not once, but twice. Went back to her boyfriend. And you think I should go after her? How stupid do I look?"

"From where I'm sitting, pretty stupid."

"Thanks for that."

"You're welcome. You would say the same thing to me." Mitch shifted his weight. "Feeling sorry for yourself is about the stupidest waste of time—"

"I am not feeling sorry for myself."

"Oh no? Then why aren't you going after Caron Hollister? You love her, don't you?"

"Yes, I love her. Even after she walked away from me, I never stopped loving her." He ignored the food sitting in front of him. "But I know when I'm not wanted—"

"Do you hear yourself? *Not wanted.* You've worn that label ever since I've met you like some sort of medal of honor. Had it long before Caron Hollister came along. The thing's pinned straight to your chest, man, and even if Caron and you were to ever get together, it would affect your relationship."

"Caron and I are not going to—"

"Fine. Let's leave Caron out of this." Mitch gripped the arms of the chair. "If anyone knows what self-pity does to a guy, it's me. People say unforgiveness is like drinking poison— that the only one you're hurting is yourself. Well, self-pity is like burying yourself alive. Every poor-me thought is like a shovelful of dirt on your grave—the grave you're digging for yourself. You're dying this slow death because instead of seeing everything—everyone—you do have, you're reckoning what you don't have."

"I'm fine, Mitch." He took a bite of chicken salad, only to have it lodge in his throat. Why hadn't his friend brought him something to drink?

Mitch continued as if Kade hadn't spoken. "When I lost my legs . . . there were days I wished you'd left me to die."

His friend's admission caused sour bile to rise up the back of Kade's throat. "No, Mitch—"

"*Yes*. If I couldn't have my life back—my life before the firefight—I didn't want it. Every negative thought was a lump of dirt thrown in my face. Suffocating me. I tried to shove you away. Lacey. My family."

"I wasn't going to desert you."

"Exactly. You wouldn't let me quit. And Lacey . . . she came back and told me she didn't care if I had two legs or four legs . . . or no legs. She loved me. And then we realized we couldn't do it on our own. It wasn't just about our relationship being strong enough for whatever the future holds. Our faith has to be strong enough, too."

"You don't talk about God much."

"Never have. God accepts I'm kinda quiet about my faith, but it's there. Lacey told me what happened to me wasn't because God lost sight of me that day." His friend's voice broke. "Look, I know you've lost a lot of people in your life. Your dad . . . that family you were close to growing up . . . even Russell Hollister . . ."

Kade refused to react as his friend counted up his losses. "It happens—"

"Yeah, it happens to all of us. But don't lose sight of what you still have—who you still have in your life. You helped me learn that truth, now I'm returning the favor."

How could Kade make Mitch understand how he saw him? "You're my hero—"

"I'm no hero. I'm a guy, just like you. Trying to make sense of life. *Trying*. If that makes me a hero, then you're one, too."

"Life's not making a whole lot of sense right now, Mitch."

"Here's a question for you, then. Does life make more sense with or without Caron Hollister? Start there. Everything else will fall into place."

"Simple as that, huh?"

Mitch picked up the plastic fork and motioned for Kade to send the plate his way. "I didn't say it would be simple. I just said it's where you start."

FORTY

• ▾ • ♥ • ▾

$\mathcal{A}$lex had kept up his side of the bargain not to tell his parents about their breakup.

At least Caron assumed he hadn't told them. She hadn't spoken to him in days, allowing Alex the space he requested.

That's what friends were for.

She'd survived Margo's wedding and then boarded the plane back to Florida without a glimpse of Kade. There was no reason not to tell her parents that she and Alex weren't getting married.

She couldn't keep delaying the inevitable. And she couldn't sit through another Sunday meal with their families, trying to explain Alex's absence.

Her text to Alex was brief: *Going to talk to my parents. Pray, please.*

His response arrived just as she pulled up to her parents' driveway: *Praying for you, friend.*

Friends.

Yes, that's what she and Alex were, and there was no reason to be ashamed of it. And there was also no reason to pretend their friendship was enough of a reason to get married.

As she expected, her parents were finishing up a leisurely Saturday breakfast. She followed the sound of their voices, along with the aroma of fresh-cooked bacon and toasted bread, to the dining room.

"Good morning."

"Caron, what a surprise!" Her mother rose and gave her a hug. "Have you had breakfast? I can fix you something."

"I had some yogurt and fruit before I came over. But some iced tea would be nice."

As her mother exited to the kitchen, her father acknowledged her with a nod, reaching for his newspaper. Now that she was here, was he going to retreat behind the headlines?

"Dad, if you don't mind, I wanted to talk with you and Mom. That's why I stopped by."

"Hmm." Her father refolded the paper.

She would take that as a yes.

Her mother returned carrying a frosted glass of iced tea. "Here you go."

"Thanks, Mom." Caron wrapped her hands around the cold glass, as if anchoring herself to something that could hold her steady in an approaching storm.

"How are you doing?" Her mother took her place at the table again.

"Fine—" Caron forced herself to stay focused. She wasn't here for casual conversation. "To be honest, I need to tell you and Dad something about Alex and me."

Now she had both her mother and father's full attention.

"We broke up."

"What?" Her mother's fork clattered against her plate. "When did this happen?"

"Why would you break up with Alex Madison?" Her father's question tangled with her mother's.

Caron chose to answer her mother's question, knowing her father would never truly understand the reasons why she and Alex weren't getting married. "We broke up several weeks ago. I asked that we wait to talk with you and with his parents until I had a little time to recover from being away for a month—and to get settled working for Dad again."

Her father shot another question at her. "And why did you walk away from a future with Alex Madison?"

Why did her father assume she was the one to end the relationship?

"I didn't walk away from him. Alex and I made a mutual decision. To be honest, he came to me and told me that he wasn't ready to get married—that he needs to handle some family issues on his own."

"Family issues." Her father waved the words away. "We all know what he's talking about. His mother's drinking shouldn't stop you two from getting married—"

"Well, it does—that, among other things." Caron eased her grip on the glass of iced tea. No need to break anything . . . well, anything else. The thought almost made her laugh. "As I said, Alex and I made a mutual decision that we are friends. And we are good enough friends to know we do not want to marry each other."

"Oh, now you're talking nonsense, Caron Amelia." Her father reached for his newspaper again.

"No, she's not, Russell."

"I beg your pardon?"

"I disagreed with you—respectfully." Her mother patted her father's hand. "It's not the first time, and it won't be the last. You know I still love you even when we disagree. Caron and

Alex made a decision. What are we going to do, force them to get married?"

"Somebody needs to talk some sense into our daughter."

"Caron is an adult. She can make her own decision about who she wants to marry. You and I did."

"She just wasted two years with him—"

Caron needed to regain control of the conversation before it deteriorated into an argument between her parents. "And that's no reason to marry Alex, either. You don't marry someone just because you dated for a certain amount of time."

"So you came here this morning to tell your mother and me that you and Alex have made up your minds not to get married—no matter what we think about your decision."

"Yes. I'm sorry if I've disappointed you—" Caron caught herself before she uttered the word *again*. She was walking through terrain littered with invisible land mines.

Her mother reached for her hand, squeezing her fingers. "Caron, of course we're not disappointed in you."

Her father stood, picked up the paper, and left the room.

"That went about as well as I expected." Caron's first sip of her tea eased the tightness in her throat just a little.

"Your father will come around. You have to admit this is a bit of a surprise. And he wants you to be happy—"

"And he has very strong opinions on what my happiness should look like." Caron forced a laugh. "I know my choices lately haven't met with his approval."

"He still loves you."

"I know he does." But even to her ears, the words sounded mechanical. Rote. "If you'll excuse me, Mom, there's one other thing I need to talk to Dad about."

As expected, her father had retreated to his office, hidden behind the pages of the morning paper.

"Dad—" Caron waited for a response. "Dad, there's something else I needed to tell you. It's work-related."

"Caron, it's Saturday. I'm trying to relax. Can't this wait until the Monday-morning staff meeting?"

"No, I'm afraid it can't."

"Why not?"

"Because I won't be at the meeting."

Her father set aside the newspaper. Then he removed his glasses, pinching the bridge of his nose. "All Realtors are expected to be at the meeting, Caron. No exceptions."

"I spoke with Nancy on Friday and . . . gave her my resignation."

"You spoke with Nancy—"

"I told her that I was going to quit. I asked her advice about whether I should wait until Monday." Caron twisted her hands together. "She said no, that speaking to her was sufficient, and since I'd only been there a few weeks, there was no need to go through the usual two weeks' notice."

"What gives Nancy Miller the right—"

"She's your partner, Dad."

Her father gripped the arms of his chair, an odd smile twisting his lips. "You enjoyed that, didn't you?"

"No, actually I didn't." Caron hid her hands behind her back. "I hope Hollister Realty Group succeeds in ways you never imagined. But it's best that I'm not a part of it."

"If this is about the home staging suggestion—"

"This is about me making my own decision about where I want to work. And about realizing that my being your employee isn't a good idea."

"And that's that?"

"Yes. Please don't take this out on Nancy. She's a tremendous asset. You made a smart business move when you made her your partner."

"I'll handle Nancy as I think is best."

"Of course. It was just a request—daughter to father."

Her father reached for the newspaper again. "Is that all?"

"Yes, thank you."

Before she'd even made it to the door, her father had disappeared behind the paper again.

.   .   .

It was an odd sort of summer when her first day at the beach didn't happen until August.

Caron's soft laugh broke the stillness of the morning, along with the faint beat of her footsteps along the boardwalk leading through the sand dunes to Henderson State Beach.

An odd sort of summer.

That would be one way to sum up the last couple of months.

She shifted her canvas beach bag on her shoulder, inhaling the Gulf breeze. At eight o'clock in the morning, she was one of the few early arrivers to the beach. She'd stake out a spot along the sugar-white sands. And then she'd walk.

Maybe the time spent allowing the music of the waves to set the rhythm of her heart would help her to pray. To hear God's voice. She'd walk in one direction until she decided to turn around and head back, and then she'd repeat the process. She could stay at the beach all day if she wanted to. And if her life wasn't any clearer by the end of today, she could always come back tomorrow and walk and talk with God some more.

She wasn't wasting time. She was making time. For herself. For God.

Talk to God. Listen. Wait.

FORTY-ONE

· ♥ · ♥ · ♥ · ♥ · ♥ ·

Was it too soon?

Alex slowed the car as Jessica's house came into view, one hand gripping the steering wheel, one hand downshifting. Was she even home? And if she did answer the door, would he be able to say anything besides "I hope you like sausage and pepperoni"?

The aroma of fresh-baked pizza filled his car—yeasty dough, tomato sauce, baked meats and cheese—but he'd refrained from snitching a piece on his way over even though he'd ordered a second basic cheese pizza as a backup. If Jessica wasn't home—or if she refused to talk with him—he'd be sitting in his apartment eating pizza for the next few days.

Okay, God, I'm here. If it's your will, at least give me a chance to say what I want to say.

Alex balanced the pizzas with one hand, heat radiating through the cardboard boxes, and rapped on Jessica's front door, even as he resisted the urge to turn around and walk away. But if the first month of counseling had taught him nothing else, it was to begin to speak up for himself. Say what he wanted to say, and accept he had no control over the outcome. He'd already told his parents that he and Caron had broken up.

After surviving that conversation, he could certainly do this.

When the door opened, it took all Alex's effort not to drop the boxes of pizza.

"Hey, Bobbie—" The smile froze on Jessica's lips. "You're not Bobbie."

"No, no, it's me. And you . . . must be going on a date."

Jessica's hair was woven into some sort of intricate braid that fell over one shoulder. She wore a shimmery blue V-neck dress that accentuated her figure in a way he'd never imagined and would find hard to forget. A pair of silver strappy heels dangled from one of her hands.

"Alex, what are you doing here?"

"I, um, brought pizza." Alex lowered his arm to prove his statement. "I'm sorry. I should have called first."

"You brought pizza?" Jessica stood there, staring at him, looking both adorable and irresistible in her confusion. "I don't understand."

He was still new at this whole being-open-with-other-people thing, but he knew it was important to the woman standing in front of him. "I wanted to see you again . . . to talk to you. And so I thought it would be fun to surprise you—and Scotty—with pizza. But I didn't think about the fact that you might be busy. Or have a date. With Bobby."

"A date—" Jessica shook her head. "Bobbie's not my date— she's my babysitter. I'm going out with some girlfriends to celebrate my birthday."

"Oh." Alex took a step forward. Stopped. "Wait—it's your birthday? Well, happy birthday. Let me just get out of your way."

Jessica grabbed his arm, pulling him into the house. "Will you get in here, please?"

"Who's at the door, Mommy?" Scotty came skidding around the corner. "Is it Miss Bobbie?"

"No, it's Mr. Alex."

"Mr. Alex is babysitting me tonight?"

"No, Miss Bobbie is babysitting you—"

As Alex knelt down, he held the pizzas aloft, bracing for the little boy's hug. Jessica rescued the pizzas, taking them from his hands.

"Where ya been, Mr. Alex? I've been asking Mom when you were coming over again."

"And I told you that Mr. Alex didn't need to come over because nothing was broken."

"That's not true. The faucet is broken."

"Not anymore. I fixed it."

"But you coulda called Mr. Alex—"

"Tell you what—why don't you talk to Mr. Alex for a few minutes while I finish getting ready for tonight, okay? And when Bobbie gets here, let her in."

Fifteen minutes later, Jessica reappeared in the living room, where Alex sat on the couch, the babysitter and Scotty now outside in the backyard.

"Bobbie's here and the pizza's in the kitchen and—" Alex did a double take. "You're wearing . . . a different dress?"

Jessica's hands skimmed the skirt of her casual floral dress. "Yes, I am."

"But why aren't you wearing the other dress?"

"Because I called my girlfriends and told them I needed to take a rain check on our dinner date tonight."

"I-I don't understand."

"Then I'll explain it to you. I was going to go out with my girlfriends, but then you showed up with pizza and I changed my plans. It's my birthday, so I figured I could choose what I wanted to do, right?" Jessica slipped her feet into a pair of purple flip-flops sitting by the front door. "Now Bobbie's here, so I thought we could go for a walk and catch up with each other and then come back and reheat the pizza. If that's okay with you—"

Alex joined her by the door. "Sounds great."

Within minutes they were walking side by side through Jessica's neighborhood. A group of kids had set up a makeshift ramp in one driveway and were practicing their skateboarding skills. An older teenage boy maneuvered a red lawn mower around the front lawn, bobbing his head to whatever music played in his headphones. The smell of fresh-mown grass filled the air.

He and Jessica walked the block, turned the corner, and continued down the next street—and still the words he wanted to say wouldn't come.

"Your air conditioner working okay?"

"I would have called your shop if it wasn't." Jessica offered him a quick smile. "And the washing machine is running fine, too."

"Great." Alex searched for another easy topic. "How's work been?"

"Busy as ever. Scotty will be starting kindergarten soon, so I'll have more free time. And he's finishing up swim lessons."

"Swimming probably tires him out."

"You would think so, wouldn't you? But the only one who ever wants a nap is me." Jessica took the lead in the conversation, asking an unexpected question. "So . . . did you ever figure out that big proposal for your girlfriend?"

"No. No, as a matter of fact, I didn't. I've been kind of busy—"

"Honestly, Alex! You can't keep putting it off. She's going to think you don't want to marry her."

"I don't."

Jessica came to a complete standstill in the middle of the sidewalk. "What?"

"I don't want to marry her. And she doesn't want to marry me, either."

"I have to admit I wasn't expecting this."

"To be honest, neither were Caron and I." Alex faced her, unwilling to keep walking as the conversation took a more serious turn. "But you're the one who challenged me to take care of myself, Jessica. Help myself if I couldn't help my mother. You were right about that . . . and about how my mother's drinking was affecting my relationship with Caron."

"I'm sorry, Alex."

"I wasn't ready to get married. I had to deal with my brother's death. My mother's drinking. My dad's unwillingness to talk about any of it—"

Jessica moved closer to him, resting her hand on his arm. "What did you do?"

"I grew up—or at least, I've started the process of growing up. I moved out of my parents' house into my own apartment. I'm seeing a counselor once a week—talking about stuff. Can't say that it's easy—'clearing away the emotional debris that's been clogging my thinking' is the way he describes it. I'm realizing my father didn't mean to abandon me back then, although that's what it felt like. He just didn't know what else to do. I'm still trying to get the right perspective on all of it—to understand it as an adult, not a ten-year-old."

"And growing up also meant you had to break up with Caron?"

"Caron and I are friends. We've always been friends. Always will be friends. Our parents always joked that we were perfect for each other, but that's not a good enough reason to get married."

"Because you're perfect for each other? You happen to be dis-agreeing with a lot of people, you know."

"Not that part—getting married because our parents thought we should. You don't get married to make someone else happy. And you don't marry someone just because they'll help you keep a family secret."

"You've talked all of this out with your counselor?"

"Yes." Alex resisted the urge to take Jessica's hand in his. Now wasn't the time. "It's been a lot to process. Sometimes I feel like somebody volunteered me to be a test dummy for a crash course on maturity."

Jessica laughed, and then covered her mouth with her hand. "I'm sorry . . . but you've got admit the way you described it was funny."

He laughed along with her. "I'm learning a sense of humor helps, too."

"So what else are you learning?"

"My counselor has helped me realize when I have my own family . . . well, I don't want secrets. Surprises, yes. But no se-crets."

Alex caught his breath as they resumed their walk, allowing silence to reign between them. His heart pounded in his chest as if he'd been running a marathon, not merely strolling through Jessica's neighborhood.

"You've been doing a lot of hard work in just a month." Jes-sica's words provided him with a second wind—the ability to keep going.

"I'm trying to figure out where I am with God, too. I hadn't even realized I was angry with him until my outburst with you."

"God's big enough to handle our anger, Alex."

"Trying to figure out what a relationship looks like when you haven't really talked to someone in a long time—when that someone is God—it's tough." Alex motioned for them to sit on a wooden bench on the outskirts of a small park. "I'm also learning all this talking about feelings . . . it's exhausting."

Jessica patted him on the back. "Don't feel like you have to tell me everything today."

"There was one more thing I've been thinking about . . . something that you said."

"Oh?"

He'd kept this part for last—and now he wasn't sure that had been the wisest decision. They'd walked and talked. He'd worn himself out just explaining some of the basic things he'd realized about himself. About God. But now he was at the trickiest part of the conversation—the riskiest—and he didn't have any emotional reserves left if things went badly.

"Alex? You okay?"

No. He wasn't okay. But the whole reason he was here today, talking with Jessica, was to tell her this next part.

Alex twisted on the wooden bench seat so he faced Jessica. "You said that when a guy proposed to you, all you wanted was for him to show up at your door with a pizza—"

Jessica's eyes widened behind the wire frames of her glasses. "Alex!"

"Jessica, I promise you, all that's in those boxes are pizzas. Nothing more." He covered one of her hands with his. "But I know how you value honesty, so I'm going to tell you exactly what I'm thinking here."

"Go ahead." The two words were a mere whisper.

"I like you, Jessica. You challenged me and forced me to look at my life and how I was living it. And you encouraged me to change it. You've always intrigued me. Being with you . . . was a glimpse of something I've always wanted. I want to get to know you better."

"Become friends, you mean?"

"Aren't we already friends?"

"Yes."

"Then we start here. See what God has for us. I hope and pray it's more. A whole lot more. Maybe even pizza and a ring down the road." He inhaled a deep breath that shifted his shoulders. "What do you think?"

Jessica slipped her hand into his. "You need to understand a couple of things about me."

"I'm listening."

"I'm a two-for-one deal. It's me and Scotty."

"Even better. Anything else?"

A smile curved Jessica's lips, causing Alex to wish he had the freedom to kiss her. "And my favorite pizza is meatlovers—the more meat and cheese the better."

Alex's laugh started low and then spread out between them. "See? I knew we were going to get along just fine, Jessica Thompson. And now that we've got that settled, how about we go home and spend the rest of the evening together—you, me, and Scotty?"

"Sounds like the perfect way to celebrate my birthday."

FORTY-TWO

· ♥ · · ♥ · ·

*I*f she kept up these daily trips to Henderson Beach, Caron might as well rent a campsite and pitch a tent. At least then she wouldn't have to leave every evening to return to her quiet, dark house.

Tonight's sunset was particularly stunning, with the sky deepening from blue to purple, the clouds' edges rimmed with a deep pink hue. The sun was a blur of gold that seemed to spill from the sky over the dark edge of the ocean.

Caron had spent hours the last several weeks walking the shore. Praying, listening for an answer to her questions about her future. Did she continue working as a Realtor, ignoring her feelings? Did she pursue home staging? At times she even practiced a halting, stumbling, all-out-there proposal for Kade Webster.

I love you.

I was wrong, wrong, wrong to walk away from you.

Forgive me.

Marry me. Please.

And she returned home every night no more certain that she should call Kade, much less ask him to marry her.

Kade was worth the risk, yes.

But after talking to Vanessa, she'd promised herself that she'd ask God what she should do. And for all her asking, the only impression she'd gotten was to wait.

Wait.

But for what? And for how long?

She refused to abandon hope that God was doing something even when she saw no evidence of it yet. She had to believe he would give her another chance with Kade, or else take away her longing for him. What had Vanessa said when they talked last week?

"God's love for you is perfect, Caron—and unconditional. It may take you a while to realize you don't have to do something—be someone—for God to love you."

Fine. For one more day, she would refuse to give in to the fear that she was disappointing God. Yes, she'd chosen wrong not once, but twice. But she had to believe that God loved her in the midst of all this waiting . . . doubting . . . struggling to trust him. And that he would give her the opportunity to finally make the right choice.

And if she never had an opportunity with Kade again, well . . . then God still loved her and he would help her accept that. Somehow.

A gentle breeze ruffled her hair, offering just the hint of relief against the mid-August heat. The sand, drenched with the motion of the waves, was still warm beneath her feet. Seagulls wheeled overhead and then moved on, their plaintive, high-pitched cries an echo of her own prayers.

She found her breathing matching the rhythm of the waves, the sun falling behind her as she headed back toward the parking area.

And then she stopped . . . her breath hitching . . . resisting the urge to rub her eyes, blink, and rub her eyes again. The man

walking toward her was no longing-of-her-heart mirage. Kade
Webster's determined stride caused the water to splash up behind him, the setting sun seeming to cast his form in a yellow
haze.

Why was he here? What should she do? Stand here, staring,
and wait? No. No more waiting. Kade had come this far—all
the way from Colorado. The sand shifted beneath her feet as
she closed the space between them, halting with mere inches
separating them.

Kade's expression was hidden behind a pair of silver-rimmed
sunglasses—but then again, her own expression was veiled behind sunglasses, too.

She removed them, slipping them into the side pocket of
her cotton dress, even as she shaded her eyes from the remaining sunlight. Honesty and transparency were uncomfortable in
more ways than one.

Someone had to speak first. It was only right she break the
silence.

But Kade spoke before her, the sound of his voice as potent
as a caress. "I was looking for you."

"How'd you find me?"

"I went to your house straight from the airport. You weren't
home—obviously. So then I drove by your parents'. Your
mother told me that you've been spending time here."

She couldn't believe he'd been brave enough to go visit her
parents alone.

"I come here every day to think."

"What have you been thinking about?"

Here was her chance. To show Kade how much she loved
him by being bold . . . confessing everything, sharing everything
she'd learned. But how did she start? It was as if all her words
had been swept out into the Gulf.

She fingered the collar of her dress. "You."

Kade reached for her hand, twining their fingers together, his touch causing her to realize how much she'd missed him all the more. "Funny thing, Miss Hollister. I've been thinking about you, too."

"You have?"

"Constantly. Mitch says I'm useless at work. And Lacey told me to get myself to Florida and fix things between us—or else."

"Kade—what happened between us—what went wrong both the first time and the second time, it wasn't your fault." Caron dropped her sandals to the sand, taking his other hand in hers.

"Caron—"

"No. You have to let me tell you that I'm sorry—terribly sorry—for choosing my dad over you two years ago."

"Caron, I didn't come here to hash that all out again—"

"Please, Kade." She touched his arm, his skin warm beneath her fingertips. "I need to say this. All of this."

He pulled her closer. "It's not necessary."

"For me it is." She resisted the urge to rest in his arms. She had to say what was in her heart. "I've realized a lot of things about myself these past couple of months. How I wasted a lot of years wanting my dad's approval more than anything else. Wanting my dad to love me, to be proud of me. But I used my father's approval like some sort of measuring stick. Was I good enough or not? And it twisted my life out of shape. I lost you, the man I loved, because I wanted my father's approval."

"That's all I need to hear."

As Kade tried to pull her into his arms, Caron braced her hand against his chest. "What? I haven't said I'm sorry yet."

"Yes, you did. And you said you love me. You want to know why I came looking for you? Because I've never stopped loving you, Caron Hollister. I let you walk away the first time . . . and then I almost let you walk away from me again. But I'm here because I couldn't make that mistake again."

Her hands gripped his shoulders as he kissed her, their lips flavored with salt. He caressed the sides of her neck with his thumbs, and then curved one hand against the back of her head, threading his fingers through her wind-tossed hair. There was no need to rush this moment, and she didn't want him to.

After a moment, Caron pulled back from his embrace. "I'm sorry, Kade—"

He pressed his fingertips against her lips. "No more apologies. I forgive you. Kiss me again and then—" He lowered his voice as he pressed a soft kiss just below her ear.

"This didn't go the way I planned."

"I beg your pardon?" Kade's question held a note of barely contained laughter. "You had something else planned for us? Background music, perhaps? A prepared script?"

"Oh, stop. I'm not complaining . . . not really."

"Well, I'm relieved to hear that."

"It's just that everyone told me—"

"Everyone?"

"Margo, to be specific. Anyway, she told me that I needed to prove to you how much I loved you since I left you the first time without any explanation . . ."

"And just how were you going to prove your love for me?" Kade's boyish grin appeared. "Fight a duel? Slay a dragon?"

"Now you're being absurd." Caron tried to push her way out of Kade's embrace.

"Oh, no you don't. Now that I've got you right where I want you, you're not going anywhere." Kade's arms tightened around her. "I've never had a woman prove her love for me before. Aren't you going to tell me what you were going to do?"

"I was going to—" Caron's voice dropped to a whisper. "—ask you to marry me."

"Well, I hate to disappoint you, but I have certain plans of my own—" Kade released her and dropped to one knee on the sand. "—and I intend to ask you first."

"What . . . what are you doing?"

"I told you—I'm proposing. Give me a minute." Kade worked something loose from the pocket of his white cotton shirt. "This always goes more smoothly in those romance movies you like to watch."

"Kade—"

"Hush. Like I said, you missed your opportunity." The laughter faded from his eyes as he took her hand again and pressed a kiss near her wrist. While looking up at her, he held out a ring, the diamond glinting in the sunlight. He then slipped the ring halfway on her finger. "Caron Hollister, will you marry me?"

"Yes. And yes. And yes." Her hand trembled as he slid the ring in place on her finger, the white-gold band adorned with a heart-shaped diamond.

"You told me once that the man who loved you would know the kind of engagement ring you'd want." Huskiness tinged Kade's words as he rose to his feet again, slipping his arms around her. "I thank God that you love me. That I have the chance to love you for always—and this ring symbolizes the love I have for you."

Caron rested her hand against his chest. "It's beautiful . . . perfect."

"So you're satisfied, then?"

"More than satisfied." She hoped the love she saw lighting Kade's eyes was reflected in her own. "And how I feel right now has nothing to do with this ring—perfect as it is—and everything to do with you."

As Kade bent his head to kiss her, a soft *thank you* whispered from her lips.

He paused, a slight smile twisting his lips. "What are you thanking me for?"

"I wasn't thanking you—I was thanking God for bringing you back to me . . . for answering my prayers . . . for all of this . . . "

"I'm thankful for all that, too—and that I can kiss you again."

"Anytime you want to, Mr. Webster."

Her words produced Kade's grin again. "I like the sound of that."

FORTY-THREE

• ♥ • ♥ • ♥ •

*F*or the first time in her life, Caron was going to have an honest conversation with her father.

Of course, it might destroy whatever tenuous relationship there was left between them . . . but then again, maybe honesty would be the beginning of something better. Something real.

Kade refused to let go of her hand. "Are you sure I can't go with you?"

"Positive." She stepped into the shelter of his embrace, even though she knew her mother was watching them. "I need to do this on my own."

"But this is our decision—"

She rested her hand against his chest, his heart beating steady and strong beneath her palm. "Yes, it is. But my dad needs to hear it from me first. Just me. You not going in there with me isn't about you being a coward. It's about me being brave."

"You'd best go on." Her mother's soft voice interrupted them. "We have dinner in an hour with Nancy Miller."

"I don't think this will take long." Caron stepped away from Kade. "And no matter what happens, you and I are getting married, Kade Webster."

He pressed a quick kiss to her lips. "No doubt about that."

"Pray for me?"

Her mother nodded. "We both will."

Leaning into those prayers, Caron whispered a few intercessions of her own as she approached her father's office. For calmness. For strength. For the right words. For courage.

"Dad?" Caron waited for her father to acknowledge her presence. "Do you have a minute to talk?"

His glasses sat halfway down his nose. "I'm just finishing up a few things before your mother and I meet Nancy Miller and her boyfriend for dinner."

"I know. Mom told me that you had plans tonight." Caron moved to stand behind the chair set just to the left of his desk. "So, can I talk with you?"

He flipped shut the folder in his hands and set it aside. "Sit down."

She'd take that as a yes.

Words, Lord. Give me the right words. Please.

As she settled into the chair, she swiped her hands down the front of her linen capris, stopping when the diamond in her engagement ring sparkled in the overhead light. She covered her left hand with her right. No need for that to catch her father's eye before the conversation even started.

"What's on your mind?"

"I've made a decision and I wanted to tell you about it."

"Does any of this have to do with your plans for future employment?"

"No. I'm still considering my options." Caron exhaled a silent breath and straightened her shoulders.

"You walked away from a perfectly good job not once, but twice."

Caron sucked in a breath, steadying herself. "The truth is, I should have stopped working for you a long time ago. Maybe it would have been better for both of us if I never worked for you in the first place."

Her father snorted, pushing away from his desk. In the past, that action would have been enough to make her reevaluate what she'd said. Leading her to question what she'd done—what she was doing with her life.

She could do this. Kade and her mother were praying for her. And this was her only opportunity to try to explain herself to her father.

"Do you know I've spent most of my life waiting for your approval?" She paused, clenching her hands together, willing her voice not to shake. "I played basketball in high school because you loved basketball and I knew . . . at least I hoped you'd come to some of my games."

"You were a good basketball player."

Now he told her that.

"Just because I was good doesn't mean I should have played basketball—not if my heart wasn't in it. And not if I was doing it to get your attention. And the truth is, I would have rather gone out for tennis. Or track. But I played basketball for four years—mostly for you." Her father sat still, making it impossible to gauge his reaction. "And I became a Realtor because you were a Realtor and I thought maybe, just maybe, you'd finally be proud of me."

"I am proud of you, Caron. You were one of my best Realtors—"

The words she'd always longed to hear from her father were as effective as the spray from a garden hose that had been knotted off near the faucet. Forced and ineffective.

"Don't say it, Dad. Not now that I'm sitting here telling you what I needed to hear all these years. And being proud of how I helped your business reputation isn't the same thing as being proud of me . . . just me. Besides, I've been wrong to stake all my hopes and dreams on your approval."

"What's that supposed to mean, young lady?"

"I gave you too much power. You're my father. What I needed from you was your love. Your acceptance. Your support of me, no matter what I did or didn't do. Instead, I didn't even stop and ask myself what my dreams were. I just followed in your footsteps, like your shadow, and lived out your dream, hoping it would be enough to get you to notice me."

Her father leaned back in his chair. "You're no longer working for me, and you've told me you don't intend to come back, so why are you telling me all this?"

Her father's words threatened to shut down the entire purpose of this conversation. She'd fought to find the courage to continue talking with him. She'd questioned who she was— who she thought she had to be. She still wasn't walking on solid ground. Some days the truth wavered, toppling over like the Jenga block game she and Logan used to spend hours playing as kids. And then she had to rebuild the truth all over again, wooden block by block.

"I'm not blaming you for this, Dad. I'm an adult and I want to take responsibility for my life and decisions."

"Meaning?"

She'd start with the simplest thing first. "What I was trying to say before was that I'm considering a job change. I never really thought about—or prayed about—my career. Now I am. I may be a Realtor. Or I might become a home stager. I may even go back to school. I don't know. No matter what, it will be my choice."

"Why do I get the idea that there's more to this sudden life transformation than a possible job change?"

Was this what a boxer felt like going in for another round against his opponent? She tried to regain focus and summon up the strength to do battle again.

"I told you and Mom that Alex and I broke up." Caron sat up straighter. "I'm happy. He's happy. You should never marry someone because it's easy. Or to please your parents."

"You two are perfect for each other."

"No, Dad, we're not. We're friends. Our families are close. But that's it." Caron kept her voice level. "Besides, I'm in love with someone else."

"What are you talking about?"

"I stopped dating Kade Webster two years ago because you wanted me to—and I always regretted it. I gave up a chance at love because I wanted your approval more—"

Her father shoved his chair back. "This is nonsense. Kade Webster is the last man I would ever let you marry."

"Dad, this is not about you *letting* me marry someone. You don't get to decide." Her diamond ring dug into the palm of her clenched fist. "Kade proposed, and I accepted. I want you to be happy for me, but I don't need your approval. Kade and I love each other and we're planning on getting married as soon as we can—"

"I won't spend a dime on a wedding for you to marry that man, Caron Amelia!"

She couldn't hold back a laugh. "The funny thing is, Dad, you won't have to. I won a wedding—a one-of-a-kind wedding in Colorado. I want you and Mom there. I . . . I can't imagine you not being there. But I have to follow my heart now."

"Follow your heart—more like making a fool of yourself."

"That's enough now, Russell." Her mother spoke from behind her.

"Do you know what our daughter wants to do?"

"Yes, I do. And I support her." Her mother rested her hands on Caron's shoulder. "And you should, too. Caron's pursuing her dreams. I'm proud of her."

"Quitting her job with me, breaking up with Alex Madison, working for Kade Webster, and now she wants to marry him? And you're fine with all this?"

"Yes, she has to make her own decisions."

"I won't attend the wedding—"

"That's your decision, sir." Now Kade appeared, coming to stand beside Caron as she rose from the chair, slipping his hand around hers. "I know Caron would want you at the ceremony, and I would hope that despite our differences, you could put that aside and be a part of your daughter's wedding—"

"Kade, I told you that I needed to do this—" Caron dropped her voice to a whisper even as she clung to his hand.

"And I was fine with that until things started sounding tense in here. I want your father to know we're in this together."

"It seems to me a lot of decisions have been made." Her father stood. "Well, I'm making the decision to end this conversation and go get ready for our dinner date."

Once her father left the room, her mother pulled her into a hug. "It's okay."

"Okay?" Caron brushed away the tears she couldn't keep from falling. "That was awful."

"You just shifted the dynamic of your relationship with your father—again. First you stop working with him. A very wise choice, even if it was sudden. Then you tell him you no longer need his approval. Also a wise choice. But your father doesn't know how to handle all of this. Give him time."

"What if he refuses to come to the wedding?"

"You and Kade haven't even scheduled a date yet. We have

time to talk this out more." Her mother smoothed Caron's hair back from her face. "And to pray."

"You're right." Caron tried to focus on the positive.

"He's a stubborn man, dealing with his own heart issues. I believe he'll come around." Her mother rested her hands on Caron's shoulders. "So what now?"

"I guess we have some plans to make."

"Wedding dress shopping?"

Caron couldn't hold back a laugh. "I knew that would be the first thing on your list."

.   .   .

"It's a good thing I never spent a lot of time daydreaming about my wedding day." Caron leaned into Kade's embrace, inhaling the scent of the Gulf breeze as they walked along the beach. The setting sun's rays lingered across the waves as the tide receded from the sand dunes covered with sea grass.

"You mean you weren't one of those teen girls who tore photos of wedding gowns and engagement rings out of bridal magazines?"

"No, I never was that girl. I was more likely to be browsing *Better Homes and Gardens* or *House Beautiful*." Caron closed her eyes, allowing the stillness of the evening to wrap around them. "However, it should make it easy when I shop for a wedding gown, right? No preconceived ideas of what I want to wear. I can try them all on and just see which one is 'it.'"

"And when are you going wedding dress shopping?"

"My mother wants to start right away, but we probably need to set a wedding date first."

"And we should decide that before I head back to Colorado tomorrow."

Caron stopped, wrapping her arms around him. "Do you have to go?"

"I am the boss, remember?"

"I remember." She stole a quick kiss. "I quite enjoyed working for you, Mr. Webster."

"Enough to work for me again?"

"Are you looking for a home stager?" Caron could barely keep the laughter out of her voice.

"I came here intending to propose. But if I go back knowing I've also expanded my business . . . well, I won't complain."

"Are you sure you didn't come out here just to talk me into working for you?"

Kade pulled her into his arms, his kiss leaving both of them breathless.

"Now that I've made it clear my proposal had nothing to do with business—"

"You certainly did."

"When do you want to get married?"

"We've already lost two years. And winning a destination wedding makes this whole plan-a-wedding thing pretty easy. I'd like to call the Peaks and see what their earliest available dates are for us to use my prize package."

"I like the sound of that."

"Because it's a destination wedding, it will be a smaller guest list. Hopefully easier to accommodate." Caron slipped from Kade's arms, reclaiming his hand as she resumed their walk. "I only hope my mom will convince my dad to come."

"Caron, a few weeks ago, we never imagined we'd be getting married, right?"

"Right."

"So don't let what your father does or doesn't do ruin our wedding day. We'll tell him that we want him there. Then we'll pray—and let him make his decision."

"I guess that's all we can do, isn't it?"

"Yes. We're making our choices. And he'll make his."

"But what if—"

"Stop." Kade pressed his fingertips against her lips. "We stay focused on today. Just today. Yes, we're planning a wedding, but we don't know what will happen the day of the wedding until the day gets here. And first we have to choose the day."

"You're right."

"I take it back."

"You take what back?"

"We do know one thing that will happen on our wedding day."

"What's that?"

"No matter what else does or doesn't happen—you and I are getting married."

FORTY-FOUR

• ♥ • ♥ • ♥ •

SEPTEMBER

Caron welcomed the splendid imperfection of her wedding day.

The gray clouds covering the San Juan Mountains threatened rain—a threat they'd made good on for the past two days. A misty rain rolled in for several hours and then disappeared. Afterward, the clouds parted, allowing the sunlight to hit the golden aspens scattered along the mountains, causing them to shimmer.

"This is one of those who-would-have-imagined-it kind of days, isn't it?" Caron's fingertips smoothed the sheer white material of the neckline of her wedding gown that transitioned into delicate Venice lace. The layers of tulle in the tea-length skirt spread out around her as she sat in a chair beside a window.

"Ye-es." Vanessa tucked a tiny spray of baby's breath into Caron's updo.

"I mean, I'm actually using that dream-come-true destination wedding I won at the bridal expo back in May."

"I know. And to think you kept telling Margo you wanted to give it back."

"And I'm marrying Kade."

"And you look stunning." Her sister-in-law added another small spray of flowers to Caron's hair.

"It's so beautiful here—I don't care if the sun is shining or not. If you'd asked me to list where I wanted to get married before, I don't think Telluride would have been anywhere on the list. But I love how rustic and romantic it is."

"Gondola rides, Jeep tours, fly-fishing . . . Telluride is definitely rustic."

"You didn't complain about the spa day—and I've noticed you and Logan have disappeared a few times."

"I'm all for romance, Caron, and I thank you for providing the perfect location." Vanessa tossed her a wink.

"Say no more." Caron sighed. "And I'm thankful my father agreed to even attend the ceremony with my mother."

"He's been . . . pleasant since they arrived—and he seemed to enjoy the fly-fishing with everyone else."

"I'm sure my mother insisted he behave himself while they were here, even though he doesn't support me marrying Kade— and won't be giving me away today."

Vanessa braced her hands on her shoulders, careful not to mess Caron's hair. "Logan's here to do that. It's a little unusual, but it will be fine—"

"Just another chance for me to realize no wedding day is perfect, right?"

"It does seem to be a theme you're embracing."

Caron stilled as Vanessa checked her hairstyle one last time, a prayer forming in her mind.

She could do this so long as she knew God was in this day. That he was with her.

"Vanessa—" Caron clasped her sister-in-law's hand. "I need to see Kade."

"What?" Vanessa took a step back. "You can't do that. It's bad luck—"

"Neither of us is superstitious. And you're my maid of honor. Isn't the maid of honor supposed to do whatever the bride needs her to do?"

"But not this—"

"Yes, this. Please. Go get Kade for me."

Despite muttering under her breath as she left, Vanessa disappeared, ordering Margo to keep an eye on Caron as she left. What, did Vanessa think Caron was going to ask her to go get Kade—and then make a run for it? She had no intention of not marrying Kade Webster today.

Whatever Vanessa told him, when Kade returned less than ten minutes later, he grinned at her, looking as handsome as she'd imagined he would in his dark brown suit complete with a white rosebud boutonnière, and ignoring Vanessa's complaint, "Well, now you've seen her before the ceremony!"

"And I'll still marry her." Kade turned Vanessa toward the door again. "Let me have some time with my future wife, please."

With a huff, Vanessa ushered the bridesmaids from the room in swirls of mauve silk georgette.

"Are you all right, hotshot? Logan's wife came marching in and demanded that I follow her, even though she thought it would ruin the whole day—"

"Yes. I'm fine. I mean, I'm not fine. But I will be once we have a chance to talk."

"You're not getting cold feet, are you?" Kade clasped her hands, his fingers warm against her skin. "Because I have to tell you, there's no way I'm letting you back out on me."

"No, I'm not getting cold feet." Caron released Kade's hands, slipping all the way into his embrace, her arms encircling his waist beneath his dark suit jacket. "I just need to change something about the ceremony."

"Change something? What?"

Being this close to Kade already steadied her thoughts. "I know my father's not going to walk me down the aisle. To be honest, I'm just thankful he's here. That alone is a miracle. And it's enough for today . . ."

"We handled that, Caron. That's why Logan's walking you down the aisle—"

Caron leaned back so she could make direct eye contact with Kade. "No, Kade. I need you to tell Logan that I don't want him to walk me down the aisle."

"Why not?"

"It just doesn't feel right. Even though my father refuses to walk me down the aisle, I don't want Logan to take his place." When Kade took her hand, she held it against her heart. She needed to make him understand everything she'd been thinking this morning. "I don't want to embarrass my father today. I don't want the guests to watch my brother escort me down the aisle and wonder why my father is sitting there with them. You and I both know this is our decision to get married today."

"If your father won't walk you down the aisle, and you don't want Logan to walk you down the aisle, then what do you want to do?"

"Let me tell you what I'm thinking. Then can we pray about it? And if you agree, will you go tell Logan about the change?"

·　·　·

It was her wedding day—and for just a few precious moments, she was alone.

She'd sent both Lacey and Margo off with a hug. Then one last moment with Vanessa, who handed off her bouquet of white roses and orchids, before walking onto the Mount Terrace area, surrounded on all sides by the San Juan Mountains.

And now, at last, it was time to walk toward Kade.

"I'll be waiting for you."

Kade's words seemed to be carried on a breeze of the brisk mountain air. Yes, she noticed Mitch and her brother. But she sought and found Kade, the one person she was looking for, her gaze never wavering from his face once their eyes locked.

•   •   •

Even though he and Caron had seen each other before the ceremony, he hadn't truly seen her. Not until this moment, when she came toward him, as his bride.

And now he couldn't look away.

At last he understood why so many people said the moment when a groom saw his bride was their favorite moment of a wedding.

He was the groom, watching Caron, his bride, approach him, her gaze never wavering from his face.

But Caron wasn't just walking toward him . . . she was declaring, in a public way, "I love Kade Webster. I want forever with him."

He and Caron had agreed she'd walk all the way down the aisle by herself. Kade had taken two steps forward before he even realized it. Before Logan stopped him with a strong grip on his shoulder. "Where are you going?"

"To get my bride."

Logan released him, stepping back next to the rest of the wedding party.

Kade ignored the whispers as he increased his pace. Caron's shimmering brown eyes widened as he came closer.

Caron stopped with mere inches separating them. "What are

you doing here? I thought we agreed you would wait for me. Was I taking too long?"

"Not at all. I just decided I wanted to escort you the rest of the way—if that's okay with you?"

Caron slipped her hand into the crook of his elbow, offering him a smile as he drew her close enough so that the scent of her perfume, intertwined with the floral aroma of her bouquet, surrounded him. "We're being extremely unconventional today, aren't we, Mr. Webster?"

"Yes, we are, Miss Hollister." He lifted her hand and pressed a kiss to her fingertips. "But it's our wedding day. Now, if you don't mind, we need to join the rest of our wedding party."

"Can't keep everyone waiting."

Whispers and laughter followed them as they made their way back down the aisle together.

"About time you two got here." Logan spoke just loud enough for the minister and guests to hear him, causing another ripple of laughter.

He and Caron had planned the ceremony so it was woven together with both joy and solemnness as they exchanged wedding rings—and then it was time for their vows.

"Kade and Caron have written their vows to one another." The minister nodded toward Caron. "Kade instructed me that it was to be ladies first."

．　．　．

As planned, Caron handed her bouquet to Vanessa, who whispered, "You can do this."

Caron couldn't resist a whispered "Thanks."

She could do this.

She and Kade had written their vows weeks ago, and she'd memorized them little by little. Practiced them as she drove around Niceville. As she worked out on her elliptical. As she lay in bed at night, waiting to fall asleep, the words appearing in her head as she transitioned to being awake in the morning.

The words were there in her head. And even more important, they were tucked into her heart—exactly what she wanted to say to Kade. And she wasn't saying them alone.

"I choose you, Kade.

"People talk of falling in love with another person. But today is about saying before our friends and family—and before the God we believe in—that I choose you as my husband."

As she paused for Kade to speak the next part of the vows, he gathered her hands closer in his, never looking away from her.

"I choose you, Caron.

"Because of you, I believe in second chances. In you, I've found the satisfaction of one my deepest longings—the beginning of a family—our family. You challenge me, enthrall me, intrigue me, and complete me."

Even though the next words she spoke were for Kade, Caron raised her voice, wanting everyone to hear her pledge. "Even as I say, 'I choose you,' I know there will be days when I will fail you. When I will speak out of anger instead of love, when I will act out of selfishness instead of kindness, when I will respond out of doubt instead of courage. But I will always remember today and that I committed my heart, my life, to you."

Kade's voice rang firm, true, as he spoke again. "I expect there will be forces and circumstances that will strive to pull us apart, but I will trust in the power of our love and in God's provision to grow us together into something new—something unbreakable."

First she spoke the last part of the vows, and then Kade repeated it to her. "We are not best friends—yet. But I look forward to becoming your best friend as we discover what marriage means. I love you—today, tomorrow, until death do us part."

Unforgettable. This moment of her wedding day was unforgettable.

While their guests enjoyed appetizers, drinks, and music at the Crystal Room back at the resort, the wedding party had climbed into gondolas that carried them over the mountains into Telluride. Once they were there, waiting Jeeps had driven them up to Bridal Veil Falls—stopping in the vale that had captivated Caron on her first visit there.

The roar of the waterfall muted the oohs and aahs of the group—as well as the murmurs of the tourists surprised to see a well-dressed bridal party appear out of a small convoy of Jeeps. Even as the photographer assembled them into a group, strangers snapped photos and took videos with their cell phones.

"Isn't this spectacular?" Caron clung to Kade's arm, her high heels sticking in the muddy ground.

"I would have to agree with you, Mrs. Webster—yes, it's spectacular." Kade leaned down and kissed her, his lips lingering on hers.

"Mrs. Webster. I like the sound of that."

"Me, too."

Vanessa leaned over. "Now I know why you insisted we all have a pair of throwaway heels."

"Exactly. No need to clean mud off the good pair."

"Hey, newlyweds! The photographer is trying to take pictures. Stop talking." Mitch stood next to Lacey, his arm around her waist.

Kade threw his arm around Mitch's shoulder. "You're next, my friend."

"I would have beat you to the altar, if Lacey hadn't insisted on a Christmas wedding."

"Oh, stop complaining—" Lacey stayed focused on the photographer, the only one who probably truly understood her challenge.

"Would everyone please stop talking—look here—and smile?" The photographer's voice rose above all the other noise.

"Sorry!"

Everyone spoke in unison and then laughed—and Caron knew the photograph would be one of her favorites of the day.

. . .

With the small gathering of family and friends, the reception in the Peaks' Crystal Room managed to be both festive and intimate. Caron and Kade moved between tables, taking the time to visit with everyone, the photographer following them and snapping photos.

As the first notes of "I Don't Dance" began, Caron followed as Kade led her onto the dance floor. She rested her head against his chest. "If it's all right with you, I don't want to talk. I feel like we've been talking with other people all night long. I just want to enjoy our first dance together."

"Say no more, wife of mine."

And she didn't. She closed her eyes and relaxed in Kade's arms. He seemed content to hold her, move to the rhythm of the music, and just be together. No words needed.

After their dance, Kade took to the dance floor with his mother, and then Caron and he cut their wedding cake, a two-layer confection—carrot cake for Kade and a more traditional vanilla with raspberry filling—decorated with lacy filigrees adorned with some of the same roses that she'd carried in her bouquet.

Caron and Kade joined Margo and Ronny at a table with

Miriam. Within seconds, everyone stopped talking and stared past her shoulder.

"What is going on?" Caron twisted around—and found her mother and father standing behind her.

A smile trembled on her mother's lips. "Your father wanted to ask you something."

"He did?"

"Well, yes." Her father's voice was subdued. "Vanessa's father and I were talking while you and Kade cut the cake. He told me that a father only gets one chance for the Father of the Bride dance with his daughter on her wedding day . . . and that I would regret missing that opportunity."

Caron sat silent, unsure of what to say. She hadn't even thought to request a song to dance with her father today. If he didn't want to even be at her wedding . . . if he refused to walk her down the aisle, why would he want to dance with her?

Her father stepped forward, holding out his hand. "So . . . Caron, would you please do me the honor of dancing with me on your wedding day?"

Even as she stood and took her father's hand, Caron blinked back tears. Her father's invitation was an unexpected gift. "I would love to."

The dance floor was empty as she walked beside her father and then stood facing him, waiting for the music to begin.

"I'm old-fashioned, you know. So I picked a classic song."

"Whatever you chose is perfect."

Her father took her hand, and she positioned herself like she used to when she was much younger, trying to learn the steps, and he would say, "Just follow me." As Dean Martin began to croon "I Wish You Love," she caught a glimpse of Kade standing with his arm around her mom, both of them smiling.

It was a dance . . . just a dance. But hidden within these moments was a glimpse of the future and what might come, given time and prayer and choosing to love.

She didn't have to figure it out all by herself. Together, she and Kade would allow God to change them into who he wanted them to be . . . starting today.

ACKNOWLEDGMENTS

• ♥ • ♥ • ♥ •

Not to us, LORD, not to us but to your name be the glory,
because of your love and faithfulness.

(PSALM 115:1, NIV)

*I*f I didn't try my family's patience a little more during the
writing of *Almost Like Being in Love*, it wasn't for lack of (un-
intentionally) trying. Writing a book is one thing. Deciding to
tear a book apart and rewrite it after you've turned that book
in to your editor is asking so much more of your family. It's
like saying, "I'm off deadline!" and then announcing, "Oops! I
didn't mean it!" Truly *my family* was extraordinarily supportive
as I wrote and rewrote this book. They are the best of the best
when it comes to loving a writer wife and mom, who is now
also a "GiGi."

I am a heartfelt believer in teams because I know the wisdom
of others makes my initial book idea all the better. My writing is
stronger because I have *Preferred Readers* who give me insight-
ful feedback about what is working and what is not working in
my story. *Shari Hamlin, Mary Agius,* and *Sonia Meeter* have
been faithful members of that team for several years.

I also value the pursuit of dreams, and the book you are
holding in your hands is a tangible expression of my writing

dream coming true. A number of people known as my *Dream Team* have invested in my life to help spread the word about my books because they believe in my dream. I will never be able to repay them for their encouragement and support. My hope and prayer is that I will be able to support their dreams, too. A special thank-you to *Casey Herringshaw,* who keeps the efforts of the Dream Team flowing smoothly—and keeps me sane as my VA.

It's always fun to create characters when I'm brainstorming a new book and decide to, oh, make my hero and heroine Realtors. And then I realize that while some of my friends are Realtors, and yes, my husband and I have bought and sold a couple of houses, that's the extent of my knowledge about that career field. Enter *the experts,* people like my friend-through-the-years *Faith Gibson,* who was a Realtor in Niceville, Florida, and my friend-thanks-to-our-daughters-playing-volleyball *Rachel Neilson,* who is a Realtor in Colorado Springs, and *Linda Turner,* a Realtor on the Emerald Coast, who became my friend thanks to her saying, "Sure, you can interview me." All three women graciously answered my questions—and believe me, I had lots of them. Rachel even read my manuscript and offered some great input. I also decided Alex Madison would be an air-conditioner repairman, and guess what? I know nothing about that, either. But thanks to my friend and fellow writer, *Alena Tauriainen,* who owns an air-conditioning and heating business in Texas with her husband, I had my expert.

Writing this book had an aspect of "new" to it—several new editors, to be specific. I've known *Beth Adams* ever since I've been a Howard author, but now she is my lead editor. She's the kind of editor who listened when I said, "I want to change the story—quite a bit," and then said, "Go ahead"—even though I messed with the production schedule. Knowing she believes in me helps me believe in myself more. *Katie Sandell* . . . what can I say? To feel a kinship with an editor is a gift. And *Ami McConnell* is the kind of editor who knows books, but also wants to know her authors—and that is priceless in the publishing world.

I continue to be thankful for the input of *Linda Sawicki,* my production editor, and *Bruce Gore,* who creates my wonderful book covers!

There are some people whose names will always show up in the acknowledgments section of my book. Not because they have to . . . but because of who they have been in my life and who they continue to be.

Rachel Hauck and Susie May Warren: The two of you are forces to be reckoned with in the writing world. Your mentorship and, even more, your friendship are gifts to me.

Rachelle Gardner: Some people would say, "Of course you acknowledge your agent!" But there's no "of course" about this. Were I to try and "acknowledge" all you've done for me while I've written this book, well, I'd need an extra page or two. You are the best of the best and I thank God for you.

ALMOST LIKE
BEING IN LOVE

Winning an all-expenses-paid Colorado destination wedding might seem like a dream come true for some people—but it only causes doubt for Caron Hollister as she evaluates if her boyfriend Alex Madison is "the one." Caron takes a trip to visit Colorado to catch her breath, but runs into the man she walked away from, Kade Webster. Spending time with Kade has Caron questioning everything. The man intrigues her—at times infuriates her—and reminds her of what she lost. Has she been settling for what everyone expects of her? Just because others believe she and Alex are the perfect couple, does that mean they should get married? And how can Caron say "I do" to one man when she's wondering "What if?" about another?

FOR DISCUSSION

1. When *Almost Like Being in Love* opens, Caron Hollister works for her father as a Realtor. Do you think her decision to

quit was the right decision, or should she have continued to work for him after he brought on Nancy Miller as his partner? What do you think about family members working together? What does it take for family members to successfully work together? Have you ever worked for a family member? How did that go for you?

2. What did you think of Caron's decision to go visit her friend Margo in Colorado rather than staying in Florida, finding another job, and facing her father after quitting? When dealing with major life changes, are you a step-back-and-evaluate-the-situation kind of person or a keep-moving-ahead kind of person?

3. Kade Webster is focused on achieving his professional dreams as a Realtor in Colorado, but that doesn't mean he forgets his friends. Mitch and Kade became friends through their time as Army Rangers, and that bond is even stronger now that Mitch faces life as a double amputee. Do you know anyone who deals with either a physical or mental challenge on a daily basis? What is life like for them? How do friends and family help them?

4. Kade convinces Eddie Kingston to let him be a part of the Peak Tour of Homes, hoping it will benefit them both in the long run. Have you ever participated in a Tour of Homes in any way—as a Realtor, home builder, decorator, judge, or just had fun as a spectator, touring the homes open to the public? What was that like? Discuss why you think these Tour of Homes events are so popular.

5. Caron's friend Margo is planning her wedding even as Caron begins to question her relationship with Alex. What are some of your experiences as a bridesmaid or maid/matron of honor? Have you ever participated in a bridal fair? Maybe won a prize,

like Caron did? How important are the relationships between a bride and the members of her bridal party? Imagine you're a bride: How do you decide who your maid of honor is? Who your bridesmaids are?

6. And then there's Alex. After a rough day dealing with his mother's alcoholism again, he thinks this about Caron: *This was one of the reasons they were so right for each other. She knew his secrets. Kept his secrets. Loved him in spite of his secrets.* What was your response to this? What happens when secrets are the foundation of a relationship?

7. Sometimes people who know us the least understand us better than those closest to us—and such is the case with Nancy Miller for Caron. How did the development of their relationship surprise you? How were Nancy Miller and Caron alike? How were they different?

8. Family knows us best, right? What did you think about Caron's brother's reaction when she told him that she'd quit working for her father? Was he speaking the truth in love or was he speaking out of turn? What about Vanessa's promise to pray for more imperfection in Caron's life? How was that prayer answered throughout the rest of the book?

9. What did Jessica symbolize to Alex? What did she provide for him that his life lacked? What did you think about their relationship at the beginning of the book? At the end of the book? Did it turn out the way you expected? Were you conflicted in your feelings about their friendship?

10. A professional crisis causes Kade to ask Caron for help. When she says yes, they are both convinced they can ignore their past romantic relationship. What would you have told

Caron to do if she'd called you for advice about whether to take a temporary job with her ex-boyfriend?

11. After quitting her job and helping stage Eddie Kingston's home for the tour, Caron begins to question whether she wants to be a Realtor. When have you questioned who you are and what you want to do with your life? How did your life change—or did it stay the same? What helped you make the decision about what you wanted to do?

12. We often hear the saying "Honesty is the best policy." Kade tried to be honest with Caron about his feelings for her. Caron tried to be honest with her father about what she wanted to do with her life—and about her feelings for Kade. Alex tried to be honest with his father (and the Hollisters) about how he was hurting. How did being honest work out for Kade? For Caron? For Alex? Have you ever had to be honest with someone—a friend or family member—about a tough or painful topic? How did you prepare for the conversation? Do you believe it's always best to be honest, or is it best to leave some things unsaid? How do you decide?

13. What did you think of the title *Almost Like Being in Love*? Why do you think the author chose this title? If you had the chance to pick a title for this book, what would you choose?

14. There's no such thing as a perfect wedding day, and that was true for Caron and Kade. What was your reaction to their destination wedding ceremony? Would you have written the scene—both the ceremony and the reception—differently? If you're married, what were some of the less-than-perfect moments on your wedding day? If you're not married, share some less-than-perfect moments from weddings you've been a part of or attended.

1. *"Am I now trying to win the approval of human beings, or of God? Or am I trying to please people?"* (Galatians 1:10). It's so easy to get caught up in the "Am I okay?" mind-set and seek approval from others, just as Caron Hollister sought approval from her father—something that affected her life for years. What are some truths that help you remember to focus on God's approval, not the approval of others?

2. *". . . You desire truth in the innermost being, And in the hidden part you will make me know wisdom"* (Psalm 51:6, NASB). Everyone has secrets. The question is: When do we keep secrets and when do we need to reveal a secret for our ultimate healing? How do you determine when keeping a secret is destructive to you emotionally? If God is calling you to "truth in the innermost being," how do you wisely move past secrets to honesty that leads to hope and new life? If you've ever helped someone cope with a secret that has been hurting them, how have you done so? What scriptural truths did you share with them?

3. One of the main themes in *Almost Like Being in Love* is the idea of two people being "perfect" for each other. If you were talking to two young people in love, what would you encourage them to be for each other? Perfect . . . or something else?

A CONVERSATION WITH BETH K. VOGT

As readers, we love to know what inspires an author's ideas in creating their books. What was the catalyst for *Almost Like Being in Love*?

Every story I write starts with a "What if?" For this novel, the "What if?" was based on the idea of parents "betrothing" their young children to their friends' kids. You know, the harmless idea that starts when the kiddos are toddlers: *Oh, I hope my daughter marries your son when they grow up!* I admit I did my own bit of harmless "betrothing" with my own kiddos—not that any of it ever happened. I mean, children grow up and have their own ideas about who they want to marry, right? But *what if* two twentysomethings buy into their parents' pressure that they are perfect for each other? Can that be the basis of a lifelong relationship? My musing turned into a Story Question, which is something else I have for every book I write: *Just because you're perfect for each other, does that mean you should get married?*

Almost Like Being in Love is connected to your first destination wedding novel, *Crazy Little Thing Called Love*. Caron Hollister, the main character in *Almost Like Being in Love*, is the little sister of Logan Hollister, the main character in *Crazy Little Thing Called Love*. What was it like to tell Caron's story?

There was only a glimpse of Caron in *Crazy Little Thing Called Love*, so it was exciting to fully develop her in this book. I'd already created the story idea and I just built the story around Caron. From the first novel I knew she was dating Alex, but I had to go back and discover the rest of the story: what were her hopes and dreams, what was the history of her broken romance with Kade, what did she want out of life. It was fun, too, because telling her story allowed me to revisit Logan and Vanessa. I don't always get to revisit my characters.

Caron struggles with being her own person because she wants to please her father so much. Why did you make that part of her story line?

Andy Stanley, the senior pastor of North Point Church, once said, "All of us are using someone or something as a mirror."

When we look in a mirror, we are checking ourselves out, asking, "How do I look? Am I good to go?" We're looking for approval. Caron's father was her "mirror"—the person she allowed to determine her value. And while Caron is a fictional character, many people use others as their "mirrors," allowing someone else to have power over their self-esteem and worth. Writing Caron's story allowed me to examine something we all struggle with.

Kade, Caron's ex-boyfriend, who becomes her boss, is a Realtor. He also runs "Mudders" with his friend and fellow Realtor, Mitch, who is a double amputee. Why did you bring those angles into the story?

Kade and Mitch are both ex-Army Rangers, too—and I've woven military angles into my other novels, such as *Catch a Falling Star* and *Somebody Like You*, because my husband was in the military. My son Josh runs Mudders and Spartan races—obstacle courses you can run solo or with a team—and my husband, Rob, and son-in-love, Nate, have joined him once. I'm purely a spectator. At one Mudder Josh ran in Aspen, there was a Wounded Warrior in a wheelchair—a double amputee. Rob and Josh told me how the team helped the Wounded Warrior conquer the course when the terrain was too rough, including one person carrying him on his back while another person carried his wheelchair. I also mention the Emerald Coast MudRun for Orphans in the book—this annual race is sponsored by Heart of the Bride, a ministry begun by my close friends, Tony and Faith Gibson.

Caron's boyfriend, Alex, is dealing with a huge family secret: alcoholism. What prompted that aspect of the story?

Alex was a complete stranger to me when I started writing *Almost Like Being in Love*. I can remember talking about him with my mentor, Rachel Hauck, trying to discover who he was. The one thing I knew was Alex wasn't as perfect as he first appeared—that there was something he was hiding. Most of us have secrets. Family secrets. Personal secrets. So often we think of keeping a secret as protection. The questions become: *Is it really best to keep a secret? How does it affect us? When and how do we bring the secret to light?* So Alex was a multilayered character for me: the "perfect" guy who actually wasn't so perfect and needed to face the harsh realities of his life.

What comes next for you?

I'm always looking forward to new, fun ways to connect with my readers—Facebook, Twitter, Instagram. I might dive into Periscope. And I'm mulling over a new story that involves a trio of sisters. They're starting to talk to me . . . It's going to be interesting.

. . . .

Beth would love to connect with book clubs that have read *Almost Like Being in Love*. You can contact her through her website at bethvogt.com, or via Facebook, Twitter, or email at beth@bethvogt.com.

ABOUT THE AUTHOR

• • • ♥ • • •

$\mathcal{B}$eth K. Vogt is a nonfiction writer who said she'd never write fiction. After saying she'd never marry a doctor or anyone in the military, she is now happily married to a former Air Force family physician. Beth believes God's best is often behind the door marked "Never." An established magazine writer and editor, she now writes inspirational contemporary romance because she believes there is more to happily ever after than the fairy tales tell us.